Praise for
*An Affair with Mr. Kennedy*

"A satisfying romance featuring a genuinely original pair of lovers and sparkling supporting characters against an unusual social and political background."

—*Publishers Weekly*

"The sexy, smart characters will appeal to modern readers as much as the suspense. Their repartee and sensuality heat up the pages, promising a treat for readers."

—*RT Book Reviews*

"A romance in every sense of that word. . . . Perfectly balanced between pace and plot but always and without a doubt character driven."

—*Bookworm2bookworm*

"A brilliant historical romance that is totally different from the type you may be used to. . . . A totally delightful and provocative story. . . . Will grab your attention and keep you enthralled all the way to the end. This one's a keeper!"

—*Romance Reviews Today*

"Sizzling hot. . . . An exciting, mysterious historical romance suspense that will steal your heart."

—*Romance Junkies*

"Intriguingly suspenseful with unique dilemmas and a number of dangerous risks. . . . Part romance and part mystery with a hefty dose of suspense, where each moment of the novel is imaginatively captivating."

—*Single Titles*

# A PRIVATE DUEL
# with
# AGENT GUNN

## JILLIAN STONE

Pocket Books

New York   London   Toronto   Sydney   New Delhi

Pocket Books
A Division of Simon & Schuster, Inc.
1230 Avenue of the Americas
New York, NY 10020

This book is a work of fiction. Names, characters, places, and incidents either are products of the author's imagination or are used fictitiously. Any resemblance to actual events or locales or persons, living or dead, is entirely coincidental.

First Pocket Books paperback edition December 2012

POCKET and colophon are registered trademarks of Simon & Schuster, Inc.

For information about special discounts for bulk purchases, please contact Simon & Schuster Special Sales at 1-866-506-1949 or business@simonandschuster.com.

The Simon & Schuster Speakers Bureau can bring authors to your live event. For more information or to book an event, contact the Simon & Schuster Speakers Bureau at 1-866-248-3049 or visit our website at www.simonspeakers.com.

Manufactured in the United States of America

10  9  8  7  6  5  4  3  2  1

ISBN: 978-1-4516-2906-4
ISBN: 978-1-4516-2909-5 (ebook)

*For my father, my son, and all the stoic, adventurous Brehaut gentlemen of Prince Edward Island.*

# Acknowledgements

The lucky-author gods smiled down on me when Kate Dresser became my editor at Pocket Books. Beyond her stellar editorial efforts, Kate has also been a champion of The Gentlemen of Scotland Yard series and I will forever be grateful for her energy and enthusiasm. Thanks also to critique partners Jodie Wilson and Charli Mac—whose comments, suggestions, and good humor have been an inspiration—and to a small but select group of excellent RWA friends: Brenna Aubrey, Judy Duarte, Kristen Koster, and Robin Delany.

I must also thank Richard Curtis, my agent—and mentor and publishing therapist—whose kindness, humor, and unflagging belief in me and my work get me through the best and worst of times.

Lastly, I would like to thank all the fans and readers who've enjoyed a bit of hot cockles and swivery with the dashing detectives of Scotland Yard. May there be more romance and adventure ahead for all of us!

# ∞ Chapter One

"Clean as a whistle, these young lovelies. Sure you won't have a taste, sir?" The dandy peacock tipped his hat and squinted to see inside the carriage.

Phineas Gunn sat in the darkness and regarded the street pimp for the briefest of moments. "Quite. Sure."

"Take another gander, sir—you'll find something comely that tickles the old Thomas." The flesh peddler cocked his head with a wink. "Rooms by the hour, right behind me." With bosoms near to bursting out of corsets, the rag-a-bed jewels of Princess Street posed enticingly for his attention.

"Bugger off." Phineas slammed the coach window shut.

Twirling a crystal-knobbed cane, the fancy man swept his walking stick behind bouncing bustles. "Special this evening—two girls, three and six." The pimp hawked his bevy of spoiled doves to every man jack and Prince Arthur prowling the backstreets of Leicester Square.

Finn gulped for air. A band of tension squeezed his chest.

Up the street, a couple of randy bloods stopped to negotiate with the flashy procurer. Finn exhaled as slowly as possible. According to the *Daily Telegraph*, at half past twelve, any night of the week, there were five hundred prostitutes working London streets between Piccadilly Circus and the bottom of Waterloo Place.

Gazing out at the blur of street smut, it appeared the newspaper's alarming calculation had proved to be nothing less than an effective advertisement. The lane was popping with customers, men whose single-minded aspiration was to gamble, drink, and fornicate the night away.

Within the smothering confinement of the carriage, his heart rate accelerated. An intense wave of fear ripped through flesh and sinew—right down to his bones.

Damn it all.

His body was playing tricks again. It seemed nothing he could think or do could distract from this sudden assault on his nerves. He inhaled another deep breath and exhaled slowly, counting to ten. The shakes often came upon him without warning or obvious cause. Finn knew very well he sat safely within the confines of his coach, yet every fiber of his body told him he was being chased down a dark alley by a raving murderer, poised to thrust a blade in his back.

He was dying and there was no way to stop it.

All his symptoms were present this evening. Chest pain, shortness of breath, precipitous heart rate. The numbness and tingling were particularly bad. *Paresthesia*, Monty called it.

In actuality, he wasn't altogether sure Dr. Montague Twombly was even licensed—more of a quack phrenologist, as it turned out. Monty had studied under a very unorthodox Austrian physician by the name of Freud. An inquiry into this new school of medicine had unearthed disturbing rumors, including the suspicion that this Freud character was a cocaine addict. Finn sighed and pushed his back deeper into the squabs of the plush upholstered coach seat.

In the middle of his search for a physician, he had simply chosen to stop. The damned talking therapy, as Monty referred to it, appeared to be working. This past summer Monty had brought him more relief than all the doctors on Harley Street combined—and there had been a good dozen over the years, all well-meaning professionals. Some time ago, Finn had discontinued the opium, and he had refused mercury treatments, but had otherwise subjected himself to the very latest in cures. From electrical currents to baths filled with ice—"shock the system back to normal," his doctors agreed—all he'd ended up with was a head cold that lasted a week.

Ultimately, the much-lauded physicians had failed to have any lasting effect on his condition.

Again, Finn held his breath, then exhaled as he counted slowly to ten.

He had made progress under Twombly, even enjoyed several months relatively free of symptoms. But the spells had returned of late. Dabbing a pocket square over beads of perspiration, he donned his opera hat, sucked in one last deep breath, and lifted the door latch.

Finn wove a path through a crush of all-night lads and eager tarts. He was no more than half a block from Leicester Square, a brief jaunt on foot to the Alhambra Theatre. "Evening, sir." The plainly dressed girl sauntered close. In the flickering gaslight he took a second look. Pretty for street quim. But her painted complexion failed to mask the pallor of frail health. And not a day over fifteen. Very likely this was a penniless, supperless girl willing to have a go for a pint and chop. She brazenly eyed him up and down. "A handsome, cocks-up gent such as yourself could use a boff before curtain rise, wouldn't you say, sir?"

"Not this evening, love." Finn slipped her a half crown and continued down the sink of iniquity that was Princess Street. Fleshbrokers, touting their whores, spilled out of every night house and café lining the block.

To escape the relentless commerce of vice, he took a shortcut between buildings. He concentrated on the glow that hovered above jagged rooftops and nearly tripped over a drunk. The electric lights of Leicester Square's theatres illuminated the sky for blocks around, but not in this passage filled with dark niches for even darker deeds.

Finn pressed past a harlot being groped by a customer. "No money, no cunny, you old sot!"

"Pardon." He jumped a puddle of unspeakable sludge. The clamor of wicked commerce gradually gave way to the echo of his footsteps on wet pavers. A wraith in the night stepped up behind and pressed a knife to his throat. "I say, Gov'nor, what's in those pockets?" For a moment, Finn imagined stepping forward into the cruel cut of the blade. The slice across his carotid artery. A steaming spray of crimson. The metallic scent of blood. This keen sense of life on the edge stirred his heart into a gallop of frenetic beats.

Bugger all, something more primal took over. Finn backed into the man with such force the surly robber staggered. Ripping the knife away, he turned it against the thug's throat and pressed the foolhardy bloke against the bricks.

Terrified, the young man's eyes darted up and down the alley. "Please, sir, I would not have hurt ye. I swear it."

Disappointed, Finn eased back. "No, I think not."

He slipped the blade inside his coat pocket. London

was chockablock with amateur thieves. Rural lads, displaced by farm machinery, continued to pour into London. Once their meager savings disappeared, they turned desperate. "I've no time for a mugger's game. Running a bit late—meeting friends at the music hall."

No doubt the young man was down on his luck and had turned to thievery. "Get yourself an honest job." Phineas pulled out his card. "Millwall docks, Isle of Dogs. Ask around for a man by the name of Tully. Tell him . . ." He studied the burly young thief in the dark. "Tell him you're no good at crime."

The stunned lad stared blankly at the card. "Yes, sir. Thank you, sir."

Exiting the alley, Finn jogged across a corner of the square. The garish lights of the Alhambra reflected off streets still wet from an earlier cloudburst. He wound his way past clusters of gentlemen assembled in front of the entertainment palace. The siren call this evening? A widely extolled troupe of ballet girls direct from Paris.

"Phineas Gunn." Hand on his hip, Dudley Chilcott's elbow swung dangerously close to skewering a passerby. "A rare sighting, indeed. I see the Ballet Royale de Musique has enticed you out of the house this evening." Chilcott took a draw on his cigar. "These ballet girls have a bad reputation, which is in most cases well deserved."

Finn did his best to ignore the dig at the rarity of his presence by acknowledging the gentlemen in Chilcott's circle. Adopting an equally disdainful pose, he arched a brow. "Then, I can only assume, Dudley, you are here hoping for a backstage introduction."

A guffaw of laughter from the circle of men prompted a grin. Trapped between Dudley Chilcott and James Oldham-Talbot, Earl of Harrow, Finn shifted uncomfortably and scanned the crowd assembled in the entryway. All of London, it would seem, was aware of his humiliating malady. The ever inebriated and opinionated earl snorted something between a laugh and a grunt. "Yes, I can't imagine Dudley lamenting the ballet corps' lack of morals." The man exhaled a puff of tobacco smoke.

"More like hallelujah," Dudley remarked dryly.

Finn's gaze rolled up and over to make note of the time, then he glanced at the earl. The Earl of Harrow reportedly enjoyed having his eyelids licked by two naked whores. An eyelid apiece, one supposed. He returned his attention to the second hand of the brass-trimmed clock above the lobby doors.

*Fifteen seconds. Thirty-five heartbeats*, Finn did the math. *Thirty-five times four equals one hundred forty beats per minute. Tolerable.* Finn released his thumb from his wrist and kept his breath slow and regular.

In actuality, he had an appointment with Scotland Yard, in the person of Zeno Kennedy, chief inspector of Special Branch. Damned intriguing to call a meeting at a music hall.

A sweep of the square through open doors brought a tall, strapping lad into view. Somewhat cheered by the sight of his brother, Finn exhaled. Dressed in frock coat and silk hat, his younger sibling wove a path through the tangled throng. Rare, to see him out of his regimentals. Rarer still, to run into each other at the Alhambra. If Finn recalled correctly, his brother's tastes ran toward table dancers in the East End. "Hardy!"

His handsome sibling waved and made his way over. "Good to see you out, Finn."

He ignored the remark. "Ballet girls? Rather tame by your standards."

"And what might those be?" Hardy grinned.

Finn stared. "Low." He turned to his circle. "I believe most of you know my brother, Cole Harding Gunn?"

"Gentlemen." Hardy nodded.

"Sans the *lady* this evening?" The Earl of Harrow quite directly referenced his brother's affair with Lady Gwendolyn Lennox, married to the very powerful Rufus Stewart, Earl of Lennox.

Hardy's gaze quickly narrowed on the earl.

"If you'll excuse us, gentlemen, I spy our host exiting his carriage." Finn whisked Hardy away before he did something rash with his fists. A quick jostle through the crowd and they were out of the hall and on the pavement. He hailed Kennedy.

Hardy shrugged off his grip. "You're meeting Zak here as well?"

Finn stared. "What manner of business could you possibly have with Scotland Yard?"

Zeno Kennedy—Zak, to his friends—greeted them both with an affable smile. "Hardy has applied to the Home Office."

His brother added another grin. "I hope to resign my commission in the Blues and join Special Branch."

Hardy often withheld information from him. A younger sibling's reaction to an overprotective, nosy brother. Still, Finn raised both brows. "And when did all this come about?"

"I didn't realize I had to ask for permission, Finn."

He studied his sibling's uncomfortable fidgeting about. A much-decorated major in the Royal Horse Guards, Hardy had been somewhat adrift since his regiment's return from Egypt. A restless type and a thrill seeker even as a small child, Hardy could ride faster and fight harder than any man he knew. So why did Finn worry so much about his little brother?

Kennedy cleared his throat. "I managed to score us a box—on loan from Lord Phillips. Shall we?" Several heads nodded their way as the famous chief inspector led them upstairs. Finn spoke quietly. "We shall see how Lady Lennox enjoys the high life on a detective's salary."

"Couldn't be worse than a soldier's pay." Hardy shrugged. "I'm under no illusion she'll leave old Rufus and his four hundred thousand for a Yard man."

Zak held back curtains and ushered them into their seats. A very attentive waiter entered the box behind them. "Shall it be supper or libations, gentlemen? Perhaps a bit of both?"

They ordered three pints and a bottle of Talisker's finest, and settled in for the evening. In the privacy of their box, amongst men he knew and trusted, Finn's nervous condition eased. "Give it up, Kennedy. What has Special Branch got in mind for me? Something interesting, I hope. I could use the diversion."

Glancing at the stage below, Zak sipped from his glass. "A couple of things, actually." The Yard man kept his voice just above the strains of music. Finn and Hardy leaned in. "A year ago, Finn, you were involved in an operation for the Naval Intelligence Department, the breakup of a ring of Spanish anarchists—*Los Tigres Solitarios.*"

"My involvement was limited to tracking a delivery of dynamite in transit from Portsmouth to France via Spain. As operations go, this one blew up, quite literally. The Deuxième Bureau—" Finn clarified for Hardy, "French intelligence—made a mess of it and then pushed the blame off on us. No lasting political ramifications, at least not from our side of the channel."

"We have reason to believe former members of *Los Tigres* are here in London, regrouping." Zak reached inside his coat pocket and dropped a slim pointed object in Finn's palm. "Have a look at this."

Finn rotated the stickpin between fingers. The facets of a large diamond caught whatever dim light was available. "Impressive. I'd like to take this bauble home for a better look."

Zak nodded. "Recently confiscated off a dead body washed up downriver. We believe the corpse to be the conspirator known as Carlos Jorge Rivera. Likely this chap decided to enrich himself and the brotherhood didn't take kindly to it." The detective swiveled toward Hardy. "I thought you might like to shadow this case with your brother. Get a taste for the work, find out if it suits." Zak caught Finn's sour expression. "Of course, if you'd rather not . . ."

"I can manage a group of surly anarchists and my little brother at the same time."

The Yard man leaned closer. "Good. And how goes the gemology consulting?"

"Brisk of late. I've been asked for a number of appraisals—all private sales."

Zak appeared to consider his statement. "Not sure you've heard, but there's a second-story man about. We suspect whoever that person is, may be connected to the anarchists." Kennedy nodded at the tiepin. "That bit of flash was purchased recently through private sale and pinched little more than a week later."

Finn twirled the gem. "Ends up on the person of an anarchist floating facedown in the Thames. It's possible whoever is selling the jewels is stealing them back for a future sale—on the Continent, perhaps." He pocketed the tiepin. "It's been done before, an old jewel thief's ploy."

Zak grimaced. "Nearly every scenario we've considered doesn't add up."

"And why is that?" Hardy asked.

"The burglar appears to be rather selective. Takes one piece and leaves piles of other valuables behind."

Finn tilted his gilded chair onto its rear legs. He gazed at the stage, which had dimmed briefly before the featured act. "I thought you were more of an opera aficionado, Kennedy. Why are we here?"

A wry grin spread across the Yard man's face. "To reconnoiter with a particular featured dancer."

From high above the stage a pale glow poured down upon the master of ceremonies. "Ladies and gentlemen, *mesdames et messieurs.* Direct from Paris, the Royal Alhambra proudly presents *Théâtre de l'Académie Royale de Musique*'s *Phoenix Unbound.*" The man in formal tails and opera hat tilted his head toward the balcony. "And where in the heavens might we find such a lovely mythical bird?"

All eyes followed as the haunting strains of harps, violins, and cellos swelled into something whimsical and evocative—Debussy, Finn thought.

A lone spotlight halted on the lithe figure of a young woman sitting on the ledge of a balcony. She wore a tightly fitted bodice and a dancer's skirt of filmy, translucent layers, which parted as she rose from her perch and raised a jaw-dropping length of leg slowly into the air—in arabesque. The very term caused a sudden shiver of uncanny intuition. Finn had dredged up the word—*arabesque*—from distant memory.

The ballerina tilted her head and opened gently wavering arms, a preening bird preparing for flight. With each flutter she loosed ribbons of red and gold silk. Her pointe slippers pawed the ledge as she traversed the upper tier, unfurling wing and tail streamers along the way.

Strains of music built quickly to a crescendo and she plunged off the balcony. The audience gasped as the diving bird swooped down over the audience attached to a delicate golden perch and gilded wire.

Hardy leaned forward. "Nice set of gams, wot?" As if in answer to his brother's crude observation, every man in the theatre lifted his opera glasses to inspect those lovely limbs. She floated across the stage, heading straight for their box. With arms outstretched, she unfurled yet another length of delicate fabric, gaily tossing it ahead of her as she reached the end of her arc.

Before he could stop himself, Finn reached out over the edge of the balcony and caught the ribbon of silk. Their eyes met in shock and surprise. Every fiber of his being came alive.

Catriona.

The roar of cheers from the male audience below barely registered. The trapeze swung the ethereal bird back over the heads of the audience and lowered her gracefully to the floor of the stage. The ballerina leaped to earth amongst an eruption of applause, and danced a series of precision pirouettes across the stage into the arms of a male dancer who lifted her high above his shoulders and rotated her slowly in the air.

Zak and Hardy joined in the applause. Without taking his eyes off her, Finn gathered the firebird's fluttering silk ribbon. She was everything he remembered, only more so. Finn sank into his chair. He had never seen Catriona dance in Spain, or France for that matter. In fact, he had hardly gotten to know her at all. Tall and willowy with large sapphire eyes and raven hair, she was so . . . achingly beautiful. Mesmerized by her every move, his mind returned to a night of unforgettable passion they had shared—Christ, how long was it now? Well over a year, at least.

Most provocatively, she slipped back down to earth in the arms of her partner. Finn was quite sure every man in the audience was aroused by her slide down the male dancer's torso. Twirling and leaping across a stage flooded with moonlight, her body moved with a light, ethereal quality—a sensuous grace—as if her feet had no real need to touch ground. Fields of gravity did not apply to this lovely creature.

She arched her back and swept an arm in the air, signaling farewell. One could feel the enchantment as everyone gasped a collective sigh. Waves of energy rippled through the room as the audience stood in ovation. She took her bows amongst a host of bravos and applause.

Zak leaned forward. "Though she dances with the Paris ballet company and has taken a French stage name, she is actually—"

"Catriona Elíse de Dovia Willoughby." Finn worked at holding himself together as he met Zak's gaze. "Born to a Spanish mother and British father, raised in both countries, attended finishing school in France. Much to the family's dismay on both sides of the channel, she auditioned for the Paris Opera Ballet and was accepted."

Hardy raised both brows. "I say, Finn, you know her?"

Zeno poured them each another dram. "According to the dossier your brother compiled on Miss Willoughby, I'd say he knows her rather well."

Finn shot Zak a cautionary glower. "Never thought you were the type to read between the lines, Kennedy."

"Quite a stunning young woman, Finn. Hardly surprising there was an affair." The Yard man gazed from one brother to the other. "My wife informs me the ladies quite often throw themselves at both of you."

Finn's gaze flicked over to his brother. "To my never-ending relief, Hardy gets most of the attention."

Zak pressed on. "As you well know, Catriona is the only sister of Eduardo Tomás de Dovia, better known by his nom de guerre: *Tigre Solitario*, Lone Tiger, the most recent and celebrated martyr of the anarchists. Killed in Béziers, a casualty of your operation, Finn, from a dynamite explosion."

Invisible bands tightened around Finn's chest, but he otherwise remained in control of his affliction. He stared at Zak. "You suspect she's working with the anarchists."

"A tool perhaps, or she could be a cunning operative. We need you to find out." Kennedy tossed back his whiskey and set the glass down.

"And what would you have me do with her?" Finn stuffed the silk ribbon in his coat pocket. "Once I find out?"

"Befriend her. Gain her trust. Turn her if you can. Both the Admiralty and Home Office would like nothing more than to have a mole on the Continent."

Hardy sat back, nearly agog. "This Scotland Yard business beats the Horse Guards by a length and half."

Zak grinned. "Most of our cases aren't nearly this—"

"Ravishing." Finn rose from his chair. "If you'll excuse me, gentlemen. I believe I have a stage door to knock on."

## ∞ Chapter Two

$B$y the thunderous applause Cate knew she had done well tonight, though she couldn't remember much about the performance. One of the girls in the wings handed her a towel. *"Merci, chouchou."* Cate dabbed at perspiration and wove a path through a blur of diaphanous pastel skirts. The corps de ballet awaited the strains of music that cued their entrance.

A rapid pulse and labored breath were normal after such a strenuous dance, but she did not recall ever being this . . . stirred up. Her mind continued to whirl a continuous *fouetté rond de jambe en tournant.* And her stomach flutters were—dear God, her body purred inside.

He had reached out and nearly touched her. A tremble vibrated from the tips of her breasts to the depths of her womb. He had caught one of her streaming ribbons, much to the elation of an audience brimming with men. The front rows were always full of randy toffs who pursued the dancers—*les abonnés,* they were called in Paris.

How dare Hugh Curzon.

And yet, how like him.

She slipped down the backstage stairs crowded with

up and down traffic, and made her way into the green room. The featured dancer's dressing rooms surrounded a wide corridor that served as kind of gentleman's salon, where admirers could approach a dancer after her performance. Some came with flowers, others with offers of a late supper.

She collected several bouquets, conversing pleasantly with her followers, men who were often nearly speechless on first acquaintance. Tonight, Cecil Cavendish, eleventh Baron Burleigh, stationed himself near her door.

"Good evening, Miss de Dovia." His bow brought him close enough to whisper. "Or may I call you Cate?"

"Of course you may. We are friends, are we not?" She offered her hand, which he kissed in European fashion. She had allowed him to take her to dinner once and to "show her off" to prominent acquaintances at a few elegant soirees. When she had confessed her real name and revealed her dual heritage, his interest had moved from mildly amused acquaintance to something more ardent and worrisome.

"Join me for supper, my dove."

She raised a brow. "Should I allow you to occupy so much of my time, monsieur? Are we not to attend the Beauforts' ball tomorrow night?"

With a plea in his eyes, Cecil's mouth formed the male version of a pout. "A quiet dinner—just the two of us?"

Cate hesitated. In actuality, she was famished. But she was also running out of expensive gowns to wear to fancy restaurants and balls. "Not Verreys. Perhaps something less public—Bertolini's?

*"Molto buono, mia bella ballerina."*

"Give me a moment." She flashed a smile and pivoted toward her dressing room. Cate took one last glance around the corridor. A wave of melancholy washed over her. If truth be told, she felt a bit deflated. Hugh was nowhere to be seen.

Cecil prowled after. "I would be honored to wait for you inside, listen to the rustle of your clothes—imagine what you look like behind your dressing screen."

"I'm afraid my dressing room would disappoint—terribly cramped." Cate deftly opened her door and winked. "Not nearly as provocative as one might imagine."

Once inside she threw the latch and rested her forehead against the door. She waited for her breathing to shift from gulps of air to something steadier.

"Must be tiring—fending off such persistent admirers."

She whirled around. The tall figure stood in the doorway to the adjoining storage room. He leaned that impressive physique of his along the frame molding and stretched. Sculpted muscle flexed under perfectly tailored clothes. Her small dressing room was suddenly airless. This man had an essence about him—something wild and fierce beneath the gentlemanly facade.

With his knee bent and his hand on a raised hip, there was an unsettling intimacy in his relaxed pose. It was as though it had been hours, not months, since they last saw each other. Yes, everything was familiar about him. Even those smoldering dark eyes that made her tingle all over.

Cate looked him up and down. "One gets used to it." A bit wobbly, she sidestepped over to the vanity bench and unpinned a crown of silver and white feathers. She met his gaze in the looking glass as her heart beat a series of *petit jetés* in her chest.

He pushed off the wall and moved in behind her. "You are even lovelier than I remember." His fingers moved down the row of hooks and eyes that fastened her costume.

She shifted away. "My dresser will be here any minute, she will—" Persistent fingers gently loosed the back of her bodice. Even as her cheeks flushed with heat, cool air wafted over skin moist with perspiration. His knuckles brushed against the flesh of her back, causing a shiver she failed to conceal.

He looked up from his unfastening duties. Deep brown eyes, the color of steaming French coffee, met her gaze in the mirror. How could she possibly have forgotten the lightness of his touch? She reacquainted herself with his strong chin and jawline, a bit swarthy perhaps, but wonderfully dangerous—or wicked. Which one was it? Did it really matter?

Reverently, he bent and kissed her shoulder. "Tell me, Cate, do you respond to lines like: ' . . . listen to the rustle of your costume and imagine what you look like . . . ' "— his breath drifted over her ear—"naked in my bed with those long, shapely legs wrapped around my waist—"

She whirled around and slapped him hard across the face. "Get out."

He straightened but made no move to leave.

Cate strode across the small room and pulled back the latch. He slammed his hand against the door. The man was a predator. So why didn't she scream for help? He had always thrilled, down to her raw, disfigured ballerina toes. Even now, he was the most masculine, feral creature she had ever encountered. And *inglés* to boot.

He leaned in close. A gentle nuzzle, just to take in her essence. And she could not help but return his interest. Hesitant at first, like two wild creatures meeting in the forest. She inhaled whiskey and bitters, hints of soap and—his scent. She looked up into heavy-lidded eyes that were far from languorous. He examined her carefully.

"When I returned to Barcelona, why didn't you meet me at Café Almirall?"

She was almost grateful when anger bubbled up inside. "You used me to get close to my brother. Then you followed him to France, where he and his *compadres* were murdered in—*asesinado en sangre fría, sangre fría, monstruo*—by you and those bloody French!"

"I do not deny we used gunfire . . ." He leaned an elbow on the door behind her and rubbed his temple. "But they were blown up by their own explosives."

"They were surrounded by British and the French agents. You knew there was dynamite in that farmhouse. And still the bullets flew." Her fists pummeled his chest.

"Slow down, Cate. *Lento, retraso, por favor.*" Firmly but gently, he grasped both of her hands and held them to her sides. Crushed between her brutish intruder and the door, she used the most insulting words she could think of. *"Hijo del perro de una puta."*

His eyes crinkled. "I'd nearly forgotten about that Catalan temper of yours."

A heavy pounding rattled the wood panel under her back. "I say, what goes on there? Miss de Dovia, are you all right?"

He pressed against her. "Sorry to see me, Cate? Worried I might interfere with your duties outside of the corps de ballet?"

She stopped writhing and blinked. "What nonsense you're talking—" She exhaled. "Please leave me alone, Hugh."

"Actually, Hugh Curzon is a name I use on the Continent—"

She angled her toe shoe and kicked him in the shin. "Ouch," he yowled.

Cate tossed her head back. "Pointe slippers can torture more than my toes, *señor*." She turned the knob. He slammed the door shut and threw the latch. She thought her heart might find a way to leap from her chest. He pushed her back against the door, and placed a hand on each shoulder.

"What do you want?" She swallowed, looking up at him.

"One kiss." His demand knocked the breath from her. She pushed away, but the more she wiggled, the more they rubbed against each other.

She had forgotten, no, she had pushed him out of her mind—what a wild and woolly creature! His hair a leonine mass of thick brown waves, his body hard and unyielding. Her gaze fell to his mouth, possibly his most intriguing feature. Well-defined lips that were full and sensuous, and when they touched hers . . .

His mouth closed in, causing a flutter of anticipation. In fact, she very much wanted his kiss. She tilted her head to give him access, but he did not take her greedily. He brushed gently, capturing her mouth in a grazing caress of soft, sensuous bites—then he licked. She shivered in his arms. *Glorioso.*

"I give you pleasure, *señorita*?"

She opened her eyes. "*Cerdo asqueroso.*"

His languid gaze traced over her features. The corners of his mouth turned up a hint of smile. "Disgusting pig . . ." The words buffeted against her cheek. "Rather enchanting in Spanish." He remained close, nuzzling, taunting, until her lips opened again for him.

This time he slid his tongue into her mouth and boldly took what he wanted. Cate closed her eyes and let him do as he pleased. In no time, he was groaning and kissing her tenderly, passionately, and, God help her, she returned his ardor with a surprising amount of intensity. Her tongue tangled with his in a thrilling chase that was . . . *muy delicioso*.

The tingle turned into a surge of desire that coursed through her body. Her knees would have buckled if he hadn't kept her pressed firmly to the door. Slowly, he released her and fell back an inch or two. Glassy-eyed, they shared each other's breath, neither able to find words.

*"Madre de Dios."* Blindly, Cate flailed about and threw the latch. To his credit, he stepped back and she opened the door. He exited the dressing room quietly—this man whose tongue had just ravaged her mouth in the most sinful way possible.

She eyed him cautiously. "By what name do you call yourself in London?"

It appeared their brief argument had captivated everyone in the salon. Cecil blurted out her answer. "Phineas Gunn?"

Her dressing room intruder approached her open-mouthed dinner date. "Rather daring of you to carry on with a ballet girl, Burleigh. Hoping for a prenuptial fling?"

Cecil poked his chin out. "I am no more engaged to Daphne than you are to Muriel Villers-Talbot."

"And according to Muriel, who so dutifully keeps me informed, your fiancée is in Paris, is she not? Purchasing her trousseau." This man with a new name towered over Cecil. "At least *my* so-called fiancée hasn't sent out the wedding invitations."

Cecil glowered.

Torn between raising a brow or bursting into laughter, Cate pressed her lips together and tried very hard not to chuckle. Much to her dismay a rather loud snort escaped. "Sorry to keep you waiting, Cecil. I'll be ready in a dash."

She opened the lid on a jar of cold cream and spoke to the wide-eyed miss in the mirror. "So, the Baron Burleigh is engaged." Based on the few strained words between the men, it would seem Mr. Gunn was nearly spoken for himself.

She closed her eyes and ran the soothing cream over darkened eyelids. When attending soirees with Cecil, she had always assumed the raised brows were due entirely to her avocation. Obviously, there was another layer here. Cate used a soft cloth to wipe away the greasepaint.

If a man was a philanderer before marriage, what might a girl look forward to afterward? She almost felt sorry for the fiancée. Daphne, he had called her.

Though her experience with stage-door gentlemen could hardly be called extensive, she knew enough to be quite sure of one fact. Men didn't change—not much anyway. They were either trustworthy or they were not. She hardly knew which one of the posturing males outside her dressing room was worse: Cecil Cavendish or Phineas Gunn, as he now called himself.

"Phin-e-as." She whispered the name under her breath. New name, same old deceiver. A man who played false for a living could never be trusted. So why then did her lips still burn from the heat of his kiss?

She once believed they had met by accident on the Passeig de Gràcia. Lugging along two large hatboxes, she had given up on a cab and decided to walk to her aunt and uncle's home. The fashionable avenue in Barcelona was as broad as the Champs-Élysées. A favorite place for aristocrats to display their riding skills and expensive carriages.

"*Perdón, señorita. Estoy . . . buscando la casa de Gaudí?*"

Shading her eyes from the low rays of the sun, she peered up at a magnificent horse and an equally imposing rider. "You are English, *señor?*" Drawing closer, Cate made out a charming grimace from a strikingly handsome man.

"Pardon my poor Spanish. I'm looking for a new residence designed by Gaudí. I believe it is on Carrer Nou de la Rambla—" Distracted, his eyes narrowed and shifted away.

Cate followed his line of sight to a teetering pony cart driven by a chubby-faced, curly-haired child that was traveling at a dangerously fast pace down the broad street. Wide eyes accompanied the girl's panicked expression and whimpering cries. Cate's heart accelerated even as the Englishman pressed his mount into action and overtook the out-of-control pony. Leaning far over his seat, he grabbed hold of the reins and slowed the animal.

Cate dropped her hatboxes and ran onto the boulevard. She positioned herself alongside of the cart just as the flushed child burst into tears. A tired old groom trotted up to join them. "*Madre de Dios, Madre de Dios. Gracias, señor.*"

"If the child cannot control the animal, you'd best take hold of these." With quite a singular glare, the gentleman on horseback handed the reins to the groom.

Cate replaced the Brit's glare with a smile and translated. She added an eye roll and shrug. "*Inglés.*"

The groom tugged on the pony's head. "*¡Adelante!*" The elder man admonished the child gently, and led the pony and cart away. The little girl wiped off a tear and stuck her tongue out at them.

"Well done, sir," she murmured. "Even if your damsel in distress thinks you a spoilsport."

He had studied her a moment before dismounting. "You speak in a decidedly British vernacular. Are you a native of Spain?"

"A Spanish mother—and my father was an Englishman like yourself."

"Was?"

"Both my parents were killed adventuring in South America."

"Sorry to bring up a sad subject."

"It happened quite some time ago." She reached up to scratch the muzzle of his horse. "You have a magnificent mount, sir."

"So I've been told." Amusement flashed in his eyes, and something else. Something much more unsettling. There was a kind of intimacy in those liquid brown orbs—as if he understood her secrets, her most personal desires.

"His name is Bhai Singh, but he answers to Sergeant MacGregor." The burr in his *r* and the soft *g* in *MacGregor* instantly brought out the Scot in the man.

He tipped his hat. "Hugh Curzon, here in Barcelona on business."

"Catriona Elise de Dovia Willoughby." She smiled at his reaction. "It seems your horse and I answer to a mélange of names."

"And which do you prefer?"

Actually, she preferred to change the subject. "You asked about Palau Güell, designed by Gaudí. You are an architect?"

"I studied architecture at university. Love to have a look at those parabolic arches and hyperbolic capitals . . . under construction." His eyes traveled over her gently. Not in a lascivious way by any means, but with definite interest. "I am fascinated by curves."

She half smiled when she shouldn't have. She should have said *buenos días* and pivoted on her heel. Instead, she offered her escort. "I live quite near Carrer Nou de la Rambla. Why don't I show you the way?"

A sharp rap at the dressing room door snapped Cate out of her reverie. "So sorry, mademoiselle, but I had to repair a torn skirt." Lucy, her dresser, swept into the room and finished unhooking her costume.

With her face cleansed of its theatrical mask, Cate dusted a bit of powder over her nose. Lucy added a pale brush of peach to each cheek and a tint of rose to her lips. "Just enough, not too much," Lucy said. Cate undressed and slipped into a simple gown. Her dresser dug in the costume chest and added a smart velvet riding jacket and silk evening hat.

"You have a flair for styling, Lucy."

The girl beamed. "Dancers can't afford much finery. I do what I can to help the corps dress for their engagements with gentlemen."

"If you can call them that." She kissed the girl's cheek and winked.

Hugh Curzon had acted the perfect gentleman that first afternoon in Barcelona. After rescuing the ungrateful child in the runaway pony cart, he'd gently prodded both packages out of Cate's hands. She'd watched him juggle reins and hatboxes. "You're sure?"

He nodded. "Lead the way, Miss Willoughby."

His large red hunter ambled along behind as they spoke of the weather and points of interest. All the things people talk about when they don't know each other well but might wish to know the other person . . . better.

When they reached her aunt and uncle's residence, he

handed her one hatbox at a time. "The Güell palace is just around the corner." She pointed down the lane.

He tipped his hat, turned away, then swiveled back. "Would you . . . have dinner with me tonight?"

She clearly remembered the flush of heat on her cheeks. "Regretfully, I have a dance lesson this evening. Besides, my aunt and uncle are very old-fashioned. I'm afraid they would insist on a chaperone."

He arched a brow. "Dance lesson?"

"While I am here in Barcelona, I wish to study the Catalan dances—the zambra mora, bolero, fandango." She remembered smiling up at him. "You are interested in the old gypsy dances, Mr. Curzon?"

"I am interested in you, Miss Willoughby." He appeared to consider what she had just revealed to him. "And if you were not here in Barcelona, where might you be?"

She smiled. "Paris. I dance with the *Théâtre de l'Académie Royale de Musique*, monsieur."

He stepped closer, his resonant voice huskier. "And if your aunt or uncle were by chance . . . *out* of town?"

"Then . . . I would ask you to meet me at nine o'clock in the square—the Plaça Reial." She dipped a brief curtsy and slipped inside the courtyard. But she hadn't missed the flash of light in his eyes. "I must go. *Talué, señor.*"

That evening, at dance class, she could not get his unsettling, deep brown gaze out of her mind, especially when she emulated Doña Marguerite's sway and roll of the hips.

Cate opened her dressing room door and shut down the memories. All that lovely romance wasted on a professional liar. And the discovery came just days after she had given herself to him. Hugh Curzon—or rather, Phineas Gunn—was a British spy. A man who could not be trusted.

## ∞ Chapter Three

"Darling, forgive me, but you are a stunner." Finn held the diamond to the light and twirled the stickpin between his fingers. A soft tap and click of the door latch meant his butler had entered the study. "Bootes, have a look at this. Note the exquisite, old European brilliant cut—near perfect clarity."

"My word." Bootes leveled his pince-nez on the bridge of his nose. "Something over ten carats, I wager."

"Twelve and half," he murmured. "A touch of azure in daylight, likely to move toward violet by gaslight." The gem was set in a delicate nest of gold filigree. "This has to be a Tavernier diamond. Note the splendid workmanship on the setting. Downright vulgar as a tiepin, wouldn't you say?

A wavering of eyelashes was all it took to read his butler's opinion of the superior gem. "I see what you mean by garish, sir. Fitting, perhaps, for a Russian prince on holiday here in British Isles."

Finn snorted. "A Russian prince would use this pretty bauble to pick his teeth."

His man's gaze narrowed, along with an uptick at the

edge of the mouth. A smirk was the closest one got to a smile from Bootes. He had always called his loyal manservant Bootes. At this moment, mesmerized by the glittering trinket, Finn could not recall why the sobriquet Bootes, nor could he remember the man's real surname— Morton, was it?

Over the last few years, he and Bootes, who functioned as both valet and houseman, had developed their own informal parlance, a bachelor's code of sorts. And Finn quite admired his butler's ability to communicate without uttering a single word. The somewhat quirky manservant spoke volumes with the slightest tilt of his chin or shift in his gaze. A serviceable and, at times, amusing accomplishment.

"Has Hardy arrived?" Finn asked.

Bootes rolled his eyes up and to the left.

"Then is he dressing?"

The butler cleared his throat. "I believe so."

They were late for the Beauforts' ball. Phineas returned the gem to its diminutive case and rose from his desk. "Is my tie straight?"

Studying his neck, Bootes made no effort to hide his satisfaction with himself. "As it was when I tied it, sir."

Finn sauntered over to Hardy's room, where his brother kept a wardrobe of clothes in a bedroom he rarely slept in. His mind wandered from stolen diamonds to Catriona de Dovia Willoughby and his heart began to race, in a good way. Every powerful emotion he had felt for her and abandoned in Spain came roaring back to life last night.

And she also knew something of his connection to her brother's demise, yet she hadn't called him a murderer. A technicality perhaps, but a relief nonetheless. And he couldn't help but wonder, had she played him in Spain?

The very idea that she was a clever operative sent to distract him while he had used her to move in on *Los Tigres*—Good God, he found the idea intensely arousing.

Finn leaned against the open doorjamb of his brother's room while Hardy attached his braces. He reminded himself that sweetly innocent young ladies did not traipse around Barcelona with strange men nor jump into bed with them.

And yet, he could have sworn she was a virgin. He cringed slightly. What was it about Cate that was so captivating—so rare? He knew full well he was a man of appetites; even so, he remained in control of himself at all times. But this lovely young woman had quickly become utterly . . . irresistible.

The assignment had ended in a hail of bullets, an explosion, and a barn full of dead Spanish insurgents. And still, he had returned to her. Rather odd for him. A highly placed anarchist had been killed, one who also happened to be her flesh and blood. In Barcelona Finn had sent Cate an urgent message, but she had not met him at Café Almirall. Not that evening, nor the evening after that. Thinking back, he remembered waiting many nights.

Finn straightened. "About ready?"

Hardy swung around and looked him up and down. "I believe we're going to slay the ladies tonight, Brother."

Finn narrowed his gaze. "With both Lady Gwendolyn Lennox and the bothersome husband in attendance, I'd have to say you're the more likely candidate to be slain." He inched over so Bootes might enter and examine Hardy's tie.

His valet grimaced at the badly done loops and retrieved a fresh cravat from the highboy. His brother lifted his chin. "Rufus is not going to call me out, and if he does I'll wing the old earl—I won't kill him."

His brother's lack of care for life and limb, propriety or

scandal, was refreshing at times, but not this evening. Finn ignored the band of tension moving across his forehead and replaced a grin with a frown. Hardy was going to get himself killed one day—or tossed into Newgate gaol for murder.

The carriage ride through Mayfair was mercifully brief. Finn could barely listen to his brother go on about Gwen. Hardy was smitten, all right, or was he just taken with the danger of it all? The stolen moments, the surreptitious meetings. The ferocious sex. Heady stuff. Investigative undercover work was likely the perfect career choice for his little brother. In some ways, he and Hardy were cut from the same cloth. They both loved fast horses and, whenever possible, faster women.

So, why did he keep returning to Cate? A twitch played at the edges of his mouth. The very thought of her sparked a fire inside strong enough to trigger a nervous spell. Happily, this evening he just felt pleasantly stimulated. If this sort of lascivious reverie over Cate Willoughby continued, he would require a good long fencing lesson tomorrow.

He and Hardy exited the carriage and entered the Beauforts' palatial town house on the square. Perfunctorily, they checked coats, hats, and extra gloves with the staff.

One last thought lingered about the fascinating young woman. She had quickly become a deeply affecting and keenly felt distraction in Barcelona. If he had been her assignment, as suspected, then mission accomplished. And this most recent turn of events—what might she be up to in London? He was certainly game to find out.

Finn ignored the heart palpitations.

Hardy broke off his chat with a couple in the concourse and joined him at the top of the stairs. "Out and about in public two nights in a row, Finn. Some kind of record for you."

"I've reconsidered." He waited for his younger brother to be announced. "I'll gladly second you in a duel with the Earl of Lennox."

Hardy snorted a laugh.

The moment he and his younger sibling entered the hall, Finn was aware of the tilting heads and surreptitious glances. They soon found themselves surrounded by a bevy of young ladies—a sea of pastel gowns and corseted bosoms. Not an entirely unpleasant predicament to find oneself in. With the exception of a few polite greetings and one or two introductions, Finn maintained a cool distance, choosing not to chat for any length of time with the young women. Generally, when he and his brother were on the town, he let Hardy do the lion's share of the flirting. Until he saw something he wanted.

"Phineas Gunn, my word, this is a rare treat."

"Anatolia." He bowed. "I must apologize for missing the reception—I blame it all on him."

The Duchess of Beaufort turned to his brother, a distinctive arch to her brow. Her cool gaze warmed considerably when Hardy took her hand and kissed it. "Such a handsome rapscallion," the duchess clucked, adding a wink to Finn. "He deserves his reputation."

A smile played at the edges of his mouth. "There is a sort of exuberant devilishness about him. At least Mother says so."

"Phineas, you terrible man!"

He turned toward the high-pitched whine with a haughty lilt. "Ah, Muriel."

"Why, I would have worn my new blue gown by Madame Mateaux had I known you planned to attend the

Beauforts' ball." She settled in beside him with a stomp of delicate foot. Muriel bobbed a curtsy. "Anatolia."

"An eleventh-hour decision." Finn wrinkled his brow. "You look lovely in . . ."

"Apricot." Muriel sniffed and prattled on to the duchess. "A gentleman would inform a young lady he was coming." She fluttered a breeze with her fan.

Finn edged closer to Hardy. "I'm quite sure I inform a woman when I'm coming."

"You always were the polite one." Hardy's wink interrupted Muriel's pout; she assumed the twitch in his brother's eye was intended for her. The blushing chit sighed a tut-tut of disapproval.

There was a time when Finn would have considered Muriel Villers-Talbot's protrusion of lower lip a charming diversion. He had briefly courted Muriel, but by God's Grace—or some other stroke of luck—he had come to his senses quickly. Unfortunately, the poor girl had never gotten over it. This past spring, at a soiree, she had maneuvered him into a scandalously intimate situation in the gallery. That he had barely escaped her entrapment served only to goad her onward.

Of late, rumors of their imminent pairing floated about like fall leaves in the wind. Muriel appeared to be campaigning the idea about that Phineas intended marriage as soon as he recovered from his pitiable nervous condition, Soldier's Heart.

A tilt of chin enhanced her sulk. "Honestly, Finn, I had no idea you were feeling right enough for a ball."

"Actually . . ." Finn lowered his voice. "I've a bit of business to attend to."

Muriel blinked. "Business?" A blur of pale plum–colored satin brushed past him. "Ah, my new friend."

Muriel snagged the dark-haired beauty into their circle. "Phineas Gunn, please meet Catriona de Dovia Willoughby. She is a *première danseuse* with the *Théâtre de l'Académie Royale de Musique*." Muriel leaned in. "She is also one of us—the British half, anyway. Isn't that right, Cate?"

Instantly, the atmosphere in the hall grew warm and stifling. He knew this because he sucked in a large quantity of the oppressive air. Finn paid no heed to an elevation in heart rate and nodded a bow. "We meet again, Miss . . . de Dovia, or do you prefer Willoughby?"

Confused or distressed or both, Muriel turned to Cate. "You two have met?"

Finn knew for certain he grinned. "Zeno Kennedy invited me to the Alhambra last night." When Muriel raised a supercilious brow he added, "On a bit of business."

An amused duchess leaned in. "My dear, I'm afraid a man's *business* is conducted just about everywhere these days."

Anatolia's innuendo breezed by Muriel. "You see how at ease I am with theatrical dancers? Finn says I can be pompous and rigid." She tapped her fan on his chest. "Don't deny it. I mean to prove to you I can be just as common and gay as—" Muriel stopped. "Oh dear." She turned to Cate. "It's not that I believe you to be common, in the vulgar sense—" With each word, Muriel dug herself in deeper.

Finn cleared his throat. Loudly.

Cate bit back a smile. A side-by-side comparison of the two young ladies proved amusing. Pleasurably plump versus lithe and lovely. Cate was nearly a head taller than Muriel. He angled closer to his brother to mumble, "Ask Muriel to dance."

Hardy was incredulous. "How will you ever return such a favor?"

Finn was not amused. "You know as well as I that you must make a show of dancing with available young ladies. Afterward, you can take Gwen for a spin around the dance floor without raising too many brows."

Hardy pivoted with a smile. "Muriel, did I tell you how delightful you are in that ruffled confection of a gown—peach, is it?"

"Apricot." She sighed.

There wasn't a woman alive who could resist him—or so Hardy believed. "The very color of your blush, I should think. Is your card open for a dance?"

In fact, Muriel's cheeks colored the very pastel of her gown. "Why, now that Finn is here—"

"I'm sure he won't mind sharing." Hardy stepped up and took her by the arm. "Shall we, dear?"

He assumed his brother steered Muriel off to the dance floor; he wouldn't know, as he was otherwise occupied staring at Cate. "Does it bother you? The pretension as well as the snide quips?"

She returned his interest for a very long time. "You are resplendent in formal attire, Mr. Gunn." She leaned in with a grin. "Please don't read anything into the compliment. It is just . . . what it is."

"A compliment." He grinned. "And if I said I had never seen a woman look lovelier in pale plum?"

Her gaze swept the room, a half smile on her face. "Then . . . I'd say I managed to change the subject." Long dark lashes fluttered above indigo eyes that returned to him. He recalled a night in Barcelona and a look of deep blue ecstasy.

Finn cleared his throat. "I presume the *première danseuse*'s card is full?"

"All the waltzes are reserved." Those extraordinary eyes sparkled with laughter when he blinked. "You're not the type of man who would be interested in anything other than a waltz."

"Here you are, my dear." Cecil Cavendish, Baron Burleigh, strode up beside Cate. He eyed Finn suspiciously. "I hope I arrived in time?"

"To rescue me from the arms of Mr. Gunn?"

Finn kept his grin stiff. "All the waltzes are taken."

"With my name." Cecil beamed as he offered his arm. "Shall we?"

The dazzling brilliance of a half-dozen chandeliers suddenly felt glaring. Finn ran a finger under the stiff points of his collar and moved to a less sparkling side of the ballroom. He reminded himself why he'd attended one of the biggest balls of the season. He was here to take silent inventory of the aristocracy's jewels. After all, it was those glittering gems and the golden fizz of champagne that put the *beau* in *beau monde*.

A quick scan of décolletés told him he was familiar with nearly all of the most extraordinary pieces in the room. At one time or other, he had either been party to the sale of or had appraised the value of the exquisite baubles. He drifted through the crowd, a good length behind Cecil and Cate as they took a turn about the room. At the far side of the hall, he caught sight of Hardy and Muriel on the dance floor. One of the new quick-step polkas—something fast and fancy. Finn marveled at his brother's ability to look dashing no matter how ridiculous the hops and skips were.

Lady Lennox also watched Hardy dance from a small

circle of friends. Drawing closer, Finn concentrated on Gwen. Dressed in something gossamer, the woman always looked ravishing. Even more breathtaking was the teardrop diamond nestled above deep cleavage. The exquisite gem dangled from several delicate strands of diamonds and pearls.

Finn inhaled a sharp breath. The necklace appeared to be something quite extraordinary, and he had not been consulted. He would have remembered a gem like this one. He needed a closer look.

The three-quarter time of the music ended on a high-spirited up note and Finn zigzagged a path to intercept his brother and Muriel as they left the dance floor.

A breathless Muriel snapped open her fan. "I must freshen up after a polka like that. If you would excuse me, gentlemen?"

Finn stabbed an elbow into his brother's side.

"Great fun, Muriel—full of vigor. We must do it again."

Finn watched Muriel until she disappeared into a sea of pastel silks and chiffon. "And how are your toes?"

Hardy remained stoic. "One has to give the young lady credit for trying."

He grabbed hold of his brother and lowered his voice. "I'd like to get a closer look at the latest bauble Lady Lennox is wearing, as well as have a turn round the floor with Cate Willoughby." A grin widened. "You, on the other hand, would like nothing more than to steal a dance with Gwen."

"Brilliant. We'll have a trade-off—just like the old days at Trinity." Hardy's eyes lit up. "Where is Miss Willoughby?"

"On the arm of Baron Burleigh. He's a bit testy with me, but you might easily cut in."

"Isn't Burleigh recently engaged?"

"He claims to be as promised to Daphne Portman as I am to Muriel."

Hardy's eyes narrowed slightly. "I wonder if Daphne feels the same way about the betrothal."

"You always were sweet on her."

Hardy exaggerated a shiver. "Brainy Miss Minx? I think not."

Finn caught the eye of Lady Lennox, who smiled. He nodded in return. As the first strains of the waltz began, the lady appeared unpartnered. Finn wasted no time closing in. He reached into her circle and she clasped his hand. "Excuse us, gentlemen." Finn whisked her onto the ballroom floor.

"Good evening, Gwen."

"Good to see you, Finn."

His eyes dropped to the gleaming strands on her chest and lingered long enough to pay two jiggling mounds a compliment. "'Torches are made to light, jewels to wear.'"

A feminine brow arched. "Do you believe Mr. Shakespeare admired such trifling gems apart from, or adorning the wearer?"

He whirled her into a series of turns. "Must it be either, or? If I choose bosom over bauble I risk life and limb from either your husband or my sibling. And as for the lovely gems—?"

The lady's mouth quirked a bit. "The earl entered my boudoir this evening and fastened the necklace around my throat." Storm clouds passed beneath mercury irises. "A reminder of his—"

"Possession?" Finn shortened his stride and steered them toward the center of the dance floor. "I must have details, madam."

Gwen exhaled quite a darling harrumph. "He purchased the necklace from a jeweler who claims it came from a chest full of gems—the dowry of a princess."

"Prussian?"

"I believe so." Her faraway gaze returned to him. "I hate it." Silver eyes shaded a darker gray as rosy lips pouted. It was obvious what Hardy saw in her pale beauty. The Gwen Lennox he knew, however, was hardly a swooning lily.

He caught a glimpse of Hardy dancing with Cate. In the space of a few more turns, they would be soon be side by side.

Finn kept his voice low. "Follow my lead closely, Lady Lennox." With his hand centered above her head, he whirled Gwen beneath his arm and stepped in the opposite direction. He released her hand to his brother as Hardy passed Cate over to him. A sliding side step brought him into position as Cate finished her twirl. He drew her into his arms, smooth as silk. If they had rehearsed the move a dozen times, it might not have come off as well. Hardy whirled the countess off with a wink.

"My, my, aren't you and your brother the clever ones." The pleasant surprise in her eyes set off an irregular series of thumps in his chest. And she danced exactly as he remembered—as light as air with a sway to her hip—like the bolero, a Spanish version of the waltz. She had shown him the steps one evening in the Plaça Reial. Finn lengthened his stride and she was with him through every fluid turn.

He tried a conciliatory smile. "Got off a bit wrong-footed last night. Perhaps we can start over?"

## ∞ Chapter Four

"Starting over implies a new beginning, which is impossible for us." Cate held his gaze well past the six beats of a complete turn.

She remembered him standing in the Plaça Reial. She had pointed to one of the sculptured lampposts in the square. "Gaudí." And he had kissed her suddenly—without any warning. A tingle had run through her body, from her lips to her toes. An unexpected intimacy from such a quietly intense man. She had thought her heart would leap from her chest.

Their attraction had quickly led to an afternoon and evening of torrid lovemaking. When the brief affair was over, she had cast the unnerving event into the furthest recess of memory. Even now he was so distractingly masculine. "I did not know they taught debauchery at the spy academy."

One side of his mouth lifted slightly. "If only there were such a such an institution—"

"You seduced me in Barcelona."

A spark flashed in those deep brown eyes. "Who seduced

whom, Miss Willoughby? As I recall, I was bewitched—" He dipped his head to make eye contact. "In Barcelona."

Cate followed every bend of his body as he lengthened his stride. A muscular leg grazed hers and she arched away to cover a tremble. They danced close. The kind of close that made it impossible not to admire the way they fit together.

Indeed, the fit had been sublime.

What on earth had come over her recently? The most obvious answer to that question held her in his arms and turned her gracefully—nay, sensuously—about the dance floor. Cate sighed. "The young woman you took advantage of in Barcelona believed you were smitten beyond measure. You are a clever operator, Agent Curzon." Her gaze narrowed. "That is, Mr. Gunn."

As if on cue, the music stopped, but he didn't let go. Even the dance of candlelight in his eyes refused to acknowledge the end of their waltz. Caught in his spell, she didn't push Finn away, not at first. Gradually, he withdrew his hand from her waist.

She dipped a curtsy and walked off the dance floor.

He took hold of her arm. "Cate."

She whirled around. "You murdered my brother."

"Let me explain—"

"I'll not warn you again, Finn." Cecil stepped between them. "Stay away from her."

He looked her escort up and down. "Sorry, I must have missed a warning somewhere." He ducked Cecil's swing.

"Cecil, stop!" she cried.

"Hold on there, Burleigh." Hardy Gunn stepped up beside his brother with Lady Lennox on his arm. "Can't we resolve this like gentlemen?"

"Give me a moment with Cate, then we'll take this outside." As Finn turned to her, an older gentleman, the Earl of Lennox, burst through the gathered circle.

"Not much of a lady, my wife." The sneering man grabbed hold of the jewels at Lady Lennox's throat and yanked harshly. Chains of pearls and diamonds cut into the neck of the beautiful countess. Cate stood frozen in horror as Gwendolyn gasped for air.

In a frenetic burst of movement the Gunn brothers sprang into action. Ignoring the shocked cries of onlookers, Finn grabbed the necklace and broke the clasp. The younger brother shoved the old man off and tucked the lady behind him. With a single well-placed blow, Hardy laid her attacker out cold on the ballroom floor.

Hardy turned to Lady Lennox. "Are you all right?"

She managed a nod, but continued to cough and appeared wobbly. The younger Gunn helped her to one of the empty chairs placed around the perimeter of the ballroom. "A glass of water—someone?"

"Come with me." Finn took hold of Cate's arm and steered her through a bewildered crowd of onlookers. He turned back to Cecil. "Be right with you, Burleigh. Perhaps you might find a second and wait for me in the square?"

Her escort swallowed hard.

Cate turned to the man hauling her toward the supper room. "Did the Earl of Lennox just try to strangle his wife in public?"

"Raving bastard." His eyes were filled with pain and something darker—fury, perhaps. Quite disconcertingly attractive on Mr. Phineas Gunn. "Cate, there are no words I can offer that will ease the loss of your brother, but I want you to know that after he was killed, I returned to

Barcelona in hopes of seeing you again—if only to apologize and explain in person."

Finn picked up a seltzer bottle and two glasses. "Hold one for me?"

She accepted the crystal flute and he poured the water. "There is nothing to explain. You used me to get close to Eduardo. Then you and your men followed *Los Tigres* to Béziers and fired upon the farmhouse."

"What happened shouldn't"—he exhaled—"have happened." Brows drawn, his gaze ransacked the room, as if he might find a better explanation hiding under the arch of a potted palm. "Still, I take full responsibility." Finn searched her face. "Cate, I didn't give the order to fire. I wanted to capture and question—"

She pivoted on her heel. "I've heard enough, Mr. Gunn." A pattern of familiar beats palpitated inside her chest. Her Catalan temper was on the rise. Soon she would be shrieking in Spanish, which wouldn't do at all. Not at the Beauforts' ball. What she needed to accomplish here must be done without notice. She could not unduly draw too much attention to herself.

Thankfully, Finn did not press the argument. Thus far, he had not come right out and accused her of an affiliation with *Los Tigres*, but these meetings—last night at the theater and now again, here at the ball—these were not chance meetings with Agent Gunn.

Her eyes narrowed to slits as she swept another glance at the man. It was clear British intelligence had set him upon her. But to what purpose? What was his game? A year ago, in Barcelona, she had been an innocent in more ways than one. She had lost her virginity to the madness of anarchy. And nearly lost her heart.

She and Finn arrived back at the scene in the ballroom

to find several guests surrounding the elder earl, still out cold on the floor. "One for Rufus." Finn lifted the glass from her hand and splashed water on the man's face. Instantly, the groggy earl opened his eyes and sputtered.

He turned to the countess. "And one for the Lady Lennox." He handed the flute to Hardy, who hovered over Gwen.

A rustle of evening gowns parted as the duchess approached. She was accompanied by a disgruntled gentleman, presumably the duke. Anatolia Beaufort flew to Lady Gwendolyn's aid while the duke took Hardy aside.

One had to admire the younger Gunn brother's audacity. Not only did he demand the earl publicly apologize to his wife, he challenged him to a duel of honor. The number of mouths that simultaneously dropped open in the crowd nearly caused a giggle. In fact, much to her dismay, a gasp of laughter escaped her mouth.

She covered her lips with her fingers and glanced at Finn. The expression on his face was unreadable, but there was something about his stance—a panther ready to spring into action in defense of his brother.

Dear Lord. Was it to be fisticuffs for Finn and Cecil? Pistols in the park, as Hardy took aim at the earl? Her sudden involvement in the Gunn brothers' imbroglio caused a wellspring of nerves to surge though her body.

When the earl finally rose to his feet, Hardy broke through the opposing circle of guests and the two men nearly came to blows a second time. One of the gentlemen referees pulled the young man aside. "Are you barking mad? If you insist on this contest, it must be quietly done."

Finn stepped into the fray. "Shall we allow a cooling-off

period of, say, a day or two? If both gentlemen still wish to proceed, I'll make the arrangements."

Hardy jerked his arm away from the man holding on to his sleeve. "I mean to see the brute finished off."


*"EN GARDE!"*

"Better to guard your bollocks, *mon ami*." Finn lunged forward and used several rapid, well-placed strokes. Having been on the poking end of a blunt épée, he knew well his instructor's ability to concentrate on the subtle, telling moves of his student.

*"Exactement*, the right riposte, Phineas—you improve." Sword master Raoul d'Artaine returned a volley of strokes that sent him into a scrambled retreat across the room.

"Stay sharp, Finn," Hardy called from one of the benches that lined the ornately paneled walls. High ceilings and chandeliers hinted at the spacious gallery's previous life as a room designed for gala receptions. Several years ago, at the height of his disability, Finn had had the room converted into a kind of gentlemen's gymnasium.

"Razor-edged, little brother." He employed a feint and reengagement from the opposite direction, using well-practiced, agile footwork. The silent gaps of cautious circling were less frequent now, punctuated more and more by the high-pitched ring of metal-on-metal rapiers.

Raoul feigned, then made a very deliberate move, foil to the inside, sliding the blade edge cleanly down Finn's sword, *a coulé*.

Long hours of practice had finally paid off. Finn's dueling skills had elevated considerably in the last year. He could hold his own with a swordsman of much greater experience. That is, unless his concentration wandered to a certain half-Brit, half-Catalan ballerina. The line of her elegant neck. Translucent nipples the color of—

Raoul deflected Finn's blade out of his hands and into the air. His sword landed with a clatter on the polished wood floor.

"Bollocks." Fisting his hands on his hips, Finn sucked in a deep breath.

Hardy hooted from the bench. "Bravo!"

Finn's glare chastened his brother's glee. "Until that unfortunate bit at the end."

Next up, Hardy leaped to his feet, flexing his épée. "Now that you've run our sword master down, let's see if I can take him out."

A glance at d'Artaine revealed the man had hardly broken a sweat. Finn turned toward a creak and click of the door. His manservant entered the room. "You have a caller, sir."

He picked up a Turkish cloth and wiped beads of perspiration off his brow. "At this hour of the morning?"

The butler's eyes rolled upward. "It's nearly half past ten."

Finn tossed the towel onto the bench. "Who, then?"

Bootes cleared his throat. "Miss Hebert is waiting in the parlor, sir."

"Evelyn?" Finn wasn't dressed to receive visitors, not that Evelyn Hebert would mind. His mistress serviced him in various stages of dishabille. They had a standing appointment here at the house. Every Tuesday—usually in the afternoon. This was Friday.

He nodded to Bootes. "I'll be down shortly."

Finn paid close attention to the sword master's critique of his footwork, then made his way downstairs. He entered the parlor and shut the door quietly. Evelyn stood at the window with her back to him. The clip-clop of horse hooves on wet streets echoed softly through the room. "Is everything all right, Evie?"

"I could ask the same question of you—Finn." She turned slowly, wearing an expression he had never seen before. Those luscious lips were set in a grim line, and her eyes almost . . . watery. Hard to read, but unsettling, nevertheless.

"Ah, the mystery that is woman." Something in his gut told him to proceed cautiously. Finn stationed himself by the arm of the settee. "Besides an impending duel or two, everything is fine, I suppose. And you?" If these vagaries went on for long, things were going to get tedious. In fact, they were already awkward.

She gnawed a bit on her lower lip. "When did you plan to tell me? I should think a gentleman would have the courtesy to tell his mistress well in advance if he planned to make a change." She approached him, eyeing his chest. He had left his shirt unbuttoned.

Incredulous, Finn stared. "And who . . . might you believe I have in mind?"

"Why, you plan to take the *première danseuse*, Catriona de Dovia, as your lover." Her lower lip jutted out. "And don't deny it, Phineas. The morning gossip is all about you and Hardy." Delicate fingers slipped into the opening of his shirt and stroked his lower torso.

Ordinarily, Evie's petting would cause a sudden surge of blood to his lower extremity. But not this time.

Gingerly, he moved her hand away. There were times it behooved one to stay abreast of the rumors. "Other than the morning tittle-tattle, what would cause you to leap to such a conclusion? I danced a single waltz with the young—"

A sharp rap from the parlor entrance seemed more

frantic than usual. The door opened a crack and his butler slipped through the narrow gap. Odd behavior, even for Bootes.

Finn's gaze narrowed. "Now what?"

The butler's eyes darted back toward the door. "A word, sir?"

Finn stepped away from Evie. "If you'll excuse me a moment?"

Out in the passageway, Bootes turned to him. "Another visitor, sir—quite insistent, I'm afraid."

"Tell whoever it is to return this afternoon." Finn began a pivot but hesitated. "What is the nature of the call?"

"A consultation, I believe. The young lady says she might be willing to consider . . . your apology." The man's eye twitched nervously. "Quite an irregular morning, wouldn't you say, sir?"

Finn turned slowly. "You have no idea." A surge of agitation throbbed through his body. He took a step, then another—before he swung around. "Might I ask you to offer Miss Hebert some refreshment? Tell her I shall only be a moment."

"Very good, sir." His manservant nodded in the direction of his study.

Finn backed down the passage and entered his private sanctuary. The young miss inside leaned over his desk for a better look through his magnifying-glass apparatus. Deep in concentration, she turned the brass-handled armature to adjust the lens.

"You can alter the height as well as the angle of the glass." He slipped in behind her. "Allow me a brief demonstration." He turned a small key on the pedestal and moved the glass up and down. "What is it you wish to focus on, Miss Willoughby?

She straightened. "A spider. Vanished under your papers." After looking him up and down her gaze settled on his chest. "Rather furry creatures up close."

This time he made an effort to button his shirt. "I'm afraid you caught me in the middle of a fencing lesson." Finn pulled his smoking jacket off a coat tree and slipped it on.

"Lady Lennox informs me you are a gemologist of sorts, Mr. Gunn. And that you often consult on private sales—appraisals—that sort of undertaking." Even in the dimly lit study her eyes shimmered like the folds of a blue satin gown.

He moved a chair closer to his desk. "Have a seat, Cate. Do you mind if I call you Cate? And you must call me Phineas or Finn."

She was simply dressed this morning. A high-collar, pleated blouse peeked out from under a velvet jacket and pinstripe gabardine skirt. Practical, with a dash of *comme des garçon* style. The way she moved in those garments made all the difference. He could barely take his eyes off a sweep of bow that settled above her bustle.

"Very well, Phin-e-ass." With an emphasis on the last syllable, she took a seat. "Rather rigid and pompous sounding. Nothing like the Hugh Curzon I knew in Barcelona."

"No, I suppose not. *That* man used you to get close to your brother. And for sex."

Those beautiful eyes narrowed sharply.

Rather than retreat behind his desk, he took the other wing chair beside her. "Your words, not mine." He crossed his boots at the ankle and stretched out tired leg muscles.

"Impossible. I would never use such coarse language."

He took a moment to admire the upward turn of her

chin and straight backbone. Perfectly British and yet, there was something so very un-English about her. The porcelain skin of a northern lass, but with a glow of color—fawn, perhaps. The welcome addition of a rose blush crept over her cheek.

"No, I suppose not." He rubbed a bristle of beard on his jaw. "I take it you have a precious gem or piece of jewelry you wish me to look at?"

Her glare softened. "Actually, there are a number of pieces, if I read my uncle's inventory correctly. The jewels are part of his estate." She stopped to moisten her lips. "He is recently passed from this life. And I am his only living relation."

"Sorry for your loss." Finn reached across his desk for a journal and pencil. "Your uncle's name?"

"Arthur George Willoughby, Baron Brooke."

"Address?"

She hesitated. "Number Nine Upper Belgravia."

"We're practically neighbors." Leafing through a volume of notes, he found a blank page to scribble on. "You were his ward for a time, if I recall correctly."

"Why yes." Eyes wider, she cocked her head. "Do you always remember odd and sundry details?"

"My memory lacks a filter. Rather helpful in my line of work." He continued to scratch a few notes to himself. "The fact that you are his sole survivor means you inherit—"

"Everything, I'm afraid." She sighed. "He left a mountain of debt."

"And what of his treasure?" He found Cate's dilemma intriguing. "Might I ask where the jewels are at this moment?"

"Scattered about London—"

A great clatter caused his interviewee to start. There was also a wail or cry. Finn sat up straight in his chair. Good God. He'd left Evie in the parlor. He set his journal on the desk and smiled somewhat stiffly.

"If you'll excuse me . . . I'll just be a moment." Finn closed the study door quietly before charging down the hallway.

A silver tray backed out of the parlor door, followed by his butler. Bootes looked up helplessly. "The lady has decided against tea, sir." The broken remnants of a cup and saucer lay scattered across the serving platter.

"So she has." Finn caught a glimpse of Evie pacing the carpet between settees. Not knowing exactly what to do, he patted his distressed butler on the shoulder.

"Good luck, sir." Bootes nodded a bow.

Finn circled Evie as he might gentle a frightened horse. "Evie . . . can we take this up another day? You are distraught and something's come up—"

She whirled around. "I know a dozen gentlemen who would gladly take your place. Handsome, rich men who send me notes and flowers—they beg for me, *mon coeur.*"

"Lower your voice, Evie, the whole house can hear—"

"Since when do you care who hears?" She lifted her chin. "You groan like a bear when you take your pleasure—in this very room." The muffled sound of a door opening and closing echoed through the house. Evie peered at the parlor door suspiciously. "Ha! She is here, is she not?"

"Miss Willoughby"—Finn hesitated—"is here on business."

"How much? How many times a week?" She spat and flew past him.

He caught hold of her skirt in the hallway. His mistress had always been passionate in bed. The sex had been heated—experimental—but he had no idea she could transmogrify into the virago before him. He dodged a slap to the face as well as her flying fists. "Evie, you will either return to the parlor or I will have to ask you to leave."

"*Et vous l'invitez dans votre maison? Bâtard!* Where are you hiding her?" Evie pulled on her skirt to break his hold. "I know she is here, *la petite putain Espagnole!*"

"I am proud of my Spanish blood, and I am no whore, madame." Cate stood in the study doorway, a defiant tilt to her chin.

Evie's up-and-down glance preceded an ear-piercing screech and a lunge. She took a swipe at Cate with her claws. With his heart thundering in his chest, Finn leaped between them. Short of breath, he managed to grab hold of each woman and hold them at a distance. Cate struck back at Evie with her free hand. "*¡Puta! ¡Usted piensa que usted es su puta Francesa!*"

Forced to shout over the snarling females, Finn shoved them further apart. "*¡Alto!* Cease fire!"

Evie's talons swept past Finn's nose, missing her feline opponent by inches. Cate batted the outstretched hand away. "*Desgraciada cretina*—daughter of a whore—*maldita bastarda.*"

A rumble of footsteps on the stairs brought Hardy into the corridor. Taking in the scene, his brother folded his arms over a shirt soaked in sweat. "I wouldn't wish to intrude on a man's pleasure—"

"Don't just stand there." Finn shoved Cate behind him and scowled at his brother. "Grab her."

Hardy lifted Miss Hebert in the air as she continued to scream and kick. "Ouch! You little—" He tossed the wailing shrew over his shoulder and headed for the door.

D'Artaine descended the stairs and met the butler recently returned from the kitchen. Both men watched the tussle with interest. "Two beauties fighting over one man." D'Artaine dipped a sweeping bow. "You have my undying admiration."

Finn glared pointedly at his butler. "Would you be kind enough to wipe that grin off your face and get the door for Hardy?"

*"Toqúeme otra vez—usted es muerto. ¡Sí, sí, usted es muerto!"* Cate yelled over his shoulder as he backed her down the passageway. She had always been ravishing when riled—especially when teased and held at the edge of pleasure. Savoring the memory, he shoved her into his study. "Stay!"

"I am not your dog, Finn. Do not think you can—"

He slammed his study door and followed a trail of French expletives down the corridor. He arrived in the foyer just as Bootes opened the front door. A familiar young woman stood on the porch looking a bit . . . huffish. "Phineas?"

Finn blinked. "Muriel?"

# Chapter Five

Cate swept up and down the room. She had unleashed the Spanish fire inside. A rarity—and she wondered how much of it had to do with this man. "*She* accuses *me* of being a whore? *¡Ella es la puta! ¡Ella es la puta!*"

Finn leaned back against the study door and pressed it shut. "Glad to know you don't use coarse language." His gaze never left her. After a lengthy silence between them he cleared his throat. "I dare not think how you might appraise Muriel."

Cate whirled around. "Why do you ask? She's not . . . here?"

"I sent her away in a hansom with Evelyn."

She stared for a moment, then snorted a laugh. "My word, as busy as a brothel in Brugge. Is it always like this?"

He approached her slowly and leaned close. "It is *never* like this." She felt his breath on her cheek.

He straightened. "As it turns out, Miss Hebert—a delightful person most of the time—can be a little . . ." He tapped a finger on the side of his head. "*Loco.*"

Cate studied him. Hot blood still thrummed through every passage of her body. "She is your French whore?"

He paused long enough to be considering a lie. "On Tuesday afternoons."

Her gaze faltered, slightly. "This is Friday."

"She heard the morning gossip about you and me. It seems Miss Hebert has grown an attachment these past few months."

She huffed a quiet snort. "Do not flatter yourself. She wants something." Cate approached him slowly. "I know of these high-priced French *putas*. They are greedy and dishonest. I do not like her for you." She enjoyed taunting him with a cynical grin. "You must trust me on this."

He stared as if he could not quite believe—her advice or her interest? She wasn't sure herself. Slowly, his liquid brown eyes narrowed. "And this counsel of yours is based on . . . ?"

She shrugged. "As you know, I did my dance study in Paris—one of the petite rats of the ballet school. I learned more than a *fouetté jeté* while I was there." She turned away and meandered through a study piled with books and odd scientific devices. The private retreat of an intellectually curious man. She noted the exotic-looking sidearms. He was also an adventurer. The stacks of technical tomes and apparatus just made him all the more attractive. "It is no surprise your French whore feels threatened. Most everyone comprehends women in theater—dancers in particular—want for nothing more than a rich protector."

Finn shook his head. "I don't believe that."

She turned back to him. "Why not?"

"Because I know you." He smiled with such sincerity her gaze faltered slightly.

She stepped away. "Shall we . . . Might we return . . ."

He motioned her to a chair and watched her take a

seat. "Before the interruption, you mentioned jewels scattered about London."

"I came here to ask if you could help me find them. I would gladly pay you a share of their worth." She retrieved a folded note from her reticule. "I found this amongst Uncle's papers."

Finn opened the letter and perused the list. "One diamond bracelet consisting of four strands of half-carat diamonds set in gold; two hundred and thirteen diamonds in toto fastened by a gold filigree heart-shaped clasp." He looked up. "These descriptions are quite complete."

"Uncle suffered from dementia in his last years. At first I thought he misplaced the jewelry. Then, at the gala opening night, I was introduced to a woman wearing a bracelet of rubies set in the shape of flowers." Her gaze swept to the list in his hand. "Number eleven."

"Could he have sold them?"

"And not keep a record of the sale? Uncle was a chronic list maker. To help himself remember, he wrote everything down—often several times. It has taken me weeks to sift through a mountain of reminders he left to himself."

She edged forward on her seat. "I believe the jewels were taken from the safe before he died."

Phineas folded the list. "You don't think someone might have—"

"Murdered him?" She tucked her lower lip under her teeth and scraped. "He was a dying man, with few servants. The most heartless thief would not have seen the need for it."

The mantel clock struck the half hour.

"I have afternoon class and rehearsal. I must go." She looped her reticule over a wrist. "Twenty percent of whatever we recover. Are you interested?"

A lopsided grin tugged at a corner of his mouth. "I rarely ask more than five percent for an appraisal. But then, this is so much more than a consult." He lifted a skeptical brow. "In fact, your quest falls somewhere between a heist, a treasure hunt, and a crime investigation, wouldn't you say?"

She found his scrutiny unsettling. "I'd rather not involve Scotland Yard."

"Then . . ." His eyes narrowed. "I shall require thirty percent."

"Seventy-five, twenty-five." She tugged on her gloves. "Do we have an understanding?"


FINN READ THE list again. He recognized several of the pieces, had even appraised one or two of the items. He returned to item number eight. "Rare blue diamond cravat pin, twelve and a quarter carats set in gold filigree."

He removed a hinged jewel box from his desk drawer and opened the case. Empty. He turned the container upside down hoping the pin would drop onto the desktop. Not a bloody thing. There was a chance he had misplaced the item. But no, that was impossible. Perhaps it had fallen out of the box and was lost—under the desk, hidden in the carpet? Finn pushed back his chair and checked a few likely spots.

He grimaced. Stolen. Right from under his nose.

And if the missing stickpin wasn't disturbing enough, he reread item fourteen. Even though the description was scrawled across the bottom of the page, it was quite the list topper. How could one forget the five strands of pearls and diamonds dripping from the throat of Lady Lennox? The infamous necklace of last evening certainly gave new meaning to the word *choker*.

Finn picked up the note and sniffed lampblack and shellac. He placed the paper under his magnifier and adjusted focus. The darker-colored script suggested the ink was fresh. No doubt a forgery and done recently. The cursive was really quite good. The words *teardrop diamond* had been crossed out and replaced with *star sapphire*. A deliberate obfuscation fashioned to look like an error.

Someone had muddled with the description of the necklace, but why? Interesting, Cate made no mention of it. Finn studied the edge of the notepaper. A fuzz of cotton fiber indicated a fresh tear. Abruptly, he rose from his desk chair and found Bootes in the foyer.

"You haven't seen my brother, by any chance?"

The butler gave a good shake to an umbrella and placed it in the hall stand. His eyes rolled upward. "Two hot baths upstairs—one of them is growing cold."

Taking two steps at a time, Phineas strode directly into his dressing room, located his evening coat, and removed five strands of pearls and diamonds from the pocket.

His pulse rate slowed considerably as he examined the broken clasp. Fisting the jewels, he exited his bedchamber and turned down the hallway. He tapped once and opened the door. "Sorry about the brawl earlier."

Hardy languished in a steaming tub, a wet cloth covering his eyes. "Good to know that nervous disorder of yours hasn't affected your cock. I say, impressive, Finn."

He settled himself against the highboy. "Do you happen to know anything about this necklace, the one Lady Gwendolyn wore last night? The slightest detail could be helpful." Five strands of shimmer and sparkle dangled from his index finger.

"The old man is always lavishing trinkets upon her. I never ask about any of it." Hardy lifted the towel and squinted at the necklace. "Ghastly thing." He sat up in the tub. "I received a wire from Gwen. All's well. Rufus left town for the estate in Shropshire—to cool off."

He stared at his younger brother. "About last night—my mistake. I dragged you into that escapade on the dance floor."

Hardy snorted a laugh. "People believe I'm the roguey one, but it's your schemes that always get us in trouble."

Finn cocked an elbow. "Yes, but I'm not the one fucking an earl's wife."

"Might I take you back more than a few years and re-mind you of your scheme to sneak into father's study and unlock the cabinet with the French nudes for the stereo-scopic? It was my youthful backside that took the brunt of that caper." Hardy scrubbed a washcloth over his toes. "I would have danced with Gwen one way or the other. Old Ruffy was soaked—cupping all night with those smarmy investors of his."

Finn scratched the stubble along his jaw. "We'll give it a few days. Lord Lennox will stand down." He opened the bedroom door. "Do not skip off and do something you'll regret. I mean it, Hardy."

"I'm back on duty. Four straight days. No leave."

"Excellent." He paused to smile at his brother. "In fact, better than excellent."

Back in his dressing room, Finn stripped off his clothes and stuck a toe in his bath. Warm enough. He sank into the water and submerged himself. Underwater, he con-templated several scenarios as to how the diamond cravat pin came to be stolen.

A number of people had seen him yank the necklace off the gorgeous but gasping Lady Lennox. Between last eve-ning and this morning, someone—the thief presumably—

had gone rummaging in his desk and run across the stickpin. He recalled Zeno's words at the music hall. *"The burglar appears to be rather selective. Takes one piece and leaves piles of other valuables behind."* He imagined a gloved hand plucking the rare item out of its case and dropping it between fleshy, feminine mounds.

Finn blew a spout of air as he surfaced in his bathwater. He lathered up his hair and rinsed. The sting of soap in his eyes didn't do much to hinder a grin.


CATE STOOD AT the ballet barre and extended her leg to the side. She executed four *tendus* front from a closed fifth position. A slow flush of heat crept from her neck to her cheeks. Phineas Gunn had witnessed a rare display of temper she was hard-pressed to explain, even to herself.

*"Dégagez à terre avec la pointe tendue."* Monsieur Didelot tapped his baton in his palm and walked the stage between rows of ballet girls at the barre. The music hall was empty but for their pianist and a cleaning crew. She was to have an additional hour of practice today with Mérante, the male lead.

"And reverse, *mes chers.*" At the end of their *tendus*, the dancers pivoted in unison. Cate checked her posture. Clearly, it was none of her business if Phineas kept a mistress.

She slid her toe out to a point, then drew her foot in. *Tendu* front. *Tendu* side. *Tendu* back. Another flush of humiliation washed over her. She had blurted out a string of profanity and curse words that would make a Portuguese sailor blush.

She bit her lip and began the *pliés*. What was it about

Phineas Gunn that encouraged the raving wanton in her? She recalled a night in Barcelona—though it had not been evening, exactly. A warm breeze had parted the curtains. Afternoon light had slanted across the hotel room and lingered on her nude body.

His tongue circled a pointed nipple.

Her knees wobbled as the memory swept through her body. "Open to me," he had whispered. His fingers moved lower—pushed deeper. She obeyed him then, and now. Cate gripped the ballet barre and widened her stance. Sweeping her arm up to third position, and lifting her chin, she tried not to think about how he had moved a finger inside her—gentle, exploring, stretching. He had paused for a moment and pulled away. "Am I the only man who has touched you here?"

She had reached out and drawn his face to hers, rubbing her flushed cheek against the stubble of his chin. "A few men have tried," she murmured.

He had studied her for a moment—evaluating, considering. She had pulled his mouth to hers and explained with her tongue how much she wanted this experience with him.

He added another finger to his exploration and his thumb also found a place to stroke. "Do you like it when I touch you here?" He discontinued the taunting, circling pleasure of his thumb. "Tell me, Catriona."

Her sex was swollen, petulant—wanting more. "Yes," she moaned. Strong arms, pulsing with life, drew her up against his hard body. With one hand, he clasped her wrists behind her—arching her, drawing her closer. He slid one finger, then two, farther, causing more shuddering and trembling.

He had boldly taken control, but he did not threaten her in any way. In fact, she felt safe with him. Perhaps more so than with any man she had ever known.

He had dipped his head and teased up a nipple. Pleasure rippled through her body. His hard organ pressed against her belly and she wondered if he would be forceful and plunge into her. Part of her wanted it—badly. He had looked up from his suckling. "I will make you very wet. It will be more comfortable until you adjust to me."

Her knees wobbled and she lost her concentration at the ballet barre. Cate took a deep breath and shook off heated memories of sensuous lovemaking. She concentrated on the dance master's words. Moving off the barre, they worked on *port de bras*.

Last night at the ball, after the gentlemen had taken their argument outside, she had stayed behind and discovered something wonderfully intriguing about Phineas Gunn. According to Lady Lennox, no one knew the jewelry of the noblesse better than Finn. The truth of it was, *Los Tigres* had disappeared overnight. She supposed they were back on the Continent, somewhere. The anarchists had left her with no help. No names of the current gem owners, or where she might go to fence the pretty baubles. She had tried several of the gem dealers of Hatton Garden, but they weren't privy to private sales. No, if she was to recover the estate's jewelry, she needed Finn.

Only this time, her encounter with Agent Gunn would remain all business. She needed his knowledge of gems and his entrée to the beau monde. Cate suspected she didn't have much time left. Very soon, *Los Tigres* would expect their share of the profits.

Abruptly, Didelot tapped his baton on the piano and

the corps executed *le révérence*, a dancer's curtsy to show respect to the teacher and pianist.

Class dismissed.

While Cate waited for Mérante, she practiced solo parts of the *pas de deux*. Eight hops backward *en pointe*, into an arabesque with a drawn-out balance. Then on to a series of *piqués*, *fouettés*, and *grand jeté*.

She landed with all the grace of an elephant. Badly done.

"Again—from the beginning of the movement, if you would, Mr. Skym?" Cate took up a position to side of the stage and waited for the piano's cue. She repeated the same combination of steps. This time she landed the *jeté* perfectly.

The hollow sound of one person clapping came from the seats in the front of the theatre. "Bravo, Catriona."

She stepped closer to the footlights. Of course it would be him. A flutter of beats leaped in her chest. She placed both hands on her hips. "What are you doing here?"

He removed his frock coat and loosened his cravat. Nervously, she adjusted her cramped toes by waggling her pointe shoe back and forth on the stage floor. He was up the steps and onto the stage before she could utter much of a protest.

"It appears you are in need of a partner." He rolled up the sleeves of his shirt.

Unsure if she should smile or frown, Cate pressed her lips together. "You realize lifts require a great deal of strength."

He raised one of those supercilious eyebrows of his.

Over six feet of pulsing sinewy muscle stood in front of her with his arms open. She sighed or huffed. "Dancers study for years to execute the lifts in this adagio. It would not be safe—" Her eyes darted about. "Male dancers touch very intimate places."

The bare semblance of a smile played at the edges of his mouth. She cringed, waiting for a crude reference to the private places he'd so expertly stroked and caressed.

"I shall do my best to control myself." His voice was huskier than usual.

She studied him a moment. "Yes, you are always very much in control."

"Until I'm not." He moved closer. "We'll work until your partner arrives. Start with something basic—elementary." He tilted his head and taunted her. "You're not afraid of me, are you, Cate?"

She bit her lip and edged closer. "Very well. Perhaps the simplest way to move into the lift is for the ballerina to step into arabesque in front of her partner."

Cate assumed the position and lifted her leg behind her, waist high. "Place one hand on my waist and the other beneath the thigh of my working leg."

Finn slipped his hand around her waist and then hesitated. "Where exactly would you like the other?"

"Reach under my skirt." Cate bit her lip to hide her amusement. "This way you will have a better grip and you won't ruin the drape of skirt."

His hand traveled gently up the inside of her thigh. A tingle shot up her leg and rippled through her body. "That's high enough." Cate shifted her weight to remain in balance. Instinctively, he steadied her.

"We shall try a *piqué de poissons*—fish dive. Lift me off the ground—not too high. Once my head is above yours, dip me quickly toward the ground and hold."

Their first attempt was far from graceful.

Hands on her hips, Cate walked off a muscle twinge. "From the lower position, you lift me up—as if you snatch me from the arms of death. Then you must dip me as though I am falling from your grasp—in a graceful swoop."

"Graceful swoop." Finn nodded. "Is there a French term for that?" His grin caused her to shift her eyes away.

Cate stepped closer. "I must keep all my muscles strong and engaged throughout the lift. If I don't press my arabesque leg against your hold, I'll fold in half and lose all stability." She cleared her throat and swallowed. "Let me feel your hands."

"Like this?" His hand slipped under her thigh and his grip tightened.

She flexed her thigh against his hold. "Do you feel me answer you?" The words were spoken in a raspy voice, one she didn't recognize as her own.

"Mm-hmm." His breath brushed against the soft hairs of her temple.

Her heart fluttered inside her chest. *"Élevé."*

He lifted on counts one and two. Dipped her on three and four. Cate swept her leg into *passé* position. He brought her upright on five, six, and returned her to earth—seven, eight.

"*Sans volume, monseiur*—quietly." He lowered her gently onto her pointe leg. Back on the ground, she turned to him. "You are better at this than I imagined."

She never knew men could grin with their eyes. At least, this one did.

"All right then, something more challenging. Nothing too high—yet." Cate tilted her head. "Perhaps you could lift me onto your shoulder?" Within one or two tries, Finn lifted her with ease—and he was both powerful and graceful. He lowered her gently to earth. Cate completed the lift with an arabesque. Standing in his arms, she arched back. "Bravo, Finn."

As a student, she had developed crushes on one or two male dancers. All that touching in places no man was allowed. And there was something deliciously wicked about engaging in such an intimacy with a man who was not a dancer. A year had passed and still the heat of her attraction to him shook her to the core. She had never been held by a dancer who moved her like this. She had trembled when his hand moved up the sensitive flesh of her inner thigh.

Without a word, he lifted her again. "If I remember correctly, your partner held you like this." He pressed her against his body and lowered her slowly.

The delicate, sensuous notes of Debussy accompanied a brief nuzzle of his nose to her bodice. A warm exhale drifted across the curve of her breast, and the rough stubble of his chin brushed the hollow of her throat.

Her toe shoes dangled inches off the ground.

Face-to-face, his half-lidded scorching gaze lowered to her mouth. The memory of his words in Barcelona taunted her. *Say yes, Cate, say yes.* Her body strained against the corset of her costume, and her stomach muscles trembled. The tingle was back. The one that aroused nipples, clenched her womb, and curled her toes.

Descending an inch at a time, her thigh pressed against his lower anatomy. A strong shiver racked his body, causing him to drop her with a thud. "Bollocks." His apology was worse, barely more than a harsh whisper. "Sorry."

She could not help but notice the bulge. "Male dancers wear a dancer's belt."

"A what?"

"I have no idea why I blurted that out." Cate shook

her head and laughed uncomfortably. "It's a kind of . . . codpiece to protect your privates."

A smile crept over his face. "Now, why would I—?"

"This is not about r-rubbing," she stammered, as a rush of heat singed her cheeks. "I could kick you by accident."

"Yes, I've experienced those toe slippers firsthand—painful to the shinbones, as well as a man's testicles, I imagine."

She really must change the subject. "The lifts look simple and elegant, almost weightless. But as you can see, they require hours of practice."

He exhaled a long loud breath. "I was better at the bolero."

She tilted her head. "Yes, I believe you were." She turned to the pianist. "Something by Strauss, Mr. Skym—adagio, please." She returned to Finn with a blush of heat to her cheeks.

"Like the waltz, the bolero is danced in three-quarter time." Finn used a mock instructor's voice. Drawing her to him, they practiced the basic pattern of the dance.

She danced a circle—more of a strut—around him. "Quick, quick—slow. Draw me to you." Finn swept her close. "Place your right leg between mine and pause." The moves returned to him quickly as they whirled around the stage. Soon they were extending the glide of their steps together.

For a large man he was graceful and very much in charge of his partner. He swiveled his body with hers—inserting his leg between hers. "Press your thigh against mine, and hold." At times, in the turns, she felt as though their bodies moved as one. *Perfecto, sensual, glorioso.* Hips swaying, legs interweaving—coming together, drawing apart.

Cate smiled. "You remembered."

He pulled her back and held her against his body. "How could I possibly forget?" The last strains of the waltz ended on a quiet note. His gaze lowered to her lips. "Lovely piece of music. 'The Kiss Waltz,' is it not?"

Her eyes fell to his mouth. She allowed herself a brief fantasy then stepped back, breaking the spell. "You never answered my question. Why are you here?"

His gaze tracked her every move. "I've had a chance to study your uncle's list and have a number of questions. If you have time before the—?"

She shook her head. "I go straight from rehearsal to the bathhouse and return in time to ready myself for evening performance." Cate ducked her head to peer through the raised piano lid. "It appears Mérante has missed rehearsal. Thank you, Mr. Skym."

"Tomorrow morning then, say ten o'clock, at your uncle's residence?" Finn asked.

"Ten is fine." She picked up a Turkish towel and patted her forehead. "You might have offered to take me to supper."

"I've a rather a busy evening ahead of me. A few errands and obligations to attend to." There was something deliberately evasive in the way he avoided her gaze. "And there is a necklace to return."

She draped the towel around her neck. "I take it Lady Lennox is recovered?"

Finn shrugged. "Hardy claims all is well. The earl has left town—cooling off in the country."

She stopped a slow pivot midturn. "You mentioned obligations?"

He stared for a moment before clearing his throat. "I think it best I settle affairs with Miss Hebert."

A smile tugged at the corners of her mouth. It would seem this *pas de deux* with Phineas Gunn was far from over.

## ∞ Chapter Six

𝔉inn sat in the darkest corner of the lady's bedchamber and listened to the padding footsteps and soft murmurs of the servants as they closed up the house for the night. A rustle of leaves whipped up by a gust of wind carried the chill of evening across Lady Lennox's sumptuously appointed four-poster bed.

He had purposely left the window ajar.

This surveillance would likely go nowhere this evening. Then again, he might catch a jewel thief.

Gwen had been a good sport about the whole thing. "Something devilishly romantic about a night visitor to my bedroom." Her reaction to the idea of a second-story man had gone from amused to angry in so many seconds. "Let the burglar have it. I shall never wear the bloody thing again."

"Yes, why not? Collect the insurance and be done with it," Finn had replied. After a good deal of flirtation and cajoling, Gwen had allowed him access to her room.

Finn had always enjoyed Gwen's pluck and he knew exactly what his brother saw in her. But this amourette with Hardy was different somehow. Gwen had encouraged gossip and flaunted the affair. Worse than that, she allowed herself to be seen in public with her lover. And his devil-may-care brother had indulged her. The fact that Gwen enjoyed a tryst now and then was entirely her own business. But she was dragging his brother into something that could end badly.

Shortly after midnight, Gwen had escorted him up to her room and unlocked her jewel safe—if one could call it that. The lady's jewelry case was more akin to a heavy, cumbersome cabinet. She leaned against the dresser as he dropped the necklace into one of the flat drawers.

"Are you planning to sleep over, Finn?"

He closed the cabinet door and met her gaze. "Sleep is not advisable when in pursuit of a burglar."

Her eyes smoldered with interest. "Mmm-hmm." More of a purr than an acknowledgment. She sidled close, like a cat looking to do a bit of rubbing against him.

He reached for the key on the crystal oil lamp in her hand. "And I'm afraid company is out of the question." He turned down the wick.

Her pout was adorable. Christ. What man with a cock between his legs wouldn't want the lovely Lady Lennox? He escorted her to the door of her bedchamber. "You'll have to sleep in the earl's bed tonight."

"First, I'd have to remember where to find it." She sighed. "I shan't be sleeping in that musty old museum piece. Too many degrading and distasteful memories." The lady wrinkled her nose. "I shall retire to a guest room."

Finn leaned against the door frame. "Good night, Gwen."

"If you happen to catch the man, please do wake me. I've never met a jewel thief." There was a tease in her smile as she backed away. "Just down the way, first door on the left."

Finn pulled up a footstool and stretched out his legs. Hooking a finger into his fob pocket, he withdrew his watch. He squinted at the hands. Half past one in the morning and not the barest stir in the air. Not since that meager bit of scratching at the window over an hour ago. The disturbance had turned out to be an ivy branch pushed about by a breeze drifting through the square.

Things were calm. Perhaps too calm. Even his pulse remained steady at seventy beats. He yawned. It was possible he was losing his edge. No doubt Monty, his unorthodox physician, would surmise it a good thing.

The hypervigilance that served him well in combat had only alienated him from civilian life. But on a night like tonight, all of his history in the northern frontier came hurtling back to mind. His body craved the tension in the same way a lotus-eater must have his opium. All of the nervous symptoms he suffered in civilian life could be traced to those bleak mountain passes northwest of Kandahar. The raids, the constant skirmishes. The only way a soldier survived was to remain yary—soldier-speak for sharp and alert.

In the fortress, on watch, he had used recitation to stave off sleep. Back then he'd favored Shakespeare, but not tonight. This evening called for something eerie, with a touch of whimsy. *"Once upon a midnight dreary, while I pondered, weak and weary. Over . . ."* He whispered a cadence of nonsense in place of forgotten words. *"While I nodded, nearly napping, suddenly there came a tapping, as of someone gently rapping . . ."*

The hair on the back of his neck sensed the movement before he saw it. A trace of shadow on the wall. He lowered his speech to inaudible, even though he continued to mouth the words. *"Tapping at Lady Gwendolyn's chamber* door. "'Tis some visitor,' I muttered, 'tapping at her chamber door. Only this, and nothing more.'"

Finn swept his gaze to the set of Palladian windows. A figure crouched on the ledge of the open windowsill, wearing a peaked cap and a rucksack over one shoulder.

Lennox House overlooked the north end of Belgrave Square. The flickering from streetlamps provided just enough illumination to observe the second-story man at work. The thief pushed up the sash and slipped through the opening in silence. From his chair set deep in the shadows of the draped poster bed, Finn admired every stealthy move.

Slight of build, with a youthful spring to his movements—possibly a chimney sweep. Used to heights and being tethered to a rope, the lads were often conscripted as parlor-jumps by master thieves.

There was a kind of fluid manner to each movement that smacked of experience. The intruder dropped into a crouched position, ready to spring to the window and escape at the first sign of discovery. Not an exhale of breath could be heard. The prowler's head turned to observe the silent lump Finn had arranged under the coverlet. A demi-mask covered the thief's upper face; all else was lost in a fog of shadow.

The trespasser's methodical scan stopped at his corner of the room. Cloaked in blackness, Finn returned the stare for an eternity of seconds. Silently, he slipped a hand into his jacket and pulled out his revolver.

The silhouetted figure rose and moved toward Gwen's dressing table. The strides were youthful, swift. Nothing more than a flicker of contour, a flash of profile. And there was a gracefulness to the motion, almost like . . . A corner of Finn's mouth edged upward.

The burglar shrugged off his rucksack and removed a tool. The lock on the jewel safe could be jimmied with a pocketknife and proved short work for the experienced thief. Drawers of exquisite jewels were pushed and pulled until, at last, the glimmering necklace was plucked from its velvet-lined tray and dropped into the bag.

Finn cocked the trigger.

The metallic click pierced the air as though it were a blast of dynamite. The robber jumped, then froze.

"Wise choice, not to run. If you had made a dash for it, I would have been forced to shoot." He remained in shadow and spoke in a raspy soft whisper. "Now then, mind telling me exactly what you're up to and who you work for?"

Finn settled back into the plush tufts of the side chair. "I advise you to start talking. Otherwise, it's off to Scotland Yard. I will likely have to wake the jailor at the CID headquarters. He can be irritable in the wee hours of the morning, woken up from a—"

"There's nothing to tell, sir." The young thief sidled toward the window.

"One more move, and I will put a bullet in your head." Truth be told, he was no fool; he'd aim for the body—if he was so inclined to shoot anyone. "Perhaps you might identify yourself?"

Rather than remove his cap, the lad pulled it lower. "Jack Pixley, sir."

Finn scratched the stubble of beard along his jawline. "No, the name doesn't feel right. Are you quite sure?"

"I think I know my own name, sir."

"Well then, just to make sure . . ." He could almost feel the nervous twitch under the demi-mask. "You will remove your cap, jacket, shirt, and trousers . . . Jack."

"Let me go, and I promise never to do it again. Give us a chance, sir."

Finn leaned forward. A pale moonbeam illuminated the barrel of his pistol. "You may leave the mask on—for privacy, if you wish."

After a few seconds of near suffocating silence, his quarry removed the cap. His brown hair was slicked back neatly. Finn motioned with the revolver and the next piece of clothing—the jacket—came off.

There was a lengthy hesitation regarding the trousers. "Must I, sir?"

"I will have your real name and who you work for."

"I work for no one—except myself."

"Drop them."

Braces loosed, the falling pants revealed long smooth thighs, delicate kneecaps, perfectly muscled calves, and nicely turned ankles he'd recognize anywhere, even in shabby work boots.

"Now then, Jack." Finn smiled. "Or might it be Jill I'm speaking with?" His pistol followed trembling fingers down the buttons of the shirt. "There really is only one way to be sure."

His subject turned away as the thin work shirt floated to the floor. Finn's gaze followed a sensuous curve of bare spine down to the firm rounded buttocks. She wore the briefest of pantalets, the kind of delicate underthing that might be worn by a courtesan.

Or a dancer.

Or a jewel thief.

The curve of each cheek bottom peeked out from under French lace. He found the sight more arousing than if she had been standing there entirely naked.

Erect to the point of pain, he rose from his chair and

approached her. "There is a line from Shakespeare: 'Our wooing doth not end like an old play; for Jack hath not Jill.'" She remained with her back to him and he could not resist. He kissed her shoulder.

"Phineas Gunn." Her voice was a husky whisper. The kind of voice a man enjoyed hearing in the dark.

"Careful, Cate. As you well know, I am able to exert a great deal of control—until I don't."

SHE MIGHT HAVE known it would be him. Cate squeezed her eyes shut and swallowed a gasp. "Mm-mm?" The hum from his lips vibrated softly against her skin. Her entire body shuddered from a sudden release of dread, fear, and the most humiliating sensation of all—desire. She arched her neck and offered him even more entrée. His lips grazed the curve of her nape and continued upward.

A shiver tingled through her, and he'd only touched her with his mouth. It was as if he deliberately goaded— teased her. He wanted her to ask for more. To admit she wanted him. And if that was what he desired, far be it from her to deny him.

She turned around, arms crossed over her chest, hands cupping her breasts. "Might I bargain for my release, sir?"

He stared at various details of her face before his gaze moved to her bosom. "A crime suspect must first be restrained before there can be any form of negotiation." Gently, he removed her hands.

Her nipples peaked, more from the heat in his gaze than the chill in the air. She raised a brow. "No handcuffs?"

"Disappointed?" His eyes continued to peruse her body. "Hands behind your back. And don't release them until I give you permission."

She clasped her hands behind her and nearly jumped out of her skin when he took a nipple in his mouth and fluttered his tongue. He lifted her off the ground and ravaged one tip then the other until she moaned from his pleasuring.

A plump nipple popped from between masterful lips. "How many men have you bedded since Barcelona?" His breath was harsh and his speech husky.

"Rather an irregular line of questioning."

He righted himself and stared. "The jailor's name is Mr. Slyce."

"Many."

He raised a brow. "How many?" His hands cupped her breasts and he rolled the sensitive, silken flesh between thumb and forefinger. A shot of something hot and wicked coursed through her. Standing in the center of the bedchamber, her trembling knees betrayed her lack of experience. Heat singed her cheeks, and she averted his piercing gaze. "None," she confessed.

His eyes lowered to her ravaged nipples and she felt his body quake. So, it wasn't just her. She suspected he was every bit as aroused as she. He dipped his head and lightly scraped his teeth over a tip of breast. She arched and gasped. *"Dios, salvame de este hombre."*

"I wonder . . ." Finn brushed his lips over the other beige rosebud. "Who needs saving from whom?" He lifted her up, using the wall to steady her back. "Straddle me with your legs." Bracing one hand against the wall of the bedchamber, he pressed his fingers into the flesh and muscle of her buttocks.

He held her at eye level. "I should impale you, right here, on my cock." He growled and carried her across the room.

"Is this the price you ask for my freedom?" She kept her legs wrapped tightly around him as he laid her down on the bed. She arched her hips to signal her willingness to receive him.

Only the glint in his eyes pierced the darkness. "And would you enjoy the gentleman's sword, as much as I would delight in the lady's sheath?" Poised above her, Finn stroked the inside of her trembling thighs. The blackguard was asking for permission.

She needed him closer. More vulnerable. Cate pressed her hand against his hard bulge. "And what do you call this great saber?"

He smiled. *"Phallus erectus."* Her fingers worked to release the impressive shaft from his trousers. Capturing his gaze, she opened her mouth and curled a moist tongue along the bottom edge of her upper lip.

As he leaned closer, she eased back onto the coverlet. "Come."

He crawled over her body like a great jungle cat ready for mating. She wove fingers into his hair and drew his head down. Her other hand dipped into his coat pocket. "Kiss me, Finn."

She withdrew the revolver.

As his lips touched hers, she swung with all her might. The butt of the pistol struck the side of his forehead. The violent crack to his skull passed though his lips and reverberated throughout her body. Suddenly, she was fearful. A ghastly grunt and a puff of air fanned across her cheek. His eyes rolled back in his head.

What if she had killed him? Dear God, she had never killed anyone before. And not Finn, please not him. He slumped on top of her—thirteen stone of dead weight.

A warm trickle of blood ran across her cheek.

## ∽ Chapter Seven

"Bloody rat bastard. I'll see both you cuckolders shot dead by dawn tomorrow." A splash of ice-cold water sat Finn bolt upright in bed. And if he was not mistaken, a raving lunatic stood over him. The worst sort of crushing, skull-splitting, stomach-churning headache forced him back onto his elbows. An entire squadron of drummers beat a throbbing tattoo inside his skull.

"Where is that brother of yours? The bloody rat bastard cuckolder."

The insult-spewing amorphous shape dipped and swung around the room, presumably in search of another—"Bloody rat bastard cuckolder," Finn croaked.

Slowly, the gray blur resolved itself into a miserable, muttonchopped, pinched-nosed character. Finn squinted an eye and the two-headed oaf resolved itself into one: Rufus Stewart, Earl of Lennox. "Such a colorful invective bears repeating, wot, Rufus?" Christ, it even hurt to grin.

The master of the house paused with a grunt.

Finn swayed to one side just as the earl's fist flew past his cheek. "Steady, old boy. I can explain." Like a ship listing to and fro in a storm, Finn righted himself. Gingerly, he probed his forehead.

The earl's second grunt was less skeptical, though puzzled. "Where is my wife?"

"You can't find Lady Lennox?" Finn blinked. "I suppose that explains your distress. If you had spoken this morning, she would have informed you I spent the night in her room"—he held up a defensive elbow—"after a ring of thieves."

The earl straightened. "What kind of cock-and-bull story is this?"

"Honestly, Rufus, do I look like I enjoyed your wife last night?" He rubbed his fingers together. Dried blood.

The earl pressed forward.

Finn retreated.

A bony finger poked at the knot on his head. "Looks as though someone got the advantage." An amused twitch formed at the corners of the earl's mouth.

"I believe my instincts were correct, though I admit the clever sneak thief got the better of me." Rufus backed off. Finn grimaced in the direction of Lady Gwendolyn's jewel case. "Check the fourth tray down. I wager the necklace is gone."

The earl slid out several drawers. "Why would a thief go to the trouble and not take the rest? This lot is worth tenfold the necklace." The suspicious look was back. "Damned irregular, wouldn't you say?"

Finn grunted. The whole scenario was damnably bad. In fact, it was worse than bad; it was nonsensical. "Rather a long story—some of it confidential." He eased his legs off the bed. "Shall we find Lady Gwen?"

Rufus scratched his chin. "Breakfast room, possibly."

How long had he and Gwen been married? At least six years. And yet the man barely knew his wife's daily routine.

"If you would—" Finn grabbed the bedpost to steady himself. "Lead the way."

The earl escorted him down the grand staircase, through several cavernous reception rooms, into a friendly alcove splashed with daylight and a pleasant flowered wallpaper.

Gwen scraped a bit of conserve over her toast. "You're home early, Rufus." She turned to Finn with a smile. "And did you catch a thief—" Her gaze moved to the side of his face. "Oh dear."

Finn dipped a look at himself in the breakfront mirror. Dark red rivulets stained the side of his face. "Caught the bloody burglar—for a moment." He swept back a tangle of hair and examined a lump the size of a golf ball. "Might I have my horse readied?"

The earl blinked. "Your horse is in my stable?"

"As I explained earlier, I have nothing to hide. Scotland Yard wants the cat burglar off the streets. Sorry, I can't be more forthcoming than that."

Somewhat chastened, the earl ordered a servant to the mews.

Finn examined the knot at his hairline. "Besides, I have an appointment."

"At this hour?" Gwen rose from the table and moved to the buffet. She dipped a lap-cloth into a pitcher of water and rang it out. "This should help." She patted the damp cloth over his beard stubble and up the side of his cheek.

"I'm going to bloody your napkin."

She smiled. "Now, why would I give a fig about a bloody napkin?" There had always been a kindness in Gwen underlying her outrageous behavior. When she pressed the cloth against the bump, he sucked air though his teeth. "Sorry." She smirked and dabbed more lightly.

"And what hour is it, exactly?" He reached in his pocket for his timepiece. "My watch has stopped."

She read the clock on the wall behind him. "Half past seven. And who wants disturbing at this hour?"

He reset his watch. "A Miss Catriona de Dovia Willoughby needs plenty of disturbing."

"Really, Finn, the ballet girl?"

The earl peered over his wife's shoulder. "Courting? With that egg on your noggin?" Rufus raised his quizzing glass for a better look. "Shall I send for Dr. Murphy? I want him fit enough to second for his brother."

Gwen faded back, her liquid silver eyes clouded over.

"A physician will not be necessary." Finn's gaze met the earl's. "Do have your man contact me."

Lady Lennox returned to her chair. "Have a piece of toast, Finn. You need your strength."

He leaned over the table, poured himself a splash of tea, and gulped it down. The very thought of Miss Cate Willoughby worsened the pounding in his skull. Everything about the young woman made him throb, either from pleasure or pain.

Had she actually outwitted and overpowered him? Frankly, he couldn't quite believe it. Rather a sly move for a ballet girl—and what a clever cover at that. If she was a foreign operative or anarchist sympathizer, what better way to move around greater Europe undetected? And what a noddy-fool she had made of him. Thieving, irritating virago.

A FLASH OF rare morning sunlight flared between the stately homes of Belgrave Square. Finn blinked from the glare. The dull throb in his head had returned. He searched his upper coat pocket and withdrew a pair of blue-tinted spectacles. Originally designed to cure certain forms of eye disease, the glasses were used by many soldiers to shade their eyes from the unrelenting sun of Egypt and India.

He hooked an armature over each ear and exhaled. Better.

The impressive facade of a nearby mansion set off thoughts of Cate scaling walls and jimmying windows. He recalled her daring high-wire act in the theatre. And it was clear she had decided to operate by her own set rules when it came to the recovery of her uncle's estate jewels. If, indeed, the list was authentic and not designed by a clever ring of thieving anarchists.

Asking for nothing more than a fast trot from his chestnut hunter, the two-block jaunt across Belgravia did nothing to clear his head. He turned his horse down a row of terrace homes on Eaton Square. If Cate Willoughby thought she was going to get away with this sort of outrageous behavior, she'd best think again.

"Nine Upper Belgravia, if I remember correctly, Sergeant MacGregor." The horse snorted and tucked his head into his chest. Smart as a whip and twice as brave, his fiery-coated steed was as sturdy as a plow horse with the added speed and stamina of the Thoroughbred. A special breed of equine. Finn tied him to a hitching post and climbed the portico steps of 9 Upper Belgravia.

A young servant opened the door, holding a pail of sudsy gray water. "Phineas Gunn." He presented his card. "I'm here to pay a call on Miss Willoughby."

She wiped her hand on a dingy apron and took his

card. "A bit early for callers, sir. The mistress has asked that you return in a few hours."

Finn pushed the dark spectacles down his nose. "Has she?" He entered the foyer. "I insist you show me to her this minute or I shall find Miss Willoughby myself."

When the maid hesitated, he pushed open every door along the hallway until he found a comfortable parlor, more of a conservatory, with a view to a garden beyond. The girl tugged on his sleeve. "Please, sir, let me take you to her. I believe Miss Willoughby is in the baron's study."

He gestured ahead, but the young servant turned down an intersecting passageway. She tapped on a door and rushed inside. "Pardon, miss, but I couldn't stop him—"

Finn stood in the door. The furnishings were a bit faded and frayed, but comfortable-looking, like the rest of the house. In fact, he found the residence rather charming after the luxury of Lennox House. "Bullyragged my way in. Don't blame the girl."

Cate sat behind a grand desk, a silver breakfast tray in front of her. "Do come in, Phin-e-ass." She emphasized the last syllable with a smile.

He ignored the inflection and handed the servant girl a few coppers. "Find a groom, and have him mind my horse." He strode into the study and headed straight for the backside of the desk. As he rounded the desk corner, Cate leaped from her chair and circled, keeping a polished expanse of mahogany between them.

"After a search of this fine-looking desk, I believe I shall arrest you on several counts of burglary." He flung open cupboards and slid out drawers as he chased her around the room.

She paused at the opposite end of the table. "I thought we had an agreement. Eighty, twenty."

He narrowed his gaze. "Seventy-five, twenty-five, and my assumption was we would locate the jewels, state your claim, and let the courts settle the matter."

"Who has time for such nonsense?" she scoffed. "I have estate taxes to pay—the overhead of two houses . . ." Cautiously, they continued around the writing table, matching each other step for step, eyes fixed. "Hardly manageable on a dancer's wages."

"Yes, I suppose *stealing* does solve your dilemma." Finn vaulted onto the desktop and Cate made a mad dash for the door. Bounding over tea trays and paperwork, he jumped to the seat of a wing chair and over the arm.

He caught her by the train of her skirt and yanked her into his arms. "There now, pretty Cate. That was a right flash-heist you pulled last night, but I'm afraid you're under arrest."

She pulled her fist from his grip and pressed her hand against his chest. "On what charges?"

He wrapped both hands around her waist. "Burglary, possession of stolen property, handling of stolen property, criminal conversion, and any other offenses I have yet to think of."

Cate ceased her wriggling and writhing, and stared at his temple. "Nasty knot. How are you feeling?"

He flicked his eyes upward. "Wicked headache, but otherwise fit enough."

She sighed. "I don't believe you're going to arrest me."

Finn peered at her over wire-framed glasses. "Just because a dear departed relation—touched by senility—concocted a list of valuable trinkets . . ." She pushed away and he pulled her against his groin.

On tiptoes, she pressed her lips to the swollen bump.

"Does not entitle you . . . to steal from every noble house in Belgravia and Mayfair."

Her brows lifted. "But the jewels have been restored to their rightful owner."

He frowned. "You mean stolen."

Cate smiled patiently. "Restored." She brushed a shock of hair off his forehead and touched the swelling. "And the list was not concocted, as you say. Uncle would never invent such a thing."

Finn swallowed. "All right then. Prove it."

Her gaze dropped to meet his. Sapphire eyes shaded with desire. Yes, he was quite sure of it. His heart quivered in his chest. Monty Twombly, quacksalver and doctor of phrenology, would call this episode of erratic beats an arrhythmia.

Finn studied her upper lip. Hard to resist the somewhat plump, well-defined peak. He dipped his head for a kiss, which she quickly broke off and wriggled out of his grasp. It pained him to let her go. All that rubbing and kissing had caused a pleasant, burgeoning effect.

Cate retreated to her chair behind the desk and dipped a spoon into blackberry preserve. "Piece of toast?"

"Nothing for me." Finn strolled around the room. "Robbery is a serious crime with a nasty change of address if you're caught." He stopped to admire a bound set of sonnets. "Have you ever paid a visit to Newgate gaol, Cate?"

Her gaze shot up from the breakfast tray. "My uncle was robbed of a number of valuable pieces of jewelry. I sometimes wonder if those thieves will ever see the inside of a prison."

Finn looked up from a small volume of Keats. "Why didn't you report the theft?"

She dropped the silver spoon in the preserve. "I most certainly did. An inspector came out from Scotland Yard and took a report."

He settled into a chair and crossed one leg over the other. "Simple enough to corroborate." He removed his spectacles and tucked them away.

A brief tap at the door brought a gray-haired woman into the room—a housekeeper of some sort. "Might you be needing anything, Miss Willoughby?" The woman eyed him with a good deal of suspicion. Word traveled fast among house servants.

"Another cup, Mrs. Mettle. And perhaps one of your powders for that knot on Mr. Gunn's head?"

The elder women squinted at his injury.

Though his gaze remained on Cate, he eased his head back to let the woman prod. "Rather touching, your sudden concern—ouch!"

Clucks and tsks accompanied more of the woman's poking. "He'll be needing a compress, as well." The elder servant backed away. "Bring him downstairs, if you would, miss."

"As you can see, we're rather informal here at Brookes House." Cate led the way down the servants' stairs. "I am forced to get by with the barest amount of help until—" She caught herself. "That is, for the time being."

Inside the kitchen, Mrs. Mettle took a damp cloth to the wound. "You mean until you are able to fence the jewels," he hissed and drew breath between his teeth.

Unmoved, the woman dipped the cloth in soapy water and continued to dab. "Listen to you—big strapping man like yourself—this'll give you something to complain about." She uncorked a small bottle and applied a tincture.

Finn yelped.

* * *

CATE BIT BACK a grin. She'd made no attempt to sell the recovered jewels. Not a single inquiry. And nary a clue how to begin or where to go. Against her better judgment, she had risked additional contact with Agent Gunn. How was she supposed to explain to him that the jewels were part of a larger covert operation? And at the same time, the gems were very much a part of her uncle's estate, and therefore she needed an idea of their worth. She still held out hope that Finn might point her toward the right sort of buyer—one who would not ask many questions.

"Fence?" She leaned over her housekeeper's shoulder. "Whatever do you mean, Finn?"

He raised a slow, skeptical brow. "A fence is a receiving house for stolen goods."

Mrs. Mettle chirped in. "I've a cousin who dabbled in a bit of crime. Led the high life for a time, now he's spending his days in Wormwood Scrubs." The housekeeper wrapped a length of clean cloth around shaved ice and twisted.

She took his hand and pressed it over the muslin pouch. "Keep a bit o' pressure on that egg, sir."

Cate held up a dropper. "Tincture of opium, just a—"

Finn grabbed her hand and jerked it away. "No laudanum."

The housekeeper stared. "Cup o' tea, then?"

He released Cate's hand and nodded. "Please. With a spot of cream."

Periodically, he displayed quite jarring episodes of temper—or nerves. She had never paid them much mind until recently. He looked at her a bit sheepishly. "I had a close brush with an opium habit after I returned from India."

She remained quiet and nodded.

He studied her from under the compress. "You did a right smart noddle on my head—for a ballet girl."

"I shall not apologize for last night, Finn."

He lowered the cloth. "Did I ask you to?"

Gently, she raised the compress up again. "Dancers are always dealing with sprains and swelling. Give it a bit longer."

"Sneaky, as well as clever—that move of yours into my coat pocket. Laudable, though mortifying."

"*You're* humiliated? And what would you call that table dance you had me do at gunpoint?" A slow grin crept across his face and she stared a bit too long at those sensual lips. A pleasant tingle fluttered through her. "You needn't answer that."

"Where are they, Cate?"

She met his gaze briefly. "I suppose it is a bit ridiculous to play coy at this juncture."

Finn lowered the compress. A larger smile created a deep line that ended in a dimple. "I would say so."

She produced a pouch from her skirt pocket. Pulling the silk cord, she rolled out the fabric, arranging the jewels on top of the satin. Finn leaned over the table.

"Two necklaces. A bracelet. A dazzling set of emerald earbobs and a diamond stickpin." Cate looked up from the array of gems. "Everything I've recovered so far."

"Stolen," he corrected her.

"Recovered."

He exhaled. "We've been down this road."

"Truthfully, I haven't tried to cash them in because I haven't a clue where to go." She hesitated. "I was hoping you might direct me to a jeweler who . . ."

Even though his grin widened, it was apparent he was not going to volunteer any names.

"Miss Willoughby will be needing a sharp swag handler. A fence, sir, just as you were saying before." The housekeeper set his tea down, along with a small pitcher of cream.

Finn stirred a drop into his cup. "Have you seen these jewels before, Mrs. Mettle?"

"Not these here, sir." She nodded at the pretty baubles on the table. "Leastwise, not while the baron was alive." She slipped a calling card out of her apron pocket. "But this man did." She slid the card across the table. "Heard them discussing the gentleman's fee in the baron's study."

Finn removed the cold compress and picked up the gilt-edged card. "Adophe Picard."

Cate immediately noticed the raised brow. "And who is Adophe Picard?"

"Perhaps the most respected gemologist alive. His father was a master jeweler. Years ago, Cartier apprenticed at his workshop." Clearly flummoxed, Finn pressed her housekeeper for more. "Are you are quite sure Picard met with Baron Brooke?"

"Oh, their business was real private-like, but I reckon he appraised the gems, sir."

Cate blinked at her servant. "You might have told me, Margaret."

"Didn't realize you were a part-time snakeman, miss—until now." The housekeeper winked.

"And if I have anything to say in the matter, that sort of risky behavior on the part of Miss Willoughby is about to come to an end." He answered Cate's frown with narrowed eyes and a grin. "All right, my dear, I will help you locate and identify the jewels. But in return, I expect due diligence. You must continue your search for proof of ownership."

He rolled up the velvet pouch and handed it over. "For the time being, I am willing to entrust the jewels to your safekeeping."

Cate suspected this was a peace offering of sorts.

He held up Picard's calling card. "May I keep this, Mrs. Mettle?"

"I've no use for it, sir. Only kept it because I thought it was pretty, all those fancy gilt flourishes."

Finn rose to leave. "See me out?"

He didn't take hold of her arm. Nor did he lightly press his fingers to the small of her back, like a gentleman. His large hand wrapped around hers, warm and reassuring. And something else; there was a kind of intimacy with this man that she quite . . . adored. Cate shook off the thought and reminded herself not to get used to anything about Phineas Gunn, no matter how tempting.

He retrieved his hat from the vestibule table and turned to her. "There's a musicale this evening at Ross House, the Marquis of Sutherland's London residence—old friend of Mother's. I will fetch you directly after your performance. We'll miss supper but arrive in time for entertainment. Evelyn Walsh, a fine mezzo-soprano, shall warble out a few arias whilst you and I do a bit of skulking about."

"Have I anything to say about this?" she huffed in protest.

Finn stepped into the street. "New rules, Cate. You co-operate with my investigation and I won't arrest you." He tipped his hat.

She slammed the door. "Wicked, arrogant devil." She stomped through the house and up the stairs. "Horrid, overbearing beast." In her bedchamber, she threw open the doors of her armoire. So what might she wear tonight?

## Chapter Eight

Finn parked MacGregor at the public stables and entered Scotland Yard in a tumult of troubled thoughts. His musings ran from lascivious fantasy to grave speculation, and they were all about Cate Willoughby. He passed Horse Guards stationed at the entrance to 4 Whitehall and headed upstairs, but turned a corner a bit too sharply and stopped short.

"Phineas Gunn."

He blinked at the man he nearly crashed into. "Rafe Lewis."

"On my way over to The Rising Sun. Care to join?" The Yard man swept back a shock of hair that perpetually fell in front of his eyes. "I believe Kennedy and Melville are there."

Finn pivoted on his heel and followed the agent downstairs. "Exactly who I'm looking for."

"New case?" Rafe opened the front door and gestured Finn through.

"A new old case." He settled in beside Rafe for the brief walk across Greater Scotland Yard. "What brings you to town? Last I heard, you and Fanny married."

"I finally won forgiveness and the darling girl said yes. Couldn't be happier." Rafe grinned. "Actually, I'm here to discuss an agent-at-large position in Edinburgh. Fanny won't let me resign—won't hear of it. Says I'll get peevish stuffed in an office all day." The good-natured agent chuckled. "She's right, of course."

Finn stole a glance at the detective, who appeared annoyingly content. Fulfilled somehow. "Lovely young woman. Mad about you, as I recall."

Rafe's grin went a bit lopsided. "If you ask me, she was entirely too keen on you."

"Fanny shamelessly used me to needle you."

"And you willingly cooperated."

Finn rolled his eyes. "A man would have to be blind to refuse her. Besides, it worked, didn't it?" He shrugged his way past a blockade of customers at the pub entrance. They found the gray-whiskered director of Special Branch, William Melville, standing amongst his men at a nearby table.

Glass in hand, Melville cleared his throat. "Gentlemen. Most of us know our intrepid protector of Queen and country as a tireless investigator, working into the wee hours without complaint, except for the occasional grunt or snort." Melville poured a pint of bitters into the soup bowl placed on the table. "To a nose brave and true. Let us drink a toast to Alfred."

The red-coated bloodhound sat in a slat-back pub chair, drooling.

"Hear hear!" A rumble of cheers went up from the men surrounding the most valuable dog in the empire. Zak Kennedy nodded to both Finn and Rafe, pointing to a few extra pints on the table.

Finn raised a glass. "And to what *auspicious* deed, do we owe this *auspicious* occasion?"

"Alfred has sired a litter of pups," Melville boasted. "And the bitch has a great nose."

"Stout lad." Rafe tipped his drink. "How many new mouths to feed?"

Melville puffed out his chest. "Seven."

Archibald Bruce, the much-touted young scientist of Special Branch, sidled over. "Hello, Mr. Gunn."

Finn's gaze shifted off the hound lapping bitters. "Mr. Bruce. It appears you will soon have an entire squadron of noses at your disposal."

Archie wiped a bit of foam off his upper lip. "We're hoping to have a son or daughter at every major port of entry."

Last year, Archie Bruce had been hired to create a crime scene laboratory. As Finn understood it, the young man had quickly established a bomb detection squad as well as a bomb dismantling and detonation facility in the East End, an unofficial adjunct of the division and, as such, sub-rosa. Archie's fledgling staff, along with Special Branch agents, had done well for the citizenry of London. Not only had they caught and jailed an assortment of anarchist dynamiters, but they had prevented quite a number of bomb attacks.

"I'm afraid Alfred has recently catapulted to the top of the dynamiters' enemies list." The young lab director added a grimace.

Finn stared. "There's a price on his head?"

Bruce nodded, gulping his stout. "Five hundred pounds."

Finn blew a low whistle.

With a nose that could identify trace particles of nitroglycerin and diatomaceous earth, Alfred was a serious threat. And London was awash with anarchists and rebels these days. American, Irish, Spanish, French—

with enclaves in every major European capital. Which brought Finn to the reason he was here. He caught Kennedy's eye.

Zak scratched the hound's ear on his way over. "Shall we grab another pint and some air?" A crowd of lunchtime guzzlers spilled out the door of the pub and onto Greater Scotland Yard.

He and Kennedy relaxed against one of the pillared gates leading to Horse Guards. "So, you have news, Finn?"

He nodded. "Through a strange bit of fortune—or misfortune, depending on how one looks at it—I was able to identify your cat burglar."

"I take it our man escaped, though you have an identity?" Zak's mouth twitched.

Finn exhaled. "*Your man* is most definitely not a he, but a she. And a most lovely one at that."

Zak straightened. "Don't tell me—Catriona de Dovia Willoughby." Much to his chagrin, the senior Yard man tossed back his head with a hoot. "And she got away."

"You should have seen this early this morning." Finn swept back his hair to reveal the injury.

Zak squinted. "Nasty knot."

He released the lock of hair and recounted his evening with Cate, leaving out the more intimate details.

Zak pressed his lips into a firm, flat line, an irritating act that hardly obscured the Yard man's amusement. "So what do you propose, Finn?"

"I'm not sure yet if she's operating on behalf of *Los Tigres* or in her own self-interest. Either way, she's going to need a fence. I'd like to give her Fabian's name, but if we bring him in on the scheme, he's going to need ready cash."

Zak nodded. "Just so happens I have a satchel full of

banknotes confiscated from an arms trafficker. I'll negotiate with Fabian straightaway." The detective lifted the brim of his hat and scratched. "It will take a few days to run down Miss Willoughby's inheritance story. Baron Brooke, you say?"

"Arthur Willoughby, Baron Brooke," he added, and accompanied Kennedy back across the yard and inside the pub. They were just in time to witness Alfred lap up a second bowl of stout. "He can do another pint." Archie grinned. "After Victoria's Golden Jubilee he swilled up several."

Finn turned to Zak and lowered his voice. "I escort Cate to a musicale this evening, on the lookout for more of Uncle's booty. I have a scheme in mind that may spur her into action."

Zak nodded. "Flush her out and follow the money."

Finn emptied his glass. "It's the only way to be sure." Having neatly polished off his bowl of stout, the hound belched.

FINN REINED HIS mount onto Horse Guards Avenue and hailed the tall, strapping urchin hawking an illustrated weekly. "Over here, lad." Hoping to make a quick tuppence for holding his horse, the boy came running.

"What's your name?"

"Charlie Doyle, sir." The young man tipped his cap.

"Detective Inspector Kennedy tells me you are a trustworthy hard worker."

The lad nodded shyly. "I do my best, sir."

He leaned over the neck of his horse. "I'd like to hire you to do a bit of undercover work. There's half a crown in it for a job well done."

"Blimey, sir." The lad's eyes sparked from his sudden good fortune as well as a chance for adventure.

Finn scratched out an address on the back of his calling card. "I want you to keep an eye on the young woman who lives here." Finn handed the card over. "Raven-haired, blue eyes, tall and attractive. She takes long, graceful strides—" Finn thought about Cate's walk and smiled. "With her toes turned out."

The paper boy scratched his head. "Hard to miss a sight like that, sir."

"Indeed." Finn sat back in the saddle. "If she leaves the house, follow her." He handed the boy several coins. "Cab fare." A quick study of the lad's face showed no sign of confusion, only eagerness.

"Once she reaches her destination, wire me at once. Phineas Gunn, Nineteen Chester Square." Finn gestured at the card and the lad turned it over.

"Yes, sir. I understand, sir."

He winked at the young hawker. "Keep a sharp eye, Charlie."

Finn pressed his heels into MacGregor's side and they made their way uptown. Bounding across Green Park, the greenest park in all of London, Finn maneuvered past the Queen's gardeners. The lawns were receiving one of their last tidy-ups of the season.

They made reasonably good time crossing town, even with the street congestion. At the public stables, he handed his horse off to a groom and hoofed it down Harley Street.

He was late for his weekly appointment with his quack physician.

A middle-aged man with a wild, unkempt head of salt-and-pepper hair opened the door with a jerk. Keen gray eyes peered over spectacles. "Your hour started ten minutes ago."

Finn slouched into his usual spot on the divan. "With a great deal of difficulty, over these last few months, I have come to understand something of your unorthodox therapy. And now I discover I must pay your exorbitant fee—to listen and make commentary—with or without my presence."

Placing a kettle on a grate, Monty paid little mind to his remark. He circled an index finger in the direction of the hearth. "I aspire to become a sorcerer by the age of eighty, able to boil water with a flick of my finger."

Finn glanced about the area. Threadbare carpets, peeling wallpaper. The treatment room was a shabby affair, nearly beyond repair. Obviously the man's practice failed to prosper.

Nevertheless, Monty beamed. "One can't really concentrate without a cup of tea at regular intervals." The man pulled up a chair. "What's on your mind, Finn?"

He took his time answering. Frankly, there was only one thing on his mind these days. He shook his head and sighed. "I am recently reacquainted with a young lady who has occupied a great deal of my time and patience."

"Rather cheeky of her." Monty tut-tutted insincerely. His physician was so easily amused.

Finn narrowed his gaze. "She kissed me this morning. Actually, she kissed an injury."

His doctor didn't hide his delight. "Disarmed by a gentle kiss." Monty settled back and crossed one leg over the other.

Finn swept a few unruly waves off his forehead. "I find her to be intensely disturbing. I'm completely on edge around her. The entire effect is unnerving."

Monty rubbed his chin. "Have you never felt . . . *agitated* by a woman?"

"Never." Finn sighed. "Irritated, often. Stymied—always. Aroused, certainly. But never this kind of lingering . . ."

"Torment?" His physician's grin couldn't have been wider or more maddening. "I must say this is progress, indeed."

Finn loosened his cravat. "How can you call such a thing progress? I'm supposed to feel better, aren't I?"

Monty opened a notebook and began penciling. "*Not* necessarily."

On the ride over, Finn had marveled at how quickly he and Cate moved from anger to affection around each other. Perhaps affection was the wrong word. Had he imagined the tenderness in her kiss? Even now he could feel the brush of her lips over the knot on his head. The one she had made with the butt end of his pistol.

"You're coming alive." Musing out loud, his doctor tilted his head to one side. "Which means you are beginning to feel things again. Emotions can be pleasant or unpleasant: positive—pleasure, for example—or negative—feelings of trepidation." Monty stared for quite a long time. "Tell me something about this young woman."

Careful not to reveal information sensitive to his case, Finn profiled his impressions of Cate and was surprised by all of the stark contrasts he was able to report. A rare beauty and accomplished ballerina. The lithe and lovely young woman was both clever and disconcertingly independent. When he spoke of her outbursts of temperament in Spanish, Monty grinned.

Silently, Finn ticked off additional notes on her perplexing situation. Possible anarchist sympathizer and put-upon heiress of a bankrupt estate. He was hard-pressed to decide what was the truth. Nor could he discern which one of Cate's possible situations provoked him the most.

The doctor poured steaming water into a chipped teapot. "In the science of magnetism, there are positive and negative charges. Just so with human interaction. Currently, your emotional body does not readily discern pleasure—that is, good agitation—from displeasure, or bad agitation. I take it the young lady has a name? A given name will do."

He sighed. "Cate."

Monty smiled. "Short for Catherine?"

"Catriona."

"Catriona. How lovely." The man steepled his fingers under his chin. "What symptoms are expressing themselves these days?"

"Sweating, trembling, shaking. Sensations of shortness of breath. A feeling of choking or smothering. Chest pain. Nausea." Finn hunkered farther down on the sofa. "Dizzy, but more of a general light-headedness—like a swoon."

Finn inhaled a breath. Everything about this new therapy was humiliating; still, he pressed on. "Feelings of unreality, detachment from myself. Fear of losing control or going mad. Fear of dying. Paresthesia—your word for the numbness and tingling sensations. Alternating chills and feverish flushes."

Monty scribbled furiously. "The full gamut, as it were. And when you are with Cate?"

"Some symptoms worsen. However . . ." Finn studied the cracks in the ceiling plaster. "Quite a few of them subside when I'm with her."

"Then, might one conclude Cate is more of a pleasurable agitation than a distressing one?"

Finn tilted his head to peer at his doctor. "Believe me, she is both."

"And do the exercises bring much relief?"

"Breathing in one nostril and out the other helps, eventually. Whenever I am outside of the house, I am in a state of moderate hysteria."

Monty reached for his hand. "No major attacks to report?" He placed his fingers on the inside of Finn's wrist and opened his pocket watch.

"In the carriage the other evening—the cabin started to close in on me. I nearly had a spell. Nothing full-blown, as long as I can escape small, dark spaces."

"Your pulse is in the normal range and quite regular." He released Finn's wrist and poured tea. Adding a dash of cream to one cup, he passed it over. "I should like you to complete the story of your experience in the Northern Territories one day."

Finn sipped the Darjeeling and sighed a bit gruffly.

"It's the key to your cure," Monty suggested, his spoon clinking softly as he stirred in cream and sugar. "Care to take another stab at it?"

His heart palpitated. "How far did I get last time?"

"A chap by the name of . . ." Monty peered over his cup to read the journal on his knee. "Abdul-Qadir Muhaddith threatened to pluck out your eyes."

## ∽ Chapter Nine

The marchioness swept up beside Cate with a wink. "I envy your choice of escort. Do not share that with a living soul."

Cate pressed her lips together, which forced a telltale dimple. "Neither a tittle nor tattle, Lady Sutherland." She took in the splendor of the recital hall. A torchère of yellow tiger lilies framed a grand piano on a low dais. The platform was surrounded by several rows of gilded chairs. Drinks in hand, guests grazed a length of buffet tables laden with delicate desserts.

The elegant hostess surveyed a circle of men standing inside the hall. "The Gunn brothers are divine, are they not?" Her narrowed gaze roamed up Finn and down Hardy.

"Very dashing to see them in their plaids." Cate's own inspection followed the woman's example.

"Descended from Pictish tribes and Norse gods." The marchioness sighed. In one fluid motion, the woman lifted a flute of champagne from the tray of a passing servant and deposited her empty.

Cate scanned a room brightened by kilts. "Quite a few Scots here this evening."

"Lord George Murray, the marquis, is a Highlander. As a consequence, our invitations often state 'traditional attire'—formal of course." The woman dipped closer. "His lordship informs me the Gunn clan are the chief trouble-makers of the North."

"Misadventure does seem to find them." Cate stole another glance at the devilishly good-looking brothers. Charming, smart, and dangerous, all wrapped up in those eye-catching skirts. In her brief acquaintance with the young gentlemen, she had observed a maelstrom of trouble swirl about them. Finn and Hardy were a formidable challenge to lesser males and a bona fide magnet to women. Worst of it was, they knew it.

Finn had not seemed overly surprised to find his brother at the recital. It seemed Hardy had shown up un-announced and uninvited. On the prowl, one assumed, for Gwen Lennox. Not that Lady Sutherland seemed to mind. Anything to give an evening of piano sonatas and selected arias a bit of a lift.

The marchioness lowered her eyelids and took another smoldering glance at Hardy Gunn. "Nothing quite like a red-blooded young man in a kilt."

Cate half expected Lady Sutherland to break into song—a few bars of "Hielan' Laddie." A smile tipped the ends of her mouth. No, perhaps not.

Sleek and sophisticated, Lucinda Murray was striking to look at. She reminded Cate of a high-strung racehorse. Reluctantly, the lady tore her eyes off Hardy and gave Cate an impatient once-over. "I understand you are related to Arthur Willoughby, Baron Brooke—dear departed soul."

"My uncle, Lady Sutherland."

"You come from such excellent stock, yet you've taken up a scandalous métier—in the performing arts of all things."

Cate's gaze flicked over to Finn. He was on his way over. She breathed a quiet sigh of relief. "It's hard to explain, actually . . ." She tried not to appear wistful. "I am passionate about dance and feel blessed to be doing the very thing I love most."

"My dear, you sound like a vicar with a calling." Finn stepped up beside her and nodded a bow to their hostess. "Good evening, Lucinda."

The marchioness rolled her eyes. "I was hoping for a naughty evening—ever since you and Hardy arrived. And Miss Willoughby, of course." The lady fashioned her signature stiff smile.

Finn waved his brother over. "Then you're in luck. Hardy is on the prowl for something equally misbehaved." He stepped back to allow the younger Gunn to move in beside Lady Sutherland.

When the marchioness lifted her hand for a kiss, Hardy leaned in close. "How might I corrupt your evening, Lucinda?" Lady Sutherland snorted a soft laugh as Hardy set her hand on his arm. "And where might a man find a tumbler of whiskey around here?"

Cate tore her eyes off the elegant couple as they receded into the crowd. "Why did you bring me here?" she asked. In a gesture that caught her completely off guard, Finn nudged her with his elbow and crooked an arm.

She exhaled a giant sigh and placed her arm in his.

"You aren't enjoying Lucinda's barbs and pricks? Come, come, Cate, the evening's just begun—plenty of room for improvement." He turned them about and headed for the back of the salon. As they passed the dessert table, Finn plucked a truffle from a tiered platter. He wrapped the round ball of chocolate in a lacy paper and slipped it into his evening jacket. "A bit of sugar for that sour temper of yours, should the need arise."

"I am not sour, I'm . . ."

"Fractious, peevish . . . in need of a caper?" He tugged her along.

"It's just that . . ." She returned the polite nod of a frail elderly couple. "A musicale is not quite as sparkling as a ball, if you take my meaning."

"Nothing of particular note, except for a few stunning ring fingers." Finn leaned in. "And, oh yes—number seven."

Cate stopped abruptly and stared. "One sixty-five-carat Ceylon sapphire; 102 cabochon sapphires totaling eleven carats; 868 brilliant diamonds totaling seventeen carats; and two emerald eyeballs weighing a carat each—all set in white gold and platinum." She pulled him closer. "*That* number seven?"

"The Panther Brooch." The twinkle in his eye sent a shiver down her spine.

"Who—where?" she stammered.

"Lucinda's jewelry box would be a likely place to start." They slipped through the dining room, past busy staff clearing the table, and back down an expansive marble corridor. Finn opened several doors before he found the servants' stairs. On the third floor, he turned the knob. Cate wriggled between Finn and the crack in the door.

"What do you see?" His words breezed past her ear and tingled though her body. Cate caught her breath. An upstairs maid moved methodically from chamber to chamber. "A servant, turning down beds." Tapping lightly on the next door in line, the girl hesitated a moment before entering the bedchamber. The door shut with a click.

Finn clasped her hand in his and led the way down the corridor. A muffled giggle came from behind closed doors as they padded down a length of carpet runner. He paused at the end of the passage and craned his neck for a quick spy down the connecting hallway. "Ah, the lady's bedchamber, if memory serves."

"Do you and your brother frequent the boudoir of every married lady in Mayfair?" Her words came out in a hiss.

"Not all of the women are married." Finn pulled her around the corner. "A widow or two, here and there."

At Lucinda's chamber door, he glanced back. "Love your nose that way."

She relaxed the wrinkle but left the frown. "Yours is a rather generous nose. De rigueur, I suppose, for one who sniggles about for a living."

"'The mark of an affable, generous, and talented lover.'" Finn pulled her close. "Cyrano de Bergerac." A cloud of perplexed thoughts appeared to whirl beneath the glimmer of his inky-black eyes. He was debating something. Would he tell her or would he not?

He cleared his throat.

She arched a brow.

"I used to enjoy a romp, now and then, when I was younger. Gave it up when I realized the idea of a tryst was more stimulating than the woman."

"Not that you gave up these dalliances on moral grounds. But then, I suppose the thrill was rather cheap." She sniffed.

Finn stared. "Ready to *steal* some jewelry, Cate?"

When she opened her mouth to protest he placed a

finger to her lips and opened the bedchamber door. A hinge whined as the door widened. He slipped through the opening and waved her in. They both froze and waited for a murmur. A rustle. A breath.

The soft blue presence of moonlight illuminated a draped poster bed and pointed the way into an alcove. Cate took the lead as they entered a plush dressing area. She opened the doors of a small armoire filled top to bottom with flat drawers, the shallow kind of trays that were often lined with velvet. The lady's jewel case.

Finn jiggled the top drawer. "Locked."

She removed two hairpins from her topknot and straightened them out. She slipped one pin into the lock and bent the other. It took several tries; each time she adjusted the zig and zag at the end of the pin.

The lock wouldn't budge. "I can't raise all the levers."

"Shall we see what Roger can accomplish?" Finn held up a skeleton key.

Cate shifted to one side. "Queer name for a master key."

"Rather ribald, actually." Finn worked the key back and forth in the hole rather suggestively. Or was she just seeing it that way? A tinge of heat crept up her neck and across her cheeks.

The key turned in the lock, but the drawer didn't open.

"The next drawer down will open," she advised. "At the back of the tray, you should find a spring-loaded latch." She pushed her hairpins back in place.

Finn pulled out the narrow shelf and felt around. "Now what?"

"Press it back until it clicks."

*Click.*

Cate released a satisfied exhale. Even in near darkness

she could make out his piercing stare. She shook her head. "Don't."

"Don't what?"

"You were going to ask where I learned such a thing." She pulled out a tray and examined the contents.

"Where did you learn such a thing?"

She shoved the drawer in. "How incredibly exasperating you are."

A scoff rumbled out of him, but he joined in the hunt. Tray by tray they systematically searched for the brooch. She worked mostly by feel, occasionally removing a piece and holding it up to the faint light. Near the bottom of the drawer stack Finn blew a soft whistle.

"Got it." The large pin glittered in the moonlight. "You'd have to have a private audience with the Crown jewels to get close to a sapphire this size." The creak of a door hinge broke the spell. He pocketed the brooch.

Shoving in drawers, they closed up the armoire. Murmured voices made it plain they were no longer alone. Finn steered her across the dressing room. A giggle and squeal accompanied a groan of bedsprings. He opened one side of the large wardrobe and pushed Cate inside. He dove in after her.

"Ouch!" Cate hissed.

"Shhh!"

"Your elbow is stabbing me."

"Sorry." He pushed silk gowns aside and inched the door to the armoire shut. A deep velvet darkness enveloped them. Finn tucked his sinewy length of body against hers. There wasn't an inch of extra wiggle room. Cate sighed. "Couldn't we crawl out a window? Shimmy down a drainpipe?"

His breath fell in steady intervals on her cheek. "Entirely too dangerous."

"What then?" Cate huffed quietly.

"We wait for Lucinda to pull the drape on the bed." Cate wondered why she bothered to ask. The man obviously knew the bedroom habits of a myriad of women.

"And what if she doesn't let down the drapes?"

"She and the marquess have worked out a kind of informal signal."

"How convenient for them." The pitch-blackness hid her frown. "I take it you and the marchioness are acquainted in the biblical sense."

"Not quite."

"Not quite?" Cate hissed softly. "How is that possible? You either have done the deed or you haven't when it comes to sex."

"Untrue. There are women with whom I might enjoy a flirtation at a soiree. Their wit, the sparkle in their eyes. An amusing moment. There are also women I enjoy a deeper friendship with. A female companion, say, who makes an excellent dinner partner. Stimulating conversation, a bit of leg rubbing under the table." He nestled close in the darkness. "Then there are the women I desire to sleep with."

Smothered amongst Lady Sutherland's silks and taffetas, there was no room for escape. And this man was so . . . unsettling. Squirming a bit, her hand landed on hard muscular flesh and froze. "Why, Miss Willoughby, you have your hand on my thigh." His husky whisper invited more, and her fingers obeyed, wrapping themselves around a hard curve of hamstring muscle. He exhaled a low-pitched groan that lifted the small hairs on her neck. Would they spend the night here—together? A soft kiss brushed her earlobe and his hand found the hard tip of her breast under layers of fabric.

Quite suddenly, she wanted him—wantonly, and all it took was a tingle. "I understand Scots pride themselves on not wearing a stitch under their kilts."

Deep brown orbs glimmered in the dark. "You could find out easily enough."

"Why on earth would I wish to do such a thing?"

"Then I suggest . . ." His kiss traveled over the tip of her nose. "You remove your hand from my thigh." Husky words landed softly on her mouth.

Cate lifted her hand until just the fingertips remained on his skin. "The Panther—in exchange for a bit of discovery."

He pulled away an inch. "Are we talking exploration as well as discovery?"

Her hand traveled farther up his thigh—over smooth buttocks covered in just enough fuzz to keep her fingertips warm. His gluteus maximus was rock hard with a slight hollow in the cheek. She marveled at how well-muscled Finn was. "Male dancers have buttocks like this—not many ordinary men."

There was a sharp intake of air in his answer. "Must be the fencing lessons . . . a lot of back and forth, parry and . . . thrust."

Slowly, she inched her way over a curve of groin muscle. A broad velvet sword sprang up to greet her, ready and waiting.

She could almost see his grin. "As stiff as the megaliths on Machrie Moor, lass." There was a burr in his speech that sent a shiver of desire through her body. She wished to impale herself upon this brawny Scot, and perhaps she would.

He lifted her petticoats and gown over her knee and swept his fingers under a satin garter. Had he read her mind, or were they just like-minded? He nibbled her earlobe. "I want ye, sorely." He kissed a spot on her neck, then licked. "Wickedly." His hand moved to the inside of her thigh . . .

"Rip it off, Hardy," Lucinda squealed. A bellowed grunt pervaded their little enclave.

"Blasted hooks and eyes," Hardy complained.

While Cate listened to the amorous acrobatics in the next room, Finn parted a few gowns and peeked through the crack in the wardrobe doors. "I believe this is our cue."

She growled. "Must we?"

He returned a growl. "We must."

Finn timed their escape from the wardrobe to the demise of Lady Sutherland's corset. He brushed a kiss over her mouth. "We shall take this up again—very soon."

## Chapter Ten

Finn rocked with the gentle sway of the carriage as they exited the south gate of Ross House and turned onto Piccadilly. "First you push me away, then you can't get enough. This could get arousing, Cate."

The carriage passed under a streetlamp, illuminating the pretty peak of her lips. He wanted to feel those lips against his again. "Have you ever kissed a man with a bit of sugar on his tongue?" He reached into his jacket and popped a confection into his mouth. "A little game Hardy and I used to play with the town girls at home." He took her in his arms and opened her mouth with a kiss. His tongue swirled the sweet taste of chocolate into her mouth.

"Mmmm." The vibration of her murmur passed into him as her lips closed around his tongue. She licked the underside of his lip for good measure. "Not terribly clever of you and Hardy—to pay for kissing lessons."

His eyes crinkled. "Perhaps not."

"I've a mind the young ladies would have schooled you both properly—without the sweets."

He held the last bite of chocolate truffle to her mouth.

"Open." Cate closed her eyes and savored. "Lady Sutherland calls you divine."

She peeked up at him. Pale moonlight edged a high cheekbone and pert nose. He tucked her into the crook of his arm. "And what is your mind?"

Her grin was visible, and it taunted him. "I say you are . . . delicious."

"Then the accolade rests squarely on the chocolate." The cabin swayed again as they rounded the park. "You are a puzzlement, Cate."

She snorted a scoff. "Not so puzzling. I haven't had a thing to eat since breakfast." As if to underscore the remark, her stomach growled.

He grinned. "Very glad that didn't happen in the lady's closet. You might have given us away."

Her eyes narrowed. "My little gurgle would have gone unnoticed over the bellowing grunts of Lucinda Sutherland."

Cate Willoughby made him smile. And not just because her acerbic wit matched her ethereal looks. He just *liked* her. Odd notion. Odder still to be so damned aroused by a woman he could so easily befriend.

Finn knocked on the roof of the carriage as they passed though Mayfair and his driver stopped at The Punch Bowl. "Be right back." He returned carrying a newspaper packet tied with string. The carriage lurched off and he fell in beside her. "An order of fish and chip for a hungry young lady."

Cate pulled off a glove and fingered the string. "Join me?"

"Thought you'd never ask." For the next several minutes they devoured steaming hot fish and potatoes, splashed with malt vinegar.

She licked her fingers and exhaled a deep sigh. "For such a dour, infuriating man, how is it you always manage to make me want to kiss you?"

Finn popped a last chip in his mouth. "Feel free to abuse my lips whenever I get too sullen."

Her gaze shifted briefly to his mouth, before she folded the newsprint. "Lady Sutherland mentioned your family. It seems Clan Gunn has quite the reputation."

"So you heard what troublemakers we are." He grinned. "Four hundred years ago, the Gunns managed to cause enough mayhem that they were appeased with a nice bit of land north of Sutherland. There was even a baronship at one time, long since forfeited. The relatives managed to hold on to the land and the estate in Helmsdale. Nothing closely resembling a castle, mind; more of a rambling pile of stones."

"Do you visit your family often?"

Finn settled in beside her. "I haven't been home in years. Mother comes down once a year to nose around a bit—check on Hardy and me, do a bit of shopping."

"Neither you nor your brother speak with much of a brogue."

"Mother's a Lowlander—insisted on the Queen's English. College and university finished off the rest of the Scot in our speech. More o' the burr comes back with a dram or two." His eyes fell to her mouth. "You've a sweet dimple when you smile, lass."

Finn dipped his head to see out the window. The carriage rounded Eaton Square, blocks from Baron Brooke's residence. He eyed his new partner in crime and reluctantly returned to the task at hand. He removed the Panther Brooch from his sporran and placed it in Cate's reticule. "We're going to need several proofs of ownership. And a provenance would help, as well."

"Provenance?"

"Rare gems have a pedigree, as does any jewelry of this caliber. I suspect the pieces on your list have a royal legacy. But whatever their history, a provenance is necessary to assure you the best possible price either by private sale or auction.

"There is a jeweler in Hatton Garden, a Hungarian chap by the name of Fabian. It's possible he might know something about your uncle's jewelry collection. He is also discreet, if you take my meaning. If we are able to locate the original thief and obtain a confession, that, and an appraisal from Adophe Picard, should give you the proof you need to resolve your claim in the courts."

"I must thank you for helping me." Deep sapphire eyes glistened in the dark. "You really didn't have to get involved in any of my difficulties."

Finn exhaled. It had been simple enough to lay the bait. So why was he feeling so miserable? No, he knew why. He wanted to believe her story. Silently he ticked off the reasons why Cate's story was viable. The jewels were very likely a legitimate legacy of Baron Brooke's estate. And why would she recover—her word—only those jewels on the list? She was either rollicking mad, or a sly little anarchist sympathizer.

Obviously, he needed some convincing. "I will continue to help you locate and identify the baron's jewels as long as we also search for proof of ownership."

Cate sighed. "I am tempted to kiss you again, but I'm rather irritated by the notion."

"Too enticing?"

"No, that isn't the word." She bit her lower lip. "You are a distraction."

Finn nearly hooted aloud. *He* was a distraction? A

pleasant tension lingered in the air between them. In the past, Finn had experienced sexual attraction with other women, but nothing quite as arousing as this lovely ballet girl. A tightness in his throat made it hard to swallow. Christ, the precocious Miss Willoughby was actually making it hard to breathe. Earlier this evening, he had experienced an enchanting intuition about her. A feeling of inevitability, which was both familiar and pleasing. He also knew, without having to ask, that she had felt it, too.

The carriage reached the end of the stately block of terrace homes and slowed. Cate peered out the window, taking particular interest in a stand of shrubbery at the corner churchyard. "Why are you having me followed?"

He didn't hesitate to lie. "Scotland Yard is having you followed, for your own protection." Honesty was impossible at this juncture, and her curiosity played neatly into his scheme.

"I thought we agreed—no Scotland Yard." She glared at him. "You told them about me? About the jewel thefts? How could you?"

"Ha!" Finn tossed his head back. "You admit you engage in thievery."

Cate looked as though she might blink back tears. "I find this most disloyal of you, Finn."

He hated himself. "Actually, it was Scotland Yard who informed on you."

Her gaze stretched into the dark corners of the coach and narrowed. "This has something to do with Eduardo."

"They believe you may be a *Los Tigres* sympathizer, involved in the recapture of your uncle's estate jewelry for resale on the Continent."

"Me?" A furrowed brow deepened, but he quite liked

her angry pout. "Any sympathy I might have had for my brother's politics died with him, Mr. Gunn."

Mr. Gunn. This was grim.

She uttered a frustrated growl. "Did you tell them about the ruin my uncle's estate is in?"

He exhaled. "Yes, of course. If everything checks out, you'll have your jewelry returned to you." His grimace tightened into a thin line. "I'm afraid I've been ordered to confiscate the items in question."

He endured a quiet sulk punctuated by a sigh. "Very well, I suppose the jewels will be safe enough at Scotland Yard." When her gaze met his again, something had changed. "Mind the jewels are returned before I am forced into receivership." Her expression was shuttered. There was a distance between them now.

"Cate, I make an excellent income from my book royalties and consultations. If you would allow me to help—"

She turned the latch and sprang from the coach.

He followed her out of the carriage and caught her arm at the door. "Cate."

"Come back in the morning." She turned to face him. "I'm tired and brokenhearted. You don't trust me."

Gently, he took the key from her hand and pushed it into the lock. "I do trust you . . . a little."

The moment the latch clicked open she slipped inside and slammed the door in his face. "¡Hombre odioso! Usted me engañó. Usted finge ser mi amigo. ¿Si no confía en mi, por qué debo confiarme en usted, Phin-e-ass Gunn?"

Finn returned to the carriage and sat on the edge of the tufted bench seat. His driver took the long way around the block to the backside of St. Peter's grounds. Absently he translated the spate of Spanish expletives. *Horrid man. Deceiver. You pretend to be my friend. If you do not trust me, why must I trust you, Phin-e-ass*—emphasis on the last syllable—*Gunn?*

She needed to be watched. Closely.


FINN COUNTED THE chimes in a groggy haze. Nine o'clock. He sat straight up in bed. A squint at the mantel clock confirmed it was true. He took a moment to gather his wits. Astonishingly, he had not been ripped from a warm bed in the middle of the night. No urgent message. No fleeing anarchist sympathizer to chase after. Finn eased out of bed and swept the window curtains back. Blinding sunshine.

So what was the matter?

After a quick washup and shave, he pulled on boots and picked up his coat. On his way downstairs, he tucked his shirt into his breeches and slipped a cravat in place as he entered the breakfast room. "Bootes."

His manservant broke a raw egg into a glass of tomato juice. "May I fix you a cure as well, sir?"

Necktie askew, his brother was down to shirtsleeves and kilt. Finn skirted the end the table and raised his sibling's eyelid. Bloodshot.

"Still alive." Hardy sputtered.

His butler, on the other hand, seemed chipper enough. Bootes moved in to examine his attire. "Bad night—or too good a night, Hardy?" Finn buttoned his waistcoat, while his manservant smoothed the knot in his tie. "Have Sergeant MacGregor saddled."

"Right away, sir."

"Hardy?" Something was wrong. His brother could suffer an elephant's hangover and still ride like the devil and shoot straighter.

"I'm not sure what came over me last night." Hardy pushed a shock of hair from his eyes and slumped back in his chair. "After you and Cate disappeared from the hall, Gwen made a brief appearance on the arm of Victor Somerset."

Finn stirred a drop of cream into his coffee and gulped. "And?"

"Had a romping good visit with Lucinda after that." Hardy tossed back the juice and egg with a grimace. "Am I a whore, Finn?"

He sampled a crisp rasher of bacon from a plate on the breakfront. "You're not lamenting your deplorable lack of morals . . ." He dipped his head to make eye contact with his brother. "Are you?"

"Of course I am." Hardy listed to one side of his chair. "Shouldn't I be?"

Finn broached the subject carefully. "Must I remind you, Lady Lennox, as dazzling as her charms are, is often all too available to young bachelors."

Hardy grunted. "Nearly every man on British soil. It's a wonder you haven't had her."

Finn made light of the implied question. "I thought I recommended her."

Hardy's groan sputtered into laughter just as his elbow slipped off the table. Bootes whisked a plate full of kipper and egg away before Hardy's face hit the table.

"I'm afraid Master Harding finished off the Talisker last night. Might you suggest a respite, sir?" The butler's eyes rolled upward.

"Come on, old sport." Finn helped his brother up and shouldered him out of the breakfast room. Upstairs, Bootes helped undress Hardy and tuck him into bed.

Even stupid from drink, Hardy's smile was charming.

"Did you sleep with Gwen? God's honest truth—on pain of blood penalty by the clan."

Finn stood above his brother and sighed. "I seem to remember a pretty little mole above her right buttock cheek."

Hardy groaned. *"Aut pax aut bellum."*

Finn returned his brother's use of the clan motto. "In peace or war, brother."

They'd duke it out later, just as they had since childhood.

Hardy reached up and grabbed his arm. "A wire came early this morning. Didn't want to wake you."

Heat rose up his neck and flamed over his cheeks. "What?"

# ∞ Chapter Eleven

Cate stared into the eyes of a strange man, a dark, swarthy type with a pronounced Eastern European accent.

"Can I help you, miss?" The man reached out and prodded her shoulder. She pulled out her pistol. "Don't touch me." She rose slowly.

The shopkeeper backed down the steps, hands in the air. "Please, don't hurt me." The man's wire-framed spectacles fogged slightly. "I came to . . . to . . . sweep." He took up the broom in the corner. "I did not expect to find anyone at my door."

Cate blinked at the shopkeeper. She must have fallen asleep on the stairs of the basement jewelry shop. "And who might you be, sir?"

"Nandor Fabian." The wiry man dipped a stilted bow. "At your service, mademoiselle." He backed through his shop door.

The numbered street sign on the building read 2 Bleeding Heart Yard. The gilded name on the door, N. Fabian, Diamonds & Gemstones. "Oh." Cate bit her lip and tucked the gun back in her coat pocket. "So sorry. You're exactly the man I wish to see."

She had stumbled upon Fabian's shop quite by accident and tucked herself into the stairwell. Dressed in traveling clothes and lugging a leather and tapestry travel bag, she had traipsed round and round Hatton Garden in search of Fabian's shop. She had finally found the small basement storefront off Greville Street, and just in time, too. In the wee hours of the morning the diamond district crawled with Metropolitan police on patrol. A young woman wandering these streets in the dead of night was suspicious enough. If they had searched her portmanteau and found the jewels, she would have been carted off to jail.

Fabian gestured to her. "Please, come inside." Cate followed, cautiously.

The jeweler lifted a sputtering kettle off an iron stove and poured steaming water into a teapot. "How do you take your tea, miss?"

All eyes, Cate took in the curious shop. "Half a lump with a spot of cream, please." The wiry man bustled about the small space dominated by two glass-fronted display cases and a workbench. Fabian added cups and saucers to the delicate tools scattered about his worktable.

Cate peered through a glass-topped cabinet to examine a display of engagement rings.

Opening her bag, she rolled out the jewelry pouch. "Might you be able to tell me something about these, Mr. Fabian?"

The jeweler appeared stunned. He even stammered. "M-May I?" He attached a brass-framed magnifying glass to his spectacles and picked up the diamond stickpin. "After being stolen from the Crown Jewels during the French Revolution, the Tavernier Blue was cut into several smaller diamonds in an attempt to prevent its proper identification."

Fabian looked up at her. The odd lens he wore had the strange effect of enlarging one eye and not the other. "May I ask how you came by such treasure, miss?"

"A family heirloom. Tucked away for many years."

The magnified eye was quite piercing. "Have you ever heard of the great diamond of Lord Francis Hope?"

Cate set down her teacup. "Yes of course, the Hope Diamond."

"Believed to be cut from the Tavernier, along with another stone, which was set as a ring for Empress Maria Feodorovna, wife of Emperor Paul I. It was subsequently given to her daughter-in-law, Alexandra. Later, it was said to have been mounted into a stickpin." He twirled the blue diamond in the gaslight.

"For months now I have heard rumors these pieces were back in circulation—all private sales." Fabian set down the pin and examined each piece in succession. With each passing second, the clock on the wall ticked louder, and Cate grew more uneasy. The mesmerized jeweler seemed to know something about each piece—what artisan crafted the jewelry, who it was made for, even the mine in India where the gems originated.

She would have enjoyed knowing something of the provenance of each piece, but she could not escape the niggling worry that she was running out of time. Cate glanced at the clock. Even if she had lost the tail placed on her by Scotland Yard, Phineas Gunn would soon arrive at her residence, find her gone, and start looking. "Mr. Fabian, have you—any idea of their worth?"

"Dare I ask . . ." Fabian tore his eyes off the gems. "Are any of these for sale?"

She nodded. "Any or all, monsieur."

He thrust himself forward. "You would sell—to me— one of these pieces?"

She blinked. "Why ever do you think I'm here?"

He shrugged. "An appraisal, perhaps. A repair?"

"A family crisis—a financial upset—forces me to part with them." Cate bit her lip. "I'm afraid only a great deal of money will solve the problem."

Fabian stood up and grabbed his hat from a hook on the wall. "I must make arrangements with my banker. How soon will you need the money, Miss Willoughby?"

"Immediately."

The jeweler studied her. "Then, I must ask for proof of ownership. A bill of sale will do."

She swallowed. "I have no documentation, per se."

He slumped onto his workbench stool. "I must have assurance these gems are not stolen."

"But—they are stolen. In a manner of speaking." She rolled her eyes. "It's a rather long story." Cate tucked the jewels back inside the velvet pouch. "Perhaps we can do business another time."

Finn had intimated this man was discreet, and implied he was the kind of dealer who might be eager to do business. Nandor Fabian tugged at the narrow tuft of goatee on his chin. "Alas, I have only limited funds in my safe."

She stopped rolling. "How much?"

> URGENT: FOR IMMEDIATE DELIVERY
> BLEEDING HEART YARD STOP
> HATTON GARDEN

Charlie's wire was brief and to the point. A time of 6:10 a.m. had been penciled under the telegram's masthead. Finn steered his horse through the light morning traffic of the diamond district and considered the situation. He'd spun a web of half-truths and outright lies last night, enough to prod Cate into action. And even though his jaw ached from the constant clenching, he felt little or no disappointment, only curiosity. And one other, unexpected reaction to Miss Willoughby's treachery. He was aroused beyond belief.

He turned into the small yard off Greville, and dismounted. Just across the quaint old courtyard Finn made out Fabian's signage, hidden partially below street level.

Sergeant MacGregor swiped a mouthful of feed from a nearby hay wagon parked in the alley. "Always on the lookout for a tasty bit."

"*Ps-s-s-st.*"

Finn peered over the far side of the cart.

Crouching behind the wheel, Charlie Doyle tipped his hat. "Hello, Mr. Gunn."

"Sorry I was delayed." It appeared the lad had stuck by his post through the night. "Good work, Charlie." Finn nodded to the shop across the yard. "Is she still with Fabian?"

Charlie nodded. "You've arrived in the nick of time, I'd say, sir."

Finn handed the reins over. "Keep an eye out while I inquire within."

As he crossed the paved yard, his pulse leaped in his chest. She had taken the bait. She was either an anarchist operator, or she was trying to sell the jewels before he could confiscate them. Either way, he was about to arrest a woman he was infatuated with, perhaps more than infatuated. The concept so disturbed him, for a fleeting moment he considered turning away.

Finn clenched his jaw. A bell tinkled as he pushed the door open. Nandor Fabian looked up from his workbench. The jeweler's hooded eyes couldn't quite hide a dash of fear. "Where is she?"

"Mr. Gunn. It has been some time. You are looking for someone?" The jeweler returned to his work.

Finn rounded the display case. "Where is Miss Willoughby? I'll not ask again." He ripped the magnifying lens off his wireframes.

The jeweler sighed. "The young lady left some time ago."

He intruded into the space between Fabian and his workbench. "You're sure of that?"

The man straightened his spectacles. "The lady claimed to have some jewelry for sale, but—"

"Open the safe. Let's see the money."

"What money?"

Had he or Nandor suddenly gone thickheaded? "The Scotland Yard *money*. You were given a sum of cash by Detective Inspector Kennedy."

"I was?" the jeweler squeaked.

"What are we doing here, Nandor?" Finn growled. "Inventing a new parlor game?"

The jeweler made a sudden move to a drawer in his workbench. Finn beat him there and removed a pistol, then flipped open the chamber.

"You see?" Fabian tried to make light of his last maneuver. "No bullets."

Finn pointed the gun up and fired. The jeweler lunged under his workbench to escape a spray of falling plaster. Finn brushed white dust off his shoulder. "It seems one bullet remained in the chamber. A common enough mistake." He fixed his glare on Fabian and fished in his coat pocket. "Good thing I can fix that." He withdrew a hand-ful of bullets.

The jeweler righted himself. "I'm telling you she left some time ago."

"How long ago?" Finn inserted six bullets, spun the chamber, and cocked the trigger.

"Perhaps an hour or so."

Enough of this. Finn pushed the jeweler against the bench and pressed the gun to his head. "I swear to God, Nandor, I'll shoot you dead. Think carefully about your next answer."

The man dripped with perspiration. Fogged spectacles slipped down his nose. "Several minutes ago."

"Liar. No one saw her leave."

He pointed frantically toward the back of the shop. "There is a backstairs."

"What did you purchase?"

Fabian's eyes shifted. Finn kept the gun barrel at Fabian's temple.

"The stickpin."

Finn waved the revolver in the direction of the back room. "Let's pay your safe a visit, shall we?" He grabbed the jeweler by the collar and pushed him into the next room.

"She drives a hard bargain, that woman. No proof of ownership. Not even false papers." Nandor bent over the floor safe. "I'll return the gem to Scotland Yard. I swear it."

"Like hell you will. With the profit you could make from that diamond, you could live like a sultan—never mind Lithuania, right here in London." Finn smiled. "I'll have the gem back."

"Hungary." Fabian twirled the dial left and the tum-blers clicked. Reluctantly, he handed over the stickpin.

"Did the young lady say where she was headed?" Finn pocketed the diamond. "Good information at this juncture could save you from deportation . . ." The stone's rarity, size, and legend had obviously proved to be too big a temptation for Fabian. "Again."

Scotland Yard had enjoyed a reasonably cooperative relationship with the part-time fence, as long as Fabian kept his dealings discreet. "In fact, I am prepared to be more than reasonable. I will forget your willful attempt to impede a law enforcement officer in pursuit of a crime." Finn leaned into the man. "Just point me in the right direction."

The sneaky-eyed jeweler nodded toward the back steps. "I told her to take Greville to Farringdon Road. She asked for directions to the telegraph office."

Finn turned back. "How much cash does she have on her?"

"All twenty thousand."

## ∞ Chapter Twelve

Cate handed the clerk a shilling.

"Off in a jiff, miss." The wire office clerk tapped a bell and put her message in a tray marked OVERSEAS. She pocketed a receipt and tuppence, picked up her portmanteau, and exited the telegraph office. Keeping to the busy side of the street, she did not walk, but trotted the two blocks to Farringdon station.

Once she paid her fare and descended the stairs, she inhaled a deep breath. The Central Line platform had begun to fill up with passengers. Hopefully, there would not be a long wait for the next train. Farringdon to King's Cross was a brief ride. She'd have another short walk to the rail station and finally, the train to Dover.

Cate grabbed her lower lip with her teeth and scraped. A four-sided clock hung from the intricate steel and glass framework of the train shed. Ten twenty-five. She was behind schedule. She had planned to slip out of London before Finn awoke. Not very likely at this point.

She peered up and down the track.

Assuming Finn rose early, he would likely make his way to her uncle's home to collect the jewels. She had left a message with Mrs. Mettle. Hopefully that would stall him long enough to give her an excellent head start. But if that little street urchin spy of his had managed to contact him last night, he could be closer.

In fact, he might be breathing down her neck.

A blast of chilly air caused Cate to jump. The stir in atmosphere signaled a train neared the station. Cautiously, she worked her way into the middle of the crowd moving forward as the car doors opened.

"SHE'S HEADED FOR the rail station at Cowcross Street and Farringdon Road." Finn lifted himself onto his horse and offered Charlie a hand up. "Up behind me."

Since Cate had likely finished her business at the wire office, he thought it best to try and catch her at the Underground station. The street traffic was light and they quickly covered several long blocks to the Underground. Charlie tapped his shoulder. "If you drop me at the Parcel Office, I can sniggle my way inside from there. If I spot her I'll give a yell: 'Hot eels here.'"

He winked at the sharp-witted young street hawker. "Eel jelly it is."

Finn parked his horse with a paper boy outside the station front and dashed inside. He descended onto the platform just as the train pulled into the station. "Bollocks." He was on the wrong side of the tracks.

Two steps at a time, he dashed back up the stairs, through a short connecting passage, and pressed through a horde of arriving commuters as he descended the stairs.

"Hot eels here." Charlie's head bobbed above the crowd.

Finn sprinted across the platform as the doors cranked

shut. "Bollocks." He punched the side of the car as the train chugged off in a hiss of steam.

Finn paced a circle around the boy. "You're sure it was her?"

"Saw her plain as day—wearing a blue traveling coat and dress. Carrying the same heavy satchel."

"All right." Finn played out several possible scenarios in his head. "I need you to follow after. Just a hunch, but she's likely on her way to St. Pancras station. Hopefully, she'll have to wait for the train to Dover."

Finn handed the boy several coins. "I'm off to the wire office. Meet you at St. Pancras." He turned back. "And next time, don't wait for me—jump on board with the lady. I'll catch up somehow."

Charlie nodded. "I will, sir."

Aboveground, Finn checked on Sergeant MacGregor, then made for the telegraph office. He entered the busy hall and took a chance on the only free clerk. "May I help you, sir?"

He noted a single wire form lay in the OVERSEAS basket on the man's desk. There was a chance Cate's message had not yet been passed on to the translating department. And if her missive had not been made into code . . .

Finn leaned across the counter. "A young lady was here, not long ago, lovely to look at—tall, wearing a blue traveling costume. She likely paid for a wire to be sent overseas. Is that the message?" He nodded toward the tray. "If so, I'd like to have a look at it." He pushed his card across the counter. "The young lady may be in danger. This is of upmost importance to the Crown."

The man read the card and raised a brow. "One moment, sir. I must clear this with my supervisor."

Finn pushed a fiver across the polished wood counter.

"Just turn the message over, and let me read it from here, while you collect your boss."

The clerk palmed the note and flipped Cate's missive over.

The message was written in a familiar cursive hand.

*Arrive Giverny late tomorrow. Quiet Woman.*

Finn reread the words. She was off to the countryside outside Paris. And she had signed the wire *Quiet Woman*. Or was the Quiet Woman the name of an inn?

CATE EXITED THE Underground and made her way along Pancras Road to the impressive rail station. Holding on to her hat, she tilted her head back to take in the curved steel arches and the orderly red bricks of the tall clock tower.

From Farringdon Station to King's Cross she had thought of nothing else but him. She had come to know the stubborn, dogged nature of Agent Gunn these last few days. Boarding the Underground train she had glimpsed a determined scowl and a promise: *I will catch you soon enough, Miss Willoughby.* The very thought sent shivers, as well as tingles, though her.

Her lower lip was raw from too much gnawing. She bit down anyway. Try as she might, she could not get Finn's fierce look out her head. And she was sure it was his fist that pounded the door as it cranked shut. Cate swallowed. No doubt he believed her to be a traitor and a thief. And perhaps she was. At this juncture, it wasn't important what Finn thought.

She spotted her contact ahead, dressed in a black overcoat. The man stood beside a balustrade overlooking St. Pancras station. "I received a rather shocking wire this morning," the man grumbled.

She leaned over the balcony. "Can I count on you?" Her query floated into the vast space above the platforms. He made eye contact briefly, then turned toward the view of the train shed below. "You realize you are very likely walking into a trap, my dove."

She knew him only by the initial *W*. And he had given her a code name, Paloma. Spanish for dove. "If there is a chance Eduardo is alive, I must see this through." She could barely hear her own speech over the hubbub.

The man's scowl warmed into a fatherly frown. "We are willing to go along with your plan—for the time being. And we will help if we can." Abruptly, the man stepped away, and then turned back. "As I can spare no one, it might not be such a terrible idea to encourage . . . Agent Gunn?" A bushy brow lifted.

She lifted her gaze to the sweeping arc of skylight overhead. "I believe his involvement to be inevitable."

The grin she received from W. was more of a smirk. "Well, that is a spot of good news." He turned and disappeared into a throng of travelers.

Cate headed downstairs to the train platforms. She was playing both sides in this game of chance—but the reward was so much greater than the risk. She blinked back a bit of excess moisture in her eyes. There was no time for regrets or tears. Not when there was a chance her brother was alive.

FINN STORMED INTO his study and unlocked his gun cabinet. "Bootes!" He removed his Purdey double rifle and his ten-gauge, double-barreled, sawed-off shotgun, known affectionately as Bully. He placed both guns on his desk, along with several cases of shells and bullets.

"You're leaving us, sir?" His manservant stood in the doorway, prepared for duty. Finn's field assignments seemed to always happen in a hurry.

"Pack the saddlebags. Field attire—plenty of clean shirts, nothing formal. Be sure to include a bedroll and canteen." He handed Bootes the ammunition boxes. "Bullets on top—and when you're done, let the groom tie everything on, along with my rifle holster."

"Very good, sir." The butler slipped out of sight.

Finn forced himself to sit down at his desk and scribbled off a message. Folding the note, he consulted the Metropolitan Rail schedule. The train to Dover was scheduled to depart at 12:25 p.m. The mantel clock read 11:45. Forty minutes to cross town and grab Cate before she escaped London.

Devil take it, Sergeant MacGregor would have to grow wings.

He might have sent Scotland Yard a message from the telegraph office earlier. Finn took in a deep breath and exhaled. The young lady was having her effect, on gray matter as well as other extremities. No matter. He would proceed under the assumption that she would not be apprehended in London. And bugger all, if he was going to end up chasing Little Miss Anarchist over every hill and dale of the Continent, he was not leaving town unprepared. He had taken a calculated chance and ridden straight for his residence. Even if her trail went cold, he was confident he would pick it up again. Over the years, he had developed contacts in France. People who had an ear to the underground.

Finn checked his coat pocket and removed Fabian's revolver. He replaced the inferior gun with his old service pistol for good measure. Sliding out several desk drawers, he removed an ammunition belt, compass, spyglass, hunting knife, and his military-issue holster.

He shrugged off his jacket and slipped both arms through the shoulder harness. With an eye on the clock, he holstered his Webley Mk1 and pulled his coat over the lot. On his way out the door Finn grabbed both long guns and flung the belt of bullets over his shoulder. He ran into Bootes in the hall.

"Packed and ready, sir."

He tugged his duster coat on and made his way to the mews. Saddled up for field service, Sergeant MacGregor snorted a greeting. Finn checked the rigging and slid his rifle into the side holster angled along his mount's flank.

"Do you expect to be gone long, sir?" Bootes handed him his slouch hat and travel papers. Finn checked the name on his passport. Hugh Curzon.

"Not long, I hope." He donned the wide-brimmed hat, grabbed the pommel, and lifted himself onto the saddle. "If I'm not home by this evening, deliver this to Hardy." He handed his manservant the note.

Bootes stepped out of the way. "Safe journey, sir."

He and MacGregor fought a snarl of traffic congestion from Piccadilly to Charing Cross Road, but when they turned for the station he thought he might have a fighting chance to catch her. He parked his horse with a stout lad and descended belowground. Crossing under the expansive vaulted ceiling of the train shed, he read the schedule board. DOVER PLATFORM 9. Due to depart in less than . . . Bollocks.

He zigged and zagged against a horde of arriving travelers, keeping his eyes peeled for either Cate or Charlie Doyle. Where was the lad?

A flap of blue traveling coat flashed just ahead. "Excuse me." Finn pressed through a knot of passengers blocking his view. "Pardon." He caught sight of the woman in blue as she entered one of the passenger cars. Stepping up his dodge and weave, Finn raced down the platform and entered the second-class passenger car. He spotted her sitting midway down the aisle.

Finn approached from behind. "Would you like me to arrest you here, or do you promise to leave the train—" He nearly choked. "You're not Cate."

An attractive middle-aged woman looked him up and down as a slow smile curved the ends of her mouth. "Unfortunately not."

The passenger car lurched as the brakes released. "Sorry to disturb." Finn tapped the brim of his hat and scanned the rest of the railcoach. Might she be hiding in plain sight? The train began a slow crawl out of the station. He checked the section of car ahead, then turned and walked every aisle to the rear baggage car. Cate was nowhere to be found.

He stepped off near the end of the platform and watched the train fade into the velvet blackness of the tunnel.

"Where is she, Mr. Gunn?" Charlie ran up beside him. "The young lady got on the train. I saw her myself."

"It wasn't her."

"No, sir. I got a good look at the lady on the train. It was her. I swear it."

"I'm telling you—" Finn glanced upward. Another flash of blue from high above the platform. He narrowed his eyes. The woman appeared to be in a hurry. He sprinted for the stairs that led to the street-level balcony. Open arches afforded passengers an excellent view as they entered the grand station.

"I see her, sir." He and the boy raced along the balustrade. Outside the station, they caught sight of her again as she climbed into a waiting carriage.

"Hold the team, Charlie." Finn flashed his revolver up at the driver. "Scotland Yard." He ripped the door open. Almost in unison the frightened females inside the coach screamed.

He dipped his head inside the cabin, swearing under his breath. "Bollocks. Bollocks. Bollocks." His cursory search ended on the young lady's companion, a matronly scarecrow who raised her umbrella. "What is the meaning of this intrusion?" The chaperone missed his head, but got off a good thwack to his shoulder.

"My apologies." He backed off and closed the door, signaling the boy to release the horses. The driver flicked his whip and the carriage swiftly pulled into traffic.

Finn rubbed his shoulder. A disquieting scene intruded upon his thoughts. An image of Cate dressed as a chimney snake. She unbuttons a man's tailored shirt and reveals a curve of breast. She turns her back. Sleeves slip off silken shoulders; trousers roll off rounded buttocks and drop to the floor.

Finn shook his head and exhaled. "You were right, Charlie."

"I like being right—what about?" The lad beamed.

"She was on the train." Another picture emerged—pure conjecture, mind, but it was the only plausible explanation. Cate cramped inside the water closet of the passenger car. She must have changed clothes. He remembered a blur of bowler hats peeking above open newspapers. He'd passed more than one gent with his head buried in the afternoon edition of the *Guardian*.

He stared into a blur of bustling street traffic. First rule of battle: never underestimate your opponent. He had underestimated Cate.

"Is something amusing, sir?"

He turned to his young helper. "I fail to find anything comic about losing Miss Willoughby."

Charlie shrugged. "You're smiling, is all."

## ∞ Chapter Thirteen

Cate leaned over the passenger rail as the steamer chugged past a majestic, tall-masted ship. She inhaled a breath of ocean air. "Heave away! Stand by to tack!" The captain's order to set sail easily carried between passing vessels. "Take them away now!" The great ship's sails snapped back at her crew and caught wind.

They were almost to port. The ferry slipped between a pair of giant stone sentinels, ancient watchtowers that had stood guard at the entrance of La Rochelle for centuries. The day-long voyage from Cherbourg had allowed her a restorative nap and time had ticked by quickly. While the ferry pilot skillfully maneuvered the boat dockside, Cate admired a jumble of colorful shop fronts. Higher up, as the view receded, tile-roofed buildings stacked themselves against the old fortress walls of the city.

She reached for her portmanteau. *"Attendez, s'il vous plaît, mademoiselle."* The call came from the pilot housing above. Cate waited at the gangway of the steamship.

The boat's captain handed over a letter. She stared at the sealed envelope in her hand. More instructions. She scraped pearly uppers over her lower lip. So far, *Los Ti-*

*gres Solitarios* had given her explicit instructions and little time to think. Their detailed travel itinerary had ended here, in La Rochelle. Until now.

She supposed she ought to feel relieved. Instructions would mean she would know what do next—where to go, who to contact. The idea of blindly following more of their directives, however, did nothing to assuage her unease. Growing suspicions and fears had kept her tossing and turning most of last night.

Yesterday, upon arrival in Cherbourg, she had booked passage to La Rochelle and taken a room at the inn. She had spent the night drifting in and out of disturbing dreams. In one strange reverie, she followed a shadowed figure, calling the name of her brother. She had pursued the amorphous creature down an endless corridor, opening and closing door after door. And just when she got close enough to reach out—the dream shifted.

Immersed in darkness and smoke, an imposing figure walked straight toward her. He wore a wide-brimmed hat pulled down over his face and a long coat. Belts made up of bullets crisscrossed his chest. The face of the stranger remained shaded, but a shiver rattled her down to her bones. He levered a double-barreled gun and fired.

Her body jerked her upright and she gasped for air. A drizzle of sweat had run down the bridge of her nose and fallen onto her lower lip. She had licked drops of perspiration away. They had tasted like tears.

Cate pocketed the letter, and checked her timepiece. Plenty of light left to explore La Rochelle. Gripping her travel case, she made her way down the gangway and onto the pier. A carriage rolled off the ferry onto the cobbled lane. She dashed around the team of horses and wound a path through luggage carts and crated goods. She nodded to a few finely dressed travelers; wealthy merchants, likely.

Yesterday, she had eluded Finn and that young street urchin spy of his—very well done, she thought. At the very least, she was confident she had delayed his departure from England. She had telegraphed a false destination in France and made it abundantly clear she was headed for Dover, then Calais. But in actuality, she had changed trains in Lambeth. Not knowing which, if any, of her ruses worked, she arrived in Portsmouth in time to catch the last ferry to Cherbourg.

Cate made her way along the broad avenue of Quai Duperré. The clear sky of her sea journey had begun to cloud over. A splash of rain fell on her cheek. More wet spots pattered softly on the pavers. She turned down an arcade-lined street and took refuge under the impressive arches of the clock tower. The exotic scents of the port town concentrated into a heady mélange in the dank stew of light rain. She sniffed: Madeira, tea chests, and the pungent scent of clove.

She opened the letter. No surprise here. More instructions, much less detailed this time. Consulting the message again, she pivoted toward the east and spied a small address sign on a building ahead. 3 Place L'Hôtel De Ville. On the corner, a waiter scurried about, moving chairs and tables under the arched walkway.

Cate brightened at the sight. It was teatime and there was a café connected to the hotel. The rumble in her stomach reminded her how long it had been since she'd had a good strong cup of French coffee and a plate of madeleines. She opened her umbrella and dashed out into the rain.

*   *   *

LIGHTNING CRACKED OVERHEAD, followed shortly by a boom of thunder. The big red horse leaped sideways, ears flicking front to back. "Aye, MacGregor, looks as though the storm's caught us." Finn spoke softly, gentling his skittish mount.

The weather had threatened a downpour since he and MacGregor stepped ashore. The storm obscured Finn's vision enough that he nearly missed the gravel drive. "Bloody hell."

Sergeant MacGregor snorted clouds of pale breath as he splashed through small puddles en route to Château Du Rozel. Finn squinted at a few cottages scattered along the coastline. Les Pieux was more of a whistle-stop than a seaside resort, barely a dot on the map. He had spent a pleasant few days with Aurélien and Gilbert last year, on his way back to London. The Clouzot brothers lived in a charming old ruin of a castle not fifteen miles from Cherbourg. It was a long shot; the two could be off adventuring in the skies somewhere. But time was of the essence, and if anyone could help him catch the wily Miss Willoughby, they could.

There had been no time to change his legend. His travel papers identified him as Hugh Curzon. The Foreign Office or Naval Intelligence would confirm his identity if questioned by French authorities. His cover assignment was more of an inquiry, a dull bit of business for the Crown. The French held a number of political dissidents at a prison called the Citadel. Disrupters of every stripe, including dynamiters. He was to contact a British chargé d'affaires there. Finn carried on his person an official offer—a proposal for an exchange of prisoners.

Unofficially, he was in pursuit of Cate Willoughby, jewel thief, anarchist collaborator, agent provocateur.

A crooked line of brilliant light met the ground up ahead. Thunder rumbled softly. The storm appeared to have moved ahead of them.

Finn had spent a restless few hours on the ferry from Portsmouth to Cherbourg trying to reconcile his past memories of the woman he hunted. A year ago, her guileless, innocent beauty had captured him, body and soul. Even now, he was bewitched by her daring—her courage. She was as desirable now as she was then— perhaps more so.

He had wrestled with his reemerging feelings for Cate the entire voyage across the channel. If dealing with his nervous condition had taught him anything, it was to take several deep breaths and evaluate the circumstances. Especially before scuttering after dangerous maidens, no matter how tempting they might be.

After losing Cate at the train station he had made his way to 4 Whitehall and found Zeno Kennedy behind his desk with his chair tilted back. The detective had glanced over the top of the Manchester *Guardian* and lowered the paper. "Let me guess—she took the bait."

"All twenty thousand."

Kennedy listened intently as Finn recounted the chase from Hatton Garden to St. Pancras station. "France is a big country. I thought I'd stop by and see if you chaps have anything new on *Los Tigres*." He slouched into a seat and stretched out his legs. "Her wire was addressed to a Claude Abeilard, Giverny, France." His gaze absently followed the cracks in the ceiling plaster. "There's something about Spanish anarchists hiding outside Paris—doesn't exactly sound right, not when they would so easily disappear in the Latin Quarter."

Zeno plucked a file from a tall stack. "This report came over from the Foreign Office yesterday—appears to be chock-full of NID intelligence." The Yard man leafed through the pages. "Nothing on *Los Tigres* by name. An illegal arms shipment was confiscated in Le Havre bound for London."

Finn pinched the bridge of his nose. "Not really their style. Anything else?"

Zeno turned a few pages. "Something here, perhaps. Two prisoners, both of them bound for Devil's Island."

"What's so special about them?"

"Country of origin: Spain. No records."

"They're in prison, aren't they? There must be records, arrests, trials, convictions?"

The detective flipped over the page. "According to the writer of this report, that is what makes these prisoners all the more intriguing."

Finn grunted. "Wouldn't be the first time the Frogs imprisoned anarchists without due process. The anonymity could indicate the men are high profile. Where are they being held?"

"In an old fortress known as the Citadel—converted to a prison ages ago—on Île de Ré, an island off La Rochelle." Kennedy glanced up from the file. "You say Miss Willoughby took the train to Dover?"

Finn leaned forward in his chair. "As an exercise, let's say Miss Willoughby got off the Dover train and doubled back to Waterloo station."

Kennedy's mouth twitched. "Where she caught a train to Portsmouth."

"Once there, she books passage to Le Havre or Cher-bourg—and on to La Rochelle." There were instincts one developed in the espionage business. Usually it was just an inkling—a niggling hunch. This one buzzed up and down his spine like a bolt of electricity. "Shall we hazard a speculation? The twenty thousand is intended for bribes. A prison official looks the other way . . ."

Finn stood up. "I'll need an assignment." He and Zeno worked out his cover story and scratched off something on letterhead that looked official. Zeno included a couple of international arrest warrants for good measure.

Detective Kennedy had sat back in his chair. "Stay in touch by wire office. Meanwhile, I'll meet with Saunders at the Foreign Office, and Hall at NID—see if I can get you names for those warrants."

Finn had spent the last night in Portsmouth and caught the early morning ferry to Cherbourg. Dutifully, upon arrival in France, he penned a brief message to 77 St. Bride Street, the unofficial wire office for Scotland Yard.

He stabled MacGregor and found a reasonably clean hotel dockside. A brief look at the harbor registry showed a cargo ship set to leave on the eventide for La Rochelle. The clerk in the harbor master's office had seemed confident Finn could book passage. Purchasing a local map, he found a café featuring mussels steamed in a curried broth. Halfway into his second plate, he had remembered the Clouzot brothers and reopened the map.

At the top of a rise, he now slowed MacGregor. Finn blinked through a drizzle of rain. The storm had passed for the most part, leaving a bit of blustery wind. He could just make out the silhouette of a crenellated parapet. Lights blazed from a rounded turret, and Finn had to smile at the welcome sight. Perhaps this was still a good idea. With any luck, he could hitch a ride to La Rochelle with Aurélien and Gilbert Clouzot.

CATE REQUESTED THE small table at the back of the dining room. "The one by the window, *s'il vous plaît.*"

"*Très bon, mademoiselle. Suivez-moi.*"

She took her seat, smoothing the swath of fabric that ended in a bow above her bustle. A grin tugged at the corners of her mouth. The money pouch was hidden in the frame above her derriere. Safe enough, for now. Her most recent instructions had been clear enough: Check into L'Hôtel De Ville. Wait to be contacted.

A cup of hot coffee would help shake off the damp chill. The steaming rich liquid would likely keep her up for hours, but she wished to stay vigilant. Or was she just trying to avoid disturbing nightmares?

There was no doubt in her mind that he would come after her—drat the man. Where exactly Finn might be at the moment, she could only wager a guess. Calais, perhaps, if she had managed to steer him off course. And if she hadn't? She pictured him by her side—on her side, even—and stirred a splash of steamed milk into her cup. Might there be a chance of that?

At least her room at the hotel was pleasantly bright, with a view to the harbor. After coffee and sustenance, she would return and unpack a few things, toiletries and a change of— A tapping noise came from the window beside her table. Cate turned toward the glass and nearly jumped out of her seat.

A smallish, reed-thin man leaned against the arched curve of the arcade. A gas lantern sputtered above, illuminating parts but not all of his face. In the flickering light he appeared more goblin than human. Hunched-over shoulders supported a largish head and a prominent, hooked nose. Small black eyes peered at her intently.

As she sat mesmerized by a sight dredged from darker childhood tales, the odd fellow reached into his coat pocket and pulled out a folded blue paper—the kind the wire services used. Thin lips on a wide-set mouth stretched into an approximate grin.

Cate looked away and sipped her coffee. A new message delivered by a gargoyle. She lifted her chin, and turned back to signal the odd fellow to come inside.

Gone.

She craned her neck and peered up and down the covered walkway. Easing back in her chair, she felt her stomach rumble. Sea travel always ravaged her stomach, and she hadn't eaten anything for . . . how long was it? More than a day, certainly. She supposed it was possible she had hallucinated the strange character.

Cate caught the eye of the waiter and asked about the dinner fare. She decided on the curried oyster bisque and *Coquilles Saint-Jacques.* Once her meal arrived, her sensitive stomach forgot about the unusual chap, or troll, or whatever he was.

She sopped up every drop of soup, using chunks of crusty bread. "M-m-mmm," she sighed upon finishing off the last bite. Next came the delicately flavored scallops in a rich cheese sauce. Every morsel disappeared—including the luscious dessert, a chocolate caramel mousse. She scraped her spoon along the edge of the parfait glass, fully satisfied and duly impressed with the cuisine of the café.

*"Excusez-moi, mademoiselle?"*

She looked up into black beady eyes.

A nervous-looking waiter hovered close by.

Cate lifted the serviette from her lap and brushed the sides of her mouth. She nodded to the café worker. "Quite all right, I believe *monsieur*—the gentleman—has a message for me.

Hat in hand, the odd character settled into a chair opposite and ordered himself a glass of wine. Not quite as threatening up close, until he sat, pulled out the envelope, and placed it on the table. The tips of three fingers on his right hand were made of metal. Fascinated, Cate leaned closer and squinted. "Are those . . ."

"Thimble fingers." The homely man shrugged.

Her gaze moved to the note on the table. "This is for me?" She opened the wire message. Two lines. Encoded. She would have to wait to decipher the message in her room. The telegram was addressed to the harbor office at La Rochelle, care of—she suspected—this man. "You have a name, then, besides Thimble Fingers?"

"I am called Dé Riquet. The accent makes the—"

"The word for thimble." Cate folded up the wire. "Clever, but not your real name, I suspect?"

Rodent-like eyes lowered. "It is not my preference."

The waiter brought the glass of wine. "Will there be anything else, mademoiselle?"

*"Un autre café, s'il vous plaît."* There would be no sleeping tonight. How could she sleep with characters like this one skulking about?

The faint clink of metal fingertips on his wineglass drew her gaze. She reached across the table and gently traced over the metal tips. Silver thimbles that had been refashioned as delicate, dangerous claws. Fascinated, her gaze connected with the reedy gent in front of her. "Tell me, Dé Riquet, how did this happen?"

## ∞ Chapter Fourteen

Cate distinctly heard a wheezing exhale from the creature. A sigh, perhaps? She supposed her question tried his patience more than caused any pain.

Silver tips stroked the side of his wineglass. "In my youth, I scratched out a living as a petty thief and pickpocket. One day a shopkeeper caught me stealing. The man was a dealer in antiquities, rare artifacts, the occasional mechanical toy.

"He dragged me back into his shop and held my hand under a handsome, working replica of a guillotine." The wiry little man struck the table with such force the cups and glasses rattled.

Cate swallowed. "How awful. What deplorable, cruel treatment of a child."

Dé Riquet tilted his head and studied her, as though evaluating how much to reveal. "Business partners can often be less forgiving than perfect strangers. The man had bought many items from me, no questions asked." He tipped the wine to his lips. "Do you have the ransom?"

She had followed her instructions to the letter, with one exception. The money was not as large as the demand note, but it would have to be enough. She was prepared to bluff her way through the first meeting and then, given assurances, she'd deliver the twenty thousand. Cate raised her chin along with an eyebrow. "Do you have my brother?"

*"ENTREZ!"* THE FAMILIAR voice welcomed. An attractive young housemaid showed Finn into a library crammed floor to ceiling with books. A six-foot model of an airship hung suspended over a reading table covered with reference tomes, charts, and technical instruments.

"Look what the storm blew in. And he's dripping all over my clean floors," the maid declared.

Gilbert poked his head over a pile of volumes. "There's a clean spot somewhere on the floor? Do point that one out to me, Inez."

The girl mumbled a retort. "I suppose we must feed the *monsieur* as well."

"We all need feeding, Inez. Must I remind you again to have cook pluck another chicken?"

The young maid huffed, and pivoted on her heel. Finn hooted under his breath. "Testy."

His friend shrugged, sheepishly. "Pretty."

"Very." He smiled. "Hello, Gilbert."

"We've been expecting you, Finn."

"I'm almost afraid to ask, but how is it possible you knew I was in France, let alone headed for your humble little plot?"

*"Bonsoir,* Phineas! Come up and have a look." The call came from high above. Aurélien waved from a balcony railing. The library opened onto the turret room. An iron staircase spiraled upward, hugging curved walls. Above an

iron deck, a glass cupola capped the tower. The dome was made up of curved panes that looked much like the sections of an orange.

Finn craned his neck. "Good God, is that what I think it is?"

Gilbert waved him ahead and they both climbed the stairs. The telescope was the largest he'd ever seen outside of the twelve-and-three-quarter-inch Merz at the Royal Observatory.

Finn stepped onto the observation deck and whistled. Gilbert cranked open a glass section of the dome. The tubular body itself must have reached fifteen feet in length, counterbalanced by framework that extended far below the iron work floor. Aurélian helped Finn into the specially rigged chair at the end of the telescope and showed him how to adjust the eyepiece. "Voilá! The clouds have parted just for you, my friend."

Finn watched spellbound as the waxing half-moon moved past the lens within a brief few seconds. "Can you keep this thing steady?"

When both brothers chuckled, Finn looked up. "What?"

"That is the moon doing the traveling." Aurélien adjusted the telescope and showed Finn the lever at the side of his seat. "The moon travels at rate of 2,288 miles per hour. But to be exact, you must also figure in the Earth's rotation at our latitude adding another 735 miles per hour."

Finn practiced raising the handle and turning the wheel until he easily tracked with the moon's trajectory. He spent the next half hour examining the giant, pocked orb, learning the names of the craters, among other lay observations, until—a shiver ran down his spine and his heart raced for a moment. "Reminds me of the desolate terrain around Kandahar."

Gilbert shook his head. "With no atmosphere, much worse!"

He exhaled a slow, controlled breath. His fleeting memory of Afghanistan had come and gone without a full-blown attack of nerves. "You blokes tracked me from Cherbourg with this?" Finn tore his eyes off the moon and stars.

Gilbert pointed to a smaller telescope at a retractable window facing west. "We receive strange deliveries daily and odd visitors." Aurélien closed several of the dome-shaped sections of window. "Present company always welcome."

"So you keep a watchful eye on the road."

To describe the Clouzot brothers as reclusive was apt, but not entirely accurate. They were stridently protective of their work and their privacy. They were also distrustful—bordering on raving mad—of all governments, including their own. He had once been a party to a rather lengthy argument on the subject. "Governments," Aurélien had insisted, "made promises of great wealth, then trapped inventors into making war machinery." A head full of dark curls had bobbed, along with a grin. "We make love, not war."

But if the Clouzots trusted you, and you appreciated scientific discussion, you were in for a rare treat. In fact, Finn had so enjoyed his visit thus far, he quite forgot to mention the reason he was here. He cleared his throat. "I have a favor to ask of you both."

*"Le dîner est servi, messieurs."*

The call came from below and Gilbert started down the stairs. "I'm famished."

"When are you not?" Aurélien snorted. "Come, Finn, you can ask your favor at supper."

He explained as much about the situation with Cate and *Los Tigres Solitarios* as the Clouzot brothers needed to know. "Scotland Yard isn't certain how deeply the young lady is involved with the anarchists but I mean to find out."

Aurélian separated a chicken leg from a roasted bird. "And this is the same young lady you mooned over the last time you were with us?"

Finn forked up a succulent piece of dark meat and turned to the other brother. "I don't recall mooning over the chit. Was I mooning?"

"You must clarify for us. This is the same girl whose brother was killed in a dynamite explosion." Gilbert sat back in his chair and rolled his eyes upward. "Granted, by some of his own contraband, but nonetheless, I believe his death made it impossible for you and the young woman to further your . . . interaction."

A strong gust of wind rustled treetops and rattled the roof tiles above. He would rather not think about that word, *impossible*. Finn's stare moved from one brother to the other. "I need the Air Commander."

"Strong air currents often follow storms this time of year." Gilbert waved a crispy *pomme frite* in the air. "There is an old saying about the mistral: it's a brutish, onerous wind that can blow the ears off a donkey."

Aurélien nodded. "The winds cross France from the northwest to the Mediterranean. Such a gale will give us cloudless skies tomorrow and luminous sunshine. We could make La Rochelle in several hours, yes?"

"Easily."

"Even better." Finn tried for a beseeching look. "So, will you or won't you? Either way, I'll need to leave for La Rochelle first thing in the morning—by sea or by air."

Gilbert leaned back in his chair and tilted his head. "I shall have to consult with my brother."

Aurélian poured Finn another glass of wine. "Much depends on how you answer the next question."

He felt a trap coming and narrowed his gaze. "All right, gentlemen, fire away."

"You do this thing—hunt down the lovely dancer . . ." Aurélian held up his glass. "For love or country?"

Gilbert raised both brows and added a grin.

Finn tilted his chair onto its back legs and consulted the number of tomes stacked in the shelves lining the walls. It seemed books served double duty in this quaint, if not eccentric little manse. Stacked on hearth mantels and on chair seats, they served as doorjambs, elbow rests, and, when piled high enough, table pedestals. Even the candelabra sat upon a large atlas.

A glance at the leather-bound spines read like the missing scrolls of Alexandria's library. One might easily draw the conclusion, based on the number of tomes, odd contraptions, unwieldy machines, and strange drawings, that the Clouzot brothers were mad savants. And they were so irritatingly . . . *French*.

Finn ran a hand through his hair. "You really insist on knowing?"


CATE STIFLED A yawn. It was late, and Dé Riquet was not offering up much in the way of information. After a good long squint at him, she suspected he was not that old. His coat, worn thin in spots, showed signs of mending in numerous places. His Van Dyke beard was patchy at best. And his hair, loosed from under a battered opera hat, turned out to be a wild mass of unruly tangles. Had he been a more winsome chap, and ten years younger, she might have described Dé Riquet as a youth in dire need of a mother.

She tried one last time to wheedle a bit of information out of him. "I take it you are sympathetic to the plight of . . . the Spanish labor union movement, Monsieur Dé Riquet?"

He set down his empty glass. "I am sympathetic to Dé Riquet, mademoiselle."

"So you are a mercenary. Up for hire—for a price."

His gaze traveled far away before returning to her. "What does it matter?"

Cate leaned forward. "Because I will pay you more. I need to know what you know."

He rose from his chair in a glower, tossing a few coins on the table. He picked up his dilapidated top hat. "I know nothing that would be of help to you, Miss Willoughby." She watched Dé Riquet wind his way though a maze of café tables.

Cate paid her bill and returned to the hotel via the arcade. She had not walked far when she realized she was closer to the rear of the hotel than the front. One gritty step after another echoed as she kept to the covered walkway. Until this moment, Cate had not been afraid to walk the streets alone. The storm had passed and people were out and about. But not here, in this less-traveled section of backstreet.

She climbed a broad set of carved stone stairs. Perhaps this was a rear entrance to the hotel. She pressed down a heavy latch and pushed hard. The door gave way suddenly, striking someone or something behind it. There was a grunt, she was sure of it.

Cate poked her head in the door. "Sorry—*je suis désolée.*"

A man lay crumpled on the tiled floor of the vestibule. Another brawny fellow stood over him, rubbing his head. He gave a kick to the downed man—a warning to stay down. Then he turned and lunged for her.

She smacked him in the face with her umbrella. A wraithlike figure moved from the shadows and grabbed her from behind. Cate swung her umbrella tip back and stabbed her assailant, then she spun herself out of his hold. She reached for the door, and stumbled into the poor bloke who rose from the floor.

She recognized the man, who swayed a bit and staggered toward her. Dé Riquet, with a nasty gash over a bloodied eye. He grabbed hold of her and slipped out the open door.

"*¡Ásgala!* Catch her!" The order came from behind, as did the large man who grabbed hold of her arm and held on. Caught in the narrow opening, her assailant slammed her against the door frame. A sharp pain stabbed the back of her head. She cried out as thousands of dark, glittering stars filled her vision. Dé Riquet's hand slipped down the length of her umbrella, and he was gone.

Vaguely, she felt someone drag her inside the building. She tried to push away, but her legs weren't working right. Like a string puppet, her knees buckled with every step. Someone tossed her over his shoulder. Her temples throbbed as blood rushed to her head. Her vision blurred. There were glimpses of a narrow corridor and a set of stairs. Her body, a large, limp rag doll, swayed with every turn in the passageway.

Cate fought to stay alert—to make sense of mumbled words. They had arrived somewhere, only where? She tried to raise her head as the floor beneath the man's boots began to whirl. Darkness finally overtook consciousness.

*    *    *

FINN PULLED HIS hat down and shouted over the howling wind. "You will see Sergeant MacGregor loaded onto the first train to La Rochelle—be sure to tip the livery attendant." He pressed several French coins into the groom's hand, along with a handwritten note. "This message must be wired ahead, as well."

"*Oui, monsieur.* I will leave right away."

Finn squinted at the young man. "And no . . ." He scratched his head. How did one say "pottering about" in French? The French dawdled. They couldn't help it.

"Phineas!" Aurélien and Gilbert waved him aboard.

Finn tilted his head back and took in the whole of the magnificent dirigible being guided out of its hangar. Tethered to the ground by safety lines held by estate workers who doubled as ground crew, the blimp bobbed and groaned eerily with each gust of the wind. He left the groom with a simple directive. "*Rapidement.*"

*Commandant d'Air Deux* was propelled by two airscrew propellers and steered with a sail-like aft rudder. The brothers' first airship had crashed due to faulty venting. "All corrected now," Gilbert had assured him.

Finn grabbed his satchel and both long guns and jogged across an expanse of lawn the length of a rugby field. At the rear of the craft, gigantic propellers churned slowly under the gondola, creating their own wind corridor. Running under the blimp, into the long shadow of the oval envelope, he felt swallowed up by the sheer size the dirigible.

Safety lines whined with each gust of wind as the airship strained at its moorings. Finn handed off his valise to one of the ground crew, and climbed the slatted steps of the ladder. The moment his gear landed on deck, Gilbert gave the order to cut ties and they nosed up into a cloudless sky. In seconds they had climbed several hundred feet in the air. As the ground receded, he took in the mesmerizing view of Cherbourg and the sparkling blue channel beyond.

"Finn." Aurélien tugged him away to review his crewing responsibilities. He learned how to adjust ballast and open and close the gas vents, as well as the finer points of gathering up tethering line. Working together, they soon had ropes coiled and ready for the next landing.

Gilbert yelled over his shoulder. "We shall set an airship speed record today, and Finn shall be our witness! First, we measure air speed alone. Then I will throttle up the engine, adding to our velocity. Then we measure again, *mais oui?*"

"I wager we make La Rochelle by early afternoon." Aurélien raised his voice above the hum of the engines belowdecks.

"Twenty francs says before noon." Gilbert grinned.

Finn swept his coat back with his fists. "If you can get me to La Rochelle by late morning, I'll gladly double that."

Aurélien lifted a metal chest behind the steerage and picked through several instruments. Finn recognized a barometer, to measure atmospheric pressure. He pointed to another gauge. "What is that?"

Aurélien carefully lifted out the strange-looking device. "It's called a cup anemometer, a wind velocity meter." The instrument featured four small hollow metal cones set to catch the wind and revolve about a vertical rod. "The revolutions of the cups calculate the wind velocity." The young inventor opened a porthole and clamped the device to the side of the gondola.

"On the Beaufort scale, I would guess we're near gale winds." He jotted down the numbers from his metering device, accounting for any added speed they received from the propellers. "Thirty-five knots and climbing. Gale certainly—if not more by midday."

"With the aid of our eight horsepower electric motor at full throttle . . ." Gilbert leaned over his brother's shoulder. "We'll soon be traveling at . . ." Aurélien returned to his calculations. "Less the airship's drag coefficient, nearly fifty knots."

"Hoo-hoo!" Gilbert and Aurélien hugged each other and pulled Finn into a three-way embrace.

"Hold on a moment." Finn scrutinized both young men as his pulse started to race. "How fast does the ship normally travel?"

"Maybe"—Gilbert shrugged—"ten knots, with a light tailwind."

Finn's stare moved between Gilbert and Aurélien until both men began to fidget. "Then what we are doing, flying at these speeds, is—"

"Dangerous, of course!" Gilbert's shoulders moved up and down and he threw his hands up. "Many would say Aurélien and I are *très fou-comme. Déments!*"

Finn nodded. "So you're telling me this bloody airship is built to putter about in the sky like a lark. And here we are, hundreds of feet in the air, flying at fifty knots."

"Not quite fifty," Aurélien assured him and opened a second chest. He pulled out a bottle of champagne. "To our next article in the *La Nature!*"

A sudden blast of mistral wind buffeted the airship. Gilbert sprang up and adjusted both the sail and the steerage. "The prevailing winds blow south, southeast. To stay on course we have to do periodic adjustments, exactly like sailing a ship on the ocean, *oui?*"

Finn took a long pull, direct from the bottle. These two were going to need all the help they could get. "If I could impose, gentlemen, I'd like a crash course in dirigible maneuvering. You never know when you might need an extra hand."

He made use of the next couple of hours in the air, learning as much as he could about the strange flying vessel. The steerage seemed to be achieved by the manipulation of a large jib sail, acting as a kind of rudder and alternating engine power to the props suspended beneath the rear of the blimp.

By mid-morning the sun glinted through the web of rigging that held the gondola to the balloon, warming the air. As the Air Commander sailed on, doing wonderfully well even in the high wind conditions, his apprehension eased some.

What a marvel this air balloon was, and he suspected many more would come after it. One day not so very long from now, people would traverse the globe in flying machines. Enthralled with the view of the coastline, Finn allowed himself a long moment of wonder.

He and Hardy had once climbed to the top of Ben Loyal in Sutherland—a high peak for the Northern Highlands. The view of his home in Helmsdale had been lovely, but nothing like this breathtaking sight. Land met sea, like a giant topographical map off the starboard side the gondola. Portside, the vast and verdant hills of the French countryside rolled endlessly eastward. And straight ahead lay La Rochelle, less than five miles away.

And Cate. She had to be there, otherwise all this risk

was for naught. Finn exhaled, feeling a bit guilty. Well, perhaps not too guilty. Even though he had placed them all in jeopardy, the Clouzot brothers had achieved their airship speed record.

"The birds have nothing over us, yes?" Gilbert wasn't frowning exactly, but he did appear less than jubilant.

"Why the long face? What's the problem?"

"We're nearly to La Rochelle, and the approach will be tricky—we're coming in too fast." Aurélien scratched his head, and the impish grin returned. "To change altitude, you see, a dirigible must adjust its air buoyancy. This new design uses a system of ballast and gas valves to adjust the overall lift of the ship. The vent valves will release lifting gas and decrease altitude while the ballast we shed will increase altitude." Gilbert pointed to the tanks mounted at each side of the gondola. "I dumped several hundred gallons of water at takeoff."

A gust of wind buffeted the gondola about and Finn widened his stance for balance. "I take it our problem is not lift with these kinds of winds."

He missed Aurélien's reassuring grin. "We will not be able to get you near to the ground without putting you or the airship in danger."

"Just get me close enough." Finn opened the door of the enclosure and leaned out over the edge of the gondola. "Another hundred feet down and I can lower myself the rest of the way using a ground tie," he yelled over the loud rush of air. "Swing me over those rooftops at the edge of the city."

Gilbert shook his head. "I do not shy from risk, *mon ami*, but this is— I cannot allow it, Phineas. One miscalculation and you slam into the wall of a building." Gilbert slapped his hands together. "Splat!"

The bottom dropped out from his stomach—and it was not due to the buffeting about by the mistral wind. Finn narrowed his gaze. "How much gas to lower me?"

"We've got enough extra gas to vent, but with these winds . . ." Aurélien frowned. "We will need to shed a great deal of ballast to take us up again, quickly. How much do you weigh, Finn?"

"Near thirteen stone."

Gilbert's lips moved in silent calculation. "It might work."

Finn's gaze slid from one brother to another. "Vent a bit of gas, gentlemen." Slinging both guns over his shoulder, he stepped onto the ledge of the gondola. "Assuming I land in one piece, how can I get ahold of you?"

"We head for our hydrogen laboratory outside Toulouse." Aurélien handed Finn a pair of goggles. "Put these on, they will protect your eyes."

Finn adjusted the protective glasses and tossed the line over the side. He wound the rope through his legs and repelled off the side of the gondola. As the craft descended, he wondered, frankly, who was crazier—the two aeronauts above releasing helium into the air, or the poor bloke dangling from a rope fifty feet below them.

Aurélien called down to him. *"Pour l'amour, mon ami!"*

## ∾ Chapter Fifteen

Finn studied what was left of the walled city and the rooftops of La Rochelle beyond. As predicted, the dirigible was coming in fast and low.

The blustery mistral suddenly buffeted him higher, then lower—so low he had to swing his legs up and over the ancient wall. His heel scraped past the crenellated stone, knocking a brick off the old parapet. The close call sent him spinning like a top on a string. Rooflines seemed to drop off sharply then suddenly grow taller as Finn whooshed through the air. The Clouzot brothers were doing their best to bring him in low enough so he might survive the fall.

Finn had adjusted his thinking about this. It wasn't the fall that would kill him, it was his air speed. He made out a chimney stack straight ahead. The word *splat* came to mind. He kicked away from an angled roof, and missed the smokestack by inches. Aurélien shouted down to him. "This is madness, Finn. We are taking you up again, hold on!" Finn caught a glimpse of a wide patch of gently pitched roofline.

It was now or never. For the briefest of moments, Finn sailed through the air.

He landed feetfirst and rolled onto his backside. The long guns strapped to his back scraped and rattled against terra-cotta tiles as he slid to the edge of the roof and over the side. He grabbed at a rain gutter, which tore away from the wall.

He landed flat on his back, in the middle of . . . shrubbery. Stunned, he didn't try to move. Actually, he wasn't so sure he *could* move. A few loose roof tiles smashed and scattered around him. He opened his eyes in time to watch his satchel careen off the roof above. He rolled to one side and the bag landed inches away.

Day turned to night as a great dark shadow passed over jagged rooftops. The Air Commander continued its breakneck descent. He heard a few shouts and cries from the citizens of La Rochelle, who doubtless cringed and pointed at the imposing airship. Finn shaded his eyes and squinted. Indeed, the Clouzot brothers were about to crash. "Jettison that ballast!" he muttered under his breath.

The sun's rays broke out from around the passing dirigible as a rainbow curtain of water dropped from the gondola. The dirigible lifted high into the air and motored off in a southeasterly direction. The ringing in his ears did not preclude him from hearing a sigh of relief from at least one witness.

He sat up and groaned. Every bone in his body felt—jarred. He rubbed down legs and arms. Realization dawned slowly. There was a chance, once the paralyzing shock wore off, that he might actually walk away from this.

*"Allez-vous bien, monsieur?"* An elderly gent with a towel draped over his arm leaned over him. Finn pushed

his goggles up and had a look around. He had landed on a rooftop terrace with tables and—he squinted from the glare of sunlight—waiters.

He rubbed stiff neck muscles, easing rattled vertebrae back into place. He was laid out in the middle of a small garden. A thick stand of low-cut hedges had broken his fall. Rather sorry-looking greenery at the moment. "Where am I? *Pardon—où suis-je?*"

CATE'S TEMPLES THROBBED and there was a knot on the side of her head that felt like, well, rather like the lump she had given Agent Gunn. So far, they hadn't laid a hand on her. It was as if they had been warned off or threatened to stay away. Frankly, it had made her wonder and caused not a small amount of trepidation.

For several hours now they had badgered her about the ransom. *"¿Dónde está el dinero?"* She had answered their question with one of her own. "Where is Eduardo?" The more they asked, the more her suspicions had grown. At one point a creeping, horrible dread had nearly overcome her. Her brother was supposed to be alive. But where was he? The demand note had been clear: Eduardo in exchange for thirty thousand.

Cate exhaled a silent sigh. She didn't have the full amount, but the twenty she had on her person would have to be enough. They'd gone round and round in circles until they fell into a sullen silence.

An iron stove in the corner threw a bit of warmth into the room. Her gaze traveled over several tall desks and a wall of crooked storage shelves, all that remained of an abandoned office. Swarthy men lounging around the stove stared at her but said very little. As best as she could make out, from their cryptic conversation, they waited for someone to arrive. A negotiator? Possibly. A torturer? Horrid thought.

She pushed the terrifying notion into the back of her mind and concentrated on the sorry cadre that surrounded her. So this is what survived of *Los Tigres Solitarios*. Cate lengthened her spine and straightened her shoulders. "Would it be possible—might you allow me to use the chamber pot? Preferably with a bit of privacy?" She tried to appear chipper. "And I wouldn't mind a cup of tea right about now."

No one moved an inch, not even Francisco—known as Curro, an old school chum of her brother's. She eyeballed the only man in the room she knew and raised a brow. Curro shuffled his feet nervously and reluctantly pushed off the thick wooden post that held up a labyrinth of open rafters overhead. They were in some sort of storehouse or guild shop.

Curro took her by the arm into an adjacent room. A thin mattress and a number of bedrolls were laid out the wood-plank floor. This was how anarchists lived. Always on the run, a new residence every few days. Curro nodded to a crude enameled pot in the corner. "I'll be outside the door," he said to her in warning, no warmth in his voice, nothing to indicate they'd known each other since childhood.

"These men are strangers to me. Who are they?" Cate spun around. "Where is Eduardo? What is going on here, Curro?"

He ducked his head back in the room. "Do what they ask, Catriona. Give them the money." He raised his voice. "*¡Rápidamente!*"

The door closed and she moved straight to the window. Open. And the gabled roofline did not seem too treacherous.

The window slammed shut, crushing her fingers.

She cried out and tried to jerk her hand out from under the frame. "Forgive my intrusion, *señorita*, but I must insist you stay." A male voice—calm and cruel—exhaled the words on her neck. He reached around her and lifted the window sash an inch.

She jerked her hand back.

Cate turned to face a devil's smile—as cold as ice, with dark eyes that peered out from under angled brows. Handsome in that Spaniard sort of way. He jerked her close and pressed his lower anatomy against her. "The money, Catriona, or I'm afraid you will never see your brother alive again."

"Let me go." She pushed against his chest to wrench herself away. Without warning, he raised his hands and let go. He leaned back against her only means of escape and smiled.

She scurried away from the fearsome, predatory man. A mouse let loose so the cat could play. "Who are you?"


"PECKER'S UP, ROGER." Finn gave his skeleton key a half turn and a good push. He heard the clink of the inside key as it fell on the floor. He peered through the door lock to the flat beyond. Predictably seedy. He slipped the key back in the lock, lined up the levers, and . . .

The door swung open.

A narrow, unmade bed filled most of the room. Finn entered the Spartan flat and picked up a fallen wine bottle. He set the empty back on a side table. No one home. He held his hand over a pile of gray ashes in a grotty tin ashtray. Warm.

A flap of a dingy curtain led Finn to an open window

and a very impressive view of the bay. There was also a near-unobstructed view of the streets below. A handy feature for the room of an ace confidence man and professional informer. Finn scanned the foot and carriage traffic in both directions. Nothing. He checked his watch. Bollocks. Sergeant MacGregor would likely arrive in the early evening, and he must arrange for a stable.

He also needed to find Cate. He'd already skulked around her room at the hotel. He'd lifted the *Ne Dérangez Pas* sign off the door and entered the ransacked bedchamber. He could not be certain, but from the amount of clothes and toilet items in her portmanteau, she hadn't done much unpacking.

"Well, well, if it isn't my old friend, Hugh Curzon—or is it Phineas Gunn this time?"

"Dé Riquet." A grin tugged at his mouth before he turned around. "Just remember it's Hugh Curzon to the French authorities." Finn looked the smarmy, thimble-fingered informer up and down. "You're looking . . . tattered, as usual."

"Sorry I didn't greet you at the door, but I like to have a look at my intruders before chatting it up." The wily rat pulled a chair over to the table. "I understand you recently flew into town."

Finn's eyes narrowed. "Word travels fast in La Rochelle."

"I have several reliable songbirds on the payroll." The reed-thin chap lifted a wine bottle from his coat and popped the cork.

"Excellent news. I'm counting on you to tell me where to find—"

Dé Riquet held up his hand. "Wait. Let me guess." The devilish runt took down two dusty glasses from a small shelf. "I've an idea you might be after a stately beauty—part English lass, part . . . *señorita.*" Dé Riquet tilted the bottle.

Finn covered his glass with his hand. "Allow me." He registered an uptick in pulse rate as he pulled out a pocket square. "Let's just say Miss Catriona de Dovia Willoughby is wanted by the Crown for . . ." No sense jacking up the man's price. Finn wiped the layer of grime off his glass. "Questioning."

He picked up the bottle and read the label. "Château Lascombes. I take it business is brisk." He was counting on Dé Riquet to have ties to the port town's baser elements. Cardsharps. Swindlers. Shysters of every sort. And, of course, anarchists. He laid a ten-pound note on the table. "Where is she?"

The homely little guttersnipe grinned. "I believe Her Majesty's Secret Intelligence Service can afford better than a tenner, monsieur." The homunculus drummed tinny fingers on the table.

He slapped down another ten and glared. "Not another sou until I get a location."

"There's an old cooperage on the south side of town, behind the dry docks."

Finn leaned forward. "She's with the anarchists then—*Los Tigres*."

"A man sought me out last week, no name, Spaniard by accent. I was to be the go-between. Pick up wires addressed to Alonso Rizal and contact the young lady when she arrived in town. They wanted assurances she wasn't followed."

Dé Riquet showed signs of a recent scuffle. "Might those cuts over your eye and those bruises be related, by any chance?"

The slight man shrugged. "I asked for more money. Miss Willoughby happened by the scuffle—I managed to get away. I assume the Spanish thugs saw their opportunity and hauled her off."

Finn stared. *Hauled her off*. Odd choice of words. "She didn't go willingly?"

Dé Riquet tossed up his hands. "Knocked out in the fray, possibly. One of the larger brutes carried her over his shoulder. They took the backstreets back to the docks."

"Take me to her." He did not miss the wary look. "Help me get Cate out of La Rochelle and I'll double that."

"Aiding and abetting." The beady-eyed runt tipped his chair back. "Requires a bit of strategic collaboration. All well and good, but the breaking and entering . . ." He shook his head. "Not really my forte. Risking my neck will cost you one hundred English pounds."

Finn kept a growl in check and passed over the banknotes. If *Los Tigres* failed to do so, he would personally wring the greedy little monster's neck when this was over. "Half now, the other half—when I recover the lady."

CATE UNFASTENED HER traveling bustle and set it down on a folded pile of her clothes. She purposefully paid no mind to the apparatus, handling the padded mound stuffed with cash as if it weighed next to nothing.

Stripped down to her corset, camisole, and pantalets, she placed her hands on her hips and exhaled audibly. "I do hope this is the end of it." Tawny mounds nearly popped out of the top of her corset. "How on earth could thirty thousand pounds be hidden in this corset? Quite impossible, wouldn't you say?"

"Unless we missed something."

She glared at the new man in command. With Eduardo

gone or kidnapped, what was left of *Los Tigres* appeared to be led by this man, Alonso. He stared—quite uncomfortably so for Cate. And this very moment he focused on the unmentionables still on her person.

Cate wasn't about to remove another stitch. "I'd like to dress now." He stepped in front of her clothes and continued his close inspection. Warily, she watched him out of the corner of her eye as he circled. She supposed the smart one had arrived, or was he just the most arrogant? He had dragged her back into the main office and ordered her to disrobe. Strangely humiliating for her—and arousing for him. A furtive glance about the room revealed men who tried not to ogle, but couldn't help themselves.

Cate bit into her lower lip. At least these anarchists weren't common thugs. She hoped. Eduardo had referred to the men as brothers who fought for a cause greater than themselves, who would readily die for their ideals.

But they were still men.

"Catriona." He shook his head and clucked. "You dress in a flimsy costume and bare your legs to gentlemen every night, do you not?" He wasn't quite as attractive when he smirked. Not handsome in the way Finn was—rugged and chiseled out of a great stone, but with lovely soft brown eyes and a sensuous mouth.

Cate ignored the tremble in her knees and stood her ground. Searching the faces of the men surrounding her, she appealed to their sense of loyalty. "Eduardo called you his brothers. And you allow this man, this new de facto leader, to treat me with such disrespect?" She met every stare until each man lowered his eyes.

Abruptly, Alonso lunged closer. "The ransom, Catriona. The sooner you hand it over, the sooner we free Eduardo."

Stunned, momentarily, she blinked. "What are you talking about?"

"I cannot deliver your brother to you if he is in prison."

FINN STUDIED THE ramshackle old factory site. An abandoned cooperage with several outbuildings and a wharf to one end of the yard. Not a soul to be seen. Nothing. A few tall weeds rustled in the wind. He moved into the shadow of a storage shed and waved Dé Riquet up to join him. "A quick bit of mapping, if you would."

The wiry character squinted across the yard. "There's an upstairs office in the main building."

"Guards?"

Dé Riquet nodded. "One at the door and one at the base of the stairs."

Finn patted down his coat and retrieved his backup—the jeweler's revolver. He checked the cylinder—empty. "Since you appear to invite physical danger wherever you go." He offered, and Dé Riquet accepted, the pistol.

Finn dug in his pocket for bullets. "Six shots. Don't waste them." Brass casings clinked against metal digits as Dé Riquet loaded the gun. "I don't mind so much, helping the young lady." The male waif sniffed. "Most lovelies pay me no mind. Miss Willoughby asked after my fingers. Even ran her hand over my thimbles."

He regarded the runt. "You knock. I'll take care of the rest." Finn crossed the yard and flattened himself against one side of the entrance. Dé Riquet approached the door and knocked. The expert confidence man pretended to search for the wire, drawing the guard farther outside. "*Merde*. Where did it go . . . ?"

Finn struck the lookout with the butt of his gun and

dragged the limp body behind a rain barrel. "Shoot anyone coming or going." Finn turned toward the door. "With the exception of Miss Willoughby or myself."

Dé Riquet nodded toward the blackness inside. "Mind your back."

Finn slipped inside a vast, dimly lit space and tucked himself into a dark niche. Dingy skylights cast patches of light on the shop floor and the office above. There—a flicker of movement in the shadows, under the open staircase. A figure slid out from under the steps. "Who goes there?" the man called.

The guard stared into the darkness, then turned away. Silently, Finn edged out of his dim corner and struck the man on the back of the head. The figure spun into his pistol, and Finn brought him down with a second blow to the skull.

Finn caught flying coattails and eased the unconscious guard to the floor silently. A mumble of voices drifted down from the rooms above. Placing one foot behind the other, he backed away from the stairs. A crisscross of heavy beams and rafters disappeared above the second-story partitions. Battered walls ended short of the ceiling at the roof trusses. Excellent. If he could find a way up, he'd have a bird's-eye view of the goings-on.

He found a coil of hemp and strung the rope over a beam. Hand over fist, he pulled himself into the rafters and through a maze of angled braces. He settled in just above the office space. "Go to hell—*bastardo asqueroso. ¡Cerdo repugnante!*"

The Spanish profanity provoked a grin. He only knew one woman with a mouth like that.

## Chapter Sixteen

"*I* no longer trust any of you." Cate blew a lock of hair off her face and narrowed her glare on Alonso. "Least of all this—leader of yours. *Él es un matón y un usurpador.*"

She saw the slap coming, but it stunned nevertheless. Her cheek blazed with heat as her head rocked back onto her shoulders. Her eyes watered and everything blurred. She blinked back tears.

She blinked again at the transverse beams, angled struts—and a man crouched in the rafters.

A familiar face peered down at her. The imposing figure dressed in long coat and slouch hat rose slowly—pistol in one hand, shotgun in the other. He winked at her.

She quickly lowered her eyes. Her heart beat erratically. Blood throbbed through her body, rivaling the heat on her cheek. She bit her lip so she might stop herself from crying out for joy. Alonso circled behind her, his eyes darting about.

He sensed something.

A blast of gunfire reverberated through the room. A few faces turned upward, most ducked for cover. Finn ran along an open beam, unloading his pistol on the men below. Bodies dropped to the ground as bullets ricocheted through the room.

The large, magnificent intruder leaped off the heavy timber and landed on a worktable. The second blast of shotgun pellets scattered the remaining men in all directions.

Seeing her chance, Cate inched toward her clothes and reached for the bustle. "Going somewhere?" Alonso pressed her against the wall and grabbed hold of the bulky padding. "Heavy for a bustle." His eyes darted toward the fracas. "Give it up, Catriona, or you will never see your brother alive again." He wrenched her arm and yanked the bustle out of her grasp.

Holding her against him, he dragged her toward the exit. Cate caught the leather strap of the bustle with one hand and dug her heels in. Smashing blows and gunshots told her Finn was fighting his way across the room. She caught a glimpse of one or two anarchists sprawled on the floor. Was Finn her rescuer or pursuer? At this moment, frankly, she didn't care. Emboldened by his nervy assault, she clung hard to the bustle full of banknotes. Alonso spun her around. The back of her head slammed into the doorjamb. "I could use some help over here," she called out.

Her gaze darted to Finn as he leveled a staggering blow to an attacker. "Be there in a jiff, darling." A number of bodies were piling up on the floor. Her free hand clung to the molding even as Alonso attempted to pull her out onto the stair landing. Through blurred vision, she saw someone jump Finn from behind.

She had to do something. She let go of the doorjamb and swiped at her abductor's face. Red lines slashed across his cheek. The sound of a grunt and an awful ripping noise came with his next yank. Cate watched in horror as the strap broke away from the bustle. A gaping tear revealed the stuffing inside. Hundreds of bills. Large denominations.

Alonso tucked the bundle under his arm and grabbed her by the waist. He spoke to the looming shadow over her shoulder. "Keep your distance or I'll send her down the stairs headfirst." He started down the stairs.

Finn charged them, gun drawn. "Might I have a word, before she takes the tumble?" The tip of his revolver stopped just short of her nose. "You never mentioned you were leaving town," he said. Finn cocked the trigger. "We had a date."

Cate blinked. "We had no such thing." She shifted against the man who heaved her downward. "Besides, something quite unexpected came up."

Alonso shoved her into Finn's arms and vaulted over the stair rail. A scuffle of footsteps could be heard below and a door banged open. Cate looked up into deep, coffee-colored eyes. Fiercely protective eyes. "Aren't you going to chase after him?"

"Why?" His grip on her tightened. "I've got what I came for."

"But he's got the money." She tried wrenching away. *Madre de Dios*. Out of one man's grip and into another's. A shot fired outside.

Finn's gaze swept from the open entry back to her. "Shall we have a look, darling?" He guided her down the stairs and out the door.

*"Pss-st."* The hissing came from the shadows of an outbuilding. Finn grabbed her hand and they jogged across the paved yard. "Over here."

That voice was familiar. Peering into the shade of the

lean-to she recognized the man crouched in the shade. "Dé Riquet?"

The shifty character stepped out of the shadows and fired his pistol.

THE SOFT CREAK of floorboards and the rustle of clothes nudged Finn awake. He cracked an eye open and blinked. A blurry figure moved about, and gradually came into focus. Miss Willoughby tucked a threadbare shirt into a pair of trousers. He recognized the surroundings. They were in Dé Riquet's seedy little flat.

The throbbing ache at the back of his a head reminded Finn he'd been out cold, possibly for some time. Inside his skull, a flash of memory filtered through a battery of drumbeats. Dé Riquet had fired his weapon. At the time, the blow to his head had felt like a gunshot. Double-crossed and dead—the last thought that entered his mind before the fading of the light. He inhaled a gulp of air. Perhaps, there might have been one other brooding reverie . . .

Finn raised both eyelids and watched his very last reflection on life place a handgun on the table. He knew the pistol by sight: his old service revolver. Cate retrieved a box of bullets from his travel bag.

Instinctively he twitched, and discovered that he was tied down. Both hands and feet were strapped to the bedposts. The tips of his fingers tingled, a precursor to an attack of nerves—or did the bindings cut off his blood flow? Racing thoughts caused his pulse to elevate, another indicator of Soldier's Heart.

He also happened to be naked.

Finn raised his head enough to check for injuries. No

bullet holes. A few bruises and scrapes. A thin red line slashed the side of his torso. The tip of an anarchist's knife must have caught him. And there was something else, an instant and impressive cockstand.

Rather stimulating circumstances, actually. He lowered his head and listened to the metallic clink of bullets and the spin and snap of the loaded cylinder. "You cannot fool me, Phineas Gunn—you are quite awake. I've heard neither a snore nor ragged breath from you in several minutes."

"You're sure it was the lack of a snore that gave me away?" He opened his eyes.

A side of her mouth ticked upward. He very much liked her mouth. It was well defined and expressive. The ends often quirked up and down with her mood, and the peak of her upper lip was so wonderfully . . . plump.

She didn't return his gaze, though she appeared to be assessing his body rather closely. Her inspection descended past his navel, stopped, and lingered.

"Miss me, Cate?" A fresh supply of blood surged into his already engorged penis. Her eyes grew wider before they snapped up to meet his.

He grinned. He couldn't help it. "You could have just asked me to take off my clothes and jump into bed. I'd have gladly—"

"We did not know the extent of your injuries," she bit out. "Dé Riquet helped undress you."

The bedposts groaned as he strained against his shackles. Finn arched a brow.

"Those are for my protection. Your odd little friend had business elsewhere." She pressed her lips together, and still a smile surfaced.

Finn guessed there was enough slack in his bindings to

right himself—possibly. Using a bit of arm and shoulder muscle, he lifted his upper body into a sitting position. A shower of stars blurred his vision and he waited for the throbbing ache in his head to subside. "Since it's obvious I'm staying put, where might you be off to, *Mademoiselle Anarchiste*?"

She looked at him as if he was either mad or thick-headed. "I'm after the twenty thousand, of course."

Some part of Cate's collusion with *Los Tigres* had gone awry. He had overheard enough at the old cooperage to surmise that much. And the money seemed to be a large part of the difficulty.

Testing, reassessing their hold, he tugged absently at his bindings. "What's going on, Cate?"

A delightful grin accompanied her headshake. "What you don't know can't hurt you."

His gaze flickered upward. "For such a talented opera-tive, you spout the most naive things. Clever of you, I sup-pose."

Exasperated, she got up and dragged the bedstand over. He noted the satchel on the floor. *His* bag. The one loaded with weapons, assorted spyware devices, and ammunition. "I see that rat Dé Riquet has gone pilfering."

"I wouldn't be so hard on him if I were you. He saved your life, retrieved your luggage, and, even now, is seeing to the livery of your horse." She opened a jar of salve and added a tincture to a basin of water. "In your delirium, you cried out for that handsome red steed of yours."

"Sergeant MacGregor is a stout-hearted mount. Quite the bullyboy."

"A sergeant no less." She wrung out a washcloth and traced over an old scar, one that started below his collar-bone and disappeared beneath a bit of chest hair. She held her mouth open slightly—in concentration. A pink tongue swept the underside of an upper lip as she gently pressed the cloth to various scrapes and cuts.

Finn wrinkled his nose. "The smell of antiseptic triggers memories." The water stung in places. "Four weeks spent in a field hospital south of Kandahar." Those were just the physical injuries. There were deeper wounds that held secrets he never spoke of. The groan of bedsprings pushed the recollection aside as she sat on the edge of the mattress.

"You were very brave today," she said. Her eyes darted up, softer and somewhat shy.

His dry throat caused a raspy answer. "Is it brave to kill another man?" When she raised a brow, he shrugged—as much as he could, tied up. "It comes down to kill or be killed. For the time being, I'd rather it wasn't me."

She tilted a glass to his lips. "Drink this."

Finn clamped his mouth shut.

She kept the tumbler raised. "It's just wine."

"No laudanum?"

"Nothing to dull the senses."

His first sip of claret went down well. "Ah, the honeyed blood of the grape—the bliss of dreams."

"Shakespeare?"

"Atticus Adams. Intrepid private investigator." Gradually, he took in more claret until he gulped thirstily. At the bottom of the glass, he sighed.

"One of your fictional characters, I presume?" She wrung out the wet cloth and studied his nude torso. Rather arousing, how she could peruse his nude body while pretending polite conversation. "Tell me, are you Agent Gunn right now, or do you prefer Curzon on the Continent?" She pressed the cloth to more scrapes and cuts, as he flinched and groaned despite the wine.

"Finn to you, Curzon to the authorities. Ah-h!" He gritted his teeth. "I can see you wish to abuse me."

"Dancers know something about contusions." Her fingers slipped into the jar of salve. "A bit of warmth and gentle massage encourages blood flow."

His throbbing prick leaped at the first brush of her hands on his chest. Gentle fingertips kneaded sore muscles and soothed bruised ribs. "I find it fascinating that you've made no attempt to cover any part of me."

Cate sat back and stared. "Has the royal Roger caught a chill?"

Her every touch caused either a groan or a sharp intake of air sucked between clenched teeth. "Goodness. Where does it not hurt?" She lay her hand on the flat of his abdomen, just below an outline of rib. A light drumming of fingertips captured his complete attention. Suddenly, all he could think about was the one place on his body he wanted her touch. "I'll let you know when you get there."

Soothing a pale green bruise, she moved lower. He inhaled a quick, sharp breath as her fingernails scraped his belly. "Here, perhaps?" The muscles of his abdomen quivered. Her eyes widened. "Dear me, I shall have to find another spot."

So far, he had experienced few ill effects from the wrist and leg restraints. His elevated heart rate was caused as much by her ministrations as by the bindings themselves. And for the sake of this fascinating bit of love play, he would tolerate a bit of nerves in hopes of even greater arousal to come.

She quirked a brow. "A bit lower, you think?"

He met her gaze. "Not so bruised, below."

Cate straightened. "Then I suppose a massage is not really necessary."

Half-crazed with lust, Finn strained against his ties. "Desperately. Necessary."

"I see." The gleam in her eye and upward tilt of her mouth spoke volumes. She knew exactly what she was doing—driving him mad. "I am told most men enjoy this." Warm, slick fingers traveled down the length of his burgeoning cock. "Do you . . . ?" Slippery with lotion, her hand wrapped around his thickness and reversed course. Near the head, she ran a finger lightly over the narrow cleft of the tip. ". . . Enjoy this?"

Any fear of a nervous attack gave way to the surge of arousal. As pleasure rushed through his body, he released a groan that was, at least in part, rutting water buffalo. Gradually, she increased the pressure of her hold, as well as the speed of her strokes. She used her other hand to sweep through his chest hair and circle a nipple. Good God, she remembered.

She leaned close and whispered. "Do you . . . darling?"

His brain had come to reside in his penis. He could think of nothing but her next stroke, and the force of his impending eruption. Every muscle tensed, every nerve ending readied.

She removed her hands from his near-to-bursting extremity. "I'm afraid I've dallied far too long." Rising from the bed, she methodically wiped slick ointment from her fingers. "I must be going."

It took a moment for an actual thought to register in his brain. "You're not quitting, are you?" He growled the words.

Cate backed away. "How badly do you want it?"

His eyes narrowed to slits.

She collected a man-tailored jacket and picked up his revolver. "As badly as I want to see my brother alive?" Her eyes darted about the room. "I need that twenty thousand, Finn—for ransom or bribes, not quite sure which at the moment."

"Untie me. I'll go with you." He tried softening his glare. "Be reasonable, Cate."

She hesitated at the door. "In London you said you thought you trusted me—a little." Rueful eyes met his briefly. "How could you ever do so now?"

She had taken him to the edge of ecstasy. And now the wicked little minx was backing out the door talking nonsense. Worse yet, she was going to get herself killed. He yanked on his bindings. "One day—very soon—I will make you pay for this, Miss Willoughby."

Dark lashes fell over a violet-blue gaze. "Oh, I do hope so, Mr. Gunn."

## Chapter Seventeen

Cate ducked her head as the bullying anarchist prodded her belowdecks. She did not know this man who had tied her arms behind her back. "*¡Vaya!*" He shoved her past several men in the galley of the ship.

Admittedly, she'd gone after the anarchists without much of a plan. Dé Riquet had mentioned a sloop anchored in the harbor with the name *El Gato del Mar*— The Sea Cat. Eduardo's prized possession, and his one pleasure. She should have waited for Dé Riquet to return to his hovel. Instead, she bolted out of the flat and hired a local to take her out to the ship—a man who turned out to be a paid lookout for *Los Tigres*.

There appeared to be very few anarchists aboard, either that or Finn had reduced their numbers by half. Could *Los Tigres* actually be down to a handful of men? How could her brother have associated himself with such ruffians? Or was this crew the last remnants of a better time—a nobler cause? The guard with the pistol at her back pushed her into a forward cabin.

The hatch slammed shut behind her and she leaped into deep shadow. A single porthole illuminated a space that was small—suffocatingly so. She squinted in the dim light. Nothing but a built-in berth and a compact writing desk. A chair sat by the door.

Something in the air shifted. Her heart jumped into an erratic rhythm. She turned and ran straight into a hard chest. Arms grabbed hold and held on. She looked up into an angular face and cold black eyes. "Alonso."

The chill in his smile, though familiar, still sent a tremble through her. "An enchanting beauty who is also tenacious. I am impressed." He tilted his head, assessing her figure. "As well as stimulated." He pressed her to him with one hand as he explored her body with the other.

Dear God, why did it have to be this reprobate again? As of this moment, she hated every member of *Los Tigres* for this, including Eduardo. Had he any idea what kind of lowly muckworms had taken over his beloved brotherhood? And how dare he resurrect himself from the dead and put her through this. More than ever she was determined to find her brother again—so she could wring his neck. She tossed her head back. "Where is Eduardo?"

"Patience, Catriona. As soon as the captain returns, we will make our departure."

"To where?"

"Once . . . we are away, *mi ángel.*"

"*Usted sabe mejor.* I am not your woman." She wrenched away but he lunged after and pressed her against the bed. Without her hands free to catch herself, she fell back onto the mattress.

"Trousers, Catriona?" His gaze raked up and down her body—an amused twitch to one side of his mouth. "Let's get rid of those, shall we?"

Alonso stood above her, smirking. Obviously, what re-

mained of *Los Tigres* was the dregs. "You have no inten-
tion of helping Eduardo." She raised her chin in defiance.
"I no longer believe he is alive. How could he be—when
you dare assault the sister of *El Primer Tigre?*" She dug
her heels into the bedding and pushed away. He grabbed
hold of her lower limbs. Pain shot though both legs as he
landed across her knees, pinning her down.

He leaned over her, into a shaft of moonlight. His black
gaze flecked with pale blue steel. "Your brother is alive—
but not for long, I'm afraid."

"How do I know that you have not made this up—this
story that Eduardo is imprisoned? It would not be the
first time you tricked me into funding your exploits. More
bombs—is that what you want? And if he is in prison,
why can't I see him—speak to him? *¿Cree usted que soy
una idiota . . . que soy estúpida? ¿Una mujer sin sentido?*"

The slap across her face struck with such force, a spray
of tears instantly covered her burning cheek.


FINN TOOK AIM. Nothing but the sound of lapping of
water. A hundred yards from the pier, a dusky sky outlined
the silhouette of the anarchists' sloop moored in the bay.
Two lookouts, fore and aft. He wagered at least four or five
more men below. And one Catriona de Dovia Willoughby.
Captive or accomplice? He still wasn't entirely sure.

Lifting the gun barrel, he angled his rifle against a stack
of old tea chests and threaded on the silencer. Dé Riquet
peered over his shoulder. "Fancy rig, that."

Finn ignored the mercenary operative. "I have a
lengthy and personal involvement in the design of this
sound suppressor—along with a considerable investment

of cash." He squinted through the site, but not before he glared at the smallish Frenchman. "Untie the skiff and get ready to scull us over."

"*Ne me blâmez pas!* How was I to know she'd tie you up?" Shaking his head, Dé Riquet backed away. "I come home to find you with this cockstand—*éléphantesque.*" Finn resisted the urge to point his rifle at the scalawag. Dé Riquet shrugged bony shoulders and disappeared down the ladder. "I don't suppose you enjoyed it any—?"

Finn braced his leg against the stack of tea chests and took aim on the lookout standing portside. The watchman peered over the side of the deck and Finn squeezed the trigger. A gentle pop from his rifle and it was over. Barely any recoil. The man dropped into the net under the bowsprit. No splash—a spot of luck there. He moved the barrel and sighted on the other guard. He held his breath.


ALONSO PATTED DOWN the outside, as well as the inside, of her thighs. "Tell me where the rest of the ransom is, and I might leave you less"—he ripped into the trousers at her hips and pulled them off—"bruised."

"Get off me." Cate tried to wriggle out from under him. "Eduardo will kill you for this." Her chemise barely covered the tops of her thighs. He grabbed both of her legs and roughly dragged her back.

Now her chemise was well up her torso. She lay there completely exposed—but not humiliated; she was too scared think about modesty.

"In a few more days, your brother will be shipped off to the penal colony at Devil's Island. Word has it, his health is failing." Alonso leered down at her. "Pray he doesn't survive the voyage."

This time he wasn't lying. She knew those cold eyes well enough by now to sense when he stalled or purposely confused the issue. Stunned by the news, she felt every ounce of fight in her simply evaporate. Tears flooded her eyes. "How could you do this—keep this from me?"

Her legs ached from the weight of his knees. He moved his hand under her chemise, revealing more of her. With his free hand, he unbuttoned his trousers.

Something pressed against her woman's mound. A shudder of revulsion ran through her. "Stop—please—" She shut her eyes.

"Look at me." He kneed her legs apart. "I'm going to take you now, Catriona. And I want to see those beautiful sapphire eyes." He poised above her. "Sorry if this hurts." A shadow moved overhead. She blinked several times to see through a blur of tears. She recognized the face that loomed above Alonso's. There was not another glare in the world quite like it.

FINN YANKED THE man's head back by the hair. "Sorry if this hurts, *bastardo*," he said.

He wasn't sure who was on top of Cate—but he was about to die. The man looked to be the same thug that had used her as a shield earlier today.

Quick as a striking snake, the anarchist wrapped his hands around Cate's neck. Finn shoved his gun between the man's legs. "In the bollocks or up the ass? Your choice." He placed a knee to the man's spine and slipped a wire around his neck. "Let go of her." There was a great deal of choking and gurgling before her violator began to fade. Finn, took the man's head in his hands and wrenched hard. The neck snapped.

He tossed the dead torso off Cate. For the second time since he entered the cabin he made eye contact with her. Wide eyes filled with terror and confusion—perhaps some relief. "Get dressed."

She rasped, then gasped for air. Once she had filled her lungs, she choked out a question. "Why didn't you shoot him?"

"Out of bullets. No time to reload." He shrugged off her surly eye roll.

"I'm afraid the trousers are in shreds." She scrambled off the bed.

"Never mind. I'll be the only one who knows you're naked under that little nothing of a slip." He kept his speech clipped, his expression blank.

He helped her stand and pulled down the chemise. "Thank you, Finn. Twice in one day—quite a good deal of rescuing." Her thin smile ended in a shiver. "Would you untie me, please?"

He shrugged out of his coat and wrapped it around her. "No."

Finn took her by the arm and she winced. "A bit bruised up?" He suppressed the urge to yank her down the galley as they climbed over dead bodies. Instead, he guided her abovedecks to the waiting skiff. He nodded to Dé Riquet. "I'll be right with you."

A moment later he was back with a knapsack he tossed down to Cate. "What's left of the Crown's money. You can buy yourself new pantalets." He sat down beside Dé Riquet and grabbed an oar. "Row like the devil."

Less than fifty feet from the pier, a thunderous explosion blasted out of the cabin of the sloop. Unfazed, Finn continued to row. "Dangerous to keep explosives on board."

She tucked her chin inside the collar of his coat. "You're rather accomplished at blowing up terrorists with their own explosives."

Finn angled his oar and steered them toward the pontoon at the side of the pier. There was a town coach waiting dockside. The moment he had her inside the carriage he was going to spank that little naked bottom raw. Cate had fearlessly approached the ragged bunch of anarchists a second time and nearly gotten herself raped. She might have been murdered, her body dumped in the bay. An icy shiver ran down his spine.

"I went back inside to retrieve my gun—my old service revolver. Stolen from me by a certain anarchist sympathizer—who is once again in my custody." The skiff bumped gently against the landing. "Turns out one of the men in the galley wasn't quite dead. He knocked down an oil lamp coming after me."

*"Kaboom."* Dé Riquet grinned.

Cate's watery eyes rolled upward. "I suppose they got what they deserve." Her sigh was more of a shudder. "*Los Tigres* will resurrect itself—with a different name and new blood. This goes on and on in Spain. The goals are always the same—they always begin with honorable intentions." Her gaze moved out beyond the flames engulfing the boat. "Somehow they never end that way."

Finn walked her down the pier, half holding her up around the waist. As they approached the carriage, he passed Dé Riquet a few coins. "We'll need a bottle of whiskey—something made in Scotland. And several bottles of ale, along with supper. In that order."

He climbed into the carriage and sat opposite Cate. He stared into her face for a long time as he contemplated various forms of punishment. The lash, the strap, the back of his hand . . . Finn exhaled a harsh sigh. No, Cate Willoughby was decidedly too old for a spanking—at least the naughty child sort of spanking.

Even though his anger clung to the fantasy of a red bottom, corporal punishment was out.

But there were many different kinds of torture, some vastly more enjoyable than others. Finn thought about the painful case of blue balls she had left him with. His gaze narrowed even as a lopsided grin emerged.

Her squirming made the upholstery squeak more than once. "You've every right to be angry with me." Her eyes darted out the window then back to him.

"You lead a charmed life, Cate."

She sniffed. "I don't feel very fortunate."

"And what if I hadn't come along when I did?" His temper teetered on the edge of explosive anger. If it weren't for the undeniable terror he'd felt at the sight of her in physical danger, he'd have her shackled at the leg and hauled into a French jail right about now. Perhaps there were ways to get his mind off the fear he'd felt, while capitalizing on the adrenaline still pumping through his system.

He leaned across the coach and placed both hands on her knees. "When we get back to the flat, let me tell you what I'm going to do to you."

## Chapter Eighteen

Cate wasn't completely nude. He'd left her stockings on. She tugged at her bindings and glared. "Mr. Phineas Gunn, aka Hugh Curzon, aka *demonio-bestia bruta, bárbaro del diablo, animal salvaje del perro, cerdo despreciable*." She gasped for air and began again. "Let me translate, you brutish fiend-beast, devil barbarian, savage dog, despicable swine—"

"Not too loud, darling." He tilted his chair back. "You wouldn't want me to have to apply a gag, would you?" His collar was open and shirt unbuttoned. Below the waist, the man was covered in leather. Deerskin hugged muscular thighs and he wore tall riding boots. Aware of her gaze, he crossed a boot over his knee. Her nudity, the bindings, and this dishabille of his charged the atmosphere with something lusty and sensual. And worst of all, it was working. *Aroused* could barely describe what she felt.

He hadn't touched her yet. But those piercing dark eyes promised he would. And she wanted him to. In fact, it was all she could think about. There was an edge of fear to these bindings—there was also something delicious and disturbing. Her womb already ached and she was aware of a stunning wetness—in those forbidden places, lower down. His gaze dropped beneath her navel and her belly trembled.

He squeezed a fresh wedge of lemon over a plate of oysters. "You're not an anarchist, Cate, nor are you a very skilled operative. You get yourself into too many—situations. This continual and, I must say, fearless confrontation technique of yours." He shook his head. "A professional would never work this way. Only an amateur could enjoy such dumb luck." He tilted a half shell to his mouth and slurped one down.

Her stomach growled.

Finn tut-tutted. "You don't eat enough. In fact, I suspect you forget to eat. Is this litheness"—an ogle traveled down her legs—"something you must maintain for dance?" Finn picked up his ale and sauntered over to the bed. "To my mind, you need a bit of feeding up."

She moistened dry lips with the tip of her tongue and eyed the bottle.

"No doubt near rape causes a thirst . . ." His dark smoldering gaze swept over her body and lingered just below her navel. He stood above her and flipped open the stopper. "Whenever I experience a close brush with death, a pint or two seems to take the edge off." He tilted back his head and took a long guzzle.

Cate closed her eyes and imagined amber liquid flowing down her throat. The mattress dipped to one side. He sat close, and pressed the cool glass against her bottom lip. Drops flavored with malt and hops filled her mouth. She swallowed as much as she could before the stream of ale ran down her chin and neck.

She opened her eyes and met his. "M-more." He tilted the bottle, and she gulped.

His gaze followed the trail of droplets to the pool of liquid in the cleft between her breasts.

Beige, translucent flesh hardened under his study. "I imagine these two would like to be kissed." Cate inhaled sharply as her chest rose and her back arched. Her traitorous, wanton body pleaded with this man in its strange, silent language of need.

Finn smiled. The first one she'd seen from him in hours.

One golden drop traveled down her chest. He moistened his finger with a pool of ale then circled an areola— first one peak, then the other. Cate writhed under his touch. "I believe I'm thirsty again."

Finn tipped the bottle and poured a spot of ale on each tip. He licked first and then suckled. Cate moaned this time. She strained against her bindings as he took to suckling one nipple and rolling the other between his fingers. A strong surge of arousal caused her entire body to buck and writhe. "Ah yes, Finn."

He raised his head. She returned his gaze, even as her chest heaved and her stomach quivered. "Ah yes, Finn, what?" He reclined beside her. "Do you desire something more?"

His grin caused her bottom lip to protrude. And oh how her womanly parts desired—more. Her eyes narrowed. "What do you want, Finn?"

"The truth." His hand slipped across her navel and inched through her curls. Her eyelids fluttered, as did her stomach muscles. A single finger moved between her labia, and was greeted by a flood of arousal. She sucked in a harsh, uneven breath. "Please—"

His hand cupped her venus mound as his finger circled the swollen nub that brought her more pleasure than she had ever known in her life. Occasionally when she danced, there were moments of ecstasy, even feelings of arousal, but this—this was as if Finn knew what her body wanted, needed. And he toyed with her pleasure. Holding back when she begged for more. Waiting patiently for her arousal to subside, so he might start again. This time he pressed farther, deeper, quickening his fingers until she was moaning again. "Make me—let me—take me there, please."

She felt fully and completely tortured by him. "I will keep you here all night if I have to," he said.

She suddenly understood. He was going to withhold her pleasure, and the more she thought about that fact, the more she could not think of anything else but her satisfaction. She was wound up as taut as a string on a Spanish guitar. Her entire body thrummed with desire. "Mother of God, pleasure me. *¡Déjame culminar!*"

"The entire story, Cate." He swiveled around and placed his feet on the floor. He tugged off his boots and hose. "No half-truths. No obfuscating." He rose from the bed and lifted off his shirt. "No excuses. No deferrals." He unbuttoned his breeches and untied his drawers, stepping out of both. "And I want . . . *fellatio.*"

Phineas Gunn was large and hard—every part of him. He stood there, in all his lionesque beauty, cock angled toward the ceiling. "Deal?"

She strained against her bindings. "Untie me."

He rested his hands on his hips, just above the magnificent groin muscle that cut down each side of his body. He moved closer. "I want your arousal to be as great as mine, therefore—you will remain bound. Afterward, I will soundly pleasure you, and then you will cuddle up against me and tell me everything." He crawled over her, but remained on his knees. The head of his cock was smooth and round—the shape of a Roman helmet. "Then we will make love again."

Everything about this man spoke of honor, courage— adventure. And yet he was gently coercing her, the devil. "Lick it, Cate."

She looked up into his eyes. "Closer."

Her tongue circled the smooth head of his cock. He rasped out a groan, already breathing hard from the feel of her mouth on his lower anatomy. He gazed down, watching her moisten her lips and move them over tightly drawn, engorged flesh. A surge of pleasure washed through her as he coaxed her to take more. "Ah, Cate, do not stop. Suck me—yes . . ." He threw his head back and groaned, pumping in and out of her. Never too deep, but still, he pressed her, gently.

Tied to the bed and at his mercy, there was the most erotic sense of—trusting this man. Just as he promised, her arousal climbed with his. Cate sucked the tip and swirled her tongue around the shaft. She wanted to pleasure him; she enjoyed pleasuring him. Finn withdrew. "Catch your breath, my love." His hand went around the shaft and stroked until she licked her lips.

"More." She waggled the tip of her tongue into the cleft at the head and tasted a pearl-sized drop of seed. Salty. And the scent was pure Finn.

His gentle, insistent domination sent yet another wave of erotic arousal through her. Never had she felt anything like this. He reached into her hair and tugged as he pushed to the back of her throat. "You're making me come," he growled. His hips thrust faster and deeper until he withdrew with a shudder. He pumped his seed onto her chest and nipples. Upright on his knees, with his head angled back and his eyes closed, he looked like a demigod kneeling at the gates of paradise. Finn inhaled and exhaled a number of deep breaths before he spoke. "That was most . . . gratifying."

"Untie me. You've had your fun—and your satisfaction."

"Ah, but you have not received yours, Cate." He reached down between soft folds and stroked her pleasure spot—still swollen. "Cranky and frustrated?" he asked in that husky bedding voice of his. Her belly quivered when he increased the speed of his fondling. "Not unlike the state you aroused in me and then walked out—into the arms of those Red Shirt rapists, who would have each taken a turn." He leaned over her body and licked a nipple. Her entire body trembled from the caress. Finn suckled the rosy tip deep, then let the nipple pop from his mouth. He backed away, but his tongue trailed past her navel and into her curls. Using both hands he parted folds. "Dusky rose petals—how many men have been here, since me?"

She met his gaze, her blue eyes glistening with desire. More than anything, she wanted what she knew would come next. From his lips and tongue. She released his gaze and her head rolled back on her shoulders. She spoke in a whisper, between harsh breaths. "There has only been you, Finn."

"If memory serves, you very much liked this." His lips met delicate swollen flesh and kissed. Gently he sucked more of her into his mouth and lapped his tongue over the spot.

Wave after wave of pleasure engulfed her. Between gasps and moans she whispered "Yes" and "More." She strained against her bindings and wriggled restlessly, arching up to answer his tongue.

"Did I get that wrong? Should I stop?" A slow grin glistened with her arousal.

"Do not stop!" His fingers flicked and circled and teased, while his tongue delved deep inside. Her orgasm began with a whimper and ended with her hips bucking and her belly shuddering. And he did not stop until she begged him to stop.

He crawled over her body and paused to admire the look of rapture on her face. Her breathing was rapid but she smiled faintly when he kissed her nose. He straddled her and untied one hand, then the other. He massaged the red marks on both wrists, before he lay down beside her.

FINN WAS HARD again. His face was still wet, glistening with female essence. The scent of their lovemaking permeated the room, so sweetly exotic. He would keep her legs bound, for the time being. He was taking no chances. The last time he had her under him in bed she smashed the butt of a pistol into his temple.

He nuzzled her neck. "Now, my darling, shall we begin at the beginning—back on Eaton Square, when you so rudely cast me aside and left town?"

There was stillness from her, but he did not feel her body stiffen or pull away. Finally she tsked. "I did not cast you aside."

"You did so."

She lifted her head. "I had no choice, Finn."

Her expression was open, honest, and her skin was luminous. She wore the look of a woman well pleasured. And he had done that to her. He exhaled a soft groan, and kissed her ear. "Please explain yourself, Cate."

"That last night in London, when I arrived home, there was a message waiting for me—from my London contact. The note stated quite plainly that Eduardo was not dead. That my brother had feigned his own demise."

"After the explosion in Béziers, *Los Tigres* must have split up—some remained in France, while others fled to London to resupply and regroup," Finn mused aloud.

She swept a glance his way. "The wire offered no details—just enough to convince me that Eduardo had been taken hostage. He was being held for ransom."

The tantalizing beauty had just made him come harder than he had in an eternity. No doubt the astonishingly erotic sex clouded his judgment, because he could think of no reason to doubt her story. He settled onto his back and stretched sore muscles. "How much?"

"Thirty thousand British pounds."

He knew she had received twenty from Fabian. A member of *Los Tigres* was found floating in the Thames last week. They found the stickpin on his person—well worth the thirty thousand, if the diamond turned out to be a Tavernier.

Her breasts swayed slightly as she propped herself up on her elbows. He pried his eyes off the translucent rosy tips. "I should have realized earlier, it's the money they're after. They care nothing about Eduardo." She sighed.

Even if the ransom numbers didn't exactly add up, at least her motives were beginning to fall in place. Her disappearance, the subterfuge, the desperation in her two attempts to bargain with the mutinous thugs. If it had been Hardy, he'd have done the same. "I'm sorry, Cate."

"Don't be sorry. I managed to get something out of Alonso before you . . ." Her gaze darted about the grotty flat, in search of the right word.

"Made sure he never raped again?"

She met his gaze and nodded. "What was that device you used on him?"

"A garrote. Spanish in origin, I believe."

She shivered. "On a more hopeful note, it appears Eduardo is in prison."

Taken aback, Finn studied her. "Where? What prison?"

"Not sure." Her brows furrowed. "Alonso spoke about a place called Devil's Island. Have you heard of it?"

A cold chill moved down his spine. He carried papers in his bag, official-looking papers that offered a trade. He and Zeno Kennedy had cooked up the proposal. Two unnamed terrorists wanted for arms smuggling in England were trussed up in the Citadel. A few months past, Scotland Yard had captured a couple of French Red Shirts on the lam. They were being held in Her Majesty's Prison Wormwood Scrubs. Simply put, a two-for-two exchange.

This sort of thing always seemed to kick up a bit of anxiety. Finn could feel his pulse rate increase. Anything to do with prison cells, confinement, dark dungeons—hellish holes in the ground. He inhaled a breath and exhaled out his nose—slowly. Might Cate's brother be one of those men?

The irony was, the documents he carried could free her brother—at least temporarily. It was all part of an elaborate cover story, but the ruse might work. And if he helped her brother escape, they would all be wanted by both the French and the British, unless . . .

He turned to Cate. "I have no wish to become an expatriate, but I might be able to help you locate Eduardo."

She sat up and flung herself upon him, flattening him

into the mattress. "You know where he is?" Her breasts pressed to his chest and she squirmed.

He wrapped an arm around her, while his free hand stroked the small of her back and her round derriere. "There is a possibility he is locked up in an old French military fortress."

Her eyes grew wide, insistent. "Where is this place?"

## ∞ Chapter Nineteen

Honestly? She loved to look at him naked. Finn rose off the bed, placed his hands to the small of his back, and lengthened his spine. She thought him a most handsomely built man. He added a groan to the stretch. Moving to the end of the bed, he picked up her foot. One at a time, he unstrapped her ankles. He tilted his head and examined black-and-blue toenails and gnarled toes.

"Please, Finn . . ." Slightly mortified, she tried to yank her foot away, but he held on. "Dancers have ugly feet," she said, adding a sigh.

Raising her leg in the air, he kissed her big toe. "You may have tortured feet, but you are lovely in all other parts." He folded her leg back at the knee, and opened her legs. Cate held her breath. Perhaps it was the way he looked at her when he opened her legs. Or was it his words? "And so . . . flexible." He leaned well over the bed and kissed the place that made her moan.

"Mm-mm." She smiled.

With a parting lick he straightened to his full six feet, two inches. He stood before her, all broad chest, sinewy stomach, and groin. And that erection. She raised her leg and pointed her toe. "*Élevé*, extend, *dégagé*." She placed her foot on his dancing cock and stroked. "*Fondu, relevé, fondu.*" Her chin dipped in time with the words. "Down, up, down."

He caught her by the leg and yanked her to the end of the bed. "And I mean to have ye again, lass." Then he did something wonderful and rare. He smiled. Gently, she tugged her foot away. "I've been dishonest with you, except for the jewelry." She sat up and rubbed her ankles.

"Confession is good for the soul. Clears the air." He retrieved a sheaf of papers from his travel bag. "By the way, where have you hidden the rest of the jewels, Cate?" He returned to bed and she curled up beside him.

"In a safe enough place."

He frowned as he shuffled papers. "I prefer very safe, but I suppose *safe enough* will have to do." His free arm went around her waist and stroked softly. "Ironically, my cover for this trip has to do with a timely suspicion by Special Branch that two Spanish anarchists—likely disenfranchised members of *Los Tigres Solitarios*—are being held by the French government."

"One of them could be Eduardo." Cate leaned her head on his shoulder and asked an innocent question, perhaps too naive. "Why would the British government be interested in Spanish insurrectionists?"

He glanced up from the official-looking papers and stared quite pointedly, as though he were trying to assess if she was playing along. "Anarchists of all stripes supply much-needed provisions to one another. If one group has access to nitroglycerin, for example, another might have arms for trade of a different nature—rifles or ammunition. Not to mention the sharing of information, perhaps the most valuable of all their resources."

"And this place they are holding Eduardo—you know where this prison is?"

Finn thumped the page. "See here—the Citadel of Saint-Martin is located on the Île de Ré. The island is just off La Rochelle." His soft brown eyes turned darker. "Cate, don't get too worked up about this. It could very well turn out to be nothing." He swept the back of his hand against her cheek. "Let's take this one step at a time."

A second twinge of guilt washed over her. "I've been a sneak and a thief. Why would you wish to help me, Finn?"

"By following you here to La Rochelle, I was able to disrupt if not permanently disable *Los Tigres*. I'd like to finish my report to Special Branch with an accurate summary of events including the whereabouts of Eduardo de Dovia—poet laureate of *Los Tigres*." He drew her close and kissed her softly. "But I do wonder—have you been dishonest with me about this?" His gaze was disarmingly sincere. "I want you to want me."

"*Madre de Dios*, how can I convince you?"

"Rather difficult at this point—after so much deceit." He kissed her again, this time deeper, and she plunged willingly into a dance of tongues.

"How do you do this to me, *cheri*?" Her heart raced with desire as his fingers probed between her legs. He turned her onto her back and hooked her leg over his shoulder. They both wanted this badly, she could hear it in their breaking voices. She opened to his cock, already hard as stone and nudging at her entrance. Their lovemaking was going to be swift and explosive this time. Her heart hammered in her chest—or was that someone was pounding on the door?

Finn froze in midthrust. As near as she could read it,

the smoldering desire in his eyes struggled with his sense of duty. She felt it herself. "Ignore it."

He pulled back gently and turned his head. "Who is it?"

"Dé Riquet—let me in."

Finn exhaled a groan. "This better be important, or I'll kill the little rat. Just warning you." He lifted himself off the bed and tugged on drawers. On his way to the door, he picked up her chemise and tossed it over.

With his hands on his hips, Finn took a moment to recover. Cate did not know much about penises. The only one she had ever known was poking out of manly drawers and twitching about. She did not like the look on his face when he stuffed it into his breeches.

He braced a shoulder against the wall and opened the door a crack. "Why are you back? I gave you enough francs for at least three whores—"

Dé Riquet pushed past Flynn. "The Chief of Police and a squad of harbor patrol are combing the quarter door-to-door. They're not far away." He dipped a polite bow to Cate. "Please, you must both leave. They are after me—but they are also looking for the two of you."

Finn picked the con artist up by his coat and pressed him up against the wall. "Say that again, little man, and try to make sense this time."

Dé Riquet held silver-tipped fingers up. *"Deux possibilités.* Someone saw us row away from the ship. Or—you didn't get them all."

"Jesus Christ, could the news get any worse?" Finn eased up on their scrawny cohort.

The sly rascal slid down the wall. "The laundress down the street says they asked her about Dé Riquet and two others—a dark-haired young woman and a British assassin."

*"Merde!"* Finn tossed on his shirt and coat and signaled Cate to dress. "I don't suppose you packed extra trousers?"

She shook her head.

"No bustles or corsets. Put on something loose you can run in." Finn barked orders even as his glare returned to their disreputable host. "How did this happen?"

Dé Riquet leaned against the wall where Finn left him. "Monsieur, you can't go around blowing up boats in La Rochelle harbor without someone noticing." Busy with ammunition and firearms, Finn missed Dé Riquet's rude gesture.

Cate snorted a laugh. *"Huevos de toro,* this little one has."

Finn hid the shorter shotgun under his coat and slung the rifle over his shoulder. He turned to the small-statured Frenchman. "I need you to get us to the stables without being seen." When Dé Riquet held out his hand, Finn leaned into him. "You dare name a price, and you will be looking for a very large thimble to stick on your neck."

FINN DUCKED HIS head around a column of the covered walkway. "Midway down you'll find a passageway into an arcade of small shops," Dé Riquet hissed. "Wind your way through. You're going to have to cross the thoroughfare without being seen. The stable is on the other side."

"We're headed for Saint-Martin, Île de Ré. How best to get there?"

"You'll find the ferry at the east end of town, but they shut down after dusk. Ask around at an inn nearby—The Quiet Woman. The proprietor also runs the ferry." Dé Riquet held up his hands with a shrug. "For the right price, he'll take you across."

Finn nodded behind them. "You ought to think about leaving town for a while," he said. The slight, unkempt man backed away. "There's a lighthouse run by a salt farmer in La Flotte. If you make it that far tonight, mention my name."

Finn reached for Cate's hand, gripping it with the intent to hold on. They made their way past a row of street vendors and small shops, most of them closing up for the evening. Just enough bustle to create cover. He pulled her into a doorway at the end of the arcade.

"You might treat Dé Riquet with a bit more civility," Cate sniffed. "After all, he's done a good bit of dangerous work."

He looked back at her. "I've given the man nearly fifty quid in the last twelve hours." He checked his timepiece. Half past ten o'clock. "I got paid less for eighteen months' duty in the Kandahar Valley." Finn peered up and down the widest boulevard in La Rochelle. Likely a busy market street during the day, at the moment the thoroughfare was a desolate stretch of cobbled pavers.

Cate nodded toward the far end of the broad avenue. "There's a good deal of bustle down by the wharf, wouldn't you say?"

He grabbed her hand again. "At the first sign of traffic, we're going to take cover either behind or alongside whatever is moving down the road." He checked back with Cate. Eager wide eyes gleamed in the dark. She wet her lips and nodded.

"All right then." Slipping onto the concourse, they dodged a fish cart then double-backed behind a dray stacked with barrels. "Hold on." Finn swept Cate behind him as a public coach and team of four nearly ran them down. They waited in a crouched position for a transport van headed in the opposite direction. Jogging alongside carts and carriages, they zigged and zagged a path across the wide thoroughfare. On the other side of the road he squeezed her hand. "Nice footwork."

She grinned. "I should hope so."

Once inside the stable, they located Sergeant Mac-Gregor and a stable boy. While Finn bridled, the groom brushed and saddled. He holstered rifles and tied on both travel bags. "Astride or sidesaddle? Never mind." He grabbed her by the waist and lifted her onto the huge chestnut horse.

He slid in behind her and encouraged her to settle that pretty derriere right up against him. This was going to be pleasant. He pulled his greatcoat around the both of them and buttoned. "There—you'll hardly be noticed."

The backstreets of town would be darker, but they would also be deserted. He and Cate could be easily noticed. Finn preferred to take his chances on the busier, gaslit avenues, where he could wend his way through traffic. The journey out of town, though tense, proved easy enough as they moved from storefronts to a peninsula of storehouses. Based on the drunks and prostitutes Finn observed on the street, La Rochelle's shipping district featured a number of rowdy pubs and whorehouses.

They soon found the ferry tied up to a quay at the east end of town. Finn pointed past the concrete pier into a black sea. "The Île de Ré is just across the straight." He turned MacGregor down a street that curved along the water.

Tucked under his coat, Cate had kept him pleasantly aroused during most of the journey. Less than an hour ago in Dé Riquet's flat she had opened to him, hooking her leg over his shoulder. Lifting her hips in invitation, she had whispered, "How do you do this to me, *cheri*?" The very remembrance made him ache for her.

On horseback, their bodies rocked together with a different kind of intimacy. Something gentler and most appealing. Reins in one hand, he pulled her against his loins. "Comfortable?" She shifted against him.

"Mm-hmm, with the exception of that hard thing poking my bum." He snorted a laugh and kissed the hair on top of her head.

Slender fingers attached to a small hand pointed out the opening of his coat. He aligned his sight with the direction of her finger. A sign hung above the inn: the stylized picture of a peasant woman without a head. "Ah—I never noticed before, but are there many inns in France named The Quiet Woman?"

Cate smiled. "Perhaps not quite as common as The Rose and Crown." She sat up straight, eyes alert. "So you did get a look at my overseas wire."

"Bribed the clerk in the telegraph office." His breath lifted the small hairs of her temple. "Hungry?"

"Famished."

Finn unbuttoned his coat. "I'm going to lower you down first—use the top of my boot as a step, that's it." He found a hitching post close to a window of the inn, where he could keep an eye on horse and belongings. "If the ferryman is willing, we'll not be staying long—a bite of something and off we go."

He opened the door and a bell jingled. The bottom floor of the inn was all pub—with a large hearth and a handful of customers scattered about the room. Finn leaned his rifle against the brass rail of bar and slipped a banknote to the young woman rinsing glasses. "I'm told I might be able to find the ferryman here. The lady and I need to get to Saint-Martin tonight."

"There is no ferryman here, monsieur." The girl smiled. "But there is a ferrywoman."

Finn blinked and spun around. "Is that so? And where might she be?" There looked to be a few men scattered about the room, but no women.

An elbow nudged his side. Cate nodded toward the girl behind the bar. "My uncle is unwell and not expected to recover. My brother and I operate the Île de Ré ferry now."

Finn studied the young woman. "Sorry to hear about your uncle, but might there be a chance I could talk you into a private charter? We'd like to go tonight, if possible."

The girl in front of him and the young lady beside him could almost be sisters. Dark hair, taller than average, slight figures. "Twenty-five francs, monsieur, and do not bother to haggle with me."

"Toss in a meal—" He waved a hand when she eye-balled him. "Whatever's left in the kitchen, and you've got a deal."

"I will have something sent out." The young woman untied her apron. "I must wake my brother. Meet us at the pier as soon as you finish."

## ∽ Chapter Twenty

Cate scooped up lentils and sausage, savoring every spoonful of pottage. The inn's baker brought in a loaf of warm bread, practically singing "Fresh from the oven." Finn tore off a hunk and dipped it in the thick soup. "Keep in mind, Dé Riquet referred us to these people," he said.

Cate hesitated before biting into a thickly buttered, well-salted slice. "And that means?"

He had a habit of rocking his head side to side in contemplation. It was becoming one of his mannerisms she most loved to watch. "They could be useful in other matters. Have you thought about what you are going to do, if indeed your brother is scheduled to be shipped off to Devil's Island?"

Cate swallowed hard. "What exactly is this Devil's Island? The name is horrid enough."

Finn settled back and finished chewing. "A penal colony in French Guiana, on the eastern coast of South America."

She set down her spoon. "I know where French Guiana is. My parents died adventuring in the Amazon rain forest."

He leaned over the table. "Cate . . . Devil's Island is all that it implies. No matter the sentence, almost no one comes back from there alive." Finn lowered his gaze and slurped down a few spoonfuls of hot broth. "The papers I carry may serve us well, at the very least they might delay matters—throw a cog in the wheel, so to speak."

Her stomach went topsy-turvy. Ravenous one moment, near to vomiting the next. Suddenly she wanted to get on with it—push on to the old fortress prison. Finn's papers could get them inside, a meeting with someone in charge. And then what would she do? Worse yet, what if Eduardo was not there? Alonso could have easily lied about Devil's Island. But a lie of such specificity? Her gut told her there was truth in his words. Cate allowed a brief internal moment of doubt. If her brother was not detained in this Citadel, she would continue her search until she found him. Her hopes had been raised from the dead; she wasn't about to let go now. "Might we take the rest of the loaf with us?" Lost in myriad thoughts, she accompanied Finn out of the inn.

"You're worried." He tucked the fresh bread loaf into a saddlebag and untied Sergeant MacGregor. "I did not mean to frighten you, Cate, but you must know the truth of the matter. Even if your brother is alive, there may be no way—"

"Don't say it, Finn." She shot him a glare.

He stopped at a fountain and let the horse drink. "That look was colder than the bite in the air, love." He pulled her into his arms. "Put your hands inside my coat."

Stubbornly, she kept her arms folded over her chest.

"Put your hands"—he dipped his head to capture her gaze—"inside my coat."

She melted against him. "I am frightened for Eduardo—for us. Look what I am dragging you into. Are you prepared to help me, Finn?"

He held her against his chest and rubbed her back. "First, we need to find out if he's even in the Citadel. Prison authorities may not want to admit they have him— you saw the papers. What we need is intelligence, beyond customary channels—the underground kind."

"You're the spy for hire. I have no idea how to go about getting that sort of information." She looked up into eyes that crinkled at the sides.

"Somehow I doubt that," Finn murmured under his breath, and turned her toward the ferry. He signaled to the young man and woman waiting on the pier. "I wager these two know a good deal about the comings and goings on the Île de Ré."

The young woman from the public room in the inn waved them aboard. "Won't be long now, sir. Boiler's near ready." She wore trousers and a heavy woolen jacket.

Finn raised a brow and nudged Cate. "It seems you two have the same fashion sense."

"Pay him no mind. He secretly likes girls who dress like boys—*comme les garçons*." Cate winked at the girl.

The ferry was of open construction, with an engine house, boiler, and a smokestack all set beside a raised pilot station. "Tether your horse here, monsieur." The young man beamed at Cate. "The seas are calm tonight, ma-demoiselle, the crossing will take but a few minutes." They moved off the moment the girl tossed off the line and jumped aboard.

Finn secured his horse, and approached the pilot be-hind the steerage. "We're headed for Saint-Martin-de-Ré. Dé Riquet suggested we spend tonight in La Flotte—there is a lighthouse keeper there?"

The young man's gaze moved back and forth between them. "My name is Bruno Géroux. This is my sister Laurette."

Finn nodded to them both. "This is Miss Willoughby, and I am Hugh Curzon, her escort."

The young woman took the wheel from her brother. "If you are friends of Dé Riquet, you will enjoy Sylvain Robideaux, he is *gardien de phare*."

Cate addressed sister and brother. "We are most anxious for information regarding the Citadel."

Finn nodded. "At the moment, our greatest concern is one of timing. Mostly regarding when the prisoners are to be shipped off." Cate knew that hesitation; Finn waited for one of them to talk. A cold wind swept off the ocean and she huddled against him.

"Normally, we do not ferry past Sablanceaux, the eastern point." Bruno pulled down his cap and stuck his in hands in his pockets. "Prisoner transport is one of the exceptions. Several days ago, we ferried men up to the fortress. The convict ship was anchored off Saint-Martin."

Laurette nodded. "A great floating prison with masts. You can't miss it."

"And might I inquire how long this floating prison remains in port, normally, before making its transoceanic voyage?" Finn asked.

"Two or three weeks. Sometimes longer."

"And this convict ship has been in port—?"

"Several weeks."

"So any day now," Finn ruminated aloud. "Thank you. You've both been most helpful." He studied the outline of dark terra firma ahead. Cate craned her neck and could make out a pier and a few flickering gaslights.

Finn turned back to the Géroux siblings. "I've a mind

to push on—make Saint-Martin tonight. This fellow Rob-ideaux. Why do you suppose Dé Riquet would have rec-ommended him? Since the two are colleagues, I can wager a guess as to the man's character, but why else?"

Bruno shrugged, shifting his gaze to his sister. "I have a thought. Perhaps more of an intuition, but here it is: You are interested in the fortress, *mais oui*? Sylvain Robideaux claims to have lived inside the walls undetected for many days."

Laurette added a bit of laughter. "He also boasts that he led the only successful escape ever in the history of *Le Citadel*."

Finn stared at the two of them. "So . . . you don't be-lieve a word of it?"

"On the contrary, he helped rescue our uncle, Fulbert Géroux." Bruno cut the motor, and his sister guided the ferry up to the quay. "Sylvain is a friend—raving mad, but . . . a hero to our family."

Finn paid their fee and something extra for the infor-mation. He also asked a few directions. Laurette called to Finn as the ferry putted away. "Stay close to your lovely woman—Sylvain has roving hands."

Bruno barked a laugh. "Arms, hands, legs, feet—tongue. *Bonne chance!*"

CATE WAVED, EVEN as Finn swept her up in his arms. "I wasn't planning on getting much sleep tonight anyway." He lifted her onto MacGregor's back.

"And why would you say such a thing? Might you be expecting a reward of some kind for spiriting us safely out of town?" Cate fell back against Finn's broad chest as he settled in behind her, resting his chin against her hair.

"I was hoping for something warm and sloppy and wholly erotic."

Cate muffled a snort with the lapel of his overcoat. "Friendly, weren't they, the Géroux siblings? And very helpful, as well." She angled her chin upward and caught a smug tilt to his mouth.

He looked down. "Are you always so trusting of people's stories, Cate?"

"Are you always such a doubter?"

"Ah. That is why you need me on this adventure of yours. For I shall play the sober, unwitting suitor who bumbles along, yet somehow manages to keep the beautiful, strong-willed heroine alive."

"No, you play the *handsome*, sober, unwitting suitor— and I am most certainly not an adventurer." Indignant, Cate looked out into the blackness of the country road, beyond the thick mane and neck of Finn's horse. Even the sound of the surf failed to soothe, for the moment. "My parents were adventurers. I am no such thing."

His incredulous hoot made her cheeks hot. "You boldly sashay into anarchists' dens. You enjoy a theatrical career, featuring a dangle in midair on gilded swing. You go about your daily life—whether in London, Paris, or Barcelona— unfettered and unchaperoned. I'd have to call you mightily adventurous. An uncivilized prig would call you worse."

"Stop taunting me, Finn, or I'll get down and walk."

"We've several miles to go yet, and you're yawning," he teased good-naturedly.

"You'd best watch out then—I'm overwrought and peevish."

Finn rubbed the top of her head with his chin. "Indeed, you are." There was something comforting about those pinpricks of beard scratching her scalp. A bit uncouth of him, but also affectionate and intimate.

"I'd give anything for a few jelly babies right about now," she sighed.

"Check my left inside pocket—there might be some seaside rock in there." Cate dug around and came up with a sack of candy sticks. She swirled one of the hard sticks into her mouth and settled back against him.

"When Hardy and I were wee lads, Father would lay on the floor between our beds—he suffered from gout—and tell us battle stories. Mostly old Gunn clan legends."

"My father told army tales." Cate lay her head against his chest. "I should like an army tale, Finn."

"Most of my service stories would give you nightmares."

"You must have at least one."

There was a long pause as he, presumably, shuffled through memories for a less gruesome tale. She had gotten the impression several times that his experience in Near Asia had been difficult. Perhaps more than difficult. Finally, he cleared his throat. "There is one . . . possibly."

Cate yawned. "Tell it, please."

"Not long after I arrived in India, I was transferred to Lahore, the Third Punjab Cavalry—made up of Sikhs, mostly, and a few British officers," he began slowly. "We received orders to reinforce Kandahar and set off straightaway. The terrain was steep, rugged—completely unforgiving. We were attacked in a narrow pass and my horse was shot out from under me.

"I heard a shout—'Behind you'—and rolled over in time to put a bullet in a man swinging a large curved sword at me. I then crawled over to the Sikh soldier who had warned me. Both his legs were shot up. He pointed to a young horse, a cannon hauler. Part of the trail had collapsed under the horse, and he was mired chest deep in bodies and loose earth. To top it off, the loose ground around us threatened to slide again, to take everything with it—cannon, horses, wounded." Finn checked his pulse mentally as he continued and found it elevated well beyond the norm. "Bullets were still flying, by the way."

She sighed. "Making you all the more brave."

Finn grunted. "Men take risks in battle. Risks they'd never take otherwise—for their comrades."

Cate tilted her chin up and grinned. "Either two- or four-legged, I presume."

"What was left of the regiment had taken cover. Pashtun snipers were picking off anyone who moved below. When the sun moved behind a mountain peak, everything in the ravine was thrown into shadow. I organized a few of our men to return fire, which gave me enough cover to get over to the trapped horse. I unhooked his rigging and slipped a bridle on him. I'll be damned if the horse didn't listen to me like he spoke English as well as you or I. Calmly, I coaxed him up out of the debris one leg at a time.

"I picked up two other injured men and the big red horse carried the three of us up the trail, where we met up with more of our men. We made the fort by nightfall. Late that evening, I got called to the infirmary. The chap who had called out—saved me and the big red horse—wanted to chat for a bit. Said his name was Sergeant Bhai Singh MacGregor. I thought he was not in his right mind—delirious—Scot and Sheikh? As it turned out, he was dying. And he, indeed, was part Scot. Adopted and raised by a Third Gurkha Rifleman named MacGregor."

"And the big red horse—you named him Sergeant MacGregor." Cate nestled into his chest. Finn rested his chin beside her temple.

"That, I did."

"Did you and MacGregor have other adventures in Afghanistan?"

"Several. But I must reserve those tales for another day. Look ahead, Cate, toward the water."

Cate straightened at the sight of the lighthouse. "This is where we find the man Sylvain."

## ∞ Chapter Twenty-one

Finn stepped back from the door, cupping his hands around his mouth. *"Bonjour! N'importe qui à la maison?"* He squinted up at the steep roofline. A row of gabled windows remained dark and closed. The residence turned out to be a two-story stone cottage, something that might accommodate the keeper and his family—but at the moment it seemed no one was home. Which was quite impossible, as a beam of powerful light swept past shoals and surf at regular intervals.

A strong offshore breeze whipped up from the shoreline. Cate pulled his coat tighter around herself. "There must be another entrance."

Finn grabbed her hand, and they circled the residence. They found a rise of wooden steps leading up to the tower door. He rapped on the door. This time he tried the latch. The door swung open almost silently and he ushered Cate inside.

He kept his arm around her and pressed her against the closed door. "I can't see a blasted thing—if you'll excuse me?" He opened and slipped his hand inside his coat— the one Cate was wearing. His hands accidentally brushed across her breasts. "Sorry for the rudeness." He could not see her expression, but imagined a delightful eye roll.

Cate sighed. "Such a lie. You're not the least bit sorry."

"No, I am not." He thought about kissing her. There was something about Cate that made him desirous of her in the most inappropriate situations. He groped around and found the deep inside pocket he was looking for. He pulled out the torch. "Ah, here you are." He toggled the switch and for good measure banged the cylinder holding the batteries against his palm. A swath of light illuminated parts of the room. A modest secretary and traveling chest occupied most of the space. "The keeper's office, is my guess." He swung the beam over Cate.

"What is that thing?" She blinked at the gadget in his hand.

"An electrical torch powered by experimental batteries. Quite a miraculous bit of invention, compliments of Scotland Yard's crime laboratory."

Finn pointed the beam up a staircase that spiraled around the cast-iron cylinder that ran down the center of the lighthouse. "Hello? Anyone on duty?" Finn called out again and waited. Nothing but whirring and clicking . . .

He turned to Cate. "What do you make of those sounds?"

She peered up through the twisting stairs. "Clockworks, perhaps?"

Finn nodded. "Let's have a look."

They reached a landing near the top of the tower, which housed a number of clockworks, large and small, all buzzing and whirling. It appeared they were in some sort of service area, just below the lantern room. A shadow played on the stairs overhead.

A figure swung over the railing and landed directly in

front of them. Finn pulled Cate away from some sort of mad, grinning gorilla. Or was this leaping figure a drunken, naked Frenchman? One covered in copious amounts of body hair. *"Ah, nuit glorieux. Les étoiles, la lune, une belle femme . . ."* The man made no attempt to cover himself and lunged closer.

Finn stepped in front of Cate. "Shall we leave it at *bonsoir?*"

"Ah—you are *Anglais!* I spend three years in Portsmouth. I shall translate. *Une nuit comme ce soir?* On such a night as tonight? *Une beauté visite mon phare?* A beauty visits my lighthouse?" The man craned his neck to get another look at Cate.

Finn stared. Accompanying the man's annoying French lesson, there was a good deal of bobbing and weaving and wild arm gestures. The strange character appeared to be in performance mode for an audience of one—Cate. Finn drew himself up to his full height and leaned over the furry little devil. "Far be it from me to dash your hopes with the young lady, but she's taken. And might I suggest you don . . . a loincloth?"

The man leaped backward. For a moment, Finn thought the wiry, athletic character might backflip and walk away on his hands. It didn't help matters any that Cate was laughing. Uncontrollably.

He silently cursed Dé Riquet's suggestion of a respite in La Flotte. "Ooof! The little man dances in the breeze," he said. The strange creature wiggled his hips side to side. "But not so little, *oui?*"

Finn looked back as Cate peeked around his shoulder. "You find gypsy circus performers with Saint Vitus Dance appealing?" He kept himself positioned between the mad Frenchman and Cate, who did not try very hard to smother her laughter at—yes, this had to be him—Sylvain Robideaux.

"Bugger this!" Finn pulled out his pistol.

Immediately, the wily man sobered. "You are here to rob me? As you can see, I have nothing to steal." He dropped his hands to display his gentlemanly wares. "Nothing but nature's jewels, *mais oui?*"

"We are not here to *steal* anything. Dé Riquet suggested we might rest here." Finn holstered the gun inside his coat. "An obvious mistake on our part. Come on, Cate."

"Did you say, Dé Riquet? One moment!" The character waved a finger and disappeared up the stairs.

"Good God, even his ass is hairy," Finn remarked as he craned his neck to peer up the curved rise of stairs. A smattering of whispers and giggles emanated from above, along with feminine laughter. The odd man poked his head over the railing. "Don't go."

Finn turned to Cate. "What do you make of this? Do you wish to stay or leave?"

She raised both brows, along with her shoulders. "I don't believe he's dangerous. Besides, I have you to protect me." Finn studied her lopsided grin, which had an infectious effect on him.

"All right," he groused, "but if he comes back wagging that little ferret in the air again . . ."

*"Bonjour de nouveau et bienvenue!"* Descending the stairs, Sylvain now wore trousers and pulled braces over his shoulders. "Please sit down—friends of Dé Riquet are friends of mine." Their host, if one could call him that, added a few lumps of coal to a small iron stove. "Wine, cognac?" He opened a glass cabinet and took down a bottle. "I am Sylvain Robideaux." There was a small cot placed

against the wall, and two ladder-back chairs. He bid them each take a seat. "And you are?"

"Catriona de Dovia Willoughby. Please, call me Cate." Every so often the man fiddled and twitched. It was distracting.

Finn examined every corner of the room, before settling into a chair beside Cate. "I am Hugh Curzon, the lady's escort. Might I ask—why do you suppose Dé Riquet suggested we pay you a visit?"

Robideaux gathered up three glasses from a sideboard and uncorked a bottle of brandy. "Let me wager a guess. You journey to Saint-Martin. Perhaps you have some sort of business at the Citadel?" He passed them each a glass of cognac and sat down. The man wasn't down a second before he jumped out of his seat and called to the ladies standing on the steps above. "Are you dressed, *mes chéris?*"

Two plainly attired but rather pretty young women descended the stairs. With a nod to Cate and a surprisingly brazen inspection of Finn, the girls gathered their coats and started downstairs. Robideaux followed after, protesting their departure.

Cate leaned across the table. "It appears we interrupted the gentleman's leisure."

At least one side of Finn's mouth cracked in a smile. "Hard to know whether we arrived pre-, mid-, or postcoitus."

Her gaze traveled warily about the lighthouse service room. "There has got to be a reason Dé Riquet sent us here," she whispered. "He must have heard the anarchists talking—something about my brother being held on this island. I believe Monsieur Robideaux can help us. And I so fear that Eduardo is about to be transported off to—"

"Devil's Island."

Finn turned toward the voice behind him. A sobered Robideaux stepped onto the landing. "Prisoners are gathered and held at the Citadel until they fill the convict ship. Then bon voyage, never to be—"

At least the man had the decency to stop, Finn thought.

Finn sipped on the excellent French brandy and studied the bedeviled fellow. It seemed nothing about this chap was quite right. His hair was arranged in a series of lopsided ragged tufts, and there was something about the mad gaze . . . One eye didn't quite track with the other. Robideaux poured himself a glass.

"Haven't you had quite enough for one evening?" Finn grumbled.

"This?" He held up his glass. "*Mais non*, Monsieur Curzon. It is the absinthe that makes me crazy."

Finn supposed that explained at least some of the man's confounding behavior. Their host settled back in his chair and stared at Cate. "How is it you don't know if your brother is in the Citadel? People are either prisoners or they are not, mademoiselle, it is not a matter of guessing."

Finn set his glass down and uncorked the cognac. "Mind if I pour myself another?"

Robideaux shrugged. "As I said, if Dé Riquet sent you, then you are my guests. What is mine, is yours."

Finn sat back with his glass and explained, "The incarceration of political prisoners is tricky and very often secretive. Anarchists sometimes fall into a gray area not covered by the War Powers Act. Nor do they enjoy a citizen's rights. And though not strictly lawful, the names of these men can be withheld. As it turns out, I have a bit of business to do with the French authorities in Saint-Martin. Might you have any contacts there?"

"We would be most grateful for your assistance—"

Cate covered a yawn. "And a bed for the night. I would love to rest my head on a pillow for a few hours."

Robideaux tossed back the last of his brandy. "You are tired. We shall talk in the morning." Once again, the wiry man leaped from his chair and led the way out of the tower.

Inside the keeper's cottage, he showed them to a small upstairs bedchamber that was clean and recently swept, clearly indicating the man employed a housekeeper.

"I'm off to bed down MacGregor and see to our bags." Finn leaned over and kissed her forehead. "Sleep well. Shall I wake you early?"

"Don't you dare." Cate flopped onto the bed, fully clothed.

## ∞ Chapter Twenty-two

A shaft of morning light angled across a small copper tub in the middle of the room. Cate shed her pantalets, testing the water with her toe. "Was your swim in the ocean invigorating?" she asked. An offshore breeze teased up a window curtain as well as dusky nipples. "Compared to a ballet girl au naturel?"

Finn's gaze lingered. "You are the very definition of the word *invigorating.*"

She sank into the water and sighed. "I shall kiss Adèle for this bath."

Finn rubbed his hair dry with a rough towel and stepped into a pair of clean drawers. "So, we're on a first-name basis with the staff now?"

"And what about you, sir—up with the cock's crow, I take it?" She dunked a washcloth in the water. "I found this small bath in the kitchen along with a housekeeper, who introduced herself as Adèle. An attractive woman, don't you think?"

"She bakes a bonny brioche." Finn flopped down on the bed and stuffed a few pillows behind him. "I do hope you had yours dripping with melted butter and strawberry conserve."

"I swooned over every morsel." Cate closed her eyes, and lay back against the rear of the tub. "According to Adèle, who insisted on practicing her English, you and our host Sylvain spoke at length this morning—in hushed tones. 'Sylvain go the village and Monsieur Curzon groom and feed his *cheval*.'" Cate perfectly mimicked the housekeeper's heavy accent.

"Lovely patois of French and English."

"And what of Eduardo?" Cate used a washcloth to soap her neck and shoulders. "We should push on to Saint-Martin soon."

"Sylvain seems to believe the transfer to the ship will take place tomorrow. He's gone to the village to see what else he can ferret out." Finn appeared to be enjoying her bath as much as she was. "If I were a painter, I would paint you this way—with those few strands of hair loosed from the knot on your head and those dancer's limbs draped over the sides of the tub."

A gentle smile lit up her face as she sponged off yesterday's grime. "Yes, and these gangly legs require a shave."

Finn reached into his travel bag bedside. Stretching further, he passed her the straight razor.

*"Merci, chéri."* Cate curled her toes over the edge of the tub and soaped her leg. She opened the razor and guided the instrument up from her ankle. "This appears to be an excellent razor. I hope you don't mind?"

"I'll give it a good stropping after you're done." Finn punched up a few pillows and leaned back. "Do all dancers groom their legs and underarms?"

"Body hair is a distraction on stage—some costumes reveal more than others." Cate grabbed her toes and pointed her leg straight up in the air. She guided the razor along the back of the extended limb.

"My word, you're flexible."

She lifted one leg then the other for a last inspection. "And getting less so every day I do not practice." Finished with his razor, she soaped her hair, then piled the tangle of wet strands on her head. She squeezed the sea sponge and a soft rain of clear water rinsed the suds down her neck and back.

She climbed out of the tub and caught him ogling again.

"Cate—what am I to do? Not look? Pretend I don't see those rivulets of water meandering down every curve?" By the time she finished drying off with the rough towel he was hard. And she noticed. And Finn noticed her notice.

"*Touché*, Monsieur Curzon." A smile tugged at the ends of her mouth. "I believe you need a washup. Unless you wish to go around smelling like a shellfish dinner." She collected a cake of soap and a basin of water and moved to his bedside. Using the sea sponge, she washed him off one limb at a time. She untied the drawstring. "Lift your derriere, sir." He raised up off the mattress and she pulled off his drawers.

She purposefully avoided the waving, randy staff that twitched with her every touch. Just when he likely thought she wasn't going to venture further—she smiled. "Now for the manly bits."

Her hand wash left him thoroughly clean and greatly aroused. Once again, she dried him off, ministering to cuts and bruises from a jar of salve. Reaching back into her portmanteau, she unscrewed a tin of scented oil. "Rosemary and lavender oil—for those tight muscles."

"I do hope you plan to rub some of that on the caber."
Finn punched up a pillow and locked his hands behind his
head. His gaze moved down her legs with a kind of raw
hunger, as though he were considering which part of her
to taste first. She pulled up the nubby cloth that barely
covered her. "Are you determined to drive me mad, Cate?"

"How impatient you are. Turn over." She applied the
lotion to his skin and massaged his neck and back muscles.

Finn groaned into the pillow. "M-mm, you are considerably improved in temperament from the peevish young
lady of last night."

"I was tired and . . ." Her voice drifted off.

"Randy. Admit it, girl—all that riding on MacGregor
and rubbing has made you lusty for me."

Cate slapped his bum.

"Do that again, please." Finn snorted a laugh and turned
over.

The door to their room opened without a knock. Sylvain stuck his head in the room. "Hoo-hoo! Have I arrived
in time or am I too late?" Their host ogled Cate, who wore
nothing but a towel. "Perhaps a ménage à trois to begin
the day?"

Finn grabbed a pillow and fired it across the room. It
hit the door hard enough to slam it shut. A few goose
feathers fluttered to the floor.

"You must both ready yourselves—quickly," Sylvain
mumbled from the hallway. "We have an appointment in
one hour's time with the British chargé d'affaires. This is
a rarity, my friends. No one knows why he is here in town.
*Une mission très réservée*—very secretive! But if anyone
can help you, perhaps this man can."

\*   \*   \*

"HOW DOES THE Mad Hatter of La Flotte get an appointment with the British chargé d'affaires?" Finn backed out of the front door carrying their travel satchels, both firearms slung over his shoulder. "After you, darling."

"Might I suggest you ask?" Cate stepped in front of him and stopped abruptly. Finn followed her stare to a rather elegant landau, top down, its tufted leather seats gleaming in the midday sun. MacGregor was saddled and tethered to the back of the fancy carriage.

Their host opened the door and waved them forward. Finn exhaled, loudly. "I thought we discussed this, Sylvain." He handed both bags to the driver. "Something a bit drab, so as not to draw attention? Did I not make myself clear?" Finn helped Cate into the carriage and fell in beside her, deliberately quashing the Frenchman's designs on sitting beside her.

Sylvain took a seat opposite, seemingly well satisfied with his choice of vehicle. "Why be drab when one can travel in style?"

Finn glared at the increasingly irritating man. "You might have a few pipers and drummers accompany us into town."

"Impossible to sneak into Saint-Martin. You'd both be noticed even if you arrived on a hay wagon. Besides, the sun shines, the weather is mild—let us enjoy." Sylvain reached under the seat and pulled out a parasol. "So you don't get spots on your nose."

Cate shook her head. "Very kind of you, but I don't freckle."

Finn stared at her, tempted to brush her cheek with the back of his hand. "Ah, but there are moments when you blush a lovely rose color." Without taking his eyes off her, he ripped the sun umbrella out of the man's hand and set it beside his long guns.

He read Cate's pointed glare perfectly. *Temper, Finn.*

Twice in so many days he'd been robbed of intimate relations with Cate. The most desirable young woman he had ever had the good fortune to know, intimately. He exhaled again—harsher still. And hang it all, he had not been able to chase her out of his mind for well over a year now.

Perhaps, if it hadn't been for the coitus interruptus, he might be the model of amiability. Tempering a frown, he leaned forward to speak man-to-man with Sylvain. "I had thought to do a bit of skulking about town. That is why I would prefer the carriage to be as inconspicuous as possible, so that my surveillance might remain, how can I put this? *Inaperçu*—unobserved."

Sylvain also leaned forward. "Ah, I did not realize, monsieur." They were nose to nose. "But, of course, you are a spy. One of those British foreign office agents—"

Finn very purposely flicked his eyes up to the driver and back. He lowered his voice. "I would prefer to keep that between us for the time being."

"I've had my suspicions." Sylvain fell back in his seat. "Dé Riquet sent you."

"If we were the truly clever sort, we'd use the landau as a kind of ruse. Spies, as you put it, wouldn't parade into town—" Finn broke off his speech to study their new cohort. Might this man's madcap facade mask a more formidable ally or enemy? There was something about the odd Frenchman—Dé Riquet as well.

"Gentlemen!" Cate sat up straight, her eyes locked on the shore ahead. "Might this be the Citadel? Oh, it must be!"

Sylvain craned his neck to see over the driver. "None other, mademoiselle."

Finn's gaze swept over the stately, imposing fortress. "I studied Vauban and his designs at university—he is considered one of the greatest military engineers of all time." He took a moment to admire the impressive arrow-shaped bastions that projected out from the massive stone walls of the enclosure.

Sylvain explained the layout. "The entire township is under the Citadel's protection. It is known as a *bastioned enceinte*. The fortified walls enclose both the village and the Citadel. The stronghold occupies the point on the eastern edge of town. It was converted to a prison more than a century ago."

Finn squinted past the great walls to the bay. "The fortress has its own docks, does it not?"

Sylvain jumped up onto the seat and pointed. "You see the entrance into the quay—just there, reaching out into the bay. The docks are used by supply boats and, of course, to transfer prisoners."

Cate hadn't spoken much. Finn traced her gaze to the basin. An immense three-masted transport dwarfed the other boats in the surrounding waters. Something about the convict ship reminded him of an old British battleship. "Might I inquire as to how you were able to procure an appointment with the British chargé d'affaires?"

Rather predictably, Sylvain shrugged. "From time to time, I do favors for the commune magistrate, as well as the *gouverneur régional*. We travel, *en fait*, to the governor's villa for your appointment."

If the tales of the man's exploits were true, that Sylvain had successfully led an escape from the Citadel, then these political connections of his made sense, especially if he was obliged to the state. Very often skilled thieves and confidence men were turned to legitimate service. Finn began to formulate a theory about the odd character twitching on the bench seat opposite.

"*Mais oui*, we are here."

Inside the walled city, Saint-Martin appeared much like the villages in the southern regions of France. Tile-roofed, whitewashed houses trimmed with pale blue window shutters. As they approached the middle of town, the carriage turned through open gates and stopped at the entrance to the Palais des Gouverneurs.

Finn spoke in low tones to both Cate and Sylvain. "Shall we get our stories straight? I am prepared to present the letters in my possession. A straightforward offer for an exchange of prisoners." He turned to Cate. "I do this with the understanding that we will return your brother to England. I will do everything in my power to see that he is treated fairly, Cate, but he must answer to the Crown's accusations."

He waited for her nod, which understandably came with a bit of lip chewing and the most adorable furrowed brow he'd ever seen attached to it. "Good."

"Also, we mention nothing about the explosion in La Rochelle harbor." When Sylvain blinked, Finn shook his head. "Not enough time to explain everything—try to stay with us."

Sylvain appeared extraordinarily calm, for once. "For the time being."

Finn checked back with Cate. "I've a mind, the local authorities might just as soon arrest the lot of us—ask questions later. Especially since we're going to be poking about asking awkward questions."

At the door, Sylvain abandoned them with a wink. "If anyone asks, you are staying at the Le Richelieu!"

The villa's lower floor was more of a reception area than a private residence. A thin, storklike gentleman approached them in the foyer, and Finn handed the man his card. "Mademoiselle Willoughby and Monsieur Curzon to see the *Attaché Britannique.*"

"Mademoiselle and monsieur, the chargé d'affaires is expecting you. This way, *s'il vous plaît.*" The man swept ahead of them, pointing to the floor. He appeared to be both butler and secretary. "Over fifty thousand hand-crafted tiles went into the design below your feet," he intoned. And tour guide.

By and large, most studies were dimly lit dens oppressed by walls lined with dusty bookshelves. But not this one. Finn followed Cate into an airy room filled with sunlight. A tall figure stood at the window with his back to them. The gentleman stared out past a garden terrace to a view of the Citadel jutting out into the bay. "Embodies the very word *formidable*, wouldn't you say?" The unmet gentleman's voice was resonant, if somewhat overly mannered.

Finn stepped closer. "Appears to form its own peninsula."

The gentleman turned slowly and examined Finn. "I am Adrian Fortesque, British chargé d'affaires." He spoke in a slow cadence, articulating each word carefully. *"Ad . . . interim."*

Finn met the man's cool, appraising gaze with one of his own. "And I am your noon appointment. Hugh Curzon, on assignment for the Home Office." He cleared his throat. "We have reason to believe the Citadel holds two unnamed prisoners, Spanish insurrectionists wanted in Britain for illegal arms trafficking." Finn paused, unsure how much more he wished to reveal. "If the French will release names, I am authorized to offer a trade. I carry papers signed by the foreign secretary to that effect."

Fortesque's gaze flickered over to Cate. Finn could not say the man's steely eyes warmed any, but there was definite interest.

"Allow me to introduce"—as Finn moved back, Cate stepped forward—"Miss Catriona de Dovia Willoughby." She reached out with her palm down.

Fortesque bowed and kissed the air above her hand, the proper English way. "Miss Willoughby." The man straightened to his full height, something just shy of Finn's own stature. Finn evaluated the man physically. Fortesque was fairly impressive in countenance. A somewhat long nose divided a pleasant, symmetrical face that featured gray eyes and an elegant, high forehead. An honest face, but then he was also a diplomat—hardly trustworthy. Finn exhaled quietly.

The chargé d'affaires appeared to be in his early forties— or was it the peppering of gray that aged him prematurely? The mane of unruly hair that fell about his face and ears was certainly reminiscent of his own, which caused a grin. Frankly, Finn wondered if this kind of tonsorial splendor was de rigueur for foreign operatives.

"Lovely name, Catriona." Fortesque's movements were smooth, almost stealthlike, as he stepped closer. "You speak the Queen's tongue, and yet . . ." His eyes drank her in. "I detect an accent."


CATE WAS USED to unseemly stares from men. Fortesque's interest was mannered, more gentlemanly, but disquieting nonetheless. What troubled her more than his leer was his power. It seemed clear he was in a position to help her greatly, if he so wished. She wondered if he was the kind of man who would take advantage, but knew, without a doubt, she would have her answer soon enough.

"Sir, though I am of both Spanish and English blood, my loyalties have always leaned toward England, whereas my brother, Eduardo—his heart is with the workers of *España*." Cate twisted a lace-edged pocket square in her hands. "He is *El Tigre Solitario.*"

"The Lone Tiger," the chargé d'affaires murmured.

Finn fell in beside her. "A romanticized moniker derived more from his tracts and speeches than actual misdeeds. We have reason to believe he may be one of two unnamed anarchists detained in the Citadel."

Fortesque straightened. "It is my understanding that that ring of anarchists was broken up last year. The man you refer to was killed during a raid—bombs set off by gunfire."

"And since it was my report you likely read," Finn added a bit of chagrin to his expression, "let me be the first one to admit that I might have been . . . mistaken."

"And your hope is that I might fa-cil-i-tate"—the man lifted a brow, as if to accent each syllable of the word—"a dialogue with the French authorities."

Cate pressed her lips together and nodded. "If you would, sir."

Fortesque studied her a few moments longer, then abruptly shifted his attention to Finn, who opened his coat pocket and handed over an official-looking envelope. "We're offering up Bonnet and Lefevre if the two unnamed men turn out to be—"

"The right *sort* of anarchists." Fortesque rounded the library table and settled into a chair. "Have a seat." He gestured to a set of wing chairs and removed the documents from the envelope.

The longer the man shuffled through the pages, the more nervous Cate became. Her gaze darted over to Finn, who appeared right enough. He winked at her. Desperate not to fidget, Cate tried to slow her intake and exhale of breath, a calmative exercise she'd noticed Finn used on occasion. She had become subtly attuned to the odd quirks of the man sitting beside her, including his breathing exercises. Something he kept to himself, the kind of thing no one would notice unless they observed him closely, as well as the kind of thing that she found incredibly endearing in such an otherwise stoic man.

Fortesque folded the papers and stuffed them back in the envelope. He looped a finger through one of the ties. "As it happens, there is a reception here this evening in honor of—me." Fortesque's grin faded quickly. "It is my understanding a director from the Ministry of Justice will attend, as well as the *gardien de prison*. I encourage you both to attend."

"Information often flows with the champagne." Finn uncrossed a booted leg and leaned across the table for the documents.

Fortesque rose from the desk and tugged on the bell pull. "Mr. Guyot will see you out. My secretary will also see that an invitation is"—he took another long look at Cate as he extended his hand toward Finn—"hand delivered."

The moment the British chargé d'affaires left the room, she leaned across the arm of her chair. "He imagines himself a bit splendid. I do hope he means to help us."

"Condescending, stiff-arsed bureaucrat." Finn grunted.

"Believe what you wish, Cate, but I've learned never to trust a chargé d'affaires—especially an *en interim*. They're temporary. They've got nothing at stake." He offered her a hand up. "He'd also enjoy a bit of alone time with you."

A sharp knock preceded the gaunt-looking secretary. "Allow me to escort you." He waved them through the door.

Cate tugged on Finn's arm. "I cannot attend a soiree this evening."

"Why ever not?"

"I've got nothing to wear."

Sylvain Robideaux sprang from behind a large potted palm, beaming. "There is to be a gala event this evening. You are invited to attend, yes?"

"It would seem so." Finn checked his pocket watch. "My lovely companion has just pointed out the obvious fact that we are woefully underdressed for a such an occasion."

"Ah, not to worry." Their ever-jubilant companion opened the carriage door. "Sylvain knows the best tailor and seamstress in all Saint-Martin."

There were times, Cate thought, when the clever Frenchman could be a great deal more than companionable; in fact, he appeared to be connected to everyone in town. "How fortunate we are to travel in your company!" She patted the comfortable upholstered seat and the Frenchman scrambled in beside her. He shouted directions to the driver. "Rue Gaspard."

A cloud bank partially blocked out the sun as they exited the long drive. Finn's expression darkened along with the sky. Obviously disgruntled with the seating arrangement, Finn slouched into the opposite bench and glowered. "We will likely have opportunity to speak with the prison warden this evening. What can you tell us about him?"

The wiry Frenchman sobered, somewhat. "Moreau's nickname is *Vipère.* "Several years ago, he was taking his evening constitutional around the fortress grounds. At one point, he stepped off the path and into one of the gardens. He emerged holding a garter snake in his hand, blood dripping down his arm. On closer inspection, it was observed that the snake's head was missing. The new warden swallowed and smiled triumphantly—teeth stained with red. It is said one of his guards fainted at the realization."

"You can't mean . . ." Cate looked from one man to the other.

Finn stared. "Jesus."

## Chapter Twenty-three

"So we're dealing with someone who will go to great lengths to make an impression." Finn loosed his collar. "Ferocious theater, at any rate."

"He's a mild-mannered character—almost meek in some ways. A former priest. Defrocked, rumor has it. He finds me amusing." Their fidgeting friend seemed less restless of late. "But there is often a predatory look in his eye, as though he challenges me to try another breakout. He ends conversations by saying, 'You must visit us again, Sylvain. Stay a little longer next time.'"

Cate stared. "He openly taunts you?"

Sylvain shrugged. "Moreau prides himself on strict discipline and, of course, no successful escapes." The Frenchman patted her gloved hand. "Something I know not to be true, by the way."

One side of Finn's mouth twitched. "I thought you retired."

Sylvain held a finger to his lips and grinned. "What more can I tell you about *Vipére*? The warden walks with a slight limp. The knob of his cane is embellished with—"

"Let me guess, the head of snake," Finn interjected.

"Ah, we are here." The carriage turned onto a charming lane lined by topiary trees, a few fashionable shops, and a café. Sylvain leaped out of the carriage and swept them both inside the dressmaker's salon.

"Our Parisian couturier, Madame Gagelin." Sylvain kissed the outstretched hand of a handsome woman dressed in a stylish gown. As if in a reverie, their odd companion bounced around the showroom without bothering with much of an introduction. "Friends of mine, madame, in dire need of your services."

Finn had observed the lines of a dress in the window. A lovely evening frock in shades of violet. Sumptuous fabrics with tonal designs draped over a narrow skirt. No lace. No bows. No need for the added frippery that British dressmakers were so fond of. The sleek bodice featured a plunging neckline with a draped diaphanous modesty panel. A man would still be entranced by a hint of cleavage, perhaps more so.

The modiste wore a measuring tape around her neck as if it were the strands of a necklace. Her gaze swept from Sylvain to Cate and landed on Finn.

He stepped forward and turned up the charm. *"Enchanté, madame."* He brushed the woman's hand with his lips—when in France, do as the Frenchmen do. Besides, he had a mind to cajole the woman into selling him the sample gown in the window. The dress would look ravishing on Cate. There were times when her brilliant blue eyes turned violet, and this gown would enhance the effect.

Finn continued, "I'm afraid we have arrived in Saint-Martin ahead of our luggage. Quite unannounced, it seems Miss Willoughby and I are expected to attend a reception this evening at the Palais des Gouverneurs."

"Of course, the soiree for the chargé d'affaires." Madame Gagelin flashed him a sultry look. "You have come to the right salon, messieurs; several of my gowns will be in attendance—a ginger and apricot confection, *très magnifique,* for Anny Ahlers. And the cut rose velvet with the raspberry satin apron—superb on—"

"Mistress of the Belgian diplomat, Chapuys." Sylvain lounged against a counter heaped with bolts of fabric. He gathered his fingers to his mouth and blew a kiss to the gods. *"Une belle poitrine."*

Madame picked up a yardstick and threatened. "Behave yourself, Sylvain."

The restless man danced away from the waving baton. "I can do better than that—I shall make myself comfortable in the lobby of the Richelieu with a bottle of cognac." Sylvain tipped his cap and exited the shop.

"The man is a nuisance—but also charming, no?" Madame swept a professional eye over Cate. "Statuesque and willowy. Any of my gowns will be exquisite on Miss Willoughby—perhaps a nip taken in here and there, and we will lower the hem." The woman took another up and down look at Cate. "Evening slippers and gloves can be dyed to match. She swept her gaze around the salon's displays. "Something in a pale buttercream . . ." Madame's gaze lingered on a yellow gown.

Finn could not hold back a tease, "Madame, it seems you name your gowns after sweets in a confectioner's shop."

*"Exactement."* The brazen women winked at him.

He nodded toward the front of the salon. "I very much admire the dress in the window."

"It will cost you, monsieur; it is the loveliest in the shop."

Finn turned to Cate. "Rather rude of me to not ask if

you had a preference, Miss Willoughby. There are several others—"

"The violet gown is lovely," Cate interrupted with a smile. When he lifted a brow, she answered with soft laughter. "Honestly, it is my favorite." The look he received took his breath away. There was something in those twinkling eyes he had not seen from her in . . . a very long time.

As an established bachelor, he had been the recipient of these kinds of stolen looks before. They invariably caused him to run in the opposite direction, as they generally included feminine designs, most often involving expectations of promise. So, why was it different with Cate? Now that he had caught a glimpse of affection in her eye, he was certain he would long for another, even chase after it.

Madame turned her attentions to him. "So tall and well muscled, I do not expect any of the tailors in town will have a sample large enough to fit a man of"—the brazen woman took the opportunity to shift her gaze from his chest to his crotch—"your measurements." The woman shot him a look seldom seen outside of bawdy houses. She swept a curtain back, revealing two young women bent over sewing machines in a dim, stuffy workroom. "This is our busiest season. From now through the end of the year, there are many gala social events. I hope you are prepared to pay, monsieur."

CATE HUDDLED AGAINST Finn under the door awning as rain pelted the sidewalk outside Madame Gagelin's shop. The landau waited in the street with its top up. Their driver, an Indian chap named Kieran, held an umbrella overhead, and they made a dash for the vehicle. Finn spoke to the driver as he steadied her climb into the carriage. "Le Richelieu, *s'il vous plaît*." He ducked inside and sat across the aisle, stretching his legs, as best he could. His gaze darted here and there before settling squarely on her face. He cleared his throat. "Well, that was . . . harrowing."

"More for you, I expect." Cate was in the mood to do a bit of goading. "I had no idea a fitting could be such a titillating adventure." She tilted her chin. "In fact, I don't believe I have ever seen anyone quite so—"

"Groped about, publicly?" Finn snorted. His sense of humor had certainly returned.

"You were blushing, Monsieur Curzon." Cate purred in a French accent, "Thirty-five and a half inches!" She fell back onto the carriage seat as if in a faint. She peeked at him and exhaled an exaggerated sigh.

"I believe it was that last inside seam measurement of Madame's that raised all the trouble." He added a charming boyish grin. "Saucy minx."

Awkward moments were rare for this man, and yet Finn had never seemed more adorable to her. Still, it wouldn't do to let him off too easily. She righted herself, tucked her arms under her chest and slowly narrowed her eyes. "French women are sluts."

"Ah, you know this for a fact." Amused by her remark, his grin widened. "Am I to understand you are a possessive woman?"

Cate shrugged a shoulder. "You imply that I'm the jealous sort, which might have some basis in truth, *if* I were spoken for, which I am not."

"I'm quite sure you could be *spoken for* if you wished it so."

She returned his gaze rather intently. "Mercifully, I do not aspire to home and hearth." Finn's eyes darkened and intensified. The carriage slowed as they arrived in front of the hotel. She had expected him to say, "What a relief, nor do I." But there were no such words forthcoming.

Exiting the coach, Finn whisked her up the hotel stairs and behind one of the pillars holding up the portico. He yanked her close. "Perhaps you just haven't been asked by the right man," he practically growled. A lock of wet hair fell over his forehead and a drop of rain landed on her cheek. His gaze moved from her lips to the wet spot below her eye. He kissed the raindrop away, then moved to her mouth. She was expecting a long, sensuous, open-mouthed kiss that would leave her all tingly and breathless, except that she was already tingly and breathless.

No kiss. No words. He found her hand and twined his fingers with hers. Easing back, he tugged gently and walked her inside the hotel.

*"Mes amis!"* Sylvain leaped up from the wing chair in the lobby and waved them over to a comfortable corner. "I have already reserved a room." The Frenchman dangled a brass key.

"Since I no doubt I paid for this bottle," Finn whisked the cognac off the side table, "which way to the room?"

"With a view—*fantastique!*" The man swept both arms to one side, inviting them to walk ahead.

Sylvain escorted them up several flights of stairs and opened the door to a grand suite. Cate's mouth dropped open. "My word, this is divine."

After a look around the spacious suite, Cate opened a door in an alcove off the bedchamber. "A private water closet."

Finn tipped the bellboy who brought up their luggage, and Cate saw the young man out. At the door she asked for a lady's maid to be sent up.

"I see that as long as we're on Her Majesty's tanner, you spared no expense, Sylvain." Finn pivoted in place as he surveyed the comfortable parlor area.

"Ah ha! Queen Victoria received a cut in room rate, compliments of Sylvain Robideaux. And this suite is worth every sou, monsieur." The Frenchman pulled back a damask drape to reveal a most startling view of the Citadel.

Finn blew a soft whistle and stepped onto an expanse of balcony. He gestured for Cate to follow. "The rain has abated, but watch yourself—the floor titles may be slippery." He held on to her hand as they took in the startling sight of the fortress. "A man could map the entire prison grounds from here. Time the watch. Notate the daily routines—schedules."

Sylvain joined them on the terrace. "This view, in combination with an ancient map demarcating secret entrances and exits, would afford such a man a very intimate knowledge of the fortress."

Finn appeared fascinated by a section of parapet walk behind crenellated walls. "You have a set of fortress defense plans?"

A sly smile crossed Sylvain's face. "A copy of the original—the only one in existence." Their mysteriously resourceful host exhaled a self-satisfied sigh. "You have the suite for the duration."

Finn tore his eyes off the prison grounds. "What duration?"

"The convict ship does not sail as usual. They claim the ship undergoes repair work. Word on the street says they await a late delivery of prisoners." Sylvain followed them back inside the suite. "This is most unusual, as the ship to my knowledge has never been delayed for prisoners."

Finn found three glasses in a cabinet by the table and poured them each a cognac. They warmed their innards with French brandy, ordered room service, and waited for dinner to arrive. A tap on the door produced a lady's maid, and Finn raised a brow. "Why?" he questioned.

She swept a few errant wisps into her topknot as she rose from the table. "For my hair."

Finn angled his head back. "Your hair looks . . . adequate."

Cate kissed the top of his head. "Glad you understand, dear." She winked at Sylvain and exited the room.


FINN ALMOST CRACKED a smile, but for the bevy of other servants that followed the young maid into the suite. Some set the table, others moved to the terrace. He tilted his head to look out the French doors. Outside, the hotel help swept water off the balcony and into a rain gutter. As they dried off table and chairs, Finn dug in his pocket for additional tip money.

Sylvan shifted in his seat. "You play the role of a person of influence well, monsieur."

Finn studied the curiously well-connected man. "Here's a theory." He sank into a wing chair and crossed a booted leg. "International prisoners are difficult to prosecute, especially terrorists; they're often wanted in several countries."

"Extradition can become a contentious matter." Sylvain toyed with his empty glass.

Finn swirled a last swallow of brandy around in his glass. "Messy, to be sure. For one thing, anarchists aren't exactly covered by the Geneva convention."

Sylvain leaned forward. "They are not prisoners of war, so what are they?"

"More like criminals with a cause. There have been rumors of late that a few governments, France in particular, are beginning to capture and hold foreign anarchists, either for future trades with other governments, or even more insidious, for transport to offshore prisons—rid the world of the troublesome rubbish."

"Many years ago, the Citadel was renowned for its political prisoners, monsieur." Sylvain proceeded to relate several instances of men being held who happened to be on the wrong side of one political imbroglio or another.

Finn swallowed the last of his cognac. "One rather glaring problem is the detainee's anonymity. No habeas corpus. No trial at all, in most cases. No records of their capture, or their incarceration. I dislike the idea of a conspiracy, particularly one perpetrated by powerful men of influence and sanctioned by—"

A knock at the door signaled dinner had arrived. Sylvain grinned. *"Huîtres, poulet rôti, et une tarte de pomme."*

"Shall I translate?" A newly coifed Cate had returned to the table. She picked up one dish cover after another. "Fresh oysters, roast chicken—" She inhaled. "And an apple tart—what lovely fare."

Finn offered her a chair. Soft waves had been artfully wound into an elegant topknot. "Quite a pretty poof you've got there, mademoiselle."

Sylvain broke off a chicken leg and waved au revoir.

Finn straightened. "You're leaving?"

"I must return to La Flotte, clean the lantern, light the lamp, and prime the clockworks." He bit into a crispy piece of skin and chewed. *"Délicieux.* I leave you to eat, dress for the soiree, and plot against warden Moreau, *oui?"* He bowed as he backed out the door. *"Bonsoir, mes amis!"*

Finn carved the bird, while Cate set out the plate of oysters. Having grown used to the near-constant chatter from their Île de Ré guide, she found the room quiet, but not uncomfortably so. She had also rekindled a fire in her belly for the man sitting across the table. Wherever Phineas Gunn went, it seemed, adventure followed. But there were other things he did, quite expertly, to cause her cheeks to blush. And there was something else—she felt protected by him, as well as valued. There was a word for that.

Apreciado *en español*.

The English word was *cherished*.

Right on cue, heat swept over her cheeks. Finn studied her quietly. "Your hair is lovely. Sorry I was so boorish about it earlier. You have my permission to stab me with your fork if it makes you feel better."

"That bit of grousing earlier?" Cate popped a baby carrot into her mouth and rolled her eyes. "Uncle, as well as *mi abuelo*, my Spanish grandfather—big grousers. I have put up with it for years. Doesn't perturb me in the least." She smiled a wily sort of smile at him.

He met her gaze for a moment. "And what of our mercurial lighthouse keeper?" He added a few more roasted vegetables to both their plates. "If instincts serve, beyond the jocular, hairy laddishness, there may lurk another Sylvain Robideaux."

Cate looked up from her plate. "Friendly or not so . . . ?"

"Not sure, as yet." Finn spooned a bit of jus over slices of breast meat. "He moves freely around the town. Well connected and well liked, it would seem. It's just—" Finn forked up a piece of chicken. "He strikes me as a man who might very well work both sides of the angle."

"No surprise there; Dé Riquet recommended him."

Finn nodded. "Sylvain has been invaluable thus far—perhaps too much so."

"You think he's steering us." Cate set fork and knife down. "What do you recommend?" she asked through a particularly delicious bite of chicken.

"For now, keep eating." Finn uncorked a fruity golden wine, which turned out to be a delightful accompaniment to a slice of apple tart.

After dinner, they took bottle and glasses into the sitting area of the suite. Finn sat beside her on the settee, hooked a finger into a waistcoat pocket, and read his watch. "Our wardrobe should arrive any time now."

He settled an arm around her. "Do you mind?"

She snuggled up against his shoulder. "I should like another war story, please."

"Ah, my dear Cate—war is a gruesome, dismal business. If there is any glory in killing, I have yet to find it." Finn sipped his wine. "Even a trained soldier cannot imagine the horror of it, not until you're caught up in an ambush, surrounded by fallen comrades—dead or crying out in pain—the unseen enemy taking shots at you from hidden positions in the hills."

She placed her cheek against his chest. "Your heart is racing. In London, Lady Lennox made reference to some sort of battle fatigue, as did Cecil." She sat up and turned to him. "If you don't mind my asking, what is the condition you suffer, Finn? Something happened to you in India—in the Northern Territories."

A part of him wanted her to know. Hardy was aware of some of it, his quack doctor had wrung out more of the story, but Cate—there was something about her that made him feel like confessing. He wondered if he would get to a certain place in the story and shut down—"suppressed memories" is what Monty had called them.

"All right." He stared at her. "But perhaps it would be best if I didn't look at you directly." Finn set his glass down on a side table and pulled her back close to his chest with both arms. "It's been called everything from extreme cowardice to battle fatigue to Soldier's Heart—quite a romantic notion, that last one."

Cate scoffed softly. "I can't imagine anyone having the nerve to call you a coward. They obviously haven't seen you perform your duties."

Finn rubbed the side of her head with his chin. "I was often sent out on patrol. Mostly we were looking for any signs of tribal movements. We knew Al Qui tari Masari was amassing an army and would likely attack the fort. The only question was when. We got into a bloody skirmish west of Kandahar and suffered several casualties. I delayed our retreat to pick up our injured—suddenly we were surrounded, and taken prisoner.

"We were held in a Pashtun village up in the mountains. As the highest-ranking officer alive, I was kept in a deep hole, underground. Each night I listened to the sound of my men being tortured. In the morning, they would lower a ladder—walk me by soldiers tied up and ready for execution."

His entire body began to tremble, just the slightest involuntary vibration. Her leg muscles quivered in a similar fashion after rehearsal. Cate sat up and turned to make eye contact. His gaze was fixed on a memory buried deep in his past.

"Blocks of wood were placed into their throats so they could not swallow. Stop me if it gets too—"

"I'm not the squeamish sort—please go on," Cate said softly.

"Then the tribal women took turns urinating into their open mouths." He inhaled a long raspy breath. "They suffocated—or drowned. Not sure which term to use . . ."

"Dear God." She grabbed hold of him.

"Sorry, I'm experiencing some dizziness, a bit of vertigo," he said. His arm dropped to her waist and she clung to him. Strong arms throbbing with life wrapped around her. He rocked her, for what seemed like a very long time.

Cate snuggled against him. "But you survived, Finn."

"Yes, I survived eight days and nights of interrogation, torture—"

"Were you injured?"

"Nothing like the men under me. Beatings mostly—and a hot metal rod jabbed at me. You've seen the scars on my chest. Not sure why they didn't kill me. At one point, most of their fighters left the village—off to ambush a search party sent after us. It turned out to be a lucky break for me and the few men still alive. We escaped that night."

"A daring rescue, no doubt." Cate tucked her legs up under her skirt. "This requires more wine, sir, as I need to be fortified for the next chapter of this adventure."

Finn marveled at Cate's response to such a lurid story. Her resilient spirit, her bravery. He knew full well that she had nearly become ill over its telling. Even all these years later, he was as good as sick over it himself. But somehow, he had choked out the horrific details of those terrible executions—something he had only done once, years ago. He had given a complete accounting of his patrol's capture and detainment to his commanding officer. Colonel Brown and several other officers had listened intently, stopping on only one occasion—for a bit of fresh air.

He dipped his chin and narrowed his eyes. "You sure you want to hear more?"

"The telling of your escape? I wouldn't miss it." Her blazing blue eyes were large and liquid. She squeezed his hand in encouragement.

"All right then." He inhaled a breath and exhaled slowly. "The screams and cries would begin as soon as the sun went down. To keep from going mad, I occupied myself digging footholds in the side of the old well they kept me in. The walls were lined with uneven stones held together with a bit of crude mortar—mostly mud. I must have been about eighteen feet down. Every night I tore at the crumbling sand and rock."

"Tricky work, to say nothing of the fall you might have taken."

Once again Finn pulled her close. "I did fall—twice." She settled into the warmth of his body. "That night I grasped at anything for a leg up. If I could escape the bloody pit, I knew the layout of the village well enough to make an attempt to free the men. Worst case, we could fight our way out and get killed in the process."

"The latter being preferable to the kind of death that awaited if you did not escape." Cate murmured her thoughts aloud.

"I had another six feet left to climb—enough to get a shoulder aboveground, so I could lift myself out of the shaft." Finn swallowed a sip of wine.

Cate angled away to look back. "Whatever you do, don't stop now, or I shall bite my fingernails."

"I only fell once that night—wrenched my ankle but it made no matter. I would have run the fifteen miles back to the fort on a broken leg. I remember poking my head up out of the hole, thinking, 'They'll shoot my head off,' and not caring if they did. As it turned out, all that was left of the tribe's warriors were a few guards, elders, and the women and children.

"A second bit of luck was it was pitch-black; the moon had set. Once I was out of the hole, I managed to crawl behind a barrier—part tent, part hovel. A row of horses were tethered to a line—including the big red lad."

Cate straightened. "Sergeant MacGregor."

Finn nodded. "I swear to you, Cate, seeing that horse nearly brought tears to my eyes—and there were a few more of our mounts there. I fished about in the dark for our tack. Much of it was strewn around the back of the shelter. I managed to bit up three horses, then I set off to find my men.

"Circling the village I came across a branch of timber, something the size of a cricket bat, which I took up as I came upon a small house—*khaneh* they call them. There was a guard at the door. I took the man out with a crack to the back of his neck and dragged the body inside the hut. Inching forward, I could just make out several bodies lying prone on sleeping mats—likely my men—and then I was jumped from behind. My assailant had a knife to my throat, leaving me only one thing to do."

"And that was?" she rasped.

"I ran backward as fast and as hard as I could, hoping to crush the man behind me into a wall—leastwise, before he had a chance to slit my throat."

"I've seen that scar, as well." Cate's hand moved through his beard stubble and down the side of his neck. Gently, she traced a thin, curved line that ran in a crescent shape toward his throat.

Finn caught her hand in his and brought her wrist to his mouth, pressing his lips to her pulse.

She swallowed. "You got your men out."

"I left the fort with a dozen soldiers and returned with less than half that number."

"You cannot blame yourself, you—"

"I was responsible for their lives, Cate. Do I blame myself for getting captured? Absolutely. Should I have abandoned those injured men—after the ambush?" Finn ran a hand through his hair. "I've been over it a thousand times and have not seen another choice in the matter. I could never have left those men behind."

Her eyes were large and round. "You did the right thing."

He frowned. "Outside of my commanders, I have never told anyone the details of the capture—until now." Gently, he turned her to him. "I should not have subjected you to such a savage accounting of war. I cannot think why I did such a thing."

Cate lifted both hands to his face and kissed him softly. "As for telling me your story—I am not shocked so much as saddened that you took so long to speak of it. Holding all those cruel memories inside." She shook her head gently. "I'm not sure how a person gets over such an event. The relentless fear, the chilling brutality, the constant uncertainty and terror. What is praiseworthy is that you have fared as well as you have—on your own—all these years."

Finn let the moment between them sink in. She had not shrunk from him, nor looked at him with pity, judging the damaged soldier that sat beside her. She had stayed and listened—even admired him. Just for good measure, Finn inhaled and exhaled slowly. And he had managed to get through the whole tale, beginning to end, without dissolving into a debilitating attack of nerves.

*Inhale. Exhale.*

Perhaps he did feel less burdened and less alone for the telling. He reached over and covered her hand with his.

"The trembling has stopped." Her smile brightened. "A good sign, is it not?"

He tipped her chin up. "Never in my life have I—"

A sharp rap on the door could only mean one thing: the delivery from Madame Gagelin's had arrived. He sighed rather loudly. Still, he was determined to finish his thought. "You are quite the most extraordinary young lady."

"As extraordinary as you, *señor. Eres mi héroe.*"

Finn raised a brow. "Now that is a tall order."

## ∞ Chapter Twenty-four

Even in the cool darkness of the carriage, Cate could feel her cheeks burn. Finn could make her blush like a school-girl. And he was the only man in the world, it seemed, who could do it. She had emerged from the bedchamber in the hotel suite, and he had risen from a wing chair. His gaze had taken in everything—from the toe of her laven-der slipper to the amethyst-colored crystals pinned in her hair. He had asked for a pirouette in dancer's language—*adagio*—and she had turned a slow pivot. When she re-turned to him, his gaze had turned feral, with eyes that glowed like a cat in the dark. It was the kind of look that made her wish the evening was not beginning, but about to end—in the large four-poster in the bedchamber. She had imagined her new gown being removed slowly, with soft caresses down her back from that generous mouth of his.

He had whisked her downstairs, past the turning heads in the lobby. Into the waiting carriage and into his arms. He kissed her hard, a ravaging kiss that took possession of her mouth and demanded more. Their tongues lashed and chased, softening into a lingering caress. She could feel his breath on her face. "You are a goddess." He slanted his mouth over hers again. "You are much adored . . ." He added the slightest tease of tongue. "And you are entirely too tempting."

A flicker of gaslight swept inside the carriage. The look in his eyes caused a quiver, one of those womanly shudders in the belly that made her want to couple with him. Have his children. Her cheeks burned with the thought.

He angled his mouth above hers. "Another kiss like that and I'm afraid I'll shred the lovely violet gown I paid more than a hundred francs for—"

"She had us over a barrel." She glimpsed a grin in the dark. "Though I suppose Madame Gagelin did move heaven and earth for us."

"She certainly managed to make of bit of heaven for you, Cate."

"And you as well, Agent Curzon—I will remember to call you Hugh now."

"That would be *very* helpful." He leaned back into the comfortable squabs of the carriage seat. "Shall we prepare a few strategies on our way to the reception? In this situation, perhaps we should try to keep our story as close to the truth as possible. The truth can be as persuasive as the best-contrived scheme, and no one ever expects it." Finn went on to outline several other scenarios, including the promise of favors. "My advice to female operatives is to never offer favors, not unless you are prepared to deliver them, and then, only as a last resort." Finn's gaze remained cool, in control—almost aloof.

She stared at him. "Do you still believe I'm some sort of agent working undercover?"

Finn dipped his head to peer out the carriage window.

"First we complete this mission. Then we get out alive. Then we discuss who works for whom."

Cate was careful not to disavow too insistently or act offended. "And if it is the man who propositions the favors . . . ?" Her question trailed off as she met his gaze.

Finn's handsome face darkened considerably. "You listen to the offer, then you use your wiles to delay—hold him off." Her undercover operative and lover seemed a bit rattled, and adorably so. She reached up and ran her fingers along his jawline to his chin.

He caught a finger and brought it up to his lips. "Should someone blow our cover story—hardly a remote possibility at this juncture, as the chargé d'affaires likely wired an inquiry to the Foreign Office—just follow my lead, like dancing the bolero." He dipped his head to peer out the coach window once more. "We have arrived."

They exited the carriage and were escorted to hall entrance. "Let's make this less painful, shall we?" Finn turned to his reception line duties and greeted their host and hostess, the Lieutenant Governor and his wife. *"Ravi d'être présent, belle soirée."* He pulled her out of line and skipped ahead until she was back in front of Adrian Fortesque. "Such a lovely evening, thank you for inviting us."

"The pleasure is all"—clearly enraptured, Adrian's gaze lowered down her décolleté—"mine, Miss Willoughby."

Finn addressed the honoree. "Delighted to attend, Mr. Fortesque." The man turned away from Cate reluctantly and nodded. "Mr. Curzon." Finn was about to move past when Fortesque raised a finger and leaned in to speak in hushed tones. "After toasts, might you and Miss Willoughby join me to discuss a . . . private matter?"

Finn tried to read him. "In the study?"

Adrian nodded to the woman in line behind Finn. That would be a yes, in foreign service nonspeak. He caught up to Cate. "Ah, we're in luck—the champagne has arrived." Finn lifted two flutes from a silver salver and handed one to Cate.

"What went on between you and Mr. Fortesque?"

"Our first intrigue of the evening. The chargé d'affaires, *ad interim*, wishes to see us privately after the toasts."

"Is this good news or bad?"

"Hard to know—the foreign service are a cagey lot."

Cate smiled her wily half smile. "Nothing like their undercover agents."

Finn scanned the room. "Amongst all the flora and fauna, might we try to find a serpent?" He led her onto the terrace, and they quickly settled into a dark corner. "Drink up." He encouraged her to take a sip of champagne and then stuffed their glasses in one of the potted shrubs.

"Someone with a cane standing by the pianoforte." Cate wrinkled her nose. "A bit too plump for our man. I envision someone a bit more—"

"Beady-eyed, long thin nose, hair slicked back, sporting a goatee . . ." Finn turned her slightly.

Her scan of the room halted on an olive-skinned man of medium stature, somewhat broad-chested with rather severe lines to his countenance. "Swarthy. Looks sinister enough." She took a second look. The man appeared a great deal less ominous when conversing. "He's likely the local schoolmaster."

"A headmaster with a shiny black walking stick?" Finn's breath lifted the small hairs on the back of her neck. "Shall we see if he slithers?"

*"Mesdames et messieurs."* The high-pitched clinking of a spoon to a crystal glass signaled the call for a toast. Finn

procured more champagne and raised his glass. "Cheers—
*à votre santé!*" He angled Cate in front of him as Fortesque
began his greeting. The man's French was as halting and
strangely cadenced as his speech was in English.

"Every time the man speaks I feel like I'm back at university, having to sit through a good stiff reading of *King
Lear*," he said.

Cate purposely backed up to Finn. He bent forward.
"Yes, darling?"

"You're right, it is Moreau." She nodded toward a small
cluster of guests as bony fingers caressed the serpent-
handled cane. She shivered and Finn squeezed her hand.

Fortesque concluded with a few words of gratitude and
disappeared into the crowd. "I believe we have an appointment in the library." Finn opened a side door and slipped
her into a narrow passageway. The circuitous route took
them through several pantries and a bustling kitchen.

*"Pardonnez-nous, la bibliothèque?"* She smiled sweetly
at the harried waiter who graciously opened several doors
and showed them out into the main corridor of the governor's palace.

Finn raised her hand to his lips. "Thank you, darling."

Cate hurried her pace to keep up with him. "Why do
gentlemen not simply ask directions?"

His only answer was a slight upturn at the edge of his
mouth. He stopped at a door and knocked.

*"Entrez."*

Finn stuck his head in the door. Fortesque stood
near the window in his usual corner of the room, hands
behind his back, only this time he faced them. Cate
stepped through the opening and Finn closed the door
quietly.

"Mr. Curzon, Miss Willoughby." Adrian studied them

both briefly. "I shall get right to the point. Say nothing to anyone regarding the offer in your documents."

Finn squared his shoulders. "Why?"

"Because I am in possession of *similar* documents." Fortesque narrowed his eyes. "Authentic ones." The stoic emissary moved to the desk. "No doubt these papers of yours were something you cooked up over at Special Branch. You will hand them over." The man waited patiently, palm open.

Finn removed an envelope from his inside pocket. "Whether we use your papers or mine, does it really matter? The last time I checked, we both work for the same side."

Fortesque's gaze darted to Cate. "And Miss Willoughby?"

Finn dropped the packet on the desktop. "She has agreed to see her brother returned to England to answer charges."

In one swift move, Fortesque opened a drawer, swept the envelope inside, and slammed it shut. Impressively done—and surprising for such a deliberative man, who continued to stare at her. He raised a brow. "Is this true, Miss Willoughby?"

Cate swallowed. "I have agreed to such an arrangement. Though it saddens me to think of my brother imprisoned anywhere, I do believe he will receive fair treatment by the British government."

Finn took a careful look about the room. "With whom have you been in communication? Salisbury's crew or Castlemaine's?

Fortesque's gaze moved to Finn. "Yes, I understand you work for both the Foreign Office and the Home Office."

"And the Admiralty." Finn returned an equally imperious gaze of his own. "On occasion."

Cate bit back a grin. The chargé d'affaires nearly always appeared taxed beyond reason—no matter the occurrence. Fortesque bit out the words, "And . . . naval intelligence."

The British emissary's eyes rolled upward. "In a few minutes, the director from the French Ministry of Justice, as well as the prison warden, will knock on the door." Fortesque unfolded a wire message and donned a pair of reading glasses. "I have been directed to make an offer for two prisoners held in a building known as the old cellblock.

"An anarchist by the name of Nicolas Crowe—" As he spoke, Fortesque glanced at Finn over the rim of his spectacles. "In actuality, he is one of ours. A counterinsurgency informant by the name of Graham 'Gray' Chamberlain." Fortesque's gaze moved over to her. "And a Spanish anarchist, risen from the dead—Eduardo de Dovia."

She could not stop the rush of tears that welled up. "Eduardo is alive," she whispered and collapsed into Finn's arms.

He moved her to a chair and handed her a pocket square. Leaning in close, he tilted her chin and spoke softly. "I'm proud of you, Cate, you didn't give up." She smiled through tears. "Have a sniffle or two, then dry your eyes." He winked. "We have work to do."

Fortesque cleared his throat. "I am prepared to confront the prison officials on behalf of the Crown, and present the offer for an exchange of prisoners."

Finn straightened. "They'll just deny they have men in custody."

"Quite. Impossible." The British emissary appeared

unruffled. "I have obtained a copy of the convict ship's manifesto, with said prisoners . . . listed." The man's grin appeared closer to a sneer. "By name."

"Well then, you've no need of our services." He pivoted to Cate. "Shall we make it an early night, Miss Willoughby?"

"Hold on." Fortesque stepped around the desk. "I'll put the press on Moreau, but we need to keep it on."

Finn's eyes flicked upward. She knew that look. He was conjuring a plan. "Introduce Miss Willoughby as exactly who she is. I'll play the amiable cousin escort." He turned to her. "You are thrilled to hear your brother is alive. Press Moreau to let you meet with Eduardo tomorrow."

Cate moistened her lips and nodded.

"Just look at those lovely eyes gleam—such an adventuress." She caught Finn's wink of encouragement.

A sharp rap came at the door. "That would be the warden." In no rush to answer, the chargé d'affaires straightened to his full height. There was a certain unflappability about the man, she'd give him that.

"One moment," Fortesque called out as he pivoted toward her. "Make the appointment for the morning. We've only got tomorrow to get the exchange accomplished. The convict ship leaves on the evening tide—with or without your brother."

*Chapter Twenty-five*

$O$utside the Governor's Palace, a wispy layer of fog covered the drive. Finn handed Cate up into the carriage. The meeting with Moreau had been mercifully brief, owing mainly to an urgent message the warden had received. He had left the meeting in haste, but not before settling a lingering kiss on Cate's hand. She had also received a most cordial invitation to the Citadel, to meet again in the morning.

Finn climbed into the carriage and reached across Cate to tug down a window shade. In doing so, he brushed against her and the scent of lavender soap filled the air. On second thought, he decided to leave the window uncovered, capture whatever moonlight filtered through the cloud drifts.

He wanted to see the pretty beige nipple as he lifted her breast above her décolleté. His gaze lingered as cool air hardened the tip. Slowly, almost reluctantly, his eyes met hers. "I've waited over a year for you—for this," he said. She answered him with a soft gasp, and arched a hard peak into his mouth. He swirled and suckled ravenously.

He uncovered the other breast and plucked the rosebud lightly between his fingers.

His hand slid down her body and gathered up her skirt, baring her upper thighs. He yanked her dress up around her waist and met her gaze. "I need to be inside you, Cate," he rasped, his voice thickened by lust. She spread her legs, giving him the access he wanted.

Finn stroked the soft inner flesh of her thighs above her garters. He kept his fingers patient, gentle. He would heighten her arousal to match his own. He slipped his hand through the slit in her pantalets and into moist folds. He watched her eyelids flutter as two fingers penetrated gently, then slid deep inside. He used his thumb to swirl over the center of her pleasure. She moaned, and of her own volition, straddled him.

He was hard as a stone and ready to take her. "Unbutton me, love."

Deftly, she opened his pants and drew him out. She stroked lightly at first and then tighter. She varied her grip and then added a bit of fingernail. He sucked in air through his teeth. The little minx was getting good at this.

Pushing up her petticoats, he opened the satin slit of her pantalets and pressed into her glorious velvet sheath. Planting himself deep, he paused and let the carriage rock them both into a state of greater arousal. "Miss Willoughby."

She licked the underside of his top lip. "Yes, Agent Gunn?"

"Might I take you quite roughly? As long as I make it up to you once we are back in the hotel?"

Her lips parted as she exhaled softly. "You may." His kiss muffled her answer, and his tongue tangled and swirled with hers. He dropped his head, kissing her neck and then lower, to bite the skin of her shoulder. Nipping at a breast, he rolled a hard tip between his teeth. The carriage hit a pothole in the road and she cried out. Gently, he licked the raw spot and whispered apologies.

He was going to come quickly and she was gloriously aroused, nearing her own pleasure. He steadied her hips above him and thrust into her like some kind of lust-crazed beast. On the edge of climax he stopped himself. He rested his forehead against her chest. His breath rasped over the firm flesh of her breasts. "Don't move a muscle."

"Pistol cocked, Mr. Gunn?"

"Ready to fire, Miss Willoughby." Finn lifted his chin and met those glorious sapphire eyes in the dark. "And no rubber goods." He lay his head back against the plush carriage seat and waited for the right moment to withdraw from her.

"Is there anything I might . . . do?"

A slow grin tugged at the edges of his mouth. "Come to think of it—that last whisper of yours in my ear at the palace. Something about a bit of lolly for the old tosser?"

"It would be one way to relieve your discontent." She darted sultry eyes at him. Her lips were puffy—swollen from kissing. He made a note to himself to kiss her hard and often. A picture came to mind: Cate's mouth exploring, taking all of him.

He dipped his head for a look out the window. The hotel was just ahead. He slumped back onto comfortable squabs and took in the delightful dishabille of her. She sat astride him, a glorious Catalan demigoddess. Her breasts were fully exposed, nipples peaked from his attentions. A mass of waves tumbled from her hair arrangement, but no matter; the more disheveled the better. For tonight, she was all his. "Change of plans. Would you mind terribly if I asked the driver to take us on a longer drive?"

A BRUSH OF derriere roused his cock and stirred Finn from a deep sleep. He opened an eye. Daybreak streamed into the bedchamber through a slit in the draperies. He was aware of Cate's soft breathing and the scent of her skin close by. He lifted the covers. She slept quietly beside him, in all her naked splendor. In answer to the chill in the air, she tucked herself into the warmth of his body. His hand went around the lissome, oh-so-flexible torso and pulled her against his lower parts.

"Good morning, Miss Willoughby." He kissed a smooth bare shoulder.

She uttered a soft "Mm-mm" and turned onto her back. Finn propped himself on an elbow to look at her, allowing his gaze to linger on her luscious mouth. Her eyes remained closed, while the loveliest smile appeared, as though she could sense she was under scrutiny. "Do you inspect the little mole on my cheek, or search for a stray, unplucked eyebrow hair?"

"There is the slightest chip on one front tooth that is about to set me upon you again. Shall we reprise last night?" He dipped his head and sucked a nipple into his mouth. He let it go with a pop. "'Mon Dieu, mon Dieu— don't stop,'" he teased, mimicking her cries of pleasure.

Cate stretched like a cat, and he slid his hand over ribs, barely felt, to cup her breast. "Does everyone call out, 'God, oh God,' in the heat of coupling?"

"Depends on who is doing the lovemaking, I suppose." Pale golden rays poured across the unkempt bed, warming their skin. Finn pressed against her and she opened her legs slowly, inviting him in. He smiled. "I believe a part of God swells below."

The lovemaking was quick to come to a finish, at least for Finn. He nuzzled the base of her throat. "It appears I am as randy as schoolboy for you." Gently, with one hand on the rubber goods, he slid his cock from her. He moved his hand between her legs and stroked her inner folds, circling the place that made her shiver and arch upward. She thrust her breasts toward his mouth and he dipped his head, happy to nibble. He stroked faster and increased pressure to the spot that made her moan unintelligible words of encouragement. Like *now*.

His mouth released a rosy pink nipple. "Are you saying you want more?" A flood of moisture met his fingers as he moved them inside her.

"*Más, por favor,*" she moaned. He delved deeper inside, then pulled out, playing at the edges of her opening. She answered him by arching her back and thrusting her hips.

"You came for me twice last night." He could feel her arousal soar to a new level. "Give me another, Cate. Come for me now." A flush rose up her chest and her expression looked as if she was barely aware of the world. There was something delightful, even joyful about watching her surrender to pleasure. Using patient manipulations, he brought her to gasping climax, then he kissed her trembling belly.

Gently, he rolled her onto her side, and she wrapped her legs around him. Her body shuddered once more and he soothed her with his hands. He ran his fingers down the small of her back and over the curve of her bottom, drawing out her *après l'amour* moment of bliss. She peeked out from the soft linen folds to smile at him. "Mm-m-m," was all she managed, but it was exactly what he needed to hear.

A muffled thud and the squeak of a serving cart filtered into their room. Finn sat up and pulled the covers over Cate. "*Mes amis!* I have arrived with *café et croissants*. A good start, *oui?*" The Frenchman poked his head in their bedchamber.

"Sylvain." Finn grunted.

Cate's answer came from under the covers. "Who else would it be?"

"The waiter is still here—shall I order something more?"

Cate sat up, holding the sheet over her breasts. "A sauté of eggs, please, and plenty of rashers fried crispy."

Propped on his elbows, Finn admired her shapely back and dimpled rump. He nodded to Sylvain. "Order enough for all of us."

The moment the door closed, Cate sprang out of bed and opened the door a crack. "Oh, and hot water, *pour le bain.*" She sat at the vanity and unpinned the rest of her hair.

"You could be a painting in an art gallery."

She brushed raven tresses, taking long strokes. "In Paris, Edgar Degas drew several sketches of me during rehearsal. He invited a few of us to his studio—to pose in the nude."

Finn rolled onto his side. "And did you?"

"I have a dancer's body, I am not ashamed of it." She looked at him through the mirror. "I can see you don't approve."

Finn tried to soften a growl. "I don't suppose I enjoy the thought of any man looking at you in such an intimate way."

"I was very young. This happened more than a year before we met in Barcelona. The artist was a perfect gentleman. I remained innocent"—she raised a brow—"until I met you, if you recall."

"I remember it well." Finn eyed her through the mirror.

A flush of color rose from her chest to her cheeks. She set her brush down and met his gaze. "How is it you are the only man who can make me blush this way?"

He rose from the bed, and she eyed his randy prick, at full tilt—again. "See what you do to me?" He leaned over, wrapping his arms around her silken flesh. Covering a breast with each hand, he let the image in the mirror do his speaking for him. *Mine*, it said. He met her gaze in the mirror.

He kissed her neck, the spot just behind her earlobe. "I have no idea why I turned into such a prig just then." A sheepish, apologetic grin surfaced. "Please forgive me."


BREAKFAST WAS DELICIOUS. "Glorious morning, wot? Let's hope the rest of the day goes as well." Finn spooned berry conserve onto a piece of croissant, and popped the warm bread into his mouth. Sated from a glorious night of lovemaking, he marveled at his good mood in the face of the tasks before them. "The meeting last night might have gone better—rather tight-lipped, the warden. And the other man—the director of justice . . ."

"Jean Luc Séverin," Cate offered.

He sipped his coffee and winked at her. "Very likely they're partners in this clandestine venture, which I suspect has little to do with justice." He studied the intrusive Frenchman, who was much more than a simple lighthouse keeper. "At least we got the warden to admit he is in custody of both anarchists." Finn sliced into a rasher. "Meek as he is, Moreau comes off as a right nasty chap—just as you observed."

"We have suspected him for years . . ." Sylvain pressed a fresh cup of coffee. "This side business of Moreau's—now it is confirmed."

The morning sun warmed the terrace patio. "Another French official with his hand out. What a surprise." Cate rolled her eyes as she forked up a bit of egg.

Sylvain poured them each another coffee. "Moreau's hand reaches into pockets in Spain, as well as Italy. But it likely doesn't stop there." He added steamed milk and a lump of sugar to his cup. "It is rumored the warden deals with the anarchists themselves, disposing of double agents, spies caught in the midst of anarchist organizations, like your Nicolas Crowe."

Cate exaggerated a shiver. "Horrid little man. I shudder to think of the kind of treatment prisoners receive."

"Then don't, Cate," Finn advised. "You're going to see your brother this morning. With a good deal of luck, and with the diplomatic press on, Moreau will release Eduardo to our custody by the afternoon." He eased back in his chair and narrowed his gaze on Sylvain. "I am curious about your use of the word *we*. Ever since Dé Riquet advised a respite in La Flotte, I have had my suspicions. Tell me, Sylvain, who are you besides a *gardien de phare* who dabbles in clockworks? And exactly who is included in this *we* of yours?"

Sylvain met his gaze. "Let us say, I am not quite as mercenary as Dé Riquet. This small island's prison—both its detainment and deportation service—has been under surveillance for many months now. You might call this a joint venture, between my government and yours. The chargé d'affaires had been planning a transaction of this very kind—"

"Then Miss Willoughby and I show up with nearly identical papers," Finn interjected, "offering a similar exchange of prisoners."

Sylvain rocked back and forth, adding a nod. "An odd coincidence, to be sure. You cannot blame us for doing a quick inquiry by wire. Not a simple thing in this town; the telegraph office reports any suspicious messages to foreign countries to the warden."

With the exception of a few overly expressive mannerisms, Sylvain Robideaux almost appeared sober. A slow grin crept over Finn's face. "Quite a cover act you've devised for yourself. Not a soul in town suspects, I imagine."

*"Un imbécile excentrique."* Sylvain winked. "As resident fool I move in and out of gatherings and events and rarely get stopped. Occasionally, I overhear things, like two anarchists being moved to the Citadel for transport overseas."

Finn slumped back in his chair. "So you were the source in the report. Two suspected anarchists being detained illegally in the Citadel at Île de Ré. You had already set this whole thing up with Fortesque, though I suppose Miss Willoughby fits neatly into your plans."

"As it turns out, invaluable. With Miss Willoughby here to attest to her brother's identity—they were forced to relent."

"Let us hope things continue to go our way." Finn sipped the last of his coffee. "I suppose it was either you or Dé Riquet who got hold of the ship's manifest?"

Sylvain waved both hands in the air. "Who else might acquire such a thing?"

As long as the Frenchman was talking, it was time to

press further. Finn rose from the table. "I want us to start working together, not at cross purposes. We share what we know from here forward. Agreed?"

The French operative nodded, and Finn entered the bedchamber. He came back with a pair of binoculars and a small tripod, which he set up on the table. "I'm not sending Cate into that meeting alone, not without a contingency plan." He adjusted the focus on the eyepiece for Sylvain, who edged over for a look.

"The prison is formidable, yes, but in effect, the Citadel was designed to keep the enemy out, not keep prisoners in." Sylvain glanced up above the binoculars and adjusted the tripod toward one of the structures in the center of the compound. "In point of fact there are many avenues out of the fort, both by land and by sea. In the event of a siege, every well-designed fortress must have ways to resupply— without the surrounding army's knowledge."

"You didn't by any chance bring that map of yours?" Finn asked.

"It's all up here." Sylvain pointed to his temple. "What would you like to know?"

"Everything."

## ∽ Chapter Twenty-six

"**I** do hope Warden Moreau will be less odious this morning." Cate's eyes fluttered upward. "The way he pranced about the room last night with that lewd sneer of his whenever he looked at me . . ." Deliberately setting aside her efforts to remain calm, she shivered. "Slithy man."

"Slithy? A bit on the mimsy side, if you ask me." Finn's gaze was rather affectionate. "The Jabberwocky will behave himself or answer to me."

She moved to kiss him and he leaned away. "*Non*, mademoiselle—lovemaking only as a reward for practice." Frustrated, she pinched him. "Ow—why do females pinch?" He was laughing. "My sister pinched."

Cate blinked. "You never mentioned a sister."

"Audrey died many years ago of a virulent meningitis. She was a snappish, bookish sort, always a bit frail. A crack wit and disarmingly charming when she wasn't torturing Hardy and me. We all doted on her." Slowly, the faraway look in his eyes was replaced by a wry grin. "She was a mighty distraction—just as you are, my dear."

Capturing both her hands, he pinned them to her sides.

The boldness of his action and the sheer proximity of him caused her pulse to elevate. He took his time. He did not kiss her mouth, but he came close. "Think of this as a dance rehearsal. You want the performance to come off well, don't you?"

"Of course I do." Cate thrust her lower lip out. "You don't believe they will allow me to see him, do you?"

The dark glimmer in his eyes settled on her lips. "I know I don't trust them." His gaze returned to hers. "I will do my best to accompany you into the meeting, but at some point, I suspect they will stop me. They'll have some excuse—one visitor per prisoner or the like. If I give them an argument they could toss one or both of us out. I want you to see your brother, so you will go on without me, but here are my rules:

"One: The moment you suspect something is wrong, ask to leave. Two: If they employ excuses—ask you to wait longer than a few minutes—leave. Three: If they threaten or touch you in any way . . ."

Cate nodded. "Leave."

He nodded. "And if you are suddenly overpowered—"

"No worry there. I'll scream bloody murder."

"If they cover your mouth, break objects, kick over furniture, *make noise*. I will get to you as fast as I possibly can."

Cate dipped her head. "And how, might I ask, will you overpower the guards?"

"Perhaps there won't be so many. Don't worry about me, Cate. Take care of yourself first. I'll find you one way or another."

"You have weapons on you—now?"

He rocked back, as if he was going to release her hands,

and then quite suddenly pressed his mouth to hers. He kissed her passionately, savagely, in a lingering, sensuous kiss. A kiss that caused her entire body to shudder. Her eyes opened to his heavy-lidded gaze. Her lips throbbed—puffy, no doubt. "I like kissing you—hard—so you can feel me hours later."

Oh, she could feel him all right. Lips, nipples, womb. It was a pleasant ache—a reminder of his passion, his expertise, and his magnificent *phallus erectus*.

He eased up on her arms. "I carry an assortment of guns and knives on me at all times. In fact . . ." He dug in his coat pocket and pulled out a small blade attached to a band of leather. He unbuttoned her sleeve and fastened the leather sheath to her wrist. "Leave a few buttons undone, in case you have to get to the blade quickly."

He had her remove the knife several times. "One last time. This time jab me with it, as quickly as you can."

She stared at him. "You are beginning to frighten me, Finn."

He dipped his head to peer out the window. The carriage turned into the single lane that led to the west entrance of the prison. He frowned. "A little fear is good. It will keep you on your toes."

Cate removed the knife and thrust it at him. He stopped her hand and moved her fist higher, toward his face. "A slash to the torso won't stop a man driven by madness or lust. Aim for an eye or the brow above. A good cut will send blood pouring and obstruct his vision." Finn gave her a nod, and a wink of encouragement. "Once more."

Cate looked to the side, out the coach window, then lunged at him with the blade. He arched backward and caught her wrist. "You employed a feint." He slipped the knife back into the sheath on her wrist and settled down beside her. "I believe that makes you dangerous enough, Miss Willoughby."

The carriage slowed and turned into a parking yard. "Why are we not driving inside the gates?" Cate asked.

"Security." Finn opened the door and helped her down. "They have to stop and search every vehicle in and out of the fortress."

Cate craned her neck to see the top of the bastion walls. "I can only imagine how one might get in or out of here once they lock up."

Finn gripped her arm a little tighter than usual. "I must confess, I wouldn't last a day in the belly of this beast."

"You can't mean it," she scoffed. "You're the bravest man I know."

The look on his face was unreadable, as usual, the countenance of a seasoned undercover man. She knew his heart must be pounding. He was walking back into that pit in Afghanistan—and she could not shake the idea that he was doing it mostly for her.

"I'd find a way to end it quickly, one way or another," Finn muttered.

Cate stepped ahead and blocked his way. "This is about Kandahar—when you were held captive."

He covered her hand with his and a lingering shudder passed through his grip, into her. "Sorry." He exhaled, adding a bit of chagrin to his apology. "Uncouth of me to worry you. Pay no attention to my ramblings."

Inside the guard station, she signed the register. Finn went next. She watched his gaze travel to the signature above hers. Adrian Fortesque.

A guard opened the iron gate and escorted them through a labyrinth of inner walls until the narrow passage gave way to an expanse of lawn. A number of pathways crisscrossed the green, most of them headed toward a cluster of buildings several stories high. Each structure featured row upon row of small barred windows. Cellblocks.

Finn leaned in. "With each turn, take in the surroundings, even small details." When she raised a brow, he explained. "In case we have to find our way out—in a hurry."

He accompanied her into the vestibule of the warden's office, where two guards appeared to be waiting for them. Just as Finn moved to close the door to the corridor, a third man slipped into the room to block their exit.

Cate surveyed the anteroom. Marble floors and columns framed both windows and entryways. The metalworks, including gaslamps, were either bronzed or gilded. In France, many departments of government were housed in royal palaces, but this was . . .

Finn leaned close. "Rather grand for a prison warden."

"A mind reader, as well," she whispered. "I had no idea you were so talented."

They approached the warden's secretary, who was sitting behind an ornately carved desk. Frail in appearance, the pale-faced gentleman rose from his chair. He peered over rimmed spectacles. "We've been expecting you, Miss Willoughby." The man's gaze slid to Finn. "And you are?"

"Hugh Curzon," Finn answered perfunctorily, scanning the men positioned about the room. "Miss Willoughby's cousin—and escort."

The man's severe countenance reminded her of something weasely. Pointed nose, beady eyes, not unlike his boss, Moreau. The smile, more of a smirk, was not particularly reassuring. "I'm afraid there is only one visitor permitted per detainee." The secretary ushered Cate ahead.

As she passed through the door she glanced back at Finn. Three guards appeared to close in around him. "No need for concern, Mr. Curzon." The secretary nodded to Finn. "Miss Willoughby will be just on the other side of this door."

She expected something akin to a throne room and was not disappointed with the warden's office. A good deal larger than the foyer, with a number of rich furnishings and an imposing desk, there was a sumptuous ease about the room while still maintaining an air of business.

"Take a seat, Miss Willoughby. The warden will be with you in a moment." Cate sat to one side of the desk and waited.

After several minutes, a whine of door hinges and a scraping, shuffling noise came from behind her. Cate peeked around the wings of her chair and gasped. "Eduardo!" Instantly on her feet, she was shocked by the sight of him. Her brother had always been wiry but he was very thin now, almost gaunt. His hair was close-cropped, and he sported a week's growth of beard, but she recognized him nonetheless.

"Catriona?" He leaned to one side, as if favoring a leg.

She crossed the room, flinging her arms around him. Nothing but skin and bones. But his arms returned her hug with a surprising amount of vigor. Cate eased away to look at him. "My God, what have they done to you?"

"Not us, Miss Willoughby." The warden walked in a cadence of three beats. Cane, step, step. Cane, step, step. "He arrived in this pitiable condition."

Eduardo's shrug nearly doubled him over. "Might have had a touch of Gaol Fever in La Santé, I cannot be sure."

"You're in pain. I must get you to a doctor." Cate

turned to Moreau. "Please, you must release him to me, immediately."

Moreau appeared mildly amused. The warden barely raised his voice. "Return him to his cell."

As quickly as Eduardo had entered the room, he was whisked away. "Do not desert me—Catriona," Eduardo called. Barely able to keep up with the guard, her brother listed terribly to one side as he was escorted out.

"Never!" she shouted. "I won't leave without you."

The door slammed shut. Cate buried her hands in the folds of her skirt and clenched her fists. She blinked at the closed door, and then turned to the warden. "He should be attended by a physician. You must let me—"

"Demanding little chit, aren't you? More British than Spanish, to my mind."

"I'm no chit, sir. I'm three and twenty."

Moreau approached her and stood too close. "Blue eyes, almost violet in color." The man reached out and stroked her cheek with the back of his fist—part caress, part threat. "Most extraordinary."

Cate veered away. "What is it you want, Moreau? What will free Eduardo?"

"It may be possible for your brother to avoid the French Guiana penal colony"—even as she retreated, the man edged closer—"if I am duly compensated for his release."

Up close, Moreau was not an unattractive man. Dark lashes surrounded fierce, almost feral eyes, golden around the pupils. Close-cropped black hair and high cheekbones helped, but there was also a cruel mouth and a severe gaze. The total effect was rather draconian to Cate's mind. "What about the offer from the chargé d'affaires?"

"Doesn't interest me," Moreau snapped. "I told Fortesque to take it up with officials in Paris. Unfortunately, by the time they make a decision, your brother will be clearing jungle on Devil's Island."

Cate stared. "And your price?"

"Twenty thousand English pounds."

The currency Finn recovered from the anarchists was a few thousand pounds. She and Finn had been spending like drunken sailors on wardrobe and the hotel suite, though she was beginning to see the sense in it. Moreau thought she had money, and money would buy her brother's freedom.

She had to find a way to delay her brother's departure, long enough to devise a stratagem. "A great deal of money, indeed. It will take time to come up with that kind of cash. Might it be possible to delay the ship a few more days?"

Moreau lunged at her, yanking her against his body. "Most anything is negotiable, mademoiselle—if you are part of the bargain."

Cate bit her lip. "I can get you the money." The harder she pushed away, the more his grip tightened. Moreau brushed his lips across the rounded mounds of breasts and she did not hesitate to scream. "Let me go!"

There immediately followed shouts from outside the warden's office. Moreau stopped his pawing and gasped. "The troublesome Mr. Curzon, I believe."

More crashes and groans. Cate imagined guards, in a semiconscious state, being tossed into walls and sliding down wainscoting. With renewed vigor she was able to push Moreau off and quickly back away.

Several loud smacks and a thud reverberated through the door.

Breathless from her struggle with the warden, Cate's

eyes darted toward the door. "Ohh, I imagine that one hurt, " she said, backing away.

"The warden's men aren't feeling anything at the moment—perhaps when they recover consciousness." Finn strode into the room under the continued protests of the warden's secretary, who trotted after him. All it took was a glare to shut the little ferret up.

"Moreau." Finn boldly stepped toward the warden, who stood his ground with only the slightest recoil.

"Be careful, monsieur, I could have you arrested."

"But you won't, will you?" At the last moment, Finn reached for her hand. She bit her lip and scurried around the cringing warden. She was quite sure this outrageous behavior of Finn's was causing her to fall deeply in love with him. Her heart raced, just from the way he looked at her—protective and possessive. "Cate, I take it you have seen and identified your brother?"

She nodded. "I have."

Finn turned to the warden. "And?"

"And," Moreau straightened, "I have given mademoiselle my terms. She has until four o'clock this afternoon."

Cate bobbed a curtsy. "You will be hearing from me, Warden."

"I'm sure your brother hopes so, Miss Willoughby." The man's sneering grin was back. "As do I."

"No need to wake the guards. We can find our way out." Finn shut the door to the warden's office and helped her over the fallen men on the floor of the vestibule. Finn gripped her arm as they half walked, half trotted down the corridor and out the door. He said nothing until they were well across the green. "I take it the warden made unwanted advances. What's his offer? You, on your back, in trade for your Eduardo's release?"

Cate darted a warning look his way. "I honestly don't believe he is excessively concerned with sexual matters. When he sees me, he . . ." She tucked her lower lip between her teeth and chewed. "He is the kind of man who wishes to dominate a woman—perhaps cruelly." She shook her head and sighed. "What he really wants is twenty thousand in small denomination banknotes."

"And the chargé d'affaires's offer?"

"We discussed the trade briefly." Cate held her straw boater in place as a gust of wind buffeted across the compound. "He couldn't be less interested."

They signed out at the gate and boarded their carriage. It was only when Finn settled in beside her that she noticed his bruised cheek and a nasty new scratch on his neck. She swallowed. "How much do we have left—?"

"A far cry from twenty thousand." He tossed his hat onto the opposite seat and pressed his fingers to his temples.

"He wants the money in his hands by four o'clock or my brother gets shipped off to Devil's Island." Finn massaged the sides of his head. "We must do something. It seems to me we have a good deal of experience in these matters in the person of Sylvain Robideaux." She fidgeted in her seat. "He knows every square inch of the fortress inside and out."

He stopped his circling and opened his eyes. "What are you suggesting, Cate?"

## ∞ Chapter Twenty-seven

$\mathcal{F}$inn shook his head. "Oh no." The thrill of the caper was written all over the beautiful, adventurous Miss Willoughby's face.

"But why not? Surely between the three of us—"

"Three?" Finn thought his eyes might bulge out of his head. "Maybe one of us might try—possibly two. Sylvain's crazy enough to give it a go. But you, you will never be a part of something so dangerous."

Cate's eyes gleamed. "You'll do it then? Break Eduardo out of the Citadel?"

What rankled him more than anything about Cate's question was its almost certain inevitability. Finn gritted his teeth. From the moment he and Sylvain had stepped onto the terrace of the hotel suite he had considered the idea as a backup plan. Under the guise of intellectual curiosity, they had quite deliberately gone over escape routes. The Frenchman had carefully kept his instruction in the realm of possible scenarios. At one point, he had asked Sylvain for detailed information about the transport of convicts to the ship. So why was he so unnerved by Cate's suggestion of a prison break?

The answer sat next to him, squirming with excitement in her seat. Instinctively his arm went around her. "All right, Cate. Suppose I told you I have a scheme—something that would be relatively easy to plan and execute on short notice, but I must insist that you stay out of it until I have your brother and the other man, Chamberlain, well out of danger."

"But I could be of use—"

"Deal or no deal, Cate?"

"Fine." She folded her arms over her chest. "No, it's not fine, but it will have to do, for now."

"And what are my thanks for going along with this madcap conspiracy of yours?"

"I suppose a kiss is in order," she huffed. "Even though I'm devil-take-it peevish about being left out." She leaned close, until her lips brushed over his in the most delicate way—a lovely nuzzle that caused an upsurge of desire to course through his body. He remained passive, and let her cover his lips with soft, openmouthed kisses. When she stayed for something deeper, with a bit of tongue, he smiled.

His arms went around her and he kissed her back—possessively. A kiss that said everything he wished to say without words. If he had his way, she would be his alone. Forever. He ended the kiss but did not release her. "When this affair is over . . . When we are back in London—"

"Will this affair of ours ever be over?" A pink tongue flicked out and moistened a lovely upper lip, and her eyes crinkled at the sides. "I hope not."

He studied her a moment, pulled her close, and placed his lips on her forehead. The carriage slowed for traffic at a cross street. Reluctant to break the spell, he nevertheless dipped a look out the window. The wire office was just up the lane. "You must excuse me, darling." He kissed the tip of her nose. "I need to send a cable to London. I'll meet you back at the hotel. I recommend an early supper—something light. We'll be too keyed up to eat later on." He was halfway out the door before he turned back. "You might compose a message to Moreau. Turn his offer down flat, so he will have no choice but to ship your brother off tonight."

"But—" A slash of pretty eyebrows crashed together.

"We need to make him nervous—force his hand." Finn closed the door of the carriage. "Do you trust me, Cate?"

She leaned out the window. "Of course I do—you know I do."

"You'll hear the rest of my plan the moment I return to the hotel."

He crossed in front of the carriage and entered the telegraph office. Wire encryption was an exacting and tedious business, but he knuckled down and ciphered off several messages to St. Bride Street, Scotland Yard's covert wire address.

"You wouldn't happen to know the map coordinates for Saint-Martin-de-Ré?"

The clerk fished around a drawer and handed Finn a chart. Finn then stood by and watched the operator tap out his messages. Lastly, he wired an urgent cable to the Clouzot brothers.

NEED AIR COMMANDER STOP
46 DEGREES 167 NORTH 1 DEGREE 326 WEST
STOP 9 PM TONIGHT STOP
IMMEDIATE REPLY REQUESTED

Finn hesitated for the blink of an eye and added two words. He stared at the words for a long moment before handing his penciled scrawl to the clerk. The words ran in and out of his brain as he waited for confirmation that the wire had been sent. He stood at the window overlooking the street, but paid little attention to a blur of pedestrians passing by.

There could be no slipups from here on out. If anything went amiss, he would not hesitate to abort such a high-risk sortie. Finn checked his watch. Nearly one o'clock. They had precious few hours to map out the details and fewer still to round up the necessary equipment and transportation. This wasn't an everyday operation for an agent of Scotland Yard—carrying out a prison break in a foreign country. His telegrams to Kennedy at Special Branch helped to ease some of his discomfort. At least the agency would be alerted to the operation, and if he happened to make balls of it—

Christ. This was complete and utter madness. Had he really gone round the bend? The fact that he even considered such a foolish escapade was proof enough he was headed for Bedlam.

Finn exited the wire office. On the more positive, rational side of the gambol, there were two high-profile men at stake here. One a much-wanted anarchist, the other a high-value mole who might still have his cover intact. He crossed the street and entered the hotel. A zigzag through the lobby found the British chargé d'affaires having a drink with a swarthy-looking chap in the lounge. Finn made the briefest eye contact with Fortesque as he climbed the stairs.

There was a third possible explanation why he embarked on this foolhardy adventure, and it began and ended with two words. The same ones he had added to the Clouzot brothers' wire.

*For love.*

Finn put his key to the door and hesitated. Suddenly, he never felt sharper or more full of bollocks. An odd bit of wisdom from Benjamin Tillet, of all people, ran through his brain: God help the man who won't marry until he finds a perfect woman . . . He entered their suite muttering the rest aloud. "And God help him still more if he finds her."

"Still grousing, Finn?" The most perfect woman in the entire world approached him. Cate had changed her clothing and freshened up. She wore a simple little frock they had purchased last minute on their way out of Madame Gagelin's. She met him at the door with a kiss and he pulled her back for another. "I ordered us a tasty meal. Come—" She tugged on his arm. "Sylvain is here as well."

He tossed his hat onto a side table, removed his coat, and rolled up his sleeves. Supper consisted of a platter of local seafood with an assortment of condiments, including chunks of bread and cheese—all of it looked quite delectable. Cate took a seat and nodded to both men. "I believe the idea is we serve ourselves from the platter. The hotel calls it *Le déjeuner de l'homme d'huître*—an oysterman's lunch." Cate demonstrated by forking up a tender piece of fish and dipping it into one of the sauce bowls that surrounded the platter. She closed her eyes and chewed. "M-mm. Delightful."

Finn turned to Sylvain. "I don't know how much Cate has told you, but we have no choice but try for the men tonight. You had mentioned they move the prisoners after dark." He dipped a forkful of fish into one of the rémoulades. "Since we have only the vaguest idea of where the two prisoners are being housed, a breakout seems more than impossible. But if we wait until dark . . ." Finn swallowed his fish and winked at Cate. "I believe we greatly increase our odds of success."

Sylvain nodded. "When they are moving the prisoners to the convict ship." He leaned forward. "They begin the transfer to the convict ship sometime after the supper bell."

"What kind of watercraft will they use?" Finn asked.

"They'll use the ship's dories. Each one carries about twelve men. Three positions, six rowers, if I remember right. The convicts do the rowing—two guards aft, one on the bow."

"The kind of action I'm thinking of would involve an ambush of sorts. We wait just outside the canal basin on the east side of the Citadel." Finn squeezed a bit of lemon over a half shell and swallowed a briny oyster. "As the dory passes by, we take out a few guards and hop aboard. Have the men row us to La Flotte."

Cate raised both brows. "And no one will give chase?"

"I expect they'll pursue us. What we need is a crew of foolhardy men and more fog. We could use the cover." Finn looked to Sylvain, who swished a tender piece of steamed eel into a curried aioli. "This time of year, the oystermen begin working round the clock—am I right?"

"*Oui*—day and night, depending on the tides." Sylvain sucked the eel into his mouth like it was a noodle. "They are either harvesting on their little flatboats or hoisting the catch aboard to take to market."

Finn broke off a crusty piece of bread, layering on a bit of soft cheese. "We'll need one of those oystermen's skiffs, and a bit of gear to look the part."

"For a sum, I can get Anton Berthelot's boat." When Finn frowned, Sylvain threw his hands up. "The man loses a day of work—what can I do?"

"I wired the Clouzot brothers about a rendezvous with the Air Commander."

Sylvain leaped from his chair with a distinctively French "Hoo-hoo! A ride in an airship—this I must experience!"

Finn cracked a smile. The hairy-arsed Frenchman was more than growing on him—he was a godsend. "I take it you're on board with us?"

"How could I miss such a thing?" Sylvain's eyes gleamed. "As for more fog tonight—who knows? Humidity remains high; it is possible. If we run into trouble, I know every small inlet between Saint-Martin and La Flotte."

"Speaking of which, Cate will take the carriage back to your place and make contact with the airship by signaling from the lighthouse."

"A double flash, regularly repeated at ten-second intervals." Sylvain picked up a champagne bottle and began untwisting wire. "I enjoy a bit of champagne with my oysters."

"How sophisticated you are, Sylvain." Cate sliced into a lemon tart. "You eat your oysters like a Parisian." She placed three narrow wedges on plates. "Assuming the prisoners will be packed shoulder to shoulder, might I ask how you to mean to single out my brother and your operative from the other men? Will you be standing on your oyster raft offshore, shouting their names as the boats slip past? I find that rather dangerous, what with three armed guards per boat."

"I suppose"—Finn stopped and thought a moment—"we could always . . ." He drained his glass of Pinot Blanc and started on the champagne. "All right, let's think this through."

A sharp rap at the door startled everyone. Finn rose

from the table and approached the door, pistol drawn. "Who is it?"

"Adrian Fortesque." The answer came through clear as a bell. Apparently, the chargé d'affaires could enunciate through heavy wooden door panels. Finn yanked open the door and looked the man up and down. "Your only friend left on Île de Ré." Fortesque stepped through the entry and nodded to Sylvain. "With the possible exception of Mr. Robideaux."

Cate rose to greet him. "Come join us. May I offer you a glass of champagne and a slice of lemon pastry?"

Fortesque rounded the table. "Champagne, *s'il vous plaît*."

"Mr. Fortesque." She offered the back of her hand, which he kissed.

Finn holstered his gun and offered the man a chair. "What brings you here, Fortesque? Certainly not a social visit?" He poured the chargé d'affaires a glass.

"I came to find out if Miss Willoughby fared any better than I with Warden Moreau."

Cate's gaze shifted to Finn and he gave her a nod. "He allowed me a few brief moments with my brother. After that, I'm afraid the meeting went abysmally. The warden barely acknowledged the official exchange offer."

"I imagine he had no difficulty discussing matters on his own terms?" Fortesque sipped a bit of champagne.

Cate colored slightly. Finn guessed it had more to do with the way Fortesque stared at her than his actual words. "Moreau made an uncouth proposition to Cate and he wants money. Twenty thousand in British sterling."

"Bold of him. He was not quite so forthcoming with a representative of the British Crown. I received no acknowledgment of our man, Chamberlain—aka, Nicolas

Crowe. Moreau persisted with the claim that he held no political prisoners."

Cate's smile was lopsided and cynical. "Moreau has his spies around town. He believes we're rich—when indeed, we are not."

Fortesque twisted up a smile of his own. "I suspect you are making . . . *alternate* plans?" The man's gaze slid to Finn.

"We are weighing our options. As you are aware, the warden hasn't allowed us much time."

"Moreau asked me aboard the convict ship tonight." The chargé d'affaires was offering up important information. "He means to prove to me that no political prisoners are being shipped out of country."

Finn shook his head and met her gaze. "He never meant to give up either man. All he has to do is forge a new manifest, add a bit of verification . . ."

Fortesque's eyes darted around the table. "He's making me into his witness. I can testify that no convicts by the name of Nicolas Crowe or Eduardo de Dovia were transferred aboard ship. Clever for a provincial."

Finn recognized all the chargé d'affaires's signals. Fortesque knew the three of them were up to something. He also thought it likely the British attaché would not interfere, and he might even be useful—more so if he knew what they were planning. "There is something you should know about the prisoner transfer this evening." He checked in briefly with Sylvain and Cate, who both gave him the nod.

"If this to be a long story full of details, allow me to order up something"—Fortesque picked up the empty champagne bottle and read the label—"*less* expensive and *twice* . . . as good."

## Chapter Twenty-eight

Cate made a great show of arranging, then rearranging, their luggage in the back of the carriage. Despite the gray weather, Finn ordered the top down on the landau, thus assuring that the residents of Saint-Martin witnessed their departure.

Once they were past the walls, they traveled until the road dipped into the shelter of a copse, where they stopped the carriage and debarked. Cate hesitated before climbing back inside. "You're sure you'll be able to identify the right two men out of all those convicts?"

"The chargé d'affaires believes he can identify his man and your brother will be somewhere close by." Finn braced both long guns behind his satchel on the opposite seat bench. "Fortesque's a clever chap; he'll find a way to ask your question."

He stretched his large frame against the open coach door. The man cut a dashing figure in his greatcoat and slouch hat. "Catriona." He reached out with one arm and hooked her close. For a few lovely moments he rocked her in his arms. She pressed her hand to his chest and leaned away, searching feral brown eyes—as deep and primal as a stag in the forest. For the next few hours, she would miss him terribly. And she was well aware his lips hovered just above her mouth.

"Would you mind terribly if I told you I've grown quite fond of you?" His words sent a wave of tingles through her body and he smiled at her wide-eyed reaction.

"Be careful, Finn." Rising on tiptoes, she pulled his mouth down to hers and kissed him softly.

They separated reluctantly. He untied his horse from the back of the carriage and mounted MacGregor. He tipped his hat. "You be careful, Cate."

She sank deeper into the tufted upholstery, rocking to and fro with the sway of the carriage. Once, she had turned around to catch a glimpse of him riding away—galloping over a rise in the road, coattails flying. Finn had taken on her burdens as though they were his own, when they clearly were not. And he no doubt risked future employment by involving himself in such an irregular operation. Unauthorized at best, criminal if they were caught. Even if they were successful their actions would be disavowed, and with good cause. Cate inhaled a sharp breath. What had she gotten him into?

To take her mind off Finn, she went over a mental checklist of duties. She was to call on Sylvain's assistants, two ladies of La Flotte, to help her prepare the lens and fuel the lantern. "A double flash, regularly repeated at ten-second intervals," she whispered aloud. The ladies would also know how to prime and start the steam-powered foghorn. The Clouzot brothers' return cable had requested a foghorn, no matter the weather conditions. And she would need to procure a small dinghy—something that would transport her, their luggage, and Finn's prized long guns out to meet the airship.

Finn's last duty in Saint-Martin was to arrange with the stable to have Sergeant MacGregor shipped on to Cherbourg. Her smile widened as she remembered his parting smile, how he flicked the brim of his hat and rode off on the big chestnut horse.

Magnificent man.

She thought perhaps she loved Phineas Gunn. Minutes ago, face-to-face with him, the words had stuck in her throat. Tongue-tied over his gentle declaration of affection, she now regretted not saying the words.

What if something happened? The rescue could go badly wrong and he might die without knowing she loved him. Cate swallowed. So many times she had strained the boundaries of her memory to recall the words from her mother and father before they sailed for the Americas. She'd been dancing in Paris when Uncle Arthur passed. Her vision blurred as a few tears welled. She removed a pocket square from her reticule and dabbed her eyes. God help her, she was determined to have both her lover and her brother returned to her alive. And for once in her life there would be a happy ending—or as happy an ending as one could hope for in this life.

FINN CROUCHED IN the shadows of the parapet walk and waited for the guard to finishing cranking open the canal gate. Twenty feet below, pole in hand, Sylvain waited in the flat-bottomed oyster skiff. Finn stole up behind the sentry on the wall and tapped his shoulder. *"Une bonne nuit pour une évasion, oui?"* The lookout whirled around to a swift punch in the jaw. The man's eyes rolled back in his head as Finn caught the collapsing guard and dragged him into the deeper shadows of the wall walk.

He signaled Sylvain to pole the skiff into the fortress canal. From a crouching position, Finn ran along the parapet walk that followed the canal inside the compound. The inlet forked into two waterways. Straight ahead, one channel opened into the prison's docking basin. To the east side of the main duct, a narrow waterway led to an old dry-dock area, long in disuse. A perfect spot from which to ambush one of the boats. If he and Sylvain pulled this off with enough stealth, they might even get well ahead of the chase.

Halfway down the canal wall, he found the set of iron rungs that led down to the water's edge. Exactly where Sylvain said they'd be. From his high perch, he took one last look around. A sliver of moon drifted closer to the horizon, promising an inky black sky. The night air was damp with mist. Finn gazed out to sea and his heart quickened. A thick blanket of fog rolled onshore. He followed the waterway and took a last squint toward the prison's boat basin. A heavy mist had already begun to obscure the torches lit along the quay. He could barely make out a number of low-slung rowboats tied to the pier. The sounds that carried through the atmosphere told him they were boarding the transfer boats and readying for departure.

Finn swung over the side of the wall and lowered himself down the iron rungs. He waited on the bottom rung for Sylvain to pull underneath. Once he was aboard they both sculled the oyster skiff into the adjunct canal and hunkered down.

"Six boats altogether. They travel in pairs." Sylvain's harsh whisper brushed the back of his neck. Finn signaled for Sylvain to crawl up beside him.

The plan was simple. Fortesque would maneuver to ride on the boat with their two men. If, by chance, their prisoners were not on his boat, he would signal a number either with words or fingers. Finn removed a pistol from the short woolen oysterman's jacket and screwed on the sound suppressor.

Sylvain eyed the silencer. "You designed this?"

"A prototype based on a recommendation I made. The device is primarily an American invention. I own stock in the company."

Finn held his hand up for quiet as the first rowboat skimmed past. "We need to scull up a bit . . ." Just as he whispered the words, the second boat's prow pushed into view. Quite clearly, they could hear Fortesque conversing with the warden. "My sister insisted on keeping all four pups. Can you imagine? Four in a London flat? Quite—unbearable."

"Good man," Finn murmured.

"I thought you did not like the chargé d'affaires." Sylvain scrambled to his knees and poled the skiff forward a few feet. As close as they could get to the main canal without being noticed.

Finn answered under his breath. "I dislike the way he looks at Cate."

The moment boat three passed, Sylvain sighed. "*Ah, l'amour.* Such wonderful torture."

The lack of nervous mannerisms from the Frenchman, of late, meant the craziness was either a complete sham, or the wily man thrived on dangerous situations. Finn was inclined to believe the latter. As the fourth boat's prow glided into view, he readied his pole and waited. When the last set of oars skimmed past they dug in and nearly rammed into the rear of the prisoner boat. Finn reached out and yanked one of rear guards off the boat and onto their skiff. Sylvain raised his pole and rendered the man unconscious, while Finn jumped aboard. He used the remaining guard as a shield, aiming his pistol at the lone guard sitting in the bow, who hesitated. Finn fired. The near silent bullet caught the man's shoulder and the guard slumped over the bow.

"You two up front, drag him back in." He shoved a few men aside and moved forward. The shock of their boarding alone should keep the men rowing—for a while. Sylvain manned the aft position and gave orders to row. *"Plus dur! Plus rapidement!"*

He squeezed onto a middle bench and did a quick look about. "We are here for Eduardo de Dovia and Nicolas Crowe." No one answered from the rear. He looked for any acknowledgment from the front; the two young men hovering over the felled guard looked back. One of them dipped his head, the other cautiously raised a hand. Finn allowed himself an exhale of relief.

Behind them there was some shouting and a bit of commotion. No doubt the last two boats were blocked by the skiff. Everything was working—almost too well. Finn turned forward and addressed the men. "The rest of you men listen up. Paddle us out of here fast. There's an airship waiting up the coast ready to fly us out of here. Cold feet? Once we're in the straight we'll toss you overboard. You can make your way to shore, or join the others bound for Devil's Island. Your choice." Finn eyeballed the convicts in front and behind. "Now, has anyone got keys to the leg irons?"

THE FOG SURROUNDED Cate like a heavy, pale gray coat. She could barely make out the sound of waves breaking softly onshore—maybe she was a hundred yards out? Smothered in thick, cold moisture, she leaned into the strokes of the oars, letting her back do most of the work—just as her grandfather had taught her. She was alone in the small dinghy, weighed down by long guns, luggage, and longing. For Finn. For her brother.

Sylvain's female assistants had been marvelously helpful, and they had quickly accomplished all the lighthouse chores. Cate gave herself a pat on the back for figuring out how to prime and start the steam-powered foghorn.

The straight was nearly as calm as glass, calmer than she had ever experienced the sea, and she had been rowing in circles for some time. Afraid to call out, hoping she would hear from Finn or from the sky. Where were these Clouzot brothers?

FINN PICKED HIS way forward and sat behind the two men in the bow. *"Cuál es el nombre de su hermana?"*

The young man with dark hair and blue eyes sat up straight. "Catriona." Finn turned to the other man. "That makes you Nicolas Crowe."

"And what if I am?" The agent spoke with a heavy Irish brogue. It seemed obvious the man wished to remain undercover. Finn leaned forward and lowered his voice. "I know one of you has the gun you took off the guard—use it only on my say-so." The prow of the rowboat slipped along still waters into a pale haze of fog.

A loud cannon boom sounded. "What the bloody hell?" Finn stood and turned. The fog was thick now—almost as thick as a London pea souper. Something whooshed through the air, striking the water not twenty feet away. "Christ, they're firing cannon at us—Sylvain?"

"The convict ship has a mounted gun on board." The Frenchman shrugged. "I forgot to mention it."

Finn ordered up fresh rowers and relieved one of the men himself. Falling in with the rowers' cadence, he shouted over his shoulder, "You forgot to mention it?"

"Lucky shot," Sylvain scoffed. As if in answer, several bullets whistled past them. Very likely the warden was on the hunt now. "Wild shots, *mon ami*, they have no idea where we are."

A diffused beam of light flashed though the mist, followed quickly by a second flash. The lighthouse signal. The boom and echo of the cannon sounded again; this time the cannon whistle was louder and the splash closer. Finn gritted his teeth and rowed harder. "Get your backs in it, lads!"

"We are close now!" Sylvain rallied the crew. *"Une fois de plus, plus rapidement!"*

Good God, Cate was out here on the water. Somewhere. Finn squinted through the thick blanket of mist. He cupped his mouth and shouted upward, "Ahoy, there."

Two more flashes from the lighthouse rippled through dense clouds to eerie effect. Like flashes of lightning, with no comforting rumble to follow after. They drifted in silence, gliding through gently lapping waves.

"Raise your oars. Steady as she goes." Sylvain's harsh whisper carried over the men's heads. The Frenchman's words were buried under the low blare of the foghorn and something else, the unmistakable groan of a ship's rigging. There, just ahead, a clearing in the mist—something moved about in the clouds, something massive loomed overhead, darkening the waters all around. The airship drifted above, and feet away, a hemp ladder descended from the sky.

The smooth underbelly of the giant hovered overhead. They rowed up alongside and Finn grabbed hold of the rope. "When I give the word, send the rest up." He climbed onto a rung and hauled himself upward.

"Gilbert, Aurélien. Where the hell are you?"

## ∽ Chapter Twenty-nine

Accustomed to the heavy stillness surrounding her, Cate swiveled toward the sound of a low moan. A rowboat drifted close by, she could feel it. Another whispered groan drifted through the mist. Her eyes darted from side to side as she strained to see through a thick curtain of gray. There it was again—a creaky whine and a splash of oar. There could only be one reason things were as quiet as they were—Finn and Sylvain were being pursued. Cate turned her small skiff silently and rowed in the direction of the faint noise.

She jumped as a number of gunshots cracked off and echoed through the atmosphere. Bullets whistled through fog and splashed just ahead of her little boat. A return volley of shots fired from the opposite direction. Cate crouched down and let the boat drift.

Not sure if she should shout out or stay quiet, she glanced over her shoulder and dipped an oar in the water. A dark shape emerged, and then the bow of a boat cut through the haze. Good God, she was headed for them at a right angle, sure to ram the boat. The figure standing at the rear of the longer crew boat turned enough for her to recognize the profile of the warden. A shiver ran down her spine. She shoved an oar in the water and sculled hard. The dinghy continued to drift forward, yet she managed to turn the small craft around in a stroke or two. In her haste, the oars caused something of a splash, loud enough for the horrid man to follow the noise.

The warden's surprised stare quickly shifted to a sly glimmer mixed with genuine glee. She laid her back into both oars. "Turn us about, quickly, Mr. Prior." Moreau's orders carried through the pale mist that enveloped her small craft. Her hands burned from the rough-handled oars, but she paid them no mind and steered farther into a drift of heavier fog.

"Miss Willoughby," he called out in a singsong voice. "Whore of the brother or the man who claims to be her cousin—which is it?" The warden continued to hurl insults and threats. She'd called him slithy this morning and she'd been right. The warden hoped to draw Finn out and recapture the escaped men. And it might work.

"Ahoy, Cate." It was Finn, yes, she was sure of it.

"Ahoy, Cate." The call came again from the west—a faint echo? She was so turned around, she hardly knew in which direction to row. The first call had likely come from Finn, and the second, an answer from Moreau. In the stillness, she was only sure of one thing. The pounding of her heart would carry through the curtain of fog and alert everyone to her presence. She took a deep breath and waited.

"Come to me, Cate—I'm here."

The warden or Finn? Cate dropped the oars in the water and turned toward the voice. "Get those black-and-blue toes over here, this minute!" The voice was husky, insistent, and all Finn. She rowed toward the voice and didn't stop until she came upon him, hanging from the clouds on a rope.

He dropped into the dinghy and wasted no time lifting her onto the ladder. He tied his long guns to another line and they were lifted above.

"Moreau is close, watch your—" she whispered, but was not able to finish her warning. Brawny deckhands hauled her up into the airship's cabin. Cate peered into the depths of the gondola. In the dim light, she could just make out a number of men hunkered down along the floor, looking plainly terrified. Others hauled luggage and guns up the ladder. She spied her brother crouched in a corner. "Eduardo," she called out and he lifted his head.

Cate remained close to the hatchway waiting for Finn. Guns fired below. And another volley. She stuck her head out of the opening. "Get up here this minute!"

"Drop the ballast." Those were the last words she heard from below. Two young men—speaking in French—pulled her away from the craft's door. "No, please!" Cate screamed. "We cannot leave him." Both young men held on as she struggled against their hold. "It is too dangerous. We cannot stay, mademoiselle."

Cate fell to the floor as the great balloon lifted them into the air at such a speed, her stomach felt as though it rose to her throat. As soon as she caught her breath and gathered her wits, she begged the two men in charge for help. "We must go back."

She searched the faces of the Frenchmen, who appeared almost as sad as she was herself. "Help me convince them," she pleaded with Sylvain. "We cannot let Finn be captured by Moreau. You don't understand, he will not—he cannot tolerate a dark cell."

"A prison cell does not sit well with any man." The last

man to climb aboard spoke to her in English—in a thick Irish accent. "He rowed away—tricked the warden into following after him."

Dazed and slightly hysterical, she sobbed. "So that we might get away."

"It seems so, miss."

Cate sank down beside her brother and huddled close. Chilled and numb from the cold, her tears came slowly at first. It wasn't long, however, before the dam burst and the real sobbing began. Her brother did his best to comfort her. "This man, Cate, you seem very attached to him."

"His name is Phineas Gunn—Hugh Curzon on the Continent." At mention of Finn's name, the Irishman briefly slid his eyes her way.

Her brother groaned. "Not the British operative? The same one that got me into this mess—"

"No lectures, Eduardo. That British operative just risked everything—perhaps his life—to break you out of the Citadel fortress. Besides, Finn says the Deuxième Bureau was at fault at the farmhouse." She hiccupped. "And I believe him."

Blinking back fresh tears, she studied the Irishman. Presumably this was Nicolas Crowe. Good-sized, nice-looking man. He might even be handsome after a haircut and a washup. She lifted her chin. "I shan't be aboard long. In my absence, might I ask you to watch over my brother?"

Eduardo protested. "Cate, I'm not a child."

"No. But you *are* ill."

"The fever is gone. I am sure to recover, I promise." He smiled weakly. "Besides, it's you who needs watching over."

Cate shook her head. "I cannot leave Finn behind. I cannot."

"Why such loyalty to an agent who would like nothing more than to see me locked up in Newgate gaol?" Eduardo stared. "Do you"—he recoiled slightly—"love this man?"

"Very much." Cate sighed. "And if you can't honor my feelings for him, say nothing at all." She took in the strange surroundings. The two men piloting the ship—the Clouzot brothers, she reasoned—appeared cheerful enough. They were also wholly taken up with a number of mechanical devices midship. Below the gondola, she could hear the putt-putt of an engine motor and another sound, that of a windmill's soft whir. Was that the propeller, perhaps? She had seen these fantastic flying machines hovering over Paris, and now she was being swept away in one. She raised her hand to Sylvain. "Help me up?"

Most of the men had settled in. Some lounged on the deck of the gondola, others peered out the observation windows. All at once, like singers in a choir, some of the men exhaled an "Ahhh!" Cate peeked over a shoulder to have a look. The airship broke through the cloud cover and putted quietly above the silver-white counterpane blanketing the earth. Overhead, a sliver of moon and stars cast enough illumination to light their way. She imagined how it might feel to have Finn's arms around her as she saw the tops of the clouds. The scratchy affection of his chin stubble at her temple. A single tear defied blinking lashes and ran down her cheek.

"Mademoiselle—Miss Willoughby?" She found both Clouzot brothers standing behind her. "I am Aurélien, and this my brother, Gilbert."

She nodded to each brother. "Finn speaks very highly of you both."

"May we speak with you a moment?" They escorted her to the dais in the center of the gondola. Several steps led up to a circular bridge surrounded by a brass railing. A panel filled with glass gauges and brass levers sat in the middle of what looked to be a kind of pilot's station. Mesmerized, Cate turned a complete circle to appreciate the view from the surrounding glass dome. Sylvain joined them near the helm. As he approached, she couldn't hold back. "What am I to do? I must return to the Île de Ré. He could be wounded—or captured." She didn't mention the other possibility, so much worse she could not bear to think of it.

Sylvain took her hands in his. "He might also be on his way to Cherbourg."

Cate could not hold his gaze for long. She didn't really believe that and neither did he, she could see it in his eyes. "I will find him, Cate, and wire you immediately. The Clouzots have agreed to drop me off, just as soon as the fog clears."

"And when will that be?

Aurélien smiled at her. "As we travel north and inland, the skies will clear." Cate nodded demurely. Inside, her heart raced with excitement as well as dread. How long would all this take? And how far north would they have to travel before the airship could set down? She needed to formulate a plan—quickly.

"*Merci*, you are all a great comfort to me." Her gaze shifted from Sylvain to the aeronauts and froze. "Eduardo!" Cate's eyes grew wide. "Wha-what are you doing?"

Her brother pointed the menacing pistol at their pilots. "Sorry to interrupt your plans, gentlemen, but this airship travels to the destination of my choosing."


FINN LAY IN a small boat drifting at sea. The sound of waves lapped against the sides of the dinghy as the surf washed him ashore. Sand and seashells scraped along the flat-bottomed skiff as it beached itself. He opened his eyes and blinked back a smear of red. A faraway voice yelled, "We've got him!" Shadowed figures lifted him out of the small boat and lowered him into another.

*"Quelle vue terrible!* He's covered in blood."

More shadowy figures played overhead. One jabbed. Another poked. "This one's not long for this world, one way or the other."

Finn let all of it fade away.

## ∞ Chapter Thirty

"She needs to go back." Eduardo waved his pistol. "No time to lose—*rápido*." Both Clouzot brothers jumped to the ship's control panel. Gilbert called out map coordinates and air speed while Aurélien reset the rudder by cranking the handle of a sizable brass wheel.

Her eyes watered. "Eduardo, I—"

Her brother narrowed his eyes. "No crying."

"Crying," she blinked back tears, *"eso es para los bebés."* Eduardo should talk. His eyes were sunken and red rimmed, yet they smiled at her.

"You're no crybaby, Cate."

Under Eduardo's watchful gaze, the Clouzot brothers turned the ship around. Aurélien eyed them over his shoulder. "We'll head for the south side of the island—less fog. We'll set down just long enough to drop you off."

Cate turned to Sylvain. "I can't do this without you."

Sylvain's eyes telegraphed adventure and something else—something more protective. "I am at your service, mademoiselle."

She turned to the Clouzot brothers. "You must carry extra clothing with you. I'll need to borrow some." She eyed Aurélien. The young man was thicker in build, but only a hair taller. "And a set of braces, if you can spare them."

Eduardo leaned against the brass rail and gestured with the gun. "See to her request." He nodded at Sylvain. "Cate seems to trust you—watch my back, and make sure she gets some privacy."

Minutes later, the gondola door opened. She paused at the open hatchway and tucked a few strands of hair under a cap. Her brother emptied the gun of bullets and handed the pistol to Gilbert. She smiled. "I love you, Eduardo."

He shot her one of those *don't kiss me* brotherly warnings. "Go get him, Cate."

She tipped her cap. "Meet you in Cherbourg." She blew her brother a kiss. "For the loan of your trousers, monsieur." She winked at Aurélien and descended the ladder. Holding on for dear life, she imagined her gilded swing at the Alhambra Theatre. A number of sand dunes dotted the strand of beach ahead. Timing is everything, she reminded herself, and let go. She landed on the back side of a dune and slid to the bottom. Sylvain came down not far away in patch of salt grass.

Once on the ground, she clambered over to Sylvain. "How far?" The Frenchman brushed himself off. "The Île de Ré is shaped a like a bent finger—many miles lengthwise, but a short distance across. Less than three miles to the other side."

As the airship ascended into clouds above them, they struck out over the dunes, which quickly turned into a difficult slog through a boggy salt marsh. Finally—joyfully—they came upon a road. Cate glanced right and left. "Which way?"

Sylvain held his index finger to his lips. "Listen—*très*

*tranquillement.*" The low vibration of a foghorn carried faintly through the mist. Cate's eyes widened. "Yours?"

"*Oui*, the only on the isle."

She and Sylvain picked up their pace, and it wasn't long before they began to catch glimpses, through the haze, of the great bastioned walls of Saint-Martin-de-Ré. "Can you get us into the Palais des Gouverneurs?"

"But, of course." Sylvain nodded. "We find out what Monsieur Fortesque knows."

"I'm nearly certain he was in Moreau's boat. He has to know something about what happened." Sylvain studied her in a way she had never experienced from him. "Prepare yourself for the worst, *mon cher*." Then, those playful eyes glimmered with a wink. "But we hope for good news, *oui*?"

Inside the township walls, Sylvain led her down backstreets and onto the palace grounds. "He has a suite in the east wing." Cate followed him up the servants' stairs and along the darker side of a dimly lit passageway. Beyond an empty second-floor parlor, they arrived at a set of double doors. "Locked." Sylvain tested the door hardware.

She raised both brows. "Couldn't we just knock?"

Sylvain rocked his head back and forth, weighing her question, then he grabbed her hand. "Come." They wound their way through the deserted sitting area, and out a set of French doors. Sylvain leaped onto a wide balcony railing and reached down to give her a hand up. "You aren't afraid, are you, Cate?

She grinned. "Out of my way, monsieur." Exactly like a prance along the balcony rails in the Alhambra Theatre. She stepped off the main terrace and onto the railing of Fortesque's private terrace.

She signaled for Sylvain to follow and crouched down

to peer through the small glass panes of the door. The sitting room was empty. Wait. She could see legs though the open bottom of a tall wing chair. The chargé d'affaires? She hoped so. A hand reached out, lifting a glass of cognac off a side table.

"What if it is Moreau?" Cate hissed. She pivoted toward Sylvain and held out her hand. "Do you have a penknife?" A moment later she inserted the blade between the paned doors and lifted the latch. Silently, she stepped inside.

"Miss Willoughby, what an unexpected pleasure."

Cate froze. The man had eyes in the back of his head. She stepped around to the front of the chair. "How could you have possibly—?" Cate stopped midsentence. The chargé d'affaires looked a bit drained.

Fortesque's eyes darted to the deep amber liquid in his glass. "It is astonishing how many household items can be used as devices to spy with." He sipped his brandy. "Or to catch the occasional intruder." Settling into his chair, he offered her a seat opposite. "Please assure me our prisoners are off to Cherbourg?"

"Safely away." She remained standing and endured Fortesque's languid perusal of her body in men's trousers. "Is Hugh Curzon alive?" The question caused her voice to shake.

The man finally settled his weary gaze on her face. "Hugh Curzon to the Navel Intelligence Division, or the man better known to Scotland Yard as Phineas Gunn? Which man would you—?"

"Is he alive?" Cate blurted out and bit her lower lip.

"He took a bullet to his head."

The bluntness of his answer caused her knees to wobble and his gaze to move away. "As you may or may not know, head injuries can be a bloody mess." Fortesque set his glass down. "As it turns out, the bullet grazed him; Moreau has him locked up in one of the infirmary cells."

"Which cellblock?" Sylvain joined her.

The chargé d'affaires tilted his head. "*E* as in *escapade*, Monsieur Robideaux. I take it you and the young lady are planning yet another breakout?"

Cate nodded. "Can we count on your assistance?"

"Insofar as a valuable operative is safely away and making his way back to London, my assignment has been— completed." Fortesque stood abruptly and walked to the vestibule table near a set of double doors.

"But what about Finn?" Cate protested. "Surely the British government would encourage you to assist us?"

He collected a number of messages off the entry table. "I am going to read these missives, have another brandy, and retire for the evening." Fortesque opened the door to his suite, and raised a brow.

As Cate walked past, she stopped. "Won't you please help us?"

Fortesque unfolded a wire envelope marked *urgent*. "Out"—he barely looked up from the telegram—"of my hands."


SHE AND SYLVAIN dipped in and out of the deeper shadows of the palace grounds and into the back alleys of town. Cate crouched behind the trimmed yew hedge. "Now what do we do?"

"I have a friend, an artisan clockmaker by the name of Périgot. He makes his living as a forger and a fence. Come, we will wake him."

A man with thinning gray hair and a wiry build answered Sylvain's knock at the door and set them down at a table in his back room. He poured them each a glass of Bergerac *rouge*—"From the land of the gods"—and listened patiently to their story without interruption. When they were done, he cleaned his spectacles with a threadbare pocket square. "The injured agent, were you able to share any information with him about the compound?" Périgot poured another glass. "The two underground passages?"

Sylvain nodded. "*Oui*, as much as I could explain from the balcony of the Richelieu."

"And you, Miss Willoughby." There was a gentle focus to his gaze, as though every detail of life must be carefully examined. "Is there anything you might wish to add? A fine point that might aid us—"

"I am a thief—a well-trained second-story cat burglar." In the dim light of the workshop, the soft patter of a hundred clocks ticking filled the air. The slightest twitch tugged up one side of Périgot's mouth.

Cate shook her head, partly out of disbelief. "I've never spoken of this to anyone."

The clockmaker's gaze shifted to a faraway place. "I knew a man once—a Spaniard. Worked the resort towns from time to time—mostly, when things got too heated in Barcelona. Here in France he went by the name *Chat de Saint*."

Cate lifted her gaze from her glass. "My grandfather."

Sylvain clapped his open mouth shut. "Does Finn know this?"

Cate swiveled the stem of her wineglass. "He has suspicions." She swallowed a velvet mouthful of wine. "I can scale those fortress walls." She reached into her trouser pocket and placed a key on the table. "And I have this."

Sylvain leaned closer and shrugged. "A skeleton key?"

Périgot's eyes twinkled. "Look a bit closer."

FINN'S HEAD FELT as though it had been set on fire. The burn traveled along the bullet path that grazed his skull. From time to time the pain faded, leaving him with the warden's words echoing in his head. "Get some rest, Agent Curzon, for you will need it." Moreau stood on the safe side of his cell: outside. "You and I will talk in the morning. I will send my guards for you—the ones with the black eyes and bruised faces."

His cell was walled on two sides with a grid of iron bars across the front. Above his bed, a single barred window let in a stream of moonlight between drifts of fog. Finn craned his neck to look out. Almost large enough to crawl out, but not quite. He had gone over and over the escape routes he and Sylvain discussed. He thought he could find his way out, if he could just get rid of these—he yanked on his leg irons. They had also chained one of his arms to the bed rail. The bed, in turn, was bolted to the floor.

He pushed a finger under the bandage that wound around his head, and scratched an itch. Sweat trickled out from under the gauze dressing. He suspected his heart rate was elevated. And that dreadful, crushing sense of impending doom had returned. His head injury would mend quickly, just like his wounds had in the Northern Territories. But he wondered, frankly, if his nerves would ever fully recover.

And he wanted to fully recover. For her. Two nights ago he had confessed everything to Cate. The whole bloody story, at least most of it. And she still wanted him. And he wanted her more than any woman he had ever known.

For a moment or two this evening, he had drifted to sleep and dreamed of his father. A conversation from years past. "Ye'll know it when you meet her, son. The lass will rob ye of your breath and ye'll not be able to eat or sleep well—'til ye wed her." Father was wrong about a lot of things. In point of fact, Finn had never slept better and his appetite was ravenous. Until now.

He had awoken gasping for air, his heart pounding like it was going to burst through his chest. Christ. And the shakes were back—which meant the sweats weren't far off. Soon the walls would close in and he'd be back in that hole in Deh Koja village. When he closed his eyes and all he could see was their faces—each one of his men as their bodies shook from lack of air—and the moment when the spark of life left their eyes . . .

For years after his capture, he would wake up in a fit of violence. The more extreme episodes had stopped, for the most part, but the night terrors still came and went. Finn lifted a shaky hand and placed a finger to one side of his nose, blocking off the air passage. He inhaled slowly from one open nostril. Switching sides, he exhaled from the opposite nostril. An odd exercise that Monty claimed regulated his breathing, which in turn slowed his heart rate. Finn laid a thumb over the inside of his wrist and felt for a pulse. One way or the other, he'd get out of here alive or dead. And if his Soldier's Heart worsened any, he wasn't sure it mattered which.

## ∽ Chapter Thirty-one

Cate emerged from the dense brush carrying several coils of rope over her shoulder. The looming fortress walls drifted in and out of sight with the fog. All the same, those ramparts taunted her as if to say, *Just try it*. Footsteps on stone echoed from above. A guard rounded a corner of the bastion that jutted out from the wall.

Keeping her eye on the man above, she made her way around the curve of the bulwark and ran straight into a tall caped shadow.

"Ah, Miss Willoughby. I was certain I'd run into you here."

Cate leaped back and nearly knocked over Sylvain, who followed close behind her. She held a finger up to her lips and flashed her eyes upward. They waited until the guard's footsteps continued north, toward the next bastion that jutted seaward.

She exhaled. "Mr. Fortesque—what are you doing here?"

"After you left this evening, I received this from Naval Intelligence." He didn't bother handing her the wire, it was too dark to read it anyway. "I shall forgo the details, for now. Let's just say . . . I have come to offer my services."

"I believe we have things well in hand." Cate raised her chin. "We appreciate the—"

"What can you offer?" Sylvain hissed, stepping closer.

The chargé d'affaires's mouth ticked upward. "The pasha's steam yacht is in port. It seems the vessel makes its way to Glasgow to undergo a refitting. I have been offered return passage as a guest of the Egyptian government. They are aware I travel with *staff*." The man backed away. "Quai de Rivaille at the west end of town. We sail at dawn."

"But if we are chased—" Cate broke off her speech and frowned. "Why should we risk an escape across town?"

"Because once you are aboard, you are—technically speaking—on foreign soil." She had never seen Fortesque grin as broadly. "Moreau can't touch you."

FINN'S SYMPTOMS WERE worse. Violent shaking—so bad his teeth chattered. Feelings of claustrophobia. Scattered thoughts, like he was losing his mind. A glimmering ghost crawled along the bars of his cell, yet no one was about.

He thought perhaps he had begun to hallucinate.

Every so often a guard strolled by his cell with barely a glance at him. The occasional snore or cough told Finn there were other men in the cells surrounding him. None of these observations could have caused the flicker of shadow from his cell window. There it was again. Finn craned his neck to look above. A bird perched on the window ledge, possibly?

A scratching sound came next. Almost a whisper at

first, then the scraping grew louder. Only it wasn't scraping, exactly. It was more like a grinding sound. His heart leaped in his chest, in a good way. If he wasn't mistaken, he was listening to the soft crush of a glass cutter.

For the second time this evening, he thought of his father—specifically his snore. Which he and Hardy could imitate perfectly. Finn opened his mouth and inhaled a deep, long rattle, and exhaled the rumble of a bear in hibernation. He strained against his irons and tried to see more of the window above. Several minutes passed before there was a brighter noise, more like—a clink.

"Finn?" The breathless voice could have been the result of a gust of wind—except it was also a familiar voice. "Finn, are you there?"

Good God, what was she doing here—risking life and limb . . . ? His heart palpitated in his chest, then sank. "You shouldn't have come back for me—go home, Cate."

"And what home would that be, Finn? Mine? Yours? Ours?"

He quelled his chattering teeth long enough to answer. "Take care of your brother. See that he retires to write seditionist tracts and advocate civil disobedience instead of bombs. Leave me."

"Shhh!" the shadow in the window admonished. She was absolutely right, this whispered conversation was entirely too dangerous to be having. How could he convince her he wasn't worth the risk without bringing the guards down on them?

A metal object scraped against the stone wall of his cell. He strained to see in the dark; a string with a key tied to the end was being lowered down to him. Finn reached up with his one free hand, and his fingers barely touched the dangling key. He stole a glance up and down the corridor to each side of his cell. No guard. He reached up again, and this time he caught the key. "Got it!"

His rescuer above released the string, and Finn went to work on the iron cuff around his wrist. The cuff released almost immediately. The leg irons proved a bit more difficult. "I can't get past one of the wards," he whispered.

"Enter as far to the left of the hole as you can. Jiggle the key up and down until you feel it slip in deeper—rather like when you deflowered me."

Finn angled the key up and down, and he was damned if he didn't feel it move farther inside. "Now what?"

"Make your turn." The key rotated.

Finn shook off one leg iron, then the other. He slipped off the bed, and sidled over to the front of his cell. His vision momentarily went black and filled with stars. He held on to the bars until the light-headedness cleared. A good length down his cellblock one of the guards turned the corner and disappeared. They had some time, yet. Standing on the prison cot, he opened the lock on the sash and held up the window.

"I've come to rescue you." Cate adjusted a strange apparatus that extended across two of the iron window bars.

"I believe that is my job, not yours." Finn stared at her, only half believing it was really Cate, and yet knowing this dark beauty was alive and real. And lurking at the window of his prison cell.

With her brows pressed together and her lips pursed in concentration, she screwed a crank handle onto the cast-iron apparatus—a jack of some sort. "You rescued me once this evening." She looked up at him and smiled. "My turn."

"How did you—? What's holding you up out there?" He was completely enthralled by her. Not only by her ingenuity, but by her cunning as well. "There's a grappling hook above, and I made a sling from rope, which my bum isn't so awfully happy about." Cate gave the handle a crank and then another—gradually, the vertical bars separated.

"I'm never going to fit through there," he warned. After a number of turns, Cate removed the device and handed it through the bowed bars. She also tossed him her rucksack. She reached out to him. "Help me." Moonlight beamed through a drift of mist, long enough for him to catch a glint in her sapphire eyes. The flexible ballerina folded her shoulders together and squeezed through the opening. Finn grabbed hold of her and pulled gently. "More!" she hissed. He gripped harder and yanked. The rest of her slipped through the opening rather easily, with only a slight delay at her sore bum.

Finn held her in his arms off the ground. "I should be angry with you for putting yourself in such danger."

She placed her hands around his neck and pulled him down for a kiss. "But you can't, can you?"

"I shall take issue with all this later—when I toss you over my knee."

"Promise?" Her lower lip protruded rather provocatively.

"Fancy that . . . I had no idea your were into hot cockles and swivery. Had you mentioned it earlier I might have—spanked you, or—" He grinned, then shrugged. "For now, we move quickly. The guard will be back soon enough."

Cate removed something small and brass from her pocket. "Remember this?"

He set her down and she placed the key in his palm. "How kind of you to bring Roger along." He reset the teeth on the key shaft as wide as possible, then reached around the lock from between the bars. He angled the key past each of the lock's wards, until he heard it scrape the back of the box. He looked at Cate. "Shall I give it go?" She nodded.

He twisted the key and the door swung open silently.

She returned a few tools to her rucksack and stuffed a bed pillow under the thin blanket on the cot. Finn reached back and she grabbed hold of his hand. They headed down the corridor, hugging the shadows. At the end of the passage he peered around the corner. Yet another corridor with a set of doors at the end, and a stairwell. He nodded her forward and they made their way downstairs. At the landing, he peered over the rail. A door swung open and a worker, kitchen help possibly, descended the stairs to the basement.

Sylvain had indicated the infirmary was in a building that housed both the dining hall and the kitchen. If he remembered rightly, the kitchen was in the basement, which had yet another subterranean level below that. From there, they would need to find the entrance to the underground escape route. "Even if we find this secret passage, we may have to turn back. Sylvain believes they've sealed the exit off at the wall."

"Not to worry." Cate raised a brow. "I have an anarchist for a brother, don't I?"

He stared at her. "You're carrying explosives?"

Her hand cupped his jawline. "I came prepared for anything." She tilted his chin toward the gaslight flickering above. "They beat you."

"Guards don't take kindly to surly prisoners."

"How are you?"

"A few cuts and bruises—

"I'm talking about your state of mind."

He stared at her. "A great deal better, now that the shackles are off."

"Finn, I need to tell you something."

He glanced ahead. "If you're going to tell me you love me—don't."

She nearly choked on her response. "Why?"

"Because I already know you do." He grabbed her hand, and they descended the stairs, staying well behind a kitchen worker.

The bustle and clamor of a prison kitchen at full tilt reminded Finn that dawn was something less than an hour away. "Let's try this way." He led them down a narrow passage, dodging a line of carts that would carry great pots of breakfast gruel and gallons of tea into the hall. "Someone's coming." They ducked under one of the carts as a worker balancing a tall stack of soup bowls swept by.

Finn held her close. "You realize your safety means more to me than—"

"Than what? Your own life?" Cate whispered. "Why is my safety more important than yours?"

"It just is, damn it." He dipped his chin to peer out from under the cart.

"You're so stubborn." She sniffed.

Another pair of trousers scurried past the cart. Finn waited a moment, then pulled Cate out from under the cart. He hit the swinging doors running and they found themselves in a great storeroom. A few wall sconces hissed and sputtered enough light to reveal that the warden kept a well-stocked pantry, chockablock full of large bags of milled grains—flour mostly. A giant cold closet took up a good section of space, along with rows of open shelves laden down with dishware and foodstuffs. The room smelled of pickler's brine and salted fish.

"It appears we have reached the end of the building." Finn's gaze swept the room and came to rest on an angled skylight. It was still dark out. "Now, if we can just find a rabbit hole in the pantry. . . ."

They split up and searched the room. Finn wandered up and down row after row of pantry shelves. "Would a trapdoor do?" Cate's harsh whisper carried across the room. He found her between stacks of barrels, and helped her roll a few out of the way. Finn yanked on the heavy cast-iron ring, and lifted the door.

Pitch-black.

"Hold on, I just passed a shelf full of lamps." He returned with one for each. The light from both lanterns revealed a set of wooden steps descending into—blackness.

Her eyes were large and round, and glowed midnight blue. "You don't suppose there will be rats down there?"

He tilted his chin down. "As large as the ones in the London Underground, I'm afraid."

Cate pushed him forward. "You first."

The moan of several horns—all cranking up at once—sounded about the room. Someone had set off the alarm sirens.

He descended the stairs with Cate right behind him. "We're going to take this passage as fast as we possibly can." The moment she was down, he climbed back up and closed the heavy door. They were surrounded by rough stone walls and suffocating blackness. Finn held his lantern high and led them down the centuries-old passage. They ran through long dry sections and picked their way through pools of sludge. It felt as though they ran for miles—when in fact, the wall was less than fifty yards away. Finn slowed their pace. "We make a right turn and then come upon . . ." He lifted his lantern. Cate added hers, stepping up beside him. "Bricked in, just as Sylvain suspected."

Cate removed a small metal pick from her jacket pocket and tapped on the wall. Holding her finger to her lips, she invited him to listen. Sure enough, three taps answered hers. Finn stared at her. "Sylvain?"

Cate nodded. "Sylvain and Mr. Périgot—a clockmaker in town, and an expert in breaking and entering. He knew my grandfather."

Finn stared at her. "Your grandfather. No doubt the man who taught you your trade?" He'd be damned if he didn't catch himself smiling at her.

"I will explain everything—later." She tapped three times again. "Right now, we must retreat many feet away."

They backed around the corner. "Plug your ears and close your eyes." Finn covered her with his body. The blast showered them with brick and mortar dust—but they were otherwise unharmed.

Coughing, Finn helped her up from the ground. "Follow my voice. Don't wait for the air to clear," a hoarse whisper echoed through the darkness. They made their way toward Sylvain's familiar voice, guiding them through the heavy haze. "This way, *mes amis*." There was light above the passage. Dawn was breaking. Sylvain's head peered down at them from above.

Finn pushed Cate up the ladder and followed on behind. "Come, quickly—the pasha's yacht departs any moment."

They were sheltered by a small stand of trees, but not for long. Finn turned toward a man he did not recognize, an older gentleman who held the reins to Sergeant Mac-Gregor. "You must be Périgot."

"At your service, monsieur—you and the beautiful *voleur de bijoux*."

Finn lifted Cate onto MacGregor and tucked himself behind her. "Take care of yourselves." He nodded to both men on the ground. "*Ce n'est qu'un au revoir, pas un adieu.*"

"'Good-bye doesn't mean forever.'" Cate laid her head back. "A rather romantic notion, Finn." He wrapped an arm around her as he headed MacGregor out of the copse. "Just a few more minutes, Cate, and we'll be safely away."

The moment they broke from the cover of trees, shots rang out.

## Chapter Thirty-two

"*Arrêtez! Prisonnier échappé!*" Two guards on horseback chased them through the narrow lanes and backstreets of Saint-Martin. Finn turned down a blind alley, guiding MacGregor through laundry lines, around dustbins, and right into a dead end.

"I'm afraid we've reached an impasse." Finn rolled the horse back and headed them directly toward their pursuers.

"Finn!" Cate pointed to a pedestrian walkway between houses—barely room for them to push through. The next lane over was a crowded marketplace. Finn merged them into a throng of shoppers, vegetable carts, and open-air stalls. "Where are we?"

Cate leaned to one side of the horse. "*Excusez-moi, le pilier avec le grand yacht?*" A woman examining an apple pointed the fruit in a northwest direction, over the rooftops of the shops behind them. Several other shoppers pointed in the same direction. "*Merci.*"

Finn steered through the open market and as soon the way cleared, he dug his heels in. MacGregor swiftly carried them into a fishpacking district, where they wound their way through eight-foot piles of sea salt along the quay. They had to be close now, and the yacht moored dockside would be an impressive-sized ship. In a break between warehouses, they caught sight of the steam yacht, along with several of their pursuers following dangerously close behind.

Cate removed Finn's pistol and handed it back to him. "You might have mentioned we were armed, darling," he said. He steered them down the alley between storehouses and came up behind their pursuers. "Drop your guns and spur your horses out of here. Otherwise I will not hesitate to shoot you."

The men rode off, but they did not drop their weapons. "Bollocks." Finn aimed his pistol and winged a man; the other two turned and fired wild shots. Finn returned fire and took off after the guards. "Let's put a bit of a scare into them." He pursued the men, hell-bent for leather, but at the last minute he turned MacGregor and headed straight for the yacht. Finn pressed his heels into MacGregor's sides and the horse flew out from the shadow of the warehouse and alongside the pier.

Cate stared in horror at the sight of the ship's gangway being retracted.

"Hold the gangway!"

"Finn, what are you doing?" She gulped.

"He can jump this, Cate. Hold on to his mane. Let him know you're with him."

She could see the men on board the yacht, particularly the gangway staff, were scrambling to get the bridge back in place. And there was a tall man shouting orders who looked a great deal like the chargé d'affaires.

Beneath her legs she could feel the powerful muscles of the great horse tense and flex. Finn lifted the reins to give MacGregor his head and urged him onward. The gangway was nearly back in place, but it was still too late. Cate grabbed hold of his mane and shut her eyes. She felt them leave the ground, milliseconds passed, and then there was a great clatter and thud as front hooves and rear legs pumped to keep them climbing up the rest of the gangway. Cate opened an eye. They had landed surprisingly far up the bridge, but the metal and wood platform rocked and swayed from the sheer force of their landing and nearly gave way. "Good boy, keep up the scramble." Cate urged the animal on, as did Finn, with calm, firm words. With only a slight hesitation, the horse pushed off the collapsing gangway using powerful rear legs and with a second, remarkable leap, MacGregor made the lower deck of the ship. Cheers went up from a crowd dockside and as well as on board.

Cate leaned over and hugged the magnificent horse around his neck. Then she hugged Finn with all her might. This brave horse and rider were meant for each other. She wondered if the two of them could make room for a third. She collapsed into Finn's arms and held on while he maneuvered the horse along the deck and away from the crowd.

Finn helped her down and they both gave the snorting, prancing equine a good rub, soothing his frayed nerves. Cate smiled at Finn. "If you weren't different species, I'd say you were both cut from same plaid." She scratched MacGregor's nose. "He has the heart of soldier."

Adrian Fortesque greeted them. "On behalf of the Egyptian and British government, welcome aboard."

"I look forward to a good tumbler full of scotch—later on." Finn trailed after the viceroy's grooms, who led the red horse away. Somewhat bewildered, Cate turned to the chargé d'affaires. "Where are they taking the horse?"

"There's a compartment belowdecks, stores the royal carriages and several of Khedive Tewfik Pasha's Arabians." Fortesque grinned. "We arrange match races for the pasha whenever he's in London. His nags win quite handily." Fortesque offered his arm. "Shall we find you a sumptuous berth, scare up a bit of ladies' wardrobe, perhaps?"

Her room was incredibly small but very well appointed. A vase of fresh flowers had been placed on a small writing desk. And there was a bed, neatly made up and built into the wall. "Drinks at eleven in the stateroom—the earliest hour they serve liquor." Fortesque turned toward the bell pull. "Tug on that and a servant will—*materialize*. I honestly don't know where they come from."

Amused, Cate tilted her head to peek behind the bell pull. "Might there be a pasha's magic lamp to rub back there?"

Fortesque hesitated at the door. "Sorry to have been such an . . . ass."

She met a different man's gaze. His usual callous expression had softened. "There were times when you might have been more . . . helpful." Her eyes narrowed before she smiled. "You did manage to redeem yourself—in the end."

Adrian stared at her the way men do when they want something badly. "You are very lovely." Steel gray eyes darted away, then returned to her. "I suppose you're mad about him?"

She nodded. "Completely, utterly mad about him."

"*That* will be enough, Miss Willoughby." Adrian tilted his head for one last, wistful look. "Shall I make a few *discreet* inquiries about wardrobe for you?"

Her cheeks warmed. "Very kind of you, Mr. Fortesque."

He caught the door on his way out. "Call me Adrian."

She grinned. "If you call me Cate."

The moment the door closed, she gave the bell pull a yank and a genie arrived.

She ordered a pot of tea and a bath, in that order. The tub turned out to be slightly larger than a washbasin, but the tea was divine. Miraculously, the genies on board appeared at her door with a simple frock and a pair of silk stockings and dancing slippers that pinched her toes. Nothing new there. Rather a hodgepodge affair, but when patched together with a blue velvet riding jacket, she looked almost—presentable.

She caught a glimpse of herself in the mirror and pinched her cheeks. Off to find her man, Cate lifted the latch on the cabin door and ventured onto the deck. She stopped several servants before she found one who spoke a smattering French. "Monsieur Curzon's cabin—*le grand Anglais, s'il vous plaît.*" From what she could piece together, Finn was still below with MacGregor; there had been an injury.

"Will you show me the way?"

The cabin boy nodded and she followed him belowdecks to a spacious indoor paddock. The compartment smelled of hay and horse dung, exactly like a barn—or in this case, a floating stable. A line of carriages were secured to one side of the space, while a row of stalls, the other. She crossed an indoor paddock covered in wood shavings. One of the stall doors was open. A stable hand held Sergeant MacGregor's head while Finn knelt on the floor, beside the horse. The horse nickered as she approached. "What happened?" Cate stroked MacGregor's nose.

Finn looked up from wrapping a rear hoof. "He ripped

a shoe off—that last scramble up the gangway did it."
Finn wiped the sweat from his forehead with his shirtsleeve. "The shoe took a piece of hoof with it. We've built
the outer wall up with a plaster cloth. He'll be hobbling
around for a bit." He tossed an unused bandage into a
nearby kit.

"Poor boy." She stroked the horse's nose.

"I can't say he minds the attention." Finn took a moment to examine her head to toe. "I miss the trousers—
that lovely view of your bum." He clapped the plaster dust
off his hands and placed his hands on his hips. "Where did
you find the dress?"

"Adrian was kind enough to arrange it."

"Adrian, now, is it?" He reached out with his hand.
"Have you had breakfast? What hour of morning is it?"

The stable hand moved around the large animal. "I'll
stay with him, sir—see that he has his water and hay."

Finn nodded to the young man. "No oats—let's keep
him as quiet as possible."

He led her up onto the main deck. Momentarily, the
sun burst from behind the cloud cover and the sea sparkled. Standing at the ship's rail, he inhaled deeply. "Ah,
fresh air, open seas—no prison cell." His eyes crinkled
from the sun and the wind ruffled his hair.

"You've removed the bandage." Cate stood on tiptoe
and he leaned over so she might inspect his wound. A dark
red streak ran from his hairline through his scalp. "Clean
wound and healing over." The fast steamer cut through a
swell of waves and her stomach roiled a bit. "Haven't got
my sea legs, as yet. Am I a bit green?" She turned her back
to the ocean.

He placed his hands on the guardrail on each side of
her. "Your eyes match the blue of the sea." He leaned

close, as if to kiss her, but did not. "And a tinge of green becomes you."

She snorted a soft laugh. "I haven't heard a word of appreciation, sir. Quite a prize I rescued, one of Her Majesty's most valuable men—"

"You're not far off, Cate." Adrian Fortesque ducked through a hatch, waving a stack of telegrams. "I have here urgent messages from every intelligence organization in Britain, all of them demanding answers or shouting directives regarding an operative by the name of Phineas Gunn, alias Hugh Curzon." He drew up beside them. "They require answers." He pointed the missives toward midship. "I recommend the lounge. There, Mr. Curzon or Mr. Gunn—whichever you prefer—you will find an assortment of telegraph pads, writing instruments, and an eighty-year-old scotch." Adrian raised a brow and a grin. "Shall we?"

After a pour of Talisker's finest, they settled in to read messages and compose answers. "Ah, here's one from Scotland Yard." Adrian picked up the wire. "Pertaining to the matter of a sloop, chartered by Spanish insurrectionists in La Rochelle harbor. There was an explosion." Adrian's cool, appraising gaze moved from Finn to Cate. "Would either of you . . . care to explain? Special Branch would love to hear about it."

Rocking his head side to side, Finn contemplated his answer. This silent evaluation of his had always intrigued her; she could almost see the clockworks turn in his head. Finally, he exhaled. "I'm not convinced the Spaniards were *Los Tigres.*"

"*Were* being the operative word." Adrian shuffled down a few missives. "It would appear the Admiralty agrees, Mr. Gunn."

Finn poured them all another swallow. "Just call me Finn—that puts us all on a first-name basis."

Adrian flashed a look over his reading spectacles. "There may be a shadow organization within *Los Tigres*— bent more toward violence and disruption than reform." He crumpled the missive and placed it in an ashtray. Rummaging in a side pocket, he removed a box of safety matches. "Would you be interested to know, I received several messages with the clear directive: bring in Agent-of-influence Crowe as well as *El Tigre Solitario*—by any means necessary."

Adrian struck a match and held it to the crumpled paper in the ashtray. "Last night, I Rogered the lock of the local wire office—tapped off a few messages of my own."

"Ah, Roger the skeleton key." Cate rolled her eyes. "So much more amusing as a verb."

Adrian blew out the match. "I telegraphed the names of those extracted and informed the Admiralty as well as Scotland Yard of your capture. I left Reginald, my aide, to wait for a response and returned to our rooms in the palace."

Finn tossed back his whiskey. "I take it you heard back."

Adrian picked up one of the missives and read aloud: "From General Frederick Roberts, 'Lend all assistance necessary to the recovery of Agent Gunn. Stop. Hero of the Battle of Kandahar and national'"—the chargé d'affaires met Finn's gaze directly—"'treasure.'" Adrian leaned forward, shaking his head. "Bloody Roberts, for God's sake— they must have bloody woken him up for that."

Cate waited for Finn's response. In fact, she and Adrian both waited. "It appears your escape from the tribal village wasn't harrowing enough." She gave him a nudge. "There's more."

Adrian slumped back in his chair. "Oh goody."

Finn shot a lethal glare across the table.

Adrian tossed his hands up in casual surrender. "I like war stories."

"As Cate mentioned, I was captured and held in a village northwest of the fort." His speech seemed measured, reluctant. "I managed to escape, along with a few other survivors. Our return was slow going. The men were in poor condition and Kandahar was surrounded by Ayub Khan's army.

"Once we made it inside the walls, we learned that General Roberts's troops were on a forced march from Kabul to Kandahar to reinforce us. Since we had slipped through the Afghan general's lines, we knew where their troops were camped. I mapped out their positions and led a sortie to clear the way for Roberts."

It was hard to imagine how he mustered the courage to do such a thing after what he'd been through. "You went back out again." Cate's voice was almost a whisper.

"The sortie wasn't a complete success but we managed to push Ayub's army into the mountains long enough for Roberts's reinforcements to arrive." He spun his whiskey glass around at the base. "We won the Battle of Kandahar—or declared it so. Six months later we pulled out of Afghanistan."

Finn stood and pushed back his chair. "Any idea when we make port?"

"Midafternoon, I expect." Adrian gathered the pile of missives and their responses. "Reggie wired the Clouzot brothers before daybreak. Suffice it to say they will be anxious to see who arrives in Cherbourg."

"If you'll excuse me." She followed Finn out of the lounge.

Sensing a shadow, Finn turned back. "I'm sorry, Cate, but that kind of heroic war talk rankles."

She grabbed hold of his hand and squeezed. "Help me to understand—please, Finn."

"Many soldiers suffered insults and terrors much greater than the ones I endured, and some of them died. For what?" Finn stopped midrant, his eyes dark and troubled, as he tried to hold back his grief and his anger. "There is nothing noble about war, Cate, not the one I experienced. But there is something gloriously noble about the soldier beside you. All this talk about national treasure—I fought for my men. As a soldier you're asked to walk the razor's edge, for God and country. But in combat, it's the bloke beside you who counts."

"Like the Punjabi soldier—the Sikh man who shouted the warning—the one who was . . ."

"Shot before my eyes," he bit out.

The realities of his war experience came crashing into her mind. She felt a bit light-headed, out of sorts. She could only imagine how it must be for Finn. Cate bit her lip and nodded. "And the soldiers you were captured with—how terrifying and brutal those executions were." She must have looked a bit forlorn, because he pulled her close and rocked her in his arms. He kissed the top of her head. "Sorry to have said anything—no one should have to think about such things, least of all—"

"Don't say it, Finn. You trusted me enough to share the terrors you'd suffered—your fears, as well as your triumphs." Cate met his gaze with a fierce one of her own. "I love you, Phineas Gunn."

There—she had finally said it. She waited for his reaction, which took an exasperatingly long time. Her eyes burned, slightly, and she stepped away, fearful he might not—"Oh, the hell with it. Just because you already know this, doesn't mean I can't—" she started.

He yanked her back into his arms and kissed her hard, slanting his mouth back and forth, coaxing her to open to him. A single brush with the tip of his tongue, and she swirled hers up to greet his. Finn lifted her off the ground and stepped through the hatchway before putting her down. In the privacy of the passage, he pressed her against the wall and nipped at her bottom lip.

Rallying to his game of kiss and release, she caught the bottom ledge of his lip with her teeth and tugged. "M-mm." His mouth skimmed over hers. "Before I rip all your clothes off and get us tossed in the brig for"—he continued to angle soft kisses over her mouth—"indecent lip-sucking, might we take this up again in private?"

He backed away reluctantly. "I'm going to run down and check on MacGregor. Then I'd like to freshen up a bit. Have you any idea where my cabin is?"

"I know where my mine is." She smiled. "Number eleven."

# ∞ Chapter Thirty-three

$\mathcal{F}$inn entered cabin eleven and his jaw dropped at the sight of her. A naked beauty had fallen asleep on her bed. His gaze slipped past the angle of her shoulder and moved down an elegant curve of spine. He lingered on a lovely rounded hip and two perfect globes of derriere before traveling down shapely legs that went on—forever.

He needed to be near her, to enter her body and experience her shudder from his touch. She was sleeping soundly and hardly stirred when he took her in his arms and stroked her smooth, tawny skin.

Cate stirred. "Am I in a dream?"

"I love you, Catriona de Dovia Willoughby. I love your shoulder, your spine, your hip, and this—" He ran his tongue along a rise of hip to her buttock cheek. "I have loved every moment ever spent with you—and I am going to make every exquisite part of your body come alive." His words buffeted softly against her mouth as he brushed his lips across hers.

She opened eyes that were desirous—of him. "With hot cockles and swivery?" Her words were coolly mysterious—even provocative, until her lips curled upward. She turned onto her side and lifted a brow. "Mind telling me what it means?"

"The cockles or the swivery?" he teased as his gaze lingered over bare peach skin. "Two bodies. Naked. Doing a bit of sheet shaking—in this berth together." Finn turned her over on her stomach and smacked her bottom for emphasis.

He laid a condom packet beside the bed, pulled off his boots, and unbuttoned his trousers. An erection strained against his drawers as Cate tugged at the strings that would loose the dragon and allow his raucous cock to spring to life. Standing at the edge of the bed, he took hold of her knees and pulled her bottom toward the edge of the mattress. He needed to see all of her. Placing himself between her legs, he opened her wide—enough to memorize every glistening detail, from the wet petals of her sex to the wanton smolder in her eyes.

"You are the most exquisitely beautiful thing I have ever seen." His hands traced light caresses up and down the insides of her thighs. "Let go, Cate—abandon every inhibition and let me pleasure you."

She flung her arms overhead and gasped as his fingers brushed lightly over moist curls and slipped into her body. He played with her arousal in stages, first with his fingers, moving rhythmically inside her—tantalizing secret places, while his thumb opened tender folds and circled her most sensitive spot. She responded by rotating her pelvis and pressing against his fingers to ease her erotic torment. "Please," she begged, but he refused her.

"Not so fast, Cate."

Bending over her, he ran a trail of kisses down the inside of each thigh—until his lips and tongue found the engorged spot between her legs to suckle and lick and circle. He delved deeper, swimming in the very juices of her arousal, delirious and intoxicated by the scent and taste of her.

He listened carefully to her every sigh, every tremble and shudder. And just as she was nearing the edge, he lifted away. In wicked, playful answer, she took hold of his shaft and stroked. He had no idea how long he would be able to last, to hold off his finish.

She urged him on, drawing his mouth down over a nipple. And he suckled and nipped and fondled until she was once more writhing beneath him. He reached for the rubber goods. "Let me," she whispered. While she rolled on the condom, he found the small of her back and slid his hands down to cup each buttock cheek. He tilted her pelvis and filled her with his stiff, smooth shaft. He did not ease himself in, but took her roughly, pumping hard and deep. And she was warm and slick and so wonderfully—flexible.

She answered every thrust, drawing him in as he groaned in response. "Take me to the end of it." She gasped, winding both legs around his hips. He slipped a finger between them—adding another level to her pleasure and sending her over the edge. Her body trembled with the strength of her climax, shuddering, then bucking under him as she breathed the words. "I do love you, Agent Gunn." In answer to her words, his own shattering release came in waves, each one stronger than the last, until he collapsed beside her.

Limbs entwined, they drifted in and out of sleep, resting in each other's arms.

After years of cutting off any uncomfortable closeness with women, he had developed fiercely possessive and protective feelings toward this young lady. It seemed he had tumbled hard into a deep and abiding love for Catriona de Dovia Willoughby.

"Darling?" he whispered, nuzzling a pretty ear.

"M-mm?" The murmured answer of a woman well pleased.

Finn propped himself on an elbow. "Since I believe you to be thoroughly sated and amiable, for the moment, might you tell me something about how you came to be such an expert cat burglar and jewel thief? No use hiding anymore; it is quite impossible to deny your skills in the matter. Especially since you have done such an excellent job at stealing my heart."

She turned onto her back and opened somnolent blue eyes. "If you must know, I come from a long line of jewel thieves, on both sides of the family."

He couldn't resist touching a smooth translucent nipple that peaked when he circled. "Go on."

"Abuelo de Dovia, in his day, was a master cat burglar—nearly invisible at his work. Not only was he never caught; in the thirty-five years he plied his trade, there were only two reported glimpses of *El Gato del Claro de Luna*—the Moonlight Cat. Sylvain's friend, the clockmaker, tells me he was known as *Chat de Saint*, in France."

"I take it he apprenticed you in the trade?"

Cate nodded. "Against all the family's wishes. Aunts, uncles—Grandmother."

Finn drew his brows together. "Why not your brother?"

She shrugged. "Eduardo did not take to it. He was always more concerned with politics and progressive reforms—from the time he was quite young." Her cheeks blushed with color. "After Father and Mother were killed, I believe Grandfather wished to leave a legacy." She rolled bright eyes that were now even bluer, if that was possible. "Odd, I know, but there is a code of sorts—pride and honor amongst thieves, I suppose."

Finn drew in a breath. "Let me guess—Baron Brooke was also involved in stolen goods: large heists, the kind one can't easily fence without causing a stir, even amongst the more talented thieves." Finn plumped up a pillow and tucked it behind them. "Peer of the realm, excellent cover—strange I never ran across him."

"I have a theory that he sold most of his gems on the Continent. Shortly after he died, someone stole the ledger he kept along with the jewels." Cate tucked herself against him and sighed. "Eduardo had to be the one to tell his comrades about the jewels—perhaps about the time this shadow group split off. This new faction may have taken some of the jewels and sold them off quite hastily through a private seller." Lost in conjecture, Cate chewed on her lower lip. "Anarchists are always in dire need of funds—but then, you know that."

"The way we catch them is by following the money or the arms deals," Finn added quietly.

She shot a shy glance his way. "I'm afraid you're involved with a gypsy thief, Agent Gunn."

Finn brushed a few hairs back from her cheek. "Actually, I believe I've fallen for a *première danseuse*, desperate to put her dear departed uncle's estate in order—a respected member of the peerage who resorted to a few discreet heists."

"You believe me then?"

Finn stared at her for quite a long moment before flashing his eyes upward. "Well, not entirely—yet. You will earn my full trust, Miss Willoughby, when you return all the unsold jewels to Scotland Yard, as was our agreement days ago."

Cate smiled one of her mysterious Cheshire cat grins.

"What?" It was good to see her face light up and hear a chortle of laughter.

"Nothing. You shall see, soon enough, sir."

A knock at the door startled them both. "We dock at Cherbourg within the half hour."

THE LATE AFTERNOON sun caused Cate to squint up and down the dock.

Dressed in gentlemen's traveling clothes, a clean-shaven Nicolas Crowe met Finn and Cate at the dock in Cherbourg. She and Finn walked over to a nearby café, one close to a wire office, and sat down with Fortesque and Crowe.

"How is Eduardo? Is my brother recovered yet?" Cate asked.

This valuable British agent was quite a handsome man—not as handsome as Finn when she compared the two, but the man had his appeal. Crowe stared at her. "I'm afraid your brother has disappeared, Miss Willoughby."

"Disappeared? I don't understand. He wasn't well."

"Eduardo was sick in Paris, we all were, but he was long recovered."

"An old prisoner's ploy," Finn muttered.

The undercover operative pulled a letter from an inside coat pocket. "He left this for you."

The seal had been broken on the folded missive. Cate frowned. "You read this?"

Crowe sighed. "I believe you will understand why I opened the letter, if you read it, Miss Willoughby."

"He's gone to Paris." She frowned. "If you believe that. Says he'd rather not be returned to British soil . . ." Her eyebrows furrowed as she read on. "Claims he was betrayed by a faction within *Los Tigres*, a ruthless group of men who are planning a very great disruption in London—on the evening of twenty-first." She looked up from reading. "That's—?"

"Tomorrow." Finn's dark gaze met hers.

Crowe lowered his voice. "I've already wired Melville and alerted him to the threat." He stared directly at Cate. "He mentions a name in conjunction with a warning. Means nothing to me, but might you know this man?"

She nodded. "Francisco Guàrdia. He and Eduardo were close for a time, almost like brothers, but there was a falling-out last year. Francisco was . . ." She chewed a bit of bottom lip. "An impatient, passionate sort of progressive—rather high-strung. At least that is what I recall of him."

Finn stopped a water boy and sent him off for a British paper. "What do you know about him, Cate? Does anything stand out? Some sort of training—was he a chemist, did he have an expertise in arms—?"

Cate straightened. "He was a marksman." She scanned the faces around the table. "Eduardo sometimes called him Sniper."

"Your brother is quite possibly handing us a valuable tip." Adrian leaned back in his chair. "If I'm not mistaken there is a contingency of high-ranked Spanish officials in London this week."

The boy ran up to Finn with a paper and was tipped handsomely. He snapped opened the *London Telegraph*, and scanned up and down. "Right you are, Adrian—two men, the Spanish prime minister, Sagasta, and the governor of Puerto Rico, Romulado Palacios Gonzales."

All three men rose from their chairs at once and headed for the wire office.

Cate read her brother's letter again and reread the last paragraph twice. He apologized for running out on her. Again. Typical. Cupping her chin in her palm, she added more hot milk to her coffee and stirred. Perhaps this was all she might ever expect of her brother. Brief encounters, hurried hellos, and good-byes. A sudden rush of loneliness swept over her.

She glanced up from her swirling spoon. Newspaper rolled in hand, Finn strode toward her across a cobbled lane. He jumped a rain puddle. A bit of mud splashed onto his boots—making him all the more dashing. This man would never run out on her. He would always protect her and care for her. He looked up and smiled. "We're off to London, my dear."

He was hers.

# ❧ Chapter Thirty-four

A secretary named Quinn tapped a courtesy knock on the door and gestured for her and Finn to slip inside Director Melville's office.

"A theatrical hall full of patrons, a skeleton crew of agents—this is a disaster before it's begun." The grumbling voice came from behind a great desk piled high with case folders. A gray-haired man with very woolly muttonchop whiskers leaned forward in a squeaky worn leather chair. He held a cable message in one hand. "And how the hell are we supposed to identify this assassin?"

Cate blinked. "I can, sir."

The man behind the desk stood up as they entered the room. "Mr. Gunn." The whiskered gentleman turned to her. "And this young lady, I presume, is the sister of Eduardo de Dovia."

Finn made introductions. "Cate, this is William Melville, director of Special Branch. And his right hand man, Chief Inspector Zeno Kennedy."

"Pleased to meet you." Cate nodded to the imposing gentlemen. The much younger man, Zeno Kennedy—she was quite sure she had heard the unusual name before, connected to the arrest of dynamiters.

Finn grabbed the last chair and offered it to Cate. "I expected to see Fortesque and Crowe here."

The man named Kennedy closed the file on his lap. "Their carriage broke down just outside of Epsom Downs, they should be along any moment."

Cate held back a snicker. Last night they had made the channel crossing to Portsmouth in a little over three hours—just as darkness fell. Standing beside her luggage, Cate had listened to the gentlemen discuss which route might be faster into town. The morning train would get them to London by no later than ten o'clock. A fast carriage with a change of team midway would certainly get them to London before daybreak. There was great deal of bickering back and forth as to whose department was going to pick up whose travel expenses.

Finally, she could stand it no longer. "Sergeant Mac-Gregor is not fit enough, as yet, for a long slog at night tied behind a rented coach. She turned to Adrian. "Why don't you and Mr. Crowe go along by carriage—roust your agents, do . . . whatever it is Scotland Yard men do in these circumstances. Finn and I will meet you in Director Melville's office in the morning."

She was tired. More than anything, she wanted a good night's sleep spooning against the warm body of the man she loved. She had crossed her arms over her chest and glared at the three of them. "I consider the matter settled, gentlemen."

It appeared she and Finn had enjoyed an excellent night's sleep and had still beaten Adrian Fortesque and Nicolas Crowe into town. She caught Finn's eye and winked.

"All right then." Melville cleared his throat. "Miss Willoughby, you say you can identify the suspected assassin?"

Finn leaned against the wall of the director's office. "Before we go volunteering Miss Willoughby for what is likely to be extremely dangerous work, might I ask if you have determined the what and the where of the assassin's scheme?"

Kennedy leaned forward. "We believe the sniper, Francisco Guàrdia, will make his attempt tonight—at the Alhambra Theatre. A place you are familiar with, Miss Willoughby."

A bit wide-eyed, she nodded.

The detective continued. "We've managed to scrounge up a set of technical drawings from an architect who recently renovated the stage. As Finn is an expert marksman himself and has been trained as a sharpshooter, I'd like you both to take a look at the schematics."

Finn reviewed the plans briefly and asked about Alfred, Scotland Yard's famous bomb-sniffing bloodhound.

Kennedy shook his head. "I'm afraid Alfred is up in the Port of Dundas—we received intelligence about a ship carrying a load of arms and explosives."

Finn stared. "What are we using to sweep the theater with?"

Melville brightened. "We thought we'd give Sofia a go. The pups can do without their mother for a few hours."

Finn stared. "Alfred's bitch?"

"I prefer paramour." Melville stiffened. "She's had some training—and she's got the best nose we've found, other than Alfred. Our good luck they took to each other."

A young man wearing a protective apron poked his head in the door. "Look who I found wandering about Four Whitehall." She spotted Adrian Fortesque and Nicolas Crowe behind the amiable chap, who waved both men inside.

"Archie Bruce, head of the crime laboratory." Finn nodded to Cate. "Please meet Cate Willoughby."

"Mr. Bruce."

The young man stared at her, quite beyond the appropriate length of time a man might stare at a lady. "Excuse me." He edged a bit closer. Cate smiled gently. She had an idea of what was coming. "But you are—you dance with—"

"My theatrical name is Catriona de Dovia, of the *Théâtre de l'Académie Royale de Musique.*"

"Yes, I attended the ballet just last week. Your featured dance was so—" The young man seemed at a loss for words.

"I'm delighted you enjoyed the performance, Mr. Bruce."

"Might we get down to business, gentlemen?" Melville moved around the long table, pulled out a chair, and nodded to Cate. "Miss Willoughby?"

They spent the morning poring over plans of the stage, as well as renderings of the Alhambra's interior. Finn used a map pointer and traced a number of potential bullet paths, or lines of sight—unobstructed views between shooter and target. "Sagasta and the governor of Puerto Rico will be seated here or here." Finn turned to Zeno Kennedy. "We'll need to confirm the exact box." After some discussion, they settled on one or two of the most likely sniper positions.

Melville paced around the table. "Next question—shall we allow our foreign dignitaries to attend the ballet as planned, or do we plant our own men?"

Finn pushed his chair back to stretch out his legs. "Risky either way—we can't have either man shot, but the use of decoys might risk discovery."

Zeno Kennedy agreed. "We lose the opportunity to catch the perpetrators."

"Unless we find a couple of ringers," Archie Bruce piped in.

Cate considered their dilemma. "What if the assassin doesn't know the prime minister on sight? What if he has to wait for a signal?" Shocked that she had blurted out her thoughts, she looked at the men, openmouthed. "I mean, I'm not completely sure I could identify Sagasta on sight, not unless I was told what box he was seated in."

Melville stopped in his tracks. "Do performers know such things? Which celebrity or notable is sitting in which seat?"

Finn suddenly tipped his chair forward. "Cate, the night you tossed the silk streamer through the air, the one I caught was meant for—?"

Cate met his gaze. "Lord Phillips. I was told it was his box, and that he was an enthusiastic patron of the ballet."

Archie Bruce beamed. "I say, that would be quite a bold signal to use."

Finn nodded. "And rather clever, if a bit theatrical. All eyes on the target, away from the shooter."

Bushy brows crashed together above Melville's frown. "For those of us who have had neither the privilege nor the delight of seeing Miss Willoughby's performance," he turned to Cate, "might you please explain?"

She sucked in a breath. "There is a *pas de deux* titled *Phoenix Unbound*. I descend to the stage on a gilded swing. There are streamers attached to my costume, meant to look like burning flames trailing after me." Cate moistened her lips a bit nervously. "The trapeze swings across the stage and comes up quite close to several balcony boxes on the opposite side of theatre. By request,

I often toss a length of silk to a gentleman in one of the boxes."

The young lab director bobbed his head. "A spectacular opening, really quite thrilling."

Melville's mouth had dropped open. "You've been gone nearly a week. Who takes over in such circumstances?"

"Miss Millicent Troy, my understudy. I would send someone over straightaway, find out if she's received any requests for this evening's performance."

"Would you now, Miss Willoughby?" The director's scowl melted into a cheerful curl. "Well, I happen to agree. It should be easy enough to discover if Sagasta's box has been requested."

"We'll want to cross-check the request with the prime minister's people." Zeno Kennedy narrowed in on Adrian Fortesque. "Might I put you on this?"

"I shall pay a call on the Spanish embassy this afternoon." Adrian's gaze landed on the agent sitting next to him. "As for Mr. Crowe—or is it Chamberlain here at home?"

"I'll take the ballet girl." It seemed Mr. Chamberlain was capable of quite a charming smile—when he wished to be charming. And it was sure to work on Millicent Troy. "And please, I am Gray Chamberlain—for the foreseeable future."

Melville grunted. "Be a damned shame if your cover is blown—two years of work down the drain."

Zeno closed one file folder and opened another. "Only time will tell. We can't risk putting Gray out there again until we know for sure." Zeno glanced across the table at Finn. "We might be calling on Hugh Curzon for a while— to fill in on the Continent."

Cate's stomach did a bit of roiling about. These men operated in a strange world filled with dangerous intrigues. Finn called himself a consultant, but there he was, right in the thick of it. He was a thrill seeker, just like her parents. She wondered, frankly, if one could settle down with a man like Phineas Gunn.

Not that she wanted to settle down, exactly. More than anything in the world she wanted to dance with a ballet company. Tour the world. Perhaps she, too, shared some of the same wanderlust as her parents. And as dedicated as Eduardo was to his causes, Cate was certain the dangers inherent in being an anarchist were a large part of the draw.

Good God. A flush of heat tinged her cheeks as she realized something she had never wished to admit to herself. Ever.

She was an adventuress.

Cate jumped when Melville grunted. "No one leaves this room until we all agree on a plan. You've got twenty minutes." Melville checked his pocket watch. "Then I'm going down to The Rising Sun for a pint and a fish pie." He glanced up at the table. "You're welcome to join."

FINN CLIMBED OUT of the hansom at 19 Chester Square. "Wait for me."

He opened the front door and took the stairs two at a time. "Bootes!" Raking through his clothes closet, his found his evening coat and flung it on the bed. He had just enough time to quickly change costume, collect his guns, and get back across town to the theatre. He had identified three likely sniper nests and wanted plenty of time to position operatives close by. Agents fitted in waiters' jackets—Cate's idea. Finn tossed off his clothes and yanked the bell pull. "Bootes! I need you up here!"

"Glad I am to have you home—Oh, sir!" His flustered housekeeper nearly spilled a washbasin full of warm water. Finn lifted the heavy bowl out of her hands while she stared openmouthed.

"Surely you've seen Mr. Doty in his unmentionables." He ran a wet washcloth across his chest and under his arms. Mrs. Doty turned her back. "Have you seen my butler about—or Hardy, for that matter?"

"The two of them worry me something terrible, Mr. Gunn. Left the house not more than half an hour ago. On their way to a duel, they said. Mr. Morton—Bootes to you, sir—is standing in as your brother's second." The distraught woman actually sobbed. "Oh, Mr. Gunn, we collected your travel bags and guns at the station—your horse as well. Everyone thought you were still off on the Continent. Please, sir, do something to stop them."

Finn said a silent prayer, then cursed Hardy, in that order. Toweling off, he yanked his dresser open. "Do you know where they went?"

Mrs. Doty sniffed. "I've a mind they didn't venture far, sir."

"Why do you say that?"

"They left on foot."

Finn pulled on a fresh shirt. Belgrave Square's private garden was large and a bit overgrown. Plenty of spots to pace off a duel. Christ, just like old Rufus to get himself gunned down in front of his own town house. "Be a dear, Mrs. Doty, and fetch my white braces and evening trousers." He raised his chin. "And I shall make a hash out of this tie."

Finn dressed and headed downstairs with his house-keeper whimpering behind him. "I don't know what I'll do if something happens to that young man." Even though Hardy teased the woman mercilessly, Mrs. Doty had a mighty affection for his brother. She pointed down the hall. "Your things are in the study, sir."

He turned at the banister and made his way down the hallway. He stopped at the umbrella stand to pick up his double-barrel rifle, the most reliable gun he owned. Inside his study he pocketed a box of shells and his Webley re-volver. Mrs. Doty watched him from the open door. "How is Sergeant MacGregor?" he asked her.

"Doing well, I believe. The groom called the farrier out, sir."

He exited the house and climbed into the waiting hansom. As they pulled away, he caught a glimpse of his overwrought housekeeper standing on the porch. Finn let down the side window. "Try not to worry yourself. Hardy's been in worse spots."

## ∞ Chapter Thirty-five

"What's going on?" Cate pushed through a crowd of hovering onlookers and leaned over the young dancer. "Millicent, what on earth?"

Her understudy was lying on the ground gasping for breath. A glance down her body ended in a horrible sight. The young dancer's foot lay at an odd angle, and the ankle bone jutted from the skin. Cate winced. It hurt just to look at the injury.

Gray Chamberlain knelt down and wrapped a towel around the bloodied leg. Cate shook her head. "How did this happen?"

He used a pocket square to secure the cloth bandage. "We were on our way downstairs—she slipped." He shook his head. "She's landed in a bad way on her ankle."

Cate stared at him. "I can see as much." He ran a hand through sandy brown hair.

"Mr. O'Donnell, we need to get Millicent to a doctor," she called out to the stage manager.

"Henry's on his way, Miss de Dovia." One of the hands pushed his way through the bystanders. The burly lad picked up Millicent as though she were a child's doll. Cate led the way upstairs and out the backstage door. She squeezed Millicent's hand. "You're in good hands, Millie. Henry will stay with you, and I'll send Francis over as well."

Cate gave the driver a Harley Street address for a doctor who treated the dancers' complaints and injuries. The big lad stuffed himself in beside Millicent and lifted the girl's leg onto his lap. Millicent rolled her eyes. "Don't you be getting any ideas, there." She turned to Cate and managed a wistful smile. "I'm afraid you'll have to go on tonight."

Her heart leaped in her chest as she stepped away. Millicent grabbed hold and yanked her back. "Be careful."

She searched her understudy's face. "What are you saying, Millie?"

The girl lowered her voice to a whisper. "I remember being jostled on the stairs, more of a push than any stumble." The hansom lurched off and Millicent let go of her hand. A confusing panoply of thoughts whirled through her mind as the cab turned the corner.

"She's right, you'll have to go on now."

Cate whirled around to face Chamberlain. "I promised Finn I wouldn't dance under any circumstances." She found it hard to meet this man's piercing gaze for long.

Cate brushed past him and headed into the theatre. What perturbed her most of all was that Chamberlain was right. No matter what she had promised Finn, she would have to go on. The entire operation had been planned around the opening movements of the dance and a silk streamer.

She could feel Mr. Chamberlain's eyes on her back as she hurried down the backstage stairs. On the floor below, a janitor mopped up smears of blood. She wondered if Millie would ever dance again. Tears filled her eyes at just the thought of it.

Cate chanced a glance behind her. Chamberlain also descended the stairs, but at a good distance behind her. The very attractive, disturbing man winked at her. There was only man in the world who was allowed to look at her that way, and he was on his way back to the theatre this very minute—togged up in evening attire and armed with his rifle.

She ran the rest of the way to her dressing room and slammed the door shut.

FINN STEADIED HIS long gun on the low branch of a small tree and took aim. Hardy stood a head taller than any of the other men gathered on the green, negotiating some finer point of rule. "Get cracking, gentlemen," Finn hissed under his breath. He needed to be back at the Alhambra, posthaste.

"Twenty paces is far enough, since the earl has forgotten his spectacles." Hardy's voice carried over a rise of grass and through the dense vegetation. Finn gritted his teeth. Lennox House was just across the square. Easy enough to send a man over to collect a pair of eyeglasses. Advantage, Earl of Lennox.

Hardy finished rolling up his shirtsleeve. "Shall we, Rufus?" He selected a pistol out of the open case and inspected his weapon.

He knew his brother well enough to know Hardy planned to aim over the earl's shoulder. But the fact remained, one could never be sure about these affairs of honor. Rufus might get off a lucky shot, and he'd be damned if his brother would get killed by that nearsighted old bugger—and for a liaison with Lady Lennox, no less. Christ, every gay blade in London had been under her skirts.

No, Hardy and Gwen were being singled out because they hadn't followed the protocols of polite adultery, and those rules were very clear. One could have an affair, just keep it discreet. And never let an attachment get out of hand.

Finn positioned his line of sight parallel to the dueler's path. It would be a quick adjustment to move his aim from one man to the other. Bootes was calling out the paces. "Seventeen, eighteen . . ." At the stroke of twenty both men turned and lowered their pistols. Finn aimed. A rustle of breeze fluttered the fabric of the earl's shirt-sleeve. He squeezed the trigger. The bullet in barrel one brushed the earl's shooting arm. Finn swiveled the gun barrel at Hardy and narrowed an eye down the sight. His brother aimed high, over the elder man's shoulder. A breath ahead of Hardy, Finn pressed the second trigger and winged his brother in the arm.

Finn shifted his gaze above his gun sight. A streak of red marred each man's shirtsleeve. He angled his rifle against the tree trunk and dipped under a branch. "Bootes! Hardy!" He called up the green. His manservant appeared pleasantly surprised to see him. "Good news, sir: both gentlemen have incurred only minor injuries."

"There you are, Finn. Finally made it, I see." A bit dazed, Rufus Lennox stared at his bloodied sleeve. "What the hell happened here?"

Finn stepped between the earl and his butler. He discreetly dropped two large-caliber bullets in Bootes's palm. "My rifle is up against a tree behind you. Reload it for me, would you?"

"Very good, sir." He caught a shifty grin from his butler.

Finn had a closer look at the earl's arm while Rufus growled. "I don't believe my honor has been satisfied."

"Feeling well enough to grouse, Rufus?" Finn inspected the man's arm. "I'd have that wound looked at."

Hardy made his way over wearing a "you don't fool me, brother" look on his face, and a shirtsleeve as red as the earl's. "Nice shooting . . ." At the last minute Hardy turned to the earl. "Rufus."

Taken aback, the earl sputtered out a return compliment.

"Excellent." Finn smiled at both men. "Now if you'll excuse me, I am expected elsewhere. I'm afraid London is awash in anarchist plots this evening." He took a moment to eyeball the earl before turning to his brother. "Scotland Yard could always use an extra hand. Interested?"

"Wouldn't miss it." One of the earl's footmen handed Hardy his coat.

"As my brother's official second," Finn backed away, "I declare the match satisfied." They were outside the garden before his brother looked at his wound. "Barely nicked the flesh." Finn tied a pocket square around Hardy's arm.

"I didn't know you were a trick shooter."

Finn ignored Hardy's jibe and climbed into the waiting hansom.

Hardy squeezed in beside him. "You might challenge Annie Oakley in Buffalo Bill's Wild West Show."

Finn stared at his brother. "How many times have we come to blows?"

Hardy leaned away. Finn leaned closer.

Hardy retreated farther—as far as one could when wedged into a narrow cab seat. "I take back the Annie Oakley remark."

"This is very important, Hardy, so listen carefully. There is going to be an assassination attempt tonight at the Alhambra—two Spanish dignitaries, or so we would like the perpetrator to believe. We've supplanted two of our own men in their place."

A rush of heartbeats forced him to inhale a breath. "Against my better judgment, Cate has volunteered to be a part of this scheme. It seems she is the only one who can reliably identify the marksman. If anything happens to me, I want you to promise me you'll take care of her. See to it she's well provided for."

"Christ, you sound like you want to marry her." Now it was Hardy's turn to stare, openmouthed. "Dog's bollocks, Finn, you want to marry her."

CATE STARED IN the dressing room mirror. "He's been gone nearly three hours," she mumbled under her breath. Lucy, her dresser, placed the feather tiara on her head.

"Did you say something, mademoiselle?" Lucy looked up from her pinning.

Feeling more than prickly, she inhaled a deep breath and moistened her lips. "Just wondering where a certain gentleman is."

"Hold still now." Lucy tilted her head to make eye contact in the mirror. "That fine looker I saw you with in the boxes?" She winked.

Cate grinned. "That would be him."

Lucy dusted her nose with powder. "A lot of good-looking toffs about this afternoon—official-looking. Nosing around asking questions, like they were from Scotland Yard."

Cate rolled her eyes. "That was because they were, Lucy."

She turned toward her capable young dresser. "Stay away from the stage tonight."

Her dresser lowered her voice, eyes like saucers. "Are there dynamiters about?"

Cate frowned. "Just—stay far back in the wings."

A knock sounded at the door. "Ten minutes, Miss de Dovia."


DOOR GLASS SHATTERED on both sides of the cab as the hansom turned onto Leicester Square. Caught in a hail of bullets, the horse screamed in panic and reared up on hind legs, raising the cab and nearly flipping it over. Finn fired his pistol over the heads of innocent bystanders. "We've lost our driver." He glanced at Hardy. "Are you hit?"

"Just the nick you gave me—" Using the butt end of Finn's rifle, Hardy cleared his window of broken glass. "We're sitting ducks here." His brother took aim. "Who am I shooting at?"

"You can't—not unless you see a target."

The blazing electric lights of the theaters brightened the square, but the glare made it hard to see where the bullets came from. Terrified theatergoers scattered in all directions as the reins fell slack and the horse charged off through the garden, taking them directly into a throng of pedestrians.

Finn reached through the shattered side window to the top of the hansom, but couldn't reach the reins. "Break out the front window," he yelled to Hardy, who used the butt end of the rifle to shatter the windshield. The hansom jerked, and they were both tossed back inside the cab as the horse bolted into the crowd. They careened through the square, and another barrage of shots hit the rear of the cab.

Bystanders flung themselves out of the path of the runaway carriage. Any moment now, the hansom would topple over in the thick of the crowd. They were well past the fountain, and rolling wildly down a side street. Finn guessed they were somewhere behind the National Gallery. Leaning out his side window, he fired behind them. Even if he didn't get close to whoever was shooting, it might serve as a bit of cover.

Ignoring his labored breath and accelerated heart, Finn reached through the cleared window and grabbed hold of the reins. Before he was able to fully collect the animal, the cab took a hard bump and lurched to one side. "Christ, we've got a broken wheel." The buzzing clatter of the spokes being sheared off the hub made one thing a certainty. Finn hit the latch and shoved Hardy out the door. The hansom screeched like a banshee in the night, then began its groaning tip over. Finn lifted himself from the opening and jumped out after his brother.

He hit the ground and rolled to a hard stop against the door of a shop front. A squint at blurred lettering read *Rare Coins and First Editions*. He craned his neck to peer down the lane. The broken wheel hub ground over street pavers, creating a swath of sparks as the toppled cab rounded a corner and disappeared.

The bones in his neck complained, loudly, when he shifted his line of sight up the lane. A dark shape climbed out from under an overturned dustbin. A single round tin rolled down the sidewalk past Finn's head. "Is that you, Hardy?"

His brother staggered to his feet and brushed off a bit of refuse.

"Where's the rifle?" Finn asked.

Hardy stared at him. "That's it? 'Where's my gun?'" His brother kicked through a pile of rubbish, foraging for the gun. "No, 'Any broken bones, Hardy?' 'Is your brain rattled?' 'Can you see straight?'"

Finn tweaked his head from side to side to pop his neck bones. Hardy pulled the rare double-barrel rifle out of the dustbin. "Look here, barely a scratch on her."

"Let's get moving." Using backstreets to reach the theatre's side entrance, they tucked into a door niche, and observed the comings and goings at the stage door. It was obvious to Finn someone didn't want him back inside the theatre. But why had he been singled out? His instincts told him that Cate somehow factored into this.

Finn glanced at his rifle. "Since I failed to ask if you had broken any bones"—he grinned at his brother—"can you see clearly? No double vision?"

Hardy shrugged. "I can shoot straight, if that's what you're asking."

"Let me rephrase that. Under pressure, how good a shot are you?"

Hardy stared. "Very good. But after those aces of yours today? Not nearly as good as you, Finn."


HEAD DOWN, MAKING no eye contact, Cate flew out of her dressing room. She swept through the green room and climbed stairs crowded with up and down traffic. Slipping behind the backdrop, she wound her way through a number of set pieces on wheels. At the far wing of the stage, she paused at a second set of steps. A rickety stair crawled up the brick wall, ending at the catwalk. High above flying backdrops, a narrow platform led to a small trapdoor, which opened onto the balcony.

"Miss de Dovia," a voice called from behind. She turned and waited, her eyes flashing daggers.

Chamberlain ignored her look and nodded upward. "Who's that?"

A stagehand perched on the catwalk above waited for her. Cate sighed. "His name is Ricky Day. He makes sure I get safely into position near the trapeze."

She elevated up onto her toes, stretching her calves. "I must go."

Chamberlain saw her up a set of stairs so narrow they had to ascend in single file. Halfway up, Cate swiveled back to him. "Just as she was taken to hospital, Millie grabbed hold of my arm. 'Watch yourself,' she said. When I asked her to clarify, she told me she hadn't tripped. She said she'd been jostled on the stairs—implying she'd been pushed."

"And so, Catriona de Dovia resumes her role." Chamberlain's jaw clenched. He stared at her. "I didn't mean to—"

"Let's get this over with, Gray."

Cate turned and ran up the stairs, a glance backward caught him nodding to the stagehand. "Take care of her. See that she doesn't fall."

The young man tipped his cap. "Not this pretty bird, sir."

"YOU CAN'T MEAN it." Finn stared at Detective Kennedy and thought he might have an apoplexy. "Cate is dancing? Who the hell authorized such a thing?"

Zeno Kennedy stared. "I did, Finn. We didn't have much

of a choice." The normally stoic Yard man appeared troubled, which did nothing to alleviate Finn's pain.

"Little more than an hour ago the understudy sustained an injury," Kennedy explained. "A fall down the back stairs—"

He thought his eyes might bulge out of his head. "And you don't find that suspicious?" Harp, violins, and cellos swelled through the theatre, and the refrain was hauntingly familiar. "Debussy—that's Cate's music."

"The time for discussion is over," Kennedy shouted over the orchestra.

"Slight change in plans." Finn shoved Hardy forward. "Here's our marksman—get him in position." Finn caught Hardy by the arm. "Remember, Cate's first cue is to identify the shooter. If we're on the beam, we jump our man. If not . . ."

Hardy held his gaze. "I take him out before he can fire."

"I'm going over. If anything goes wrong in the crossfire, I want to be close enough to—" Finn turned away.

"To do what, Finn?" Kennedy called after him.

He raced up the main aisle in orchestra seating. Vaguely, Finn was aware of the master of ceremonies' crooning, "And where in the heavens might we find such a lovely mythical bird?" Finn pushed past a crowd of gentlemen taking their seats and launched himself up a set of carpeted stairs.

The balcony seating at the Alhambra consisted of exposed boxes at the railing, a narrow corridor for traffic with additional rows of seating behind the boxes. From behind a velvet drape Finn watched Cate's arabesque. He was as enthralled as the gentlemen sitting in the front boxes. Halfway down the aisle, he spied Gray Chamberlain stationed in a dark corner, dressed in a waiter's jacket.

Finn caught the agent's attention and waved him over. "Seen anything?" Finn spun the chamber of his revolver.

"There's a gentlemen with a peculiar-looking cane— might be a device of some kind." Gray nodded to a man sitting alone.

Finn confronted the man directly. "What goes on here, Chamberlain?"

The agent scanned the audience before he answered. "Someone either wants Cate taken out—not sure why— or they're going to try to pin the assassination on her, implicate her in some way."

He stared at Gray. "You don't believe she could be involved?" Finn's gaze shot across the room. As Cate approached the gilded swing, a graceful, outstretched leg parted a sea of pale rose tulle. He nodded across the theatre. "The moment she releases the swing, we move down to the boxes." She placed a toe slipper on the bar.

Tilting her head, she opened gently wavering arms—a preening bird preparing for flight. With each flutter she loosed ribbons of red and gold silk. Strains of music built to a crescendo as she stepped onto the gilded trapeze and plunged off the balcony.

While the audience oohed and gasped, Finn moved down to the aisle that serviced the boxes. The soaring bird swooped over the orchestra seats, heading straight for their box. Finn paid careful attention to Cate's expression. They had arranged to give her as many swings as she needed to make an identification—within reason. Arms outstretched, she did not unfurl a length of silk fabric as she reached the end of her arc.

Their eyes met for the briefest of seconds. She shook her head.

Was that *no, he's not here* or *no*— Finn made a quick

appraisal of the audience on his side. Nothing. Not a single man had even moved forward in his seat. He quickly checked with Gray, who shook his head.

He swiveled back to Cate as her arc neared the opposite balcony. Good God—she tossed the silk in the direction of their decoys. The assassin's bullet would come from behind at close range.

A barrage of shots rang out. Finn stared in horror as Cate's leg buckled and she slipped off her swing. A stream of red ran down her pale stocking. Momentarily stunned, a panicked audience deserted their seats and crowded into the aisles.

As if in a dream—where seconds move like minutes— he watched Cate catch hold of the bar. Finn moved toward the railing as the trapeze swung the injured bird back to him. She dangled precariously off the swing as it headed straight for him.

Without a great deal of forethought, Finn timed his leap over the balcony edge to the arc of the trapeze, and grabbed hold of the rope. Far below, theatergoers trampled over each other to reach the exits. The added weight and the force of his landing caused the aerial equipment to buck and swing erratically. He lowered himself down to the bar and grabbed hold of her with his free arm. "I've got you, Cate."

The swing gradually lowered over the heads of the few remaining spectators and dropped Cate and Finn down to the floor of the stage. A crowd of concerned dancers instantly gathered around them. Finn pulled Cate into his arms and inspected the bullet wound. Despite the pain there was a spark in her eye. "Did we get him?"

Christ, he hadn't even gotten a decent look at the suspect. Finn looked up into a deserted balcony. "Not sure. There are some bloody good agents after him, though, I can promise you that." Finn ripped open her hose to have a look. Blood oozed, but no spurting—a good sign. He looked up. "Do you hurt badly?"

She shook her head. "A terrible sting at first. Most of my weight was on the leg and it slipped out from under me." He searched the pocket of his dress coat and pulled out the red streamer he had caught over a week ago, here at the Alhambra. "A fitting bandage, for such a beautiful injured bird."

While concerned dancers and stagehands hovered, he wrapped the silk around her thigh and tied it off. One of the ballet girls leaned in. "You gave us such a fright, Miss de Dovia, you could have been killed."

Finn picked her up in his arms and headed offstage. She called out over his shoulder, "Hard to kill a moving target."

He carried her out of the theatre and to the end of the alley before he spoke. "You disobeyed me." Leicester Square was still in utter chaos, teeming with police. "Not a cab to be found," he muttered, and turned down a side street, picking up his pace.

"Are you going to carry me all the way to Harley Street?"

"If I have to." Finn hugged her closer. "Cate, my love, when were you going to tell me you are a double agent?"

All the mystery and beauty of her sea-blue gaze confronted him. "When did you figure it out, Finn?"

He hoisted her up to adjust his grip and continued on to Piccadilly Circus, where they would surely find a ride. "My suspicions have waxed and waned for some time— until this evening." A drift of fog crept over the street, and Cate shivered in his arms.

"All I ask of you, until we have this leg tended, is that you answer the query, darling."

Cate sighed. "I suppose I was being cautious. What if you and I had a lovely amourette, as well as a spot of adventure, and went our separate ways?" Her bottom lip protruded and her eyes narrowed, an unsettling combination. "Was it really advisable to reveal anything more to you than necessary?"

Finn grimaced. "First rule of an intelligence agent: protect your identity and your allegiance at all costs."

She nodded. "And twice as true for a double agent." He observed a wince of pain, but she covered it well with a flirty grin. He paused before crossing Shaftesbury just to look at her. She was alive. And she was as lovely as she was dangerous. Finn lifted her close and kissed her. He made it long and sensuous—a very unpublic kind of kiss. And when it was over, he didn't let go.

## ∽ Epilogue

$\mathcal{F}$inn set her down, smoothing layers of pale rose tulle over tawny flesh. "Doctor's orders." He lifted her foot off the ottoman and tucked a pillow under her ankle. But for the hint of crisp white bandage around her thigh, both limbs were bare. "A few days off that leggy leg and you'll be back at your ballet barre, Miss de Dovia."

His manservant entered the study and placed a tea tray on a side table. "Will that be all, sir?"

"Thank you, Bootes," Finn answered without taking his eyes off her.

Cate had scrubbed off the theatrical mask in hospital. She was fresh faced, a bit disheveled, and so lovely she made his loins ache. She leaned over the side of her chair and inhaled. "I love a good steep of Earl Grey."

"I've sent for a few of your things—some proper clothing, a few unmentionables. I hope you don't mind." Finn settled into a nearby chair. "I'd like you to stay on here, for a few days. Humor me—let me watch over you."

Thick dark lashes shaded her gaze. She lifted her skirt and examined the bandage. "So you believe this bullet was meant for me?"

"Our escapade in France, in particular La Rochelle harbor, was more than enough to blow your cover." Finn dropped his head to one side and pushed a long lock of hair behind his ear. "Incredibly brave—as well as reckless—of you to go onstage last night." His gaze darkened. "The moment your understudy took the fall, you must have known you were a target. Why, Cate?"

"There really was no choice, was there? Not if we wanted to get Francisco."

"Now that we have the assassin in lockup, and all Yard men duly credited in the press—including my brother—mind if I ask a few more questions?"

"You are free to ask." She cozied into her chair. "I may not be at liberty to answer."

"Fair enough." He leaned forward in his chair. "How does Chamberlain fit in? Or is it Nicolas Crowe?"

"He appears to be a highly valued agent. Other than that, I haven't a clue."

"They . . . or should I say *we* certainly went to a great deal of trouble to recover him."

She met his skeptical gaze with a sly smile. "Honestly, Finn, he's an enigma. Weeks ago, I was called in to a meeting. The name Nick Crowe was mentioned." Finn raised a brow and she rolled her eyes. "There is a room on the third floor of the Admiralty. I only know it by the number on the door—thirty-nine."

"No doubt some secret section over at the Admiralty." Cate appeared to be a part of an ongoing operation he knew nothing about. Frankly, it rankled. "Quite a tricky business, operating for and against your brother. How exactly did you come to the work, Cate?"

"I was approached by an agent in Paris, from the Naval

Intelligence Division. They needed someone who could gain access to *Los Tigres* quickly, and I wanted answers. I had just lost my only brother under rather brutal circumstances." Her gaze moved far away. "I wanted to find out what happened to Eduardo—who might have betrayed him, what had actually happened that day at the farmhouse."

Finn poured two cups of tea. "I know so many intimate things about you: what makes you smile, what makes you irritable—what makes you moan." He looked up from pouring. A lovely peach color blushed her cheeks. "But I have no idea how you take your tea."

She smiled. "A spot of milk and half a sugar."

"It seems clear that the splinter group set up the ambush in France." He settled back in his chair with a cup. "How long have you suspected?"

"Long before the explosion, Eduardo shared his own suspicions with me. He was worried, Finn. So when he was killed, it seemed like the right thing to do—to go after the men who killed my brother. I had no wish to save *Los Tigres*. I do hope you know I am not political—"

"No, you are a ballerina who claims she is not adventurous."

Cate snorted a soft laugh.

"For a time, I did not know if it was Scotland Yard or the Deuxième who fired everything they had at a farmhouse they knew was full of explosives." Her eyes darted about as she moistened her lips. "In Barcelona, what part of us—?" She choked a bit on her words as her gaze met his.

"Are you asking if you were a part of my assignment?" Finn exhaled, more from relief than anything else. "I contrived to meet you. I had no idea I'd have my heart broken by the baby sister of an infamous anarchist."

She stared, eyes wide and dewy. "I didn't meet you at the Plaça Reial . . ." She looked away. "I was in mourning—"

"I wanted to comfort you, Cate." Momentarily he was back in Barcelona, sitting in the Café Almirall alone, his heart aching for her. For himself.

She leaned forward. "I know." She squeezed his hand.

They fell into silence. Absently, Finn's gaze moved from the mantel clock to a stack of unopened correspondence. "And what of this?" He picked up a package on his desk, still in its shipping wrapper. "Stamped and dated the day you left town, and it is addressed to me, from you."

"Seven days ago." She craned her neck. "You haven't opened it?"

Finn stretched his legs, crossing them at the ankle. "I thought I'd let you tell me what's inside."

"The jewelry is all there—except for the pin I sold to Fabian, which I assume Scotland Yard has recovered." She met his gaze over a tipped cup. "I wanted you to believe I'd stolen it."

He leaned on an elbow, cupping his chin. "Why on earth would you do such a thing?"

She returned his gaze, with eyes slightly narrowed. "I wanted to arouse your curiosity, Agent Gunn."

"You never fail to arouse me . . . Agent Willoughby." As it turned out, this young woman excited him in so many interesting ways. "You also managed to intrigue all of Scotland Yard."

She peered over the arm of her chair. "Are those ginger biscuits?" Finn picked up the small plate and offered her the selection. She sampled a pale brown biscuit. "M-mm, they're chewy." After a bite or two, a pale pink tongue licked a sprinkle of icing sugar off her lips.

He stirred his tea and waited for Cate to elaborate.

"The splinter group stole the jewels—aided by information gleaned from Eduardo in happier times. As you already have surmised"—Cate appeared to choose her words carefully—"the jewelry thefts helped to pull you and Scotland Yard into the game. The NID is desperately shorthanded. W.—my contact at the Admiralty—gave me the go-ahead to enlist you to help steal them back. I had no idea where the intrigue might lead, but it seemed like a perfect way to gain entrée to *Los Tigres*. Then the message arrived."

"Eduardo was alive."

Cate met his gaze and nodded.

He wasn't sure whether to grin or frown. "Shamelessly used by another underfunded government agency." All parts of Finn were on full alert and aroused. "And if, by chance, I was caught and tortured, I couldn't possibly jeopardize your cover." The idea of Cate as an undercover operative had always stimulated. He continued to stare. "Last evening was clever by half, Cate. You had to make it look as though you were part of the assassination team, as well as play a key role in thwarting it."

She smiled. "Once we substituted the decoys, I worried less. After that, it was more about how to keep a certain British agent away from the theatre long enough to have the assassination attempt come off as authentic—as well as put Francisco behind bars."

"Steely Agent Willoughby. I suppose there was no way to know for certain if your cover was blown." His eyes narrowed some. "That ambush you arranged nearly got Hardy and me killed. Nevertheless, I'll take the little side operation of yours as a compliment."

Cate swallowed the rest of her biscuit. "I'm afraid some of the characters who work for the Admiralty can be rather . . . zealous."

Finn studied her. "And this W. chap—your contact—could he be William Henry Hall? Steel gray beard, white at the temples . . ."

She set cup to saucer and raised a brow.

"It seems you work for an arm of intelligence," he lowered his voice, "even more secretive than my own." Finn set his tea aside and rose from his chair. "Allow me?" Slipping his hands around her waist and under her knees, he lifted her. "Arms around my neck, that's it." He angled her legs carefully around the furnishings. "I don't believe I ever told you how attracted I am to double agents."

"Is that so?" Her eyes sparkled with interest.

"Indeed, I get these powerful urges—rather like a stag in rutting season." He nodded at the doorknob of his study. "Would you mind, dear?"

Amused, Cate twisted the knob and pushed the door open.

"There is yet another puzzle I could use your help with, my love." Finn bounded down the hallway and up the stairs. "Might an incorrigible, part-time double agent and *première danseuse* find a way to live happily under the same roof as an equally difficult intelligence agent with a nervous affliction?

"Once again, darling?" She turned the knob of his bedroom door and he kicked it open.

"You are so much more than an intelligence agent, Finn."

Puzzled, he angled his head to read her expression. "Meaning?"

"You are a warrior—honorable, heroic, and perfectly modest about all of it." He placed her on the counterpane of his bed and lay down beside her. "However, Agent Gunn"—she stroked his cheek—"'tis your soldier's heart I love the most."

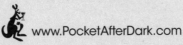